HER
MOUNTAIN
PROTECTOR

BY
PATRICIA THAYER

MILLS & BOON

First published in Great Britain 2013
by Mills & Boon, an imprint of Harlequin (UK) Limited,
Eton House, 18-24 Paradise Road, Richmond, Surrey TW9 1SR

© Patricia Wright 2013

ISBN: 978 0 263 90091 0
ebook ISBN: 978 1 472 00451 2

23-0313

Harlequin (UK) policy is to use papers that are natural, renewable and recyclable products and made from wood grown in sustainable forests. The logging and manufacturing processes conform to the legal environmental regulations of the country of origin.

Printed and bound in Spain
by Blackprint CPI, Barcelona

Originally born and raised in Muncie, Indiana, **Patricia Thayer** is the second of eight children. She attended Ball State University, and soon afterwards headed West. Over the years she's made frequent visits back to the Midwest, trying to keep up with her growing family.

Patricia has called Orange County, California, home for many years. She not only enjoys the warm climate, but also the company and support of other published authors in the local writers' organisation. For the past eighteen years she has had the unwavering support and encouragement of her critique group. It's a sisterhood like no other.

When she's not working on a story, you might find her travelling the United States and Europe, taking in the scenery and doing story research while thoroughly enjoying herself, accompanied by Steve, her husband for over thirty-five years. Together, they have three grown sons and four grandsons. As she calls them: her own true-life heroes. On rare days off from writing you might catch her at Disneyland, spoiling those grandkids rotten! She also volunteers for the Grandparent Autism Network.

Patricia has written for over twenty years, and has authored more than forty-six books. She has been nominated for both a National Readers' Choice Award and the prestigious RITA® Award. Her book *Nothing Short of a Miracle* won an *RT Book Reviews* Reviewers' Choice award.

A longtime member of Romance Writers of America, she has served as President and held many other board positions for her local chapter in Orange County. She's a firm believer in giving back.

Check her website, www.patriciathayer.com, for upcoming books.

To the strongest and the most stubborn woman.
I'll miss you every day, but I'm happy you're
with Dad now.

Love you, Mom. Rest in peace.

CHAPTER ONE

REGINA WILLIAMS rolled over and stared up at the peeling paint on the ceiling of her bedroom and smiled.

Two weeks. That was how long she and Zack had been living in the little bungalow on Cherry Street. Even with the endless projects to do, and the sparse furnishings, they'd found joy moving into their very first home.

Of course, there were thirty years of payments ahead, even with Lori's help as co-signer and a good interest rate. That was as far as Gina would let her wealthy big sister go. She had to do this on her own. She had to prove to herself and her son they could be independent.

She had a good start, with her staging business and thrift shop and new friends and now, a wonderful place to live. Destiny, Colorado, was a great small town to raise her seven-year-old son. Zack was thriving in school and he was making friends. He was finally coming out of his shell, and maybe putting their old life where it belonged. In the past.

She climbed out of bed, slipped on her robe as she walked into the hall. She hesitated at Zack's door, then decided to put on coffee first. In the kitchen, she drew back the curtains at the French doors that overlooked the backyard.

This was the view that had sold her on the house—also the acre of land out back. Springtime in Colorado was an array of color and she had already planned out her flower garden in her head.

Right now she'd better get her busy day started. Coffee made, she walked down the hall, knocked on her son's door and opened it. "Rise and shine, kiddo." No response. Zack had always been a slow starter. She went across the hall to the bathroom and turned on the light, then the shower.

"Come on, Zack," she called. "I need to get to work and you have school." She walked back to the bunk beds, to find the top bunk empty. So she glanced under to the lower bed, but no child.

"Zack," she called, and pushed around the blankets. "Honey, we don't have time to play around. So come out of hiding."

Fear began to build as she glanced around the room. That was when she saw the curtains blowing from the open window. She rushed over to find the screen missing.

"No, God. No!" Her heart stopped then started racing as she frantically checked the closet, then under the bed, calling her son.

"Zack. Oh, God. Where are you? Please come out." Even as she pleaded, something in the back of her mind told her that her worst nightmare had come true. She returned to the bed, jerked back the blankets and found the proof. A crumpled piece of paper.

A familiar feeling of helplessness hit her. Hard. Instinctively Gina knew it was a note from her ex-husband. A shiver ran through her as she picked it up and read, *"I found you, babe. Now I got what you want. You'll be hearing from me."*

*   *   *

Grady Fletcher parked his truck in front of Destiny's sheriff's office and glanced up and down First Street. Mid-morning and the main street was busy with people going about their business, paying no attention to him. Just how he liked it.

He pulled up the collar of his coat and climbed out. He checked the area once again. Although he knew he was safe, old habits died hard. "Stay," he said to his trusted companion.

The German shepherd, Scout, sat in his spot in the backseat. The retired military working dog's ears perked up, waiting for his command. Grady gave a hand signal and the animal lay down. "Be right back, boy."

Grady was adjusting to his new life, too. Suddenly becoming a civilian after twenty years in the army wasn't an easy transition, especially after his last tour of duty. So temporarily living at his grandfather's old cabin was a good thing. It gave him time to heal physically and think about the future. He'd loved the solitude he found in the San Juan Mountains until he found there was a trespasser on his land.

He was going to let the sheriff handle it.

Grady walked through the front door and the room was a buzz of activity. He removed his cowboy hat and looked around. He could sense something was wrong. That was when he caught sight of the small dark-haired woman seated next to the desk. Worry was evident on her face, along with her tears. He decided his business could wait and started to leave when Reed Larkin came out of his office.

The woman stood and hurried to the sheriff. "Please, Reed, we need to start looking for Zack right now."

"And we will, Gina. First, I had to issue an Amber Alert on the boy, and find a description of Eric's last-known vehicle." He glanced over the paper. "That was a 1998 primer-gray Ford truck, Colorado license." He read off the numbers. "I have all the state agencies involved in the search, Gina."

That description sparked Grady's interest. He walked up to the twosome. "Maybe I can help."

They both turned to him, but his attention went to the pretty brunette with the wide green eyes. Grady quickly turned to the sheriff, shielding his injured side.

"Hey, Grady, I haven't seen you in town for a while."

"There's been no need, until today. You're looking for a gray truck? I might know where you can find it."

Gina forced herself to draw in her next breath as she looked up at the giant of a man. He had a head full of sandy-brown hair that curled in thick waves. His dark eyes were deep-set and edged with tiny lines. His chiseled jaw was firm and clean-shaved. She caught a glimpse of an angry red scar on the side of his neck.

Gina gasped. "Where?"

Suddenly the man turned his intense gaze on her. Her first instinct was to back away from the intimidating man, but she forced herself to listen to what he had to say.

She forced herself to move closer. "Did you see a little boy, Mr...?"

"It's Fletcher, ma'am. Grady Fletcher. There's a truck with that description on my grandfather's property. But I haven't seen anyone."

The sheriff spoke up. "This is Gina Williams, Grady. Her seven-year-old son has been taken by his father. Eric Lowell was recently released from prison for drug possession and abuse. He kidnapped the boy from his home sometime during the night. We believe he's dangerous, so any help would be appreciated. Where did you see the vehicle?"

Grady nodded. "On the northeast section of my grandfather's property," he told them. "The truck is partly hidden off the road just below Rocky Top Ridge."

Reed Larkin frowned. "Where your granddad's old mines are?"

The man nodded. "As far as I can tell the truck has been there a few days. I came in to report it. I figured they were thinking the mine is abandoned, or they're trying to jump Fletch's old claim."

"Oh, God," Gina gasped and turned to the sheriff. "Eric's been in town that long, stalking us?"

"It's okay, Gina. We're going to get him." He looked back at Grady. "When was the last time you saw the truck?"

"At dawn this morning," the man said.

Reed nodded. "Did he see you?"

"Not unless he was out walking around early. There wasn't anyone in the truck when I found it."

"Good, we have a possible location," the sheriff said. "My bet is he's holed up in one of the old mines. Can you take us there, Grady?"

He shrugged. "It's pretty rough terrain, but my dog might be able to pick up the trail. Are you and your men experienced hikers?"

Larkin nodded. "We've all had survival training. I hope the weather holds out today."

They started to walk away. Gina went after them. "Wait," she called. "Please, take me with you."

Reed went to her. "Gina, no. You can't handle the climb."

She blinked. "You have no idea what I can handle, Reed. My son is up there with a man who swore he'd get even with me. I'm not going to stand by and wait while he takes his revenge out on Zack."

The sheriff shook his head. "It's not safe."

"I can do this. And I know Eric. I know what pushes his buttons. Besides, he doesn't want Zack, or he'd be on the road heading for parts unknown."

She exchanged a glance with Grady Fletcher. "He wants me." She stood straight. "And as long as my son is safe, I'm willing to make a trade."

Minutes later, Grady stood out of the way as the sheriff made arrangements to leave. It hadn't taken long for Reed to give in to the mother's plea. Grady didn't like this plan, not one bit. Take this woman with them. No way.

He shook his head. He didn't need this problem. All he had to do was take them up to the mine, then leave the sheriff to handle the rest. Right. He wasn't made that way. In the army he'd become a take-charge-guy as a means of survival. But that was before the explosion, before he gave up his career. He shoved the memory aside and turned his thoughts to the problem at hand.

This Lowell must be a crazy bastard to come in and steal his own kid. It definitely could turn out badly.

Just then Gina Williams came out of Reed Larkin's office. She'd changed into hiking boots laced up at the bottom of her jeans. A sweatshirt under a quilted down vest would keep her warm against the cool day. She had her hair pulled back into a ponytail and a wide-brimmed hat to protect her from the elements. Springtime in Colorado was unpredictable. It could mean anything from rain to a full-blown snowstorm.

A blonde woman walked out behind the boy's mother. He recognized her as Lorelei Hutchinson Yeager. She'd pretty much owned this town since her father's death last year. Grady knew about the Hutchinsons only because of his grandfather's stories. Old Fletch had a strong dislike for any members of the town's founding family. It had something to do with disagreements over land rights.

Grady stood straighter when the two women walked his way. Ms. Williams had a stuffed toy in her hand.

"Mr. Fletcher, this is my sister, Lori Yeager. Lori, Grady Fletcher."

He nodded. "Mrs. Yeager."

She managed a smile. "It's Lori. And I can't tell you how much I appreciate your help finding my nephew. Zack means the world to us. If there's anything you need, let Reed know."

Gina looked at Grady. "The sheriff said you have a dog who can track."

He wasn't about to explain that he'd been through hell and back. "Scout was a military working dog. We're both retired now."

Gina held up a floppy-eared rabbit. "This belongs to Zack. Do you think he could pick up his scent?"

Since Scout's injury, he hadn't been put to the test. "It's worth a try."

She hugged her sister and they all walked outside. The sheriff and his two men had loaded up the white four-wheel drive SUV. After instruction to lead, Grady climbed in his own truck and Scout greeted him.

"Looks like we got some work to do. You up to it, fella?"

Surprisingly the animal let out a bark as the passenger-side door opened and the pretty Gina Williams peered in. "The other car is full. Would you mind if I rode with you?"

* * *

It seemed to take forever to get to their destination. The longest twenty minutes in Gina's life, but thanks to Grady Fletcher she now had hope of finding Zack.

She tried to calm herself as she stole a glance at the beautiful scenery along the gravel road leading to the dotting of tall pines in the distance. A stream ran alongside the winding path. She thought of Zack. Was he warm enough? Had Eric hurt him? She tensed. He'd better not have.

Suddenly she felt a nudge on her arm. She started to pull away, then discovered it was Mr. Fletcher's dog. "Hey, fella."

She looked at the man who filled up the truck cab, making Gina very aware of his presence. "Is it okay if I pet him?"

He gave her a curt nod. "It seems Scout wants the attention."

She ran her hand over the shepherd's soft, nearly black coat. "He's a beautiful dog. You said he's a military dog?"

"Yes. He served overseas until last year."

"Were you with him?"

Another curt nod.

Gina continued to rub the dog's fur. She found it gave her comfort, but nothing could stop the fear she felt for her son. She'd thought she'd been so careful. That Eric would never find them.

Out of the blue, Mr. Fletcher said, "Tell me about your…about Eric. How experienced is he with survival skills?"

"Really good. Every year, he'd go with his brothers during hunting season." She had been glad when he was away because it had meant she was safe from his abuse. "Don't put anything past him, Mr. Fletcher."

She couldn't forget the times she had, and he had made her pay. *Oh, God, Zack,* she cried silently. "Eric wasn't supposed to find us here. Destiny was our safe place." She worked to hold it together, but wasn't doing well. "We didn't tell a soul that we'd moved here. We changed our names while he was in prison." She released a sigh. "Why can't he leave us alone?"

For a long time the man didn't say anything, then added, "The sheriff will get him and he'll go back to prison."

"I pray that happens. Right now, all I'm concerned about is my son's safety."

Grady went across the stream, then drove several yards off-road, coming to a stop under a tree, next to some large boulders at the base of hillside. Before he could shut off the engine, Gina jumped out of the truck and had started up the hillside when she felt his hand on her arm.

"Hey, you just can't go running off half-cocked. At least wait for the others."

Before she could argue, a rifle shot rang out, and something hit the tree above their heads.

With a curse, Grady pushed Gina to the ground and covered her body with his. He had to get her out of there. He grabbed her close, hearing her gasp, then rolled them over and over until they were behind the tree.

Gina landed on her back and was swiftly aware of this large man. He braced his arms on either side of her head so his full weight wasn't on her. Still, she was very mindful of the fact of his powerful size. Oddly, she didn't feel panicked or threatened. She had her son to worry about.

He raised his head and those dark brooding eyes locked on hers. "You okay?"

She managed a nod. Again she caught sight of the scarred skin covering the side of his neck.

Another series of shots rang out over their heads. He moved her just as the sheriff's vehicle pulled up and parked in front of them as a shield.

Reed climbed out of the truck. His men scrambled to find cover behind large boulders. The sheriff reached them. "You two okay?"

Grady moved off the woman, trying to forget the awareness he felt. Their gaze connected for an instant before she sat up. This was trouble in more ways than he could count.

"I'm fine, but my son isn't. So I need to go up there."

She started to stand and Grady pulled her back down. "Lady, I know you aren't thinking clearly right now," he growled. "And running up there isn't going to get your son back. That maniac is holding a high-powered rife on us, and he wants you to pay."

Before Grady could stand, Gina Williams gripped his arm. "I don't care how you do it, Mr. Fletcher—just get my son out safely. Please." Tears filled those mesmerizing green eyes. "My life doesn't matter without Zack."

"We'll do whatever it takes to get the boy out of there." Grady moved away, praying he could keep his promise.

I'm so scared. Mom, help me.

Wiping away more tears, Zack sat up on the blanket and began pulling at the ropes that held his wrists and feet together. He had to get away before his dad got back. Struggling with the ropes again, he wished he were strong enough to break free. With only a little light from the lantern, he glanced around the dark cave, but couldn't see anything.

He was all alone.

He bit down on his lip, trying not to cry again. He had to get out and find his mom before Dad hurt her again.

"I got to get loose," he whispered and began to wiggle his hands back and forth feeling the burn, but continuing to fight to get out of the ropes. Using his teeth, he loosened the knot and finally his hands came out. Excited, he untied the ropes at his ankles. He stood, careful not to make any noise. He grabbed the lantern and headed toward the light in the opening. Outside he heard rifle shots so he turned and ran off in the other direction. Far away from danger.

CHAPTER TWO

GRADY stood behind the large boulder as he scanned the rocky rim with binoculars. He followed the dark figure of a man as he moved cautiously among the trees and brush. He'd seen a picture of the suspect and recognized him.

He nudged the sheriff beside him. "Lowell's up there, but I can't see any sign of the boy. Can you?"

Reed looked through his glasses, then said, "No, no sign of Zack, but that's definitely Eric Lowell. We can't rush him. The boy could get hurt. If this guy came all this way to take his son away from his ex-wife, he isn't going to give up easily."

"He'll never give up."

Grady looked over his shoulder to see that Gina approached them.

"I thought you promised to stay in the vehicle. It's not safe here."

She shook her head. "He's got Zack. My child isn't safe with him."

The panicked look on her face tore at Grady. It sent him a painful reminder of what he'd lost. Only he never deserved to have a family in the first place.

"You've got to let me go up there, Reed. Make a trade. Eric wants me. He wants to punish me. Please,

Reed," she pleaded. "Eric knows he's going back to prison. So he has nothing to lose." She wiped the tears that escaped her eyes. "I can't let him hurt Zack. I can't."

When she started to walk into the clearing, Grady grabbed her right arm as another rifle shot rang out. He pulled her back against the rock wall and shielded her. Grady had to work to get his breathing and heart rate under control. That was too close. This lunatic was playing for keeps. "Lady, you've got to stop with the crazy stunts," he growled.

She tossed him a stubborn look. "It doesn't matter. Nothing matters without my son."

"What do you think will happen to Zack if you get yourself killed? You need to let the sheriff handle this."

"Okay, but you don't understand. I can't leave my son up there." She nodded to the ridge. "I promised Zack. I promised him I wouldn't let his dad hurt us again. Please, you've got to help me."

He hated that this woman got to him. As much as Grady wanted to, it was impossible to walk away from this. He turned to Reed Larkin. "What's your next move, Sheriff?"

"I wish I had an answer. I can't take a chance that he'll harm the boy." Larkin gave him a hard look. "You know the area, Fletcher. Is there a back way in?"

Grady nodded, remembering the summers he'd tracked after old Fletch. "You can come in along Miner's Ridge. It's pretty narrow, and it'll take about fifteen minutes, but if Lowell is focused on watching for his ex-wife, we might be able to catch him by surprise. Give me a little time to scope the area."

Grady started to walk back to his truck to arm himself when Larkin stopped him. "I can't ask you to do this."

"You didn't. I volunteered."

"Then I'll need to deputize you first. Do you have a problem with that? I can't let a civilian get involved."

Grady paused as he looked at this woman still gripping that floppy-eared rabbit. Suddenly memories of his past life flashed before him, the picture of the stuffed animals that lined the shelf in his infant son's room. Toys the baby never got the chance to see or play with. He quickly shook it away. "Do what you need to do."

After the sheriff had sworn him in, Grady hurried back to his vehicle and opened the door. Immediately the shepherd stood in the backseat. Scout hesitated. The dog hadn't worked since Afghanistan when he'd been injured. Yet since they'd returned home, Grady had adopted Scout, hoping to get involved in some search-and-rescue operations. It was a good time to test him.

"Come on, boy. We've got a kid to find." The shepherd jumped out of the backseat and waited for his next command.

Grady reached back inside the vehicle, took the Glock from under the driver's seat and tucked the gun in the waistband of his jeans against his back. He was going to be prepared for anything.

Reed appeared. "I see you don't need me to issue you a weapon." The sheriff looked concerned. "I'm going to send one of my men with you."

"No. Alone. I'll move faster and with less chance of being seen." He stared at the sheriff. "You have to trust me on this."

"Okay." Reed Larkin handed him a small radio. "Here, you'll need this to communicate with us."

Grady took it, then walked over to Gina Williams, seeing the fear on her face. "I'll do everything I can to bring the boy back. So don't try anything stupid, or the sheriff will send you back to town. Let us handle this."

She nodded. "Just hurry. Please!"

Grady settled her in the truck and then he went to the sheriff. Grady knew these mountains. His grandpa had taken him around every mine and cliff along this face of the mountain range. He glanced at his dog. "Come on, boy, let's find Zack." He prayed that his words would come true. Maybe this time he would be there when someone's child needed him.

Gina watched as Grady and Scout started up the back side of the mountain. She began to pray that they would be able to get to her son before any harm came to him. She closed her eyes and could feel her ex-husband's slap across her face just as if it were happening again.

But it never stopped at just a slap. There were also those closed fists that slammed into her body. A tear dropped to her cheek and she quickly wiped it away.

No! She wasn't going to let Eric win again. She was going to make a life for her son here in Destiny. Zack was going to have a happy childhood. She wasn't going to let Eric hurt her little boy again. Even if she had to stop him herself.

"Gina."

She opened her eyes to see Reed standing next to the truck. "I wish I could tell you everything is going to be all right, but I can't. Only you know your ex. Has he ever hurt his son?"

"He hadn't until the last time. That's when Eric learned that he could inflict more pain on me by making Zack his target."

Reed's nostrils flared. "I swear, Gina, we'll do everything possible to get Zack away from him. Grady Fletcher is retired army. He's served overseas and is combat trained." The radio squawked. "That's Fletcher."

He pulled the radio out and spoke into it. "Larkin, here."

"I've reached the mine. He could be inside, or Zack could be there. Since I can't see Lowell, I don't know. You need to draw him out."

"Roger." The sheriff looked at Gina. "We need to draw Eric out in the open."

"Use me," she said, and started out of the truck. "I can distract him." She wanted Grady Fletcher to get a good shot at him.

"Give me a few minutes," the sheriff said, then signed off. "Gina, don't do anything foolish. Your ex isn't worried about leaving here. He wants revenge on you."

"I don't care. Zack is the only thing that matters."

"But he needs his mother, too."

"Just not a mother who's let him down so many times," she breathed. "But not this time, not any more."

Grady was pressed flat against the rock wall as he moved toward his target. He gave the hand signal for Scout to stay behind and continued around the boulder. There he heard the sheriff call to Lowell.

"Hey, Eric, your wife wants to talk to you."

Nothing. There was no movement, no sign of the guy. "Come on, you bastard," Grady breathed.

Then he heard Gina's voice. "Eric!" she called. "Eric, please talk to me. I know you don't want to hurt Zack. So I want to make a trade. Zack for me."

Lowell finally spoke. "I'm not falling for that," he told her.

Grady got a location. The kidnapper was just on the other side of the boulder. He looked down at Scout to see the animal's ears go up. He gave a hand signal to stay. The animal obeyed.

Again, Gina called out. "Please, Eric. I'll do whatever you want. Just don't hurt Zack. Please."

"I like to hear you beg, Gina," Lowell said. "Come on, convince me some more."

That was when Grady saw him. The man came out just enough to get into his line of sight. He looked to be around six feet tall. His body was lean and strong, probably from working out in prison. Grady wasn't impressed. Not by a man who used his strength to beat up on women. He just hoped the guy wasn't too smart.

Lowell called his ex-wife a few choice names. "Tell me what you want, wife. You always want something." The man moved toward the ledge. He knelt down for protection. "I'll need more than just you, if you want my son. That big sister of yours inherited a boatload of money. I want a cut."

"How much?" Gina asked without hesitation.

"A few million should get me where I want to go. I'll also need transportation."

There was a pause, then Gina said, "It's going to take some time."

"You got an hour," he told her.

Grady saw his chance and took it. He came out behind the guy, just as he turned around. Grady managed to knock Eric's rifle out of his hand, but that didn't stop him.

Lowell charged at him, landing several blows, then Grady got in a good one, knocking the man down. He called to Scout once he had subdued Eric on the ground in a choke hold.

"I got him," Grady yelled down to the sheriff, then to Lowell he said, "I wouldn't move if I were you." He nodded toward the growling dog. "Scout will catch you. And I haven't fed him today."

Eric cursed but didn't put up a fight as Larkin and his men showed up. One of the deputies took charge and cuffed Lowell. Larkin finished reading him his rights when Gina Williams showed up.

She ran to her ex. "Where is Zack?" she demanded.

"Go to hell," he said. His words were slurred, his eyes glassy. Drugs, in all likelihood.

Grady walked up. "Let's check the mine," he said, taking out his penlight and heading to the opening that had once been boarded up but now showed signs of some of the boards having been pulled away. He stepped through the slats, Larkin and Gina right behind him.

"Come, Scout," he called to his dog.

The shepherd immediately went into the darkness and Grady turned on the flashlight, and followed.

Gina cried out, "Zack! Mom's here and you're safe. Zack!" There wasn't a sound, then a bark from Scout. They walked carefully through the maze of rocks and mining equipment. Then they reached the wide opening. That was where they saw the light and sleeping bags and camp lanterns. There was a pile of ropes abandoned on the blanket.

Gina searched around. "Where's Zack?"

"Not sure," the sheriff said. "Maybe Eric moved him." He flashed the light around the cave and over the piles of blankets to the empty food containers. Then he picked up the knotted ropes. "Do you think Zack could have got away?" He glanced at Grady. "Is there another way out?"

Grady had to think a minute. Then he heard Scout's bark again. "This way." He started off and the others followed. They were led through a maze of rocks until they saw some light and were outside in the back of the cliff. There was no sign of the boy.

"Where is he?" Gina demanded.

Not waiting for an answer, she returned to the front of the cave. Marching over to her ex-husband, she began pounding him with her fists. "Where's Zack? Tell me. Damn you, tell me."

Lowell tried to move, but the deputies held him there. "Get her the hell away from me."

When Reed Larkin finally pulled Gina back, Grady could see her tears on her face. He was about ready to give her something to beat the SOB with.

Gina couldn't hold back any more and sobbed. "Where's my son?"

An evil grin appeared on the jerk's face. "Hell, Gina, I hid him so deep, you'll never find him."

Suddenly Grady reached out and gripped Eric's shirt, getting the man's attention. "You'd better hope that's a lie, because if anything you said has one ounce of truth in it, I'll personally take care of you myself. So I suggest you don't push any more of my buttons, or I'll bury you so deep no one will find you," he said through clenched teeth, then he finally released Lowell, causing him to stumble backward.

"Hey, he threatened me," Eric cried.

"I didn't hear anything," the sheriff told him, and the deputies agreed. "Maybe you better talk, and fast."

"Who the hell are you?"

Fletcher moved closer. "Your worst nightmare. I've done two tours of duty in Afghanistan. I know a lot of ways to torture someone, and get rid of the body."

Lowell's eyes grew wide. "I swear, I left Zack back

in the cave and he was tied up when I came out. I don't know where he is now."

Grady got in his face again. "I'd better not find out you're lyin'."

Eric cringed, looking like the coward he was. "Sheriff, get him away from me, I told you everything I know."

"Take him down to the truck," Reed said.

After the deputies took Lowell off to the vehicle, Gina turned to the sheriff. "We've got to go look for Zack."

"We will, Gina," Reed promised, and turned to Grady. "Could Scout find the boy?"

"We can try." Grady looked around the dark area, but Scout wasn't there. He put two fingers in his mouth and whistled. "Scout. Come." There wasn't even the sound of a bark. Now it was time for Grady to panic.

"Please, don't hurt me," Zack cried as the big wolf came toward him. He raised his shaking hand and waved, hoping the animal would leave his hiding place. "Just go away. Please."

Zack took off running. He wasn't sure what he was more afraid of, the animal or his dad finding him. He climbed the rough hillside, and went through a group of trees, but every time he looked back the big wolf was still following him. He tripped on a rock and cried out as he fell. He rolled over and saw his bloody palms. It hurt so bad, but he wasn't going to cry. He just had to get away.

He got up and started to walk again, hoping he could find someone who would get him back to his mom. He looked up at the sky. It was getting late and it was going to be dark soon. That scared him. Nighttime was when bad things happened. He glanced over his shoulder to see the wolf was still following him. Zack climbed over the next rock and stopped. There was a coyote, then soon there were three of them.

Suddenly the wolf following him took off after the wild dogs. The animals fought, and soon the coyotes ran away, but not the wolf, who came back to him. Afraid, Zack backed away, but the animal still came closer. Then he saw a collar and a tag hanging from his neck. "You're a dog?"

As if he understood, the animal barked at him.

All at once the wind began to blow and Zack hugged himself. It began to rain, and lightning and thunder weren't far behind.

The dog barked again and started off, but stopped and waited for him. Maybe the dog was taking him home. Zack went after him, but they came to another mine and the dog slipped inside, showing him the way.

Shivering, he went inside the dark old mine. He didn't know what else to do. Inside, he stayed close to the opening, and the fading light, but couldn't help but be curious by all the treasures. An old mining car sat on tracks. He wished there were some blankets to keep him warm. It began to pour rain outside and he stepped back. The dog came up beside him, and Zack stood very still, then he reached down and petted him. His fur was soft.

"Good dog," Zack managed to say.

The animal nudged him away from the entrance and Zack sat. The dog sat, too. "Can I see your collar?" Zack carefully reached for the silver tag and read the letters.

"U.S. Army. Your name is Scout. Wow, you're an army dog. You can protect me."

Scout laid his head on Zack's leg, and he was beginning to feel a little better. Now, if only his mom would find him.

CHAPTER THREE

THREE hours later, and exhausted from the search, everyone stood next to the sheriff's vehicles to figure out the next move. They'd had to wait out the heavy rain, then had gone back out and combed the area once it let up, but any trail of her son had been washed out.

"But we can't leave Zack out there," Gina cried.

A frustrated Reed Larkin said, "Of course not, Gina, but it's getting dark. I need to go back to town and get more volunteers and we'll start out again at first light. The men need to eat, and get some rest."

"It could be too late by then," Gina argued.

The sheriff turned to Grady Fletcher. "Is there a chance your dog might be with Zack?"

Gina was hopeful. "Is that true?"

Grady nodded. "Scout might have got the boy's scent and gone after him. If the dog couldn't get the boy to follow him back to us, he'd stay."

She was hopeful. "So Zack's not alone out there?"

"It's a possibility," Grady told her. "I don't know for sure." He hesitated. "Scout had some injuries while in Afghanistan."

Gina frowned. "Injuries? So you don't know how he'll act? Could he harm Zack?"

Grady shook his head. "Scout wouldn't hurt anyone

unless he's given provocation. If he found your son, he's been trained to stay with him. He'll protect him with his life."

The sheriff stepped in. "I know I can't get you to go back to town, Gina, but I can call Lori."

"No, I don't want her out in this weather. She's pregnant and Jace is out of town."

"So you're going to spend the night in a truck?" the sheriff argued. "And there's more rain expected."

"I'll be all right." She turned to Grady. "That is, if you'd be willing stay, too. Of course I'll pay you for your time."

The man straightened. "I don't want your money. I'll stay for the boy and for my dog. But a better plan might be to go to my grandfather's cabin up the road. At least dry off and get something to eat."

Reed Larkin stepped in. "That's a good idea, Gina. You can't just keep wandering around these mountains. You'll get lost. That isn't going to help Zack."

How could she leave her son? "How far away is the cabin?"

"About a half mile from here," he offered. "You'll at least be close by, and if Scout leads the boy out, he'll bring him to the cabin."

She looked back at Reed. "Go, Gina," he told her. "You're chilled to the bone. I'll be back at first light."

It had been a long time since she'd trusted a man, outside of her new brother-in-law, Jace, and a few of the townspeople. It looked like she didn't have much of a choice.

"Thank you, Grady," Gina said. "I promise I won't be a problem."

Grady knew that wasn't true. Gina Williams had already caused him the kind of trouble he didn't need right now. "I know. And you'll at least dry off and get some food in you."

The sheriff stopped Grady. "I'll be back at dawn." He handed him his card. "If anything happens before then call my cell phone."

Then the men loaded into the vehicles and drove down the road.

"Come on, let's get you warmed up." Grady helped Gina into the truck, then turned on the heater, trying to stop her shivering. The temperature had already dropped with the fading daylight, and with the combination of the rain, it was damn cold. He, too, was worried about the boy, praying he had found cover.

He drove along the bumpy road that led to the old log cabin that he'd called home for the past three months. In the dim light, the place didn't look much better than when he'd officially moved in a few months ago, knowing his grandfather needed a lot of help for his recovery.

After parking the truck, he got out to help his guest, but she'd already jumped down by the time he reached her. He climbed the steps to the porch that sorely needed to be replaced. It was one of the many things on his list. He would get to that in time. But it meant he wasn't exactly ready to have guests.

He unlocked the door and swung it open and allowed Gina to step inside. He followed and quickly went to the back room and switched on the compressor, then returned and turned on the table lamp.

"Oh, my," she said. "It really is rustic."

He glanced at her. "There's a generator for the refrigerator and lights, but wait until you need to use the facilities. They're still out back."

She shrugged. "Then maybe I should head there now."

With a nod, he showed her the little house toward the back of the cabin. He waited on the porch as the last of day turned into night. It only took a few minutes before she came hurrying back to the cabin.

Inside again he watched her examine her surroundings in the main room. A huge stone fireplace and rough log walls were as far as the rustic charm went. It got worse with the old sofas and two chairs that were covered in a faded fabric. A big scarred table took up most of the kitchen area. He'd like to get rid of a lot of it.

Old Fletch had had the entire space crowded with furniture. His grandfather never threw out anything. Thank goodness he hadn't inherited that trait from the old man. Since he'd heard about his grandfather's accident, he'd been doing double duty. Once he'd arrived here from Texas, he'd been going to the nursing home to oversee Fletch's recovery from his broken hip. He'd also been trying to clean up this place by hauling things off to the dump.

He handed her a blanket and lit the logs in the fireplace. "It'll be warm soon."

"I'm fine, really," she said, unable to stop her shivering. "I can't tell you how much I appreciate you letting me stay here. I just need to be close by."

"I understand." He went into the kitchen area. "I'm going to reheat some stew I made last night."

"Please don't feel you have to wait on me." She stood by the fire. "I'll probably just sit right here."

"I'm going to eat, so you might as well."

She nodded. "Okay, what can I do to help?"

He nodded toward the cupboard as she came into the kitchen area. "The bowls and spoons are in there."

Gina did as he asked. She was surprised at the cabin, especially the array of furniture crammed inside. The cabinet that held the dishes was an antique. "You have a lot of…things."

"It all belongs to my grandfather. He's been in a nursing home. I've been trying to clear out most of this stuff since I came here a few months ago."

She looked at him. "Are you selling the furniture? I might know of someone who's interested."

"In this junk?"

She raised an eyebrow. "Your grandfather has some nice pieces. This cabinet is probably an antique. It's a Hoosier." She glanced over the scarred wood. "It might need work, but it's worth some money."

He turned up the flame on the camp stove and set the pan on top. "Really?"

Gina once again saw on his neck the long burn scar that ran past his collar. She didn't want to stare, but it was hard not to. "You said Scout was injured by a bomb. Were you with him?"

He stopped, but didn't answer for a while. Then he looked at her with those dark brooding eyes. "Are you asking if that's where I got my scar?"

She nodded.

"Yeah. It's not pretty, but I was one of the lucky ones."

Grady tried not to think about that day, or the two men he'd lost.

"I'm sorry. It must have been horrible."

"Yeah, war usually is."

Grady thought back to the two young soldiers, Jimmy and Vince. After he'd been well enough to leave the hospital, Grady had made a trip to West Virginia to visit Jimmy Prescott's family, then he'd gone on to Georgia to see Vince Johnson's kin.

Gina drew his attention back to the present. "What about you?" she asked. "Do you have any family?"

He didn't like where this was headed. "You sure are full of questions."

She shrugged. "Seems you know everything about me and my sordid past."

He frowned. "It's not sordid. You did nothing wrong. The man beat you. There's nothing lower than that. You did the right thing by sending him to jail."

"Not as soon as I should have," she admitted. "I had the misconception that I could love Eric enough to make him stop." She raised her chin. "He just didn't love me enough to want to. Now, my son is paying for it."

He stopped himself from going to her. She didn't need the kind of comfort he was willing to give. "Hey, we all have regrets," he told her. Hell, he had a boatload of them. "Sometimes love isn't enough." Removing the pan from the stove, he carried it to the table and emptied the stew into the bowls. "Sit down. You need to eat."

She did as he asked. "I'm really not hungry."

He sat across from her. "Eat anyway. You need strength to hike around the mountains. I don't need to have to carry you out of there tomorrow."

She took a small bite and chewed slowly. "You're good at giving orders."

He swallowed a spoonful of stew. "I've had a lot of years to practice."

Those deep green eyes widened and he felt a stirring of awareness. "How long were you in the army?"

He watched her take another bite. "I went in the day I turned eighteen, and got discharged last December. Twenty years." When had he suddenly become such an open book?

"You don't look old enough."

And she looked far too young for him to think about anything beyond helping to find her son. So he needed to stop the direction of his thoughts. "Spoken like a respectful youngster."

She raised an eyebrow. "I'm not so young."

"What, twenty-five?"

"Twenty-seven…my next birthday."

Still far too young for him. Think of her as a kid sister. That didn't work, either. He was drawn to her intriguing eyes once again, then his gaze lowered to her mouth and he felt the reaction like a slam in the gut. He glanced away. It had been nearly two years since he'd reacted so strongly to a woman. Not since his marriage had fallen apart. Definitely not since the accident. He stood. "Do you want any more?"

"No thank you. I'm finished."

"Okay, if you need to use the bathroom again, I suggest you go now." He looked out the window. "It's started to rain again."

She nodded. "I'm fine."

Well, he wasn't. So the sooner they found the boy the better. Then he could get back to his life.

"You think you can get away from me? Think again, bitch."

Gina huddled in the corner, trying to protect her body from Eric's vicious blows. "Please stop!" she cried, praying he'd tire and let her alone.

"Never. I'll always find you. You'll never get away. Never." He stepped back, stumbling drunkenly.

Zack suddenly appeared. "Stop hurting my mom," he cried, and began hitting his dad. "Go away. Leave us alone."

Eric grabbed the boy, swung back his fist and she screamed. "No! Don't hit him! No!"

"Gina! Wake up"

She felt someone shaking her. She finally opened her eyes and saw the large figure leaning over her. She gasped and pushed him away. "Please, don't," she cried and scurried to the end of the sofa.

Grady stepped back and raised his hands in surrender. "Hey, it's me, Grady. You had a bad dream. I woke you, that's all. I'm not going to hurt you, Gina. You're safe here."

Gina brushed her hair back, trying to slow her breathing. "Oh, God, Grady, I'm so sorry." She glanced up to see the man standing there in the dark shadows in a pair of Levi's and a T-shirt over a well-toned body. "Please tell me I didn't hit you. Are you all right?"

In the shadowed light, Grady stared back at her, knowing it best to keep his distance. He wished he could get his hands on Lowell again. "Question is, are you?"

She nodded, but avoided any eye contact. "The nightmare must have been triggered by Eric taking Zack."

At least she'd got a few hours of sleep. He'd covered her with a blanket before going into the one bedroom in the cabin.

She finally looked at him. "Is it light enough to start searching again?"

He nodded. "I expect by the time we have some coffee, it'll be daylight." He sure wasn't going to get any more sleep.

After Grady dressed in fresh jeans and a shirt, he made coffee and they pulled on their coats and headed to the truck. It only took a few minutes to get back to the original spot where Eric's truck had been parked the day before. Where Gina Williams's nightmare had started.

Grady ended the call to the sheriff and put his cell phone back into his pocket. "Larkin said they'll be here in ten minutes."

"I can't wait." Gina opened the truck door. "I'm going to head up." She was out of the cab.

Grady jumped out and went after her. He grabbed her by the arm, and she immediately jerked away. He raised his hands in surrender.

"Sorry. I just don't want you to run off. You don't know the area and could get lost, too. Besides, I want to check out another mine, the Lucky Penny." He pointed to a different direction. "We didn't get to it last night."

"Why not?"

They started climbing the slope. "For one thing, it was too dark and it's a lot farther."

"Why do you think Zack could be there?"

"Scout knows the mines around here. I've been working with him there on some search-and-rescue training."

Gina was frustrated. Her son had been out in the elements all night and all she wanted was to find him. "Okay, let's go there."

He nodded and they started their hike to the Lucky Penny.

She managed to keep up with him. "Do you think Zack would follow your dog to safety?"

"Your son seems pretty resourceful. He was smart enough to get untied and run away from his dad, then he's smart enough to stay out of the weather."

"But he doesn't know that he's safe from his dad. He might still be hiding."

Zack was shivering when he woke up. He'd been cold all night, even with Scout sleeping beside him, keeping him warm. He was still next to him now. He wished it were his mom with him. He was so scared and his scraped hand hurt.

"What do we do, Scout? I don't want my dad to find me. He's mean, and he hurts Mom." He stroked the dog's fur. "He'll hurt me, too, because I ran away." He brushed away a tear, hating to cry.

The dog got up and gave a bark.

Maybe Scout could protect him. But his dad had a gun. He wiped away more tears. "Why can't my dad just leave us alone?" he said, making a fist. "I don't want to go away and have to hide again. I like living in Destiny with my mom, Aunt Lori and Uncle Jace and my cousin Cassie."

The dog cocked his head as if he were listening to every word.

"We have a new house and I'm gonna try out for baseball next month. I get to have a birthday party this year." He didn't care about that. He only wanted his mom.

The animal made a whining sound and looked toward the cave opening.

Zack was suddenly afraid again. What if his dad got his mom, and hurt her? He didn't know what to do.

Suddenly the animal jumped up and went to the opening, then he looked back and barked. He came back several times, and nudged at him before he ran outside.

"Wait, Scout," Zack cried and took off after him. Once he was outside, the sunlight nearly blinded him. The dog barked again, then he heard a voice calling his name.

He tried not to cry, but he couldn't help it. "Mom!" he yelled, and followed Scout. "Mom!"

* * *

Gina stopped when she heard the sound. She grabbed Grady's arm. "I hear something."

Grady paused and the next sound was that of a dog barking. He put two fingers in his mouth and let loose with a loud whistle. He was rewarded with another bark.

"This way," he said. "It's coming from the Lucky Penny." He pointed toward their left, then took her hand and helped her climb up the slope. When they reached the cluster of boulders, a dog and child appeared.

Her heart was beating wildly. "Zack," she cried, and ran to her son.

"Mom," he cried, throwing himself into her arms.

"Oh, Zack." The tears poured out of her as she hugged him tight, breathing in his familiar smell. Even with the mixture of dirt and sweat, it was heavenly. "Oh, thank goodness you're safe." She pulled back and did a quick examination. "We were so worried. Where did you go?"

The child looked worried. "When I got untied, I was afraid Dad would come back to get me. So I ran away. Where is he?"

"Oh, honey." She smiled. "Don't worry. Sheriff Larkin has your dad in jail. Mr. Fletcher helped capture him." She hugged her son again. "He's never going to hurt us again. I promise, Zack. I promise. You must have been so scared."

Her son pulled away. "I was at first." He glanced down at the dog. "Scout came and stayed with me." His brown eyes widened. "Mom, he's a military dog."

She managed a nod. "I know. He's trained to find people and I'm so grateful that he found you."

"He kept me warm all night long." Zack looked at Grady. "Is he your dog?"

"Yes, he is." Grady stood next to the animal, who sat

perfectly still. "We've been in a lot of tight situations together. Scout was trained to find bombs. I guess now he can add little boys to the list."

Gina had completely forgotten about the introductions. "Zack, this is Mr. Fletcher. He's helped me search for you."

"Thank you. I'm glad you had Scout." Zack went over to the animal. "Can I pet him?"

"I know Scout would like that."

Grady watched the affection between the two. This was a new experience for Scout. A child was hard to resist, could even be distracting. Grady glanced at Gina Williams. So was his mother.

"Maybe we should head back down," he said. "You need to get warm and checked out to make sure you're okay."

They started walking down the slope just as the sheriff's vehicle appeared next to his truck. The next ten minutes were chaotic as Grady stood back and let the paramedic look over the boy. Then they all piled into the vehicle.

"I can't thank you enough for all you did, Grady." She smiled for real this time and he found he liked it too much. "My son is everything to me," she managed to say.

"Then you'd better go tend to him." Scout sent a bark toward his new friend in the SUV. Grady watched Gina get into the vehicle and drive off. Suddenly he was alone once again, and realized it wasn't what he truly wanted at all.

Be careful what you wish for.

CHAPTER FOUR

Four hours later Gina stood at her sister, Lori's, family room entrance and watched her son sleeping on the pull-out sofa bed. She still felt shaky, thinking about the thirty-six-hour ordeal. Worse, how things could have turned out.

A tear fell against her cheek. Zack was back safe with her. She had so many people to thank; one in particular, Grady Fletcher. The stranger who had put everything else aside and led the sheriff to Eric, then had stayed with her the entire time, keeping her sane until they found Zack. And Scout. What a special dog to protect her son.

"Is he asleep?" Lori whispered as she came up behind her.

Gina nodded, and followed her sister into the kitchen. "I promised I'd stay close by."

Lori motioned for her to take a seat at the large kitchen island. "I think we're close enough to hear him if he wakes."

Technically her half sister, Lorelei Hutchinson Yeager was a pretty blonde with big brown eyes and a generous heart. Last fall she'd come to Destiny when she inherited her estranged father's fortune. She'd fallen in love and married a building contractor, Jace Yeager, and moved into his house with his daughter, Cassie. Just recently they'd got a big surprise when Lori learned she was pregnant.

Gina glanced around the newly remodeled room. Jace had done a great job of refinishing the fixer-upper home, especially the kitchen. The large space had custom maple cabinets, granite counters and top-of-the-line stainless-steel appliances.

Gina was proud she'd helped Lori add some special touches with the burnt-orange paint and bright yellow accents.

Lori set a cup of hot tea in front of her. "Here, drink this."

"Thanks," Gina told her. "You should sit down, too. You have to be tired."

"I'm fine. Really."

When Gina was growing up, Lori had been more than a big sister. She had filled in where their mother couldn't or wouldn't. Still Gina had become a rebellious teenager when she'd met wild boy Eric Lowell. Lori had never deserted her though, especially when things had got rough and Eric had begun knocking her around.

Last fall when Lori had come to Destiny to claim her inheritance from her father, Lyle Hutchinson, she'd sent for Gina and Zack, hoping they all could start a new life here together. Then somehow Eric had found them.

Gina felt the emotions churning up again, but this time she couldn't push them away and she began to sob.

Lori shot around the island and pulled her sister into her arms. "Oh, honey. Let it out. You've been through hell the past two days."

Gina cried until her throat was raw and she finally wiped away the last of her tears. "I thought we were safe. How foolish could I be to think Eric would leave us alone?"

"Well, he's going to be staying away now. He'll be in jail. If the kidnapping charge doesn't stick, shooting at the sheriff and at you should carry some weight."

Heavens, she prayed that would work. "He's got off before."

"This is his third offence, Gina. That hateful man took my nephew and he isn't going to get away with that. Not this time."

Gina thought back to all the people who'd helped her in the past few days. The entire town had volunteered. They'd cooked meals, asked to be deputized and searched for Zack, or just prayed for his safe return. Once again she thought of the one man who had truly helped her find her son.

"Lori, what do you know about Grady Fletcher?"

Her sister blinked at her question, then smiled. "Not much, only that he's been in the bank a few times. I know more about his grandfather, Joe Fletcher. The old miner is recuperating from a broken hip at Shady Haven Nursing Home. Since Grady was listed as next of kin, he's been handling things until Fletch gets back on his feet. I'm not sure that's going to happen since his grandfather has to be in his eighties."

"So he doesn't live here?"

Lori shrugged. "It would be nice if he did. From what Reed told me about what happened on the mountain, I'd say Grady is a take-charge kind of guy. And for what he did for Zack, he's pretty high on my list of good people. Not bad-looking, either."

Gina wasn't surprised by her sister's assessment. She hadn't had much time to notice, but once the dust had settled, she had taken a look at the handsome man. "You'd better not let Jace hear you talk like that."

Lori smiled. "He has nothing to worry about. I only have eyes for my husband."

"That's good to know."

They turned around to see Jace Yeager standing in the doorway. The tall, dark and handsome man was smiling at his wife. "Because I'm kind of crazy about you, too."

Lori rushed across the room, wrapped her arms around him and rewarded him with a tender kiss. "I thought you weren't coming home until tomorrow," she said.

"My family needed me. So I made it happen." He walked over to Gina and pulled her into a big hug. "I'm so sorry I wasn't here for you and Zack."

She nodded. "It's okay, Jace. We got him back and that's all that matters."

That was when they heard a child's cry from the other room. Gina jumped up and hurried to the sofa bed.

"It's okay, honey." She sat on the edge of the bed and pulled her son into her arms.

There were tears in her son's eyes. "Mom, I dreamed Dad was coming after me."

"Never. He's never going to get near you ever again." She looked up at Lori and Jace. "Hey, Uncle Jace came home so he could be with you."

Jace walked to the sofa. "That's right, partner. I heard you had a rough few days."

The child nodded eagerly. "Yeah, I got tied up in a cave."

Gina saw her brother-in-law stiffen, working to control his anger. He kept his voice calm. "Man, that's bad. I'm proud of you for being smart enough to handle it."

He messed the boy's hair. "So you spent the night in a cave."

The boy's eyes grew wide. "Yeah, but Scout was with me. He's a big German shepherd. I didn't get scared too much because he was there to protect me from other animals and bad people."

"Sounds like Scout is a pretty neat dog."

Again the child nodded. "He was in the military. He's a hero like Grady." Zack looked at his mom. "I wish I had a dog like Scout. I wouldn't be afraid then."

All eyes turned to Gina. "Yeah, Mom," Jace mimicked. "A dog would be good protection."

Gina had always planned to get her son a dog once they were settled. Her house had a fenced-in yard. "I guess a dog wouldn't be a bad idea."

Her son nearly jumped into her arms. "You're the best mom in the whole world."

Those words were enough to completely sell her on the idea, and to remind her how close she'd come to losing her son. "And you're the best son in the whole world."

The next morning was Saturday, and as Gina promised, she drove her son out to the cabin to thank Grady. Even for her small all-wheel-drive vehicle, it was slow going over the pitted dirt road. She wasn't sure that she was headed in the right direction until she came through a grove of trees and finally saw the cabin in the clearing.

"Oh, boy." It wasn't much of a clearing. More like a junkyard. Something she hadn't noticed when she was here before. Suddenly she was rethinking her decision to come, wondering if Grady Fletcher just wanted to be left alone.

"Grady might be busy, Zack. I'm not sure if we should just drop in on him."

"Come on, Mom. We don't have to stay long. I want to give Scout my present."

They'd spent all morning shopping for a reward for the dog. "Okay, but if he doesn't have the time, then we leave. Mr. Fletcher is a busy man."

Then the cabin door opened and the German shepherd came out and greeted them with a bark, but stayed on the porch. Gina's heart skipped a beat when the tall man stepped through the door. He was dressed in jeans and a dark thermal shirt, showing off his muscular build. Her body reacted, not in fear but in awareness. Well, darn.

"Scout!" her son called and jumped out of the car. Zack took off running to the dog before she could stop him.

Grady stood rooted on the porch, surprised to see Gina Williams again. Then she stepped out of her car and he found his heart suddenly beating faster. He wasn't happy about that, or about the lack of sleep he'd had since the night she'd invaded his cabin.

Dressed in jeans tucked into boots and a sweater and thermal vest, she reached into the backseat and took out a cellophane-wrapped basket.

She walked toward the steps. "I hope we're not disturbing you."

She didn't want to know the answer to that. "I can take a break." He looked down at Zack. He was glad that the boy looked to be doing well. "Hey, Zack. How are you feeling today?"

He stood on the bottom step, and Scout sat eagerly on the porch waiting for a command to go greet his new friend.

"I had a nightmare last night, but then I pretended that Scout was with me and felt better." The boy waited. "Mom said I need to ask you first if I can pet Scout 'cause he might be in training." Both kid and dog looked up at him waiting for an answer.

"When he's not working he can play. And he's not working now."

Zack grinned. "I got Scout a present. Mom got you something, too." He pulled a long tug rope with a handle on the end from the bag he was carrying. "Is this okay?"

It was okay for Scout, but he didn't want anyone bringing *him* presents. Especially a distracting woman with a little boy. "Yeah, it's okay, but Scout can pull pretty hard."

"I know he's really strong."

Grady pointed to a cleared spot. "Go over in the yard."

The bright sunlight seemed to highlight all the junk that littered the area. Two rusted-out vehicles, a mess of mining equipment. "I've been trying to clear away most of this stuff, but couldn't do much until the snow melted."

Gina nodded. "I'm sure you can get a lot for the scrap metal."

"I might have hell to pay from my grandfather, but I've got someone coming here in a few days. I'm hoping it will all be cleared out." He sighed. "Then I plan to cart some stuff out of the inside so I have room to move around." He shook his head. "I don't know how the man didn't kill himself. What am I saying? He broke his hip."

The boy called Scout and they ran off to the yard. That meant he was left alone to deal with the mother.

Gina carried the basket up the steps. "I wanted to talk to you about that."

"About what?"

"Your furniture. Well, your grandfather's that is." She stepped onto the porch. "I have a thrift store in town called Second Best. If there are things you want to get rid of, I can sell them for you on consignment…."

That surprised the hell out of him. "That's what you do for a living?"

She nodded. "I kind of fell into it. I started by staging my sister's business complex, then she asked me to decorate some bank-owned properties. I got the idea for a store when I ended up with all this furniture people left behind." She nodded toward the cabin. "Seems like you have extra furniture, too. If you want to get rid of some things, I'd be happy to have a look."

"I'll check with Fletch when I visit him the next time."

"Good." She held out the package in her hands. "I also brought you a little something."

Though embarrassed by her gesture, Grady couldn't refuse her gift. "You didn't have to."

"It's not much. Really. Just some turkey and ham and cheeses from the sandwich shop in town. We wanted to thank you for everything you did. Especially having to put up with me."

Spending time with her hadn't been a burden. Finding her son had been the good part. "Hey, I was in the military for years, so I'm used to taking orders."

She made a face, but it didn't take away from her beauty. He doubted anything could. "Was I that bad?"

"You were just willing to do whatever it took to get your child back. I'm glad everything came out okay." He motioned her toward the door. "Please come in."

First, Gina glanced at Zack to see he was okay with

Scout then turned and told Grady, "He makes a great babysitter."

"Scout hasn't been around kids much, but I can see that I don't have anything to worry about. And since I've adopted him and am training him for search and rescue, I was impressed with how well he did finding Zack."

"Will you be staying here after your grandfather comes home?"

"My plans are to go back to Texas, San Antonio, outside Lackland AFB. That's where I plan to do my training with my partner."

"I see." Gina wasn't sure of what else to say as she crossed the threshold so she concentrated on her surroundings. In the daylight, she was able to get a better look. There was some junk, but she'd been right the night she stayed here. There were several good pieces, too. "Do you know what you'd like to keep?"

When she heard his sigh, she realized how close he was standing to her. "About half this," he told her. "I can barely move around as it is. "I'm going to throw out two of the sofas."

She set the basket down on the table. "Which two?"

He pointed out the two worst of the three. "I'll take them," she told him.

"You're kidding?"

"No. They're older, but the frames look to be in great shape. I can reupholster them and sell them in the shop."

"They're yours," he assured her.

Gina examined all the different antique pieces that interested her. He told her no when she asked about the Hoosier cabinet. She'd expected that, but she got a nice sideboard and two end tables to sell on consignment. And he just gave her the old rocking chair.

"Is there more?"

He arched a brow, and she caught a gleam in those dark brown eyes. Then a smile tugged at the corner of his mouth and there was a strange feeling in her stomach.

"Show me?" Her voice was a little throaty.

He didn't say a word as he walked to the doorway leading to another room. She followed tentatively as he opened the door and she stepped through into the next room.

She immediately saw the huge bed that took up most of the limited space. She got closer to the metal frame to see that it was brass, heavily tarnished, but definitely brass. "Oh, my. This is quite something."

"Oh, yeah, it is," Grady agreed. "And my grandfather was very proud of this bed."

"I take it he had it for years."

He nodded. "Ever since I can remember. And I spent a lot of summers here as a kid. Fletch was so proud that he bought it with one of his first gold strikes."

Gina walked around to the other side. "Of course he wouldn't want to sell it?"

He shrugged. "It does take up a lot of room, but probably not."

She glanced around. Like the other space the room was crowded with furniture. "There would be more room to move around if you removed one of these armoires." She went to one cabinet and examined the hand-carved detail on the doors. "This is a lovely piece. I'm not an expert, but I could have an appraiser look at it."

He hesitated, so Gina moved on to the other cabinet. "This one is nice, too. Not as well made, but I could sell it for you if you want."

This was the last thing Grady thought he'd be doing today. When Gina Williams showed up on his doorstep, he didn't think they'd end up in his bedroom. *Whoa, don't go there.*

"Grady?"

He shook off the thoughts. "Sure, I'll check with my grandfather and get back to you. Just leave me the bed and something to put clothes in. Right now my focus is working on the outside."

"Well, I should let you get back to it. I'll go."

She turned to leave and Grady reached for her arm. Then hearing her gasp, realized his mistake. He also saw the panicked look in her eyes and released her. "Sorry. I didn't mean to startle you."

"It's okay. I'm still a little jumpy."

"No, I had no right to grab you like that. Look, you don't have to leave. It's just my frustration with all this stuff in the cabin. Hell, I don't know what to do with fifty years of junk around here. I wouldn't know an antique if it bit me."

"Are you trying to get ready to sell this place?"

He shook his head. "No, but my grandfather can't continue to live like this if he wants to come back here. I'm training dogs, and since I'm staying here longer than planned, I need to build temporary kennels.

"First, I need to clear an area outside. A guy is coming Monday to haul off all the things in the front yard. So the inside of the cabin isn't a top priority."

She smiled. "You're going to train more dogs for a living."

He wanted to make a living at something he enjoyed, and that was working with dogs. "Since I'm retired from the army, I need to do something. Of course, Grandpa

Fletch could be a handful." He couldn't abandon the old man who had always been there for him.

"Sounds like a interesting man."

"He has his moments. I'll ask him about the furniture the next visit, because I can't concentrate on the cabin until then." This bedroom was getting smaller by the minute. Her scent drifted in his direction, reminding him of the things he'd lost, that he'd chosen to walk away from.

She followed him back into the main room. "Then we're out of your hair."

She headed for the door, then paused and turned back to him with those sparkling green eyes. "I have an idea. How about if when you get the okay from your grandfather, I'll handle organizing the inside of the cabin for you?" She walked back to him so he got the full effect of her beauty. Her flawless skin and perfect mouth. All that thick brown hair brushing her shoulders made his hands itch to touch it.

"There's no need for you to do that."

"I know, but you rescued my son. There's no way I can repay you for that. Please, let me help you."

He'd pretty much been a loner since his marriage had ended. His choice. And this woman wasn't helping his solitude. "Do you have someone to help you cart off this stuff?"

She nodded. "There's a man who works for my brother-in-law. He does pickups and deliveries for me, too."

He sighed. "Okay, let me check with Fletch and I'll get back to you."

Just then Zack came rushing inside. "Boy, Grady, your dog is really smart."

Grady wasn't used to having kids around. "He's been well trained."

"By you?"

"No, I'm not his first handler. A soldier named Vince Richards worked with him while in Afghanistan."

"Why do you have him?"

Grady shot a glance at Gina, then said, "Because Scout is retired and I adopted him. I've also adopted two more military dogs. They should arrive next week."

The boy's eyes widened. "Wow. I wish I could have a dog like Scout. Mom said I could get a puppy."

Grady arched an eyebrow. "A dog is a lot of responsibility and work."

The boy nodded. "I know. Mom said I have to feed him and take him for walks."

And Gina added, "And make sure he doesn't have accidents in the house."

"And I want him to protect me, too." Zack turned to Grady. "Can you help me teach a dog to do that?"

Grady hesitated, knowing the boy was still traumatized over what had happened. "I'll see what I can do."

CHAPTER FIVE

GRADY drove his truck through the gates of Shady Haven Nursing Home. With the brick and red-cedar shingles, the two-story building looked like a mountain resort. That was only part of the facility, too. There was also a drug rehab center on the far side of the property. And they'd added a newer section, the senior assisted-living apartments.

He walked through the double doors and the inside was just about as impressive. A large reception area had a fireplace and gleaming hardwood floors. In an adjoining room, Grady could see several patients in wheelchairs. One of them was old Joe Fletcher.

He walked in past residents playing games at different tables. His grandfather was playing cards, no doubt taking their money, too.

"Hey, Fletch, what are you up to?"

The thin man with the leathered skin glanced in his direction. "Hey, Grady." He smiled. "Good to see you. Hey, everyone, this is my grandson. Master Sergeant Grady Fletcher."

He pulled up a chair, swung it around and straddled it. "Come on, Joe, I'm retired now. It's just Grady."

"But you're a hero." Those same dark eyes looked back at him. "I heard about the boy."

Grady was surprised. "That was an accident. I found someone trespassing on your land. I told the sheriff."

The old man gave him a toothy grin. "I'm proud, son. Now, can you break me out of here?"

"Whoa, you aren't even healed yet. You need physical therapy." He leaned forward. "And about coming home. It's a death trap there."

Those bony shoulders lifted in a shrug. "So I've collected a few things."

Grady arched an eyebrow. "A few! I'd say, in certain circles you could be known as a hoarder." He sobered. "I need to get rid of a few things so you can get a walker around the place."

The old man grumbled some, then said, "Whatever you think is best, son. Just leave my bed alone."

It was a few days before Gina heard from Grady when he gave her the okay to come out. It took another day before she could get Mac Burleson and his brother, Connor, to drive up to the Fletcher place. They both had other jobs, working for her brother-in-law at Yeager Construction. She couldn't pay them the same money as Jace and she didn't need them too often.

She was reluctant to come along, not knowing if Grady really wanted her there. She also wondered if it was his burn scars that kept him out of town and on the mountain. Somehow, she thought he might just be a solitary man by nature. No sign of a wedding band. Of course, that didn't mean there wasn't someone special. Maybe he was at a loose end since he retired from the army and had to stay here until his grandfather got better.

She shook away any personal thoughts of Mr. Fletcher. It was none of her business. She was interested only in his furniture, not him. She pulled her car up next to the familiar truck, leaving room for Mac's vehicle. She climbed out and that was when she noticed the changes.

The rusted old cars that littered the yard were gone, along with the mining equipment. The grass had even been mowed. Along with the Burlesons, she went up the walk and saw the new wooden steps to the porch. The door opened and Grady came out.

"Good morning," she greeted him, trying not to notice how the long-sleeved T-shirt hugged his wide shoulders and flat stomach. "Looks like you've been busy."

"There's a possibility of snow flurries tonight. I needed to get things done."

"Well, we're here to help. Grady, this is Mac and Connor Burleson."

The men shook hands and then quickly started with their tasks. The brothers loaded the two old sofas onto the truck bed, and went back for some smaller pieces that Grady had told her to take. In about thirty minutes the job was finished. Mac and Connor tied the furniture down, and then they were on their way back to town.

Back in the cabin, Gina began rearranging the furniture that was left behind. She placed the sofa toward the fireplace and tucked a large quilt over the back, then put a braided rug in front of it to cover the rough wooden floor. Since there was room now, she pulled the kitchen table away from the wall and placed a checkered tablecloth she found in the cupboard over the scarred surface.

She stood back and examined her work. "Not bad."

"It looks a helluva lot better than it did."

She turned to see Grady. "Sorry, I hope you don't mind that I moved some things around."

He shook his head. "No. You made it look so much

better and I can get around the room now. More importantly, my grandfather will be able to."

She thought it looked cozy. "Well, I should probably get back."

Grady looked at her. "If you have a few minutes, I've got something to show you."

Gina was surprised and intrigued. "Sure." She followed him out the door to the side of the cabin. That was where she saw a high fence and the small building.

"You built a kennel."

"It's temporary."

She saw Scout. He barked and came to the fence to greet her. Soon another shepherd came into view. A lighter color, more golden. "That's Beau." Then two others appeared. "And that's Rowdy and Bandit."

"Oh, Grady. They're beautiful. Can I pet them?"

"I want to work with those two awhile first." He gave a hand signal and the dogs sat, and he managed to retrieve the smaller shepherd named Bandit. Once outside, the lovable animal was all over her. "Well, aren't you a lover."

"Hey, stay back," Grady ordered. It worked, but the little guy began to whine when she moved away.

"I thought you were only getting two dogs."

"When I picked these two up at the Durango airport, my partner, Josh, told me about Bandit. He didn't complete the program, but I didn't want him to go into a shelter." Grady turned that dark gaze on her. "If you're serious about getting a dog for Zack, this guy would be a good one for him."

Gina looked back at the dog. He had the gold and black markings of a shepherd, with two circles around his eyes. "Is he safe for kids?"

"These dogs are socialized before they even start

with any other training. I'd never recommend him if he wasn't safe. Of course he needs a little discipline, but yes, he'd be a good companion dog for Zack. And a good watchdog for the house, too."

"Is Zack old enough to handle a big dog?"

"Owning any pet is work, Gina."

She was a little surprised when he said her name. He'd never been that personal before.

"If you have a yard, and can afford to feed him, Bandit will be a great dog for a child. But only if you feel you want a pet."

She refocused on the cute dog. "Okay. Okay, you sold me. What do I owe you for him?"

He shook his head. "Nothing, Josh and I are just glad that we could find him a home. I would like to hold on to Bandit for a few days, just to see what needs to be worked on. I'll bring him into town this weekend. Will you be home?"

"I work Saturday, so is Sunday okay?" At his nod, she went on to say, "Plan on staying for supper." She began to laugh like a silly girl. "Oh, Zack is going to be so excited, especially since you've picked him out. He hasn't stopped talking about Scout and you." She added silently that she'd done her fair share of thinking about this man, too.

Sunday afternoon Grady drove his truck off Main Street onto Cherry Street, a tree-lined street with well-kept family homes. The Williamses' house was a green clapboard bungalow with a large front yard and spring flowers that edged a big porch.

He pulled up to the curb and parked his truck and glanced around. This reminded him of another lifetime. He'd once had a home that looked a lot like this. It had taken them a while before he and Barbara had been able to get their first place, especially since the army had moved him around every few years.

Then he'd been stationed in Texas to stay for a two-year stint. But he hadn't stayed, he'd left to go back to fight a war. He closed his eyes, not wanting to remember the rest. Maybe because he wanted to forget the pain of a bad marriage, and the child he'd never know.

He leaned back against the headrest, recalling the whirlwind romance with the pretty blonde, Barbara Dixon. They'd met at a nightclub while he was on leave, he'd ended up going home with her, and had just stayed. They'd married within weeks, just days before he was deployed.

Nearly a year later he'd come home from overseas and found they were strangers. They were. In all fairness, he hadn't worked that hard at being as social as Barbara needed him to be. He'd tried over the next year to be as attentive as he could.

She struggled with him being gone so much, but he felt helpless to change it. Their marriage suffered for it. Then while deployed again in Afghanistan, Barbara shocked him with the news that he was going to be a father. Excited, he hoped to be home when his child arrived into the world. Then complications had set in and Barbara had gone into labor a month early. He'd got emergency leave, but by the time he arrived home, it was too late. He couldn't even share the loss with his wife. She wanted nothing to do with him. His son was gone. The marriage was over, maybe before it had even had a chance.

Grady shook away thoughts when he heard his name and looked to see Zack running toward the truck. Scout barked from the backseat, causing a chain reaction from Bandit.

"Okay, boys, I want you two on your best behavior." He climbed out of the truck. "Hey, Zack. How's it going?"

"Fine." He nodded toward the truck. "Who's with Scout?"

"What?" He turned and looked at the dogs. "Well, how did he get in my truck?" Grady opened the back door and signaled for Scout to come out. He was grateful that Bandit stayed, but obviously he wanted to get some attention, too.

"You call him out." Grady showed the boy a hand signal.

Zack motioned and Bandit jumped out of the truck. "I did it." He glanced over his shoulder. "Mom, did you see what I did?"

Gina walked up to them. "I saw. Boy, this sure is a pretty dog."

Grady could only stare at her. Gina Williams was the pretty one. She was dressed in jeans and a blue sweater, showing off her trim figure.

"What's his name?" Zack asked, drawing his attention back.

"This is Bandit."

"Wow! That's a cool name. Are you going to train him to rescue people, too?"

Grady shook his head. "No, I have Scout. And my two other dogs, Beau and Rowdy, are back at the cabin. This guy is pretty young and he needs a home."

"Really? Can anyone adopt him? I mean even a kid?"

Grady nodded again.

Zack looked at his mother. "Mom, can we adopt Bandit and have him live with us?"

She acted like she was thinking it over. "That depends. Are you sure this is the kind of dog you want?"

"Yes! He almost looks like Scout."

"A dog is a big responsibility."

Grady took over. "You'll need to feed him, Zack. Not just when you have time, but every morning and evening." He petted the shepherd. "He needs to be walked, and most importantly, clean up after him."

"Oh, I promise I will." He turned to his mother. "I really promise, Mom. Every day."

Something tightened in his chest. This boy had been through a lot in his short life. He had been braver than most adults. "Bandit will need his training reinforced."

Grady glanced at Gina. "He hasn't been worked with much. So he's not as good at taking orders as Scout."

The boy nodded. "I'll work with him, I promise."

Grady nodded. "Then I guess he's yours."

The boy threw his small arms around Grady. "Thank you, Grady. I promise I'll love him and take care of him."

"I know you will, son," he said, feeling a funny tightening in his chest.

Then Zack moved away and went to his mother and hugged her. "Oh, thank you, Mom."

Grady moved away from the touching scene and went to the truck bed and picked up a large bag of food and a dog bed.

There was the sound of a horn and he looked up to see an SUV pull up behind his truck. Gina's sister, Lori, got out, along with a man he recognized as Jace Yeager. A young girl climbed out of the backseat and went straight to Zack and Bandit.

So this was going to be a family dinner. Great.

The sisters hugged and Lori turned toward him. "It's good to see you again, Mr. Fletcher."

"It's Grady, ma'am," he said and saw the resemblance between the sisters. The hair and eye color might have been different, but the shape of the face, and the flawless skin was shared between the two sisters.

"I'm Lori, remember? This is my husband, Jace." The two men shook hands. "And that's our daughter, Cassie." Lori glanced at her husband. "Brace yourself, she's gonna want a dog now."

"She's got a horse," Jace argued.

The attention turned back to Grady and Lori said, "I don't think I ever thanked you for finding Zack."

"No need. I've been thanked enough."

"Maybe so, but I have to say it again. Thank you, Grady Fletcher." She quickly changed the subject. "How is your grandfather doing?"

"He seems to be recovering nicely."

"Is he up for visitors?"

"Who wants to see him?"

"I wanted to stop by and speak with him about some land that there's a question about."

"If this has anything to do with Billy Hutchinson, I'm not sure I want you stirring up any trouble."

"No trouble, Grady. It's righting a wrong that my grandfather did years ago. Once I took over the bank, I discovered a title to a piece of land that I believe belongs to Joe Fletcher. Maybe when he's feeling better I can correct this…mistake."

Gina stood back and watched the change in Grady's demeanor. How different he'd been with just Zack and her. Now that the group was bigger, he seemed tense. He wasn't comfortable around people.

Grady didn't have time to reflect on Lori Hutchinson

Yeager's confession as they herded both kids and dogs to the backyard. Grady followed Gina to put away the bag of dog food in the cupboard on the utility porch. The oversize dog bed was placed next to the clothes dryer.

"I doubt Bandit will be sleeping in here," she said. "I know Zack wants him to be in his bedroom."

Grady nodded. "This dog has been kenneled at night, but I'm sure there won't be a problem with Bandit sleeping in Zack's room. Just not in the bed."

"Okay, but you have to tell Zack, along with any other rules about caring for the dog."

"I will." He looked into her green eyes and started to get distracted. "How's Zack doing?"

"Better each day, but he still isn't sleeping in his own room. Jace is going to replace the windows and put in higher ones so Zack will feel safe again. Right now he's sleeping in another room that I've been using as my office." He saw her watery eyes. "And we have an appointment tomorrow to go and talk to a therapist about what happened."

Grady tensed. He'd love to get his hands on Lowell again. *Who does that to a child?* "He's gone through a lot. It'll take time."

He couldn't help but think about what Gina had gone through, too. The years of abuse from a man who claimed he loved her. "What about you? How are you handling this?"

She looked surprised at the question. "I'm okay, as long as Zack recovers from this."

The sounds of giggles coming from the backyard got Gina's attention. She smiled and his heart skipped a beat. "I guess having a dog is a start. Thank you."

"Not a problem," he told her, wondering why her praise meant so much to him.

"Come on, Grady, let's join the fun."

She started out the door, but he hesitated. It had been a long time since he'd done any family things. He'd never been very good at it. The army had been his family. And now he didn't even have that. He wasn't sure what he had.

An hour later Gina, Grady, Jace and Lori were sitting on the patio finishing their hamburgers while the kids played with the dogs.

Gina loved that her family was all together, at her house. She'd never expected to have someone like Grady Fletcher sit beside her, but he seemed on edge all during the meal. Finally he'd gotten up and taken Zack out to teach him how to work the dogs.

She glanced at her son, running around the yard with his dog. Zack was so happy.

Grady had given them some tricks to work on and that was all it took. The kids started burying things, and soon the dogs were retrieving toys and returning them. Bandit got distracted pretty easily, but some training would help that.

Gina's attention went to the ex-soldier standing alone. Did he have a problem being around a lot of people? She'd noticed how his demeanor had changed when her sister and her family had arrived.

Lori turned to her husband. "Mark my words, Cassie will ask for a puppy before we get back home."

"If you really want one, I bet Grady can find you one."

Jace groaned. "Don't give your niece any ideas." He hugged his wife. "We're hoping a new baby will distract her from wanting any more pets."

They all three laughed as the back gate opened and

Gina saw Claire and Tim Keenan walk in. Gina rushed over to greet them both with a hug.

"I hope we're not intruding," Claire said, holding out a covered dish.

Gina hugged the two. "Claire and Tim, of course you're not, you're always welcome. Please, join us."

"Oh, no, we just wanted to drop off this pie and tell you how happy we are that both you and Zack are back safe."

"I insist you stay. We're about to have some coffee and now some pie."

"I can go for that," Tim volunteered as they walked toward the others on the patio.

Gina introduced Grady, letting him know they owned the Keenan Inn, a historical bed-and-breakfast in town.

"Sheriff Larkin is married to their daughter, Paige, who is an attorney. Their oldest daughter, Morgan, is the mayor. Their youngest daughter, Leah, is a photo journalist. They all came back to Destiny to raise their families."

After they shook hands, Tim said, "Sounds like a Chamber of Commerce ad." The older man smiled. "I remember you, but it's been a while. You were just a kid. Old Fletch used to come into town and bring you along."

Gina watched as Grady nodded. "That wasn't very often," he admitted. "He didn't like people much."

So that was where he got it from. Was Grady a loner like his grandfather, or was it the scar?

Tim Keenan laughed. "No, he didn't. Most of the old miners kept to themselves. I think they were afraid someone would jump their claims if they left them for long."

Grady gave a rare smile. "Yeah, I used to hear a lot

of those stories. I feel bad I wasn't around to help him more."

Claire added, "Rest assured, the Shady Haven Nursing Home is a wonderful facility. I volunteer there, so I see how happy their patients are." She smiled. "I hope you don't mind, but I stop in to see your grandfather from time to time."

"I appreciate it." Grady was ashamed that his own personal problems had interfered with spending more time with his grandfather. "I didn't get to see much of him the past few years."

Claire smiled. "Fletch understood, and let us know on more than one occasion that you were defending our freedom," she told him. "And we, too, thank you for your service."

He nodded. "I'm retired now."

Tim stepped in. "I hear you're already starting a new career, training dogs for search and rescue." He looked out toward the shepherds. "Are those two of them?"

"Just the one," Grady said as he pointed to the bigger dog. "That's Scout."

"He found Zack," Gina added. "The other younger one is Bandit, he's Zack's new dog."

Claire looked from Gina toward Grady. "That's really nice of you to get the boy such a special dog. Are you planning to move here permanently?"

"No. I'm going back to Texas once Fletch is settled and on his feet again."

"Oh, do you have family there?"

Grady knew where this was going. Mrs. Keenan was already putting Gina and him together as a couple. "No, it's just me." He glanced around. He needed to leave, and soon.

Suddenly as if Gina saw his distress, she interrupted.

"Oh, we need some plates for our dessert," she said, then rushed into the house.

Grady knew that he couldn't get away as easily. What was he thinking, getting involved with them? He wanted to come here and sit on the mountain while his grandfather recuperated. Why couldn't he be left alone?

Over the past several nights his solitude had been invaded by a lost boy and a beautiful single mother. None of which he needed at this point in his life. Probably never. Gina Williams had her own issues. So did he. She needed a patient guy who wanted a family. Grady didn't do family. He'd tried and failed, never again. He'd stick with animals.

"They're beautiful dogs." Tim Keenan came up to him. "Were they overseas, too?"

"Scout was. He's completed his service so I was able to adopt him. Bandit didn't make the program, but he's still an excellent dog."

"Even better that Zack gets to have one, too." Tim shook his head. "That boy has been through hell, and he was just starting to open up when this all happened. I think Bandit will be a great therapy dog for him."

"I'm glad I could help. I need to get back before dark." He stood and whistled for Scout. The dog stopped then ran toward him and sat. Grady said goodbye to everyone as he started to leave.

"Don't be a stranger in town," Tim said as he walked with him to the gate. "Get to know people here in Destiny. You'll find we're pretty easy to get along with."

Grady just wasn't sure he wanted to form any attachments. He'd be leaving soon. Definitely the best idea before he got distracted by one pretty brunette.

CHAPTER SIX

THREE days later Gina stood at the front window of her shop on First Street. The Second Best Thrift Shop had an ideal location right off the town square.

She could see the large fountain and park, along with several other storefront shops. Destiny Community Bank was across the street, next door was Paige Keenan Larkin's law office and the Rocky Mountain Bridal Shop. The sheriff's office was on the next block along with the U.S. post office.

Gina had been lucky to get a space in a prime location. The front of the shop was her thrift store. The showroom was still a little sparse, but once she cleaned up the pieces she'd gotten from Grady Fletcher, it should add a lot to the window display.

Her thoughts turned to the man who had upset her tranquillity. She still didn't know much about the ex-army master sergeant who lived on the mountain. Only that he'd seen war, and had to have suffered greatly with his obvious burns. She'd seen the pain in his eyes. Yet, from the way he stood back from people, she somehow doubted it was all physical.

Still he hadn't hesitated to help find Zack. That alone made Grady Fletcher pretty special. The part that bothered her was that she found she was drawn to him.

She'd spent just over twenty-four hours with the man, and oddly, she felt safe around him. Given her past record with men, she hadn't found it easy to trust. And she might never find it easy.

She couldn't help but recall the width of Grady's shoulders and chest. Her breath caught in her throat as she remembered his gentle touch, with her, Zack and his dogs.

She shook away the direction of her thoughts. She was in no way ready to think about a man in her life. Besides, Grady Fletcher would be leaving for Texas soon. That right there should make her keep her distance. Not that he would ever want her, not with all her baggage. Not with her fears of intimacy. She could never measure up to what Eric wanted in a wife or a lover. He'd let her know time and again that she couldn't please him.

She shook away the memories. No, she didn't need a man. She was happy with her life as it was. She was independent and had her family.

Most importantly, Zack. This was his first day back to school since the ordeal. Even though she'd talked with her son about the situation, she knew it would be a long time before he got over the events of those harrowing twenty-four hours. Their new dog helped a lot.

She smiled, thinking about Bandit. He'd been the best medicine ever. Boy and dog had been inseparable the past two days. So there had been sad faces this morning when she'd taken Zack to school. Maybe she should go home at lunch to check on Bandit, just to make sure he was okay.

Gina checked her watch. Right, she needed to get to work herself, so she walked toward the back of her store. In the work area she saw the two sofas from Grady's cabin. Marie, her young helper, was already removing the dirty, worn fabric.

"How bad is it, Marie?" she asked the young mother of a twelve-month-old little girl, Sophie.

The tall, willowy blonde was about Gina's age. She had an easy smile and a real talent with a sewing machine.

"Not bad. The frame is solid and with new padding and fabric it will look great."

"That's what I was thinking when I saw it." Gina grinned. "And it was free." She eyed the other sofa. "How about you reupholster this one, and I'll do the camelback sofa? Since I can't pay you what you're really worth, how about you take sixty percent of the sale?"

"Oh, Gina, you don't have to do that."

"Yes, I do. I'm barely paying you now. And don't tell me you can't use the money."

Marie's husband was finishing college and could only work part time. "But how many bosses let an employee bring her kid to work?"

Not many that Gina knew of, remembering when she herself had tried to find work with Zack in tow. "Hey, a business should supply a daycare, even if it is a small storage area in the back of the store."

"It's perfect. And thank you for that."

"Let's just get these sofas finished so we can sell 'em."

Marie looked toward the wide doorway that led out to the alley. "I think we have a visitor."

Gina turned around. She couldn't be more surprised to find Grady Fletcher. He looked big and intimidating. Did he do that on purpose?

She put on a smile and went to him. "Grady. It's nice to see you again."

He gave her a nod and stepped through the doorway as if he wouldn't be welcome. "Didn't mean to disturb you, but I thought I'd come around back to drop off some things I found in the shed."

"Oh, really?" Gina glanced over her shoulder. "Marie this is Grady Fletcher. Grady, Marie, my jack-of-all-trades."

"Nice to meet you, Grady."

Grady tipped his cowboy hat. "Ma'am."

He turned his attention back to Gina, causing her to feel nervous. "As you can see, we've started tearing apart the sofas you gave me."

He walked over. His gaze searched the furniture. She wondered if that was how he looked when he inspected the troops.

"Looks like a lot of work."

"It'll be worth it once they're finished. Right, Marie?"

"Right," the pretty blonde agreed. Gina planned to put them in the front display window. She put on a big smile. "Of course, they won't be there long, once we work our magic."

"Well, good luck with that."

Gina pulled his attention back. "You said you have some more furniture?"

Grady nodded, wondering what he was doing here. One look at Gina Williams, and already he was distracted. She looked fresh, young and so pretty. Dressed in those nice-fitting jeans and a denim blouse, she could pass for a teenager. Too young for him. And it seemed every time he got near her, he couldn't seem to act normal.

"I was clearing out the shed when I found some

things." He pointed over his shoulder. "They're in the truck."

She smiled and his heart began to pound hard. "May I see them?"

"Sure."

They walked out to his truck. Scout spotted her and barked in greeting from the backseat.

"Well, hello, fella." When the dog stuck his head out the open window, she went to him and began to pet him. "Oh, I know a little boy who misses you," she told the animal.

"How is Zack doing?"

She turned to him. "Good. He went back to school today, but as a mother, I worry. What if the kids start saying things? Teasing him?"

Grady leaned against the truck door, then realized he was close enough to inhale her soft scent. "I would think the kids would be more interested in Zack spending the night in a silver mine, more than his dad kidnapping him."

She looked up with those moss-green eyes. "Thank you for that, but I can't help but be overprotective."

"You have good reason to be. But now, you know you and your son are safe from your ex."

She sighed. "You can't imagine how good that feels. We can finally concentrate on making a life for ourselves."

He wondered if that included finding someone to share that life. It wouldn't take long for the men in this town to come sniffing around.

She smiled. "Like you are," she added.

He nodded, but he wasn't sure what his permanent plans were. "Thanks to my grandfather I have a place to live for now. On the downside, Old Fletch is a packrat—my immediate future is filled with a lot of work clearing out the place."

"Your grandfather is a man after my own heart." She rubbed her hands together excitedly. "So what did you bring me?"

He couldn't help but smile. "I don't know if this stuff is even worth bringing in." He walked to the truck bed and unfastened the tarp and pulled it back, then let down the gate.

"Oh, my," she said, and began to climb up on the bumper. Grady reached out, gripped her waist and boosted her up into the truck.

Gina froze momentarily, but then realized this was Grady touching her. She trusted him—as much as she would ever trust a man—not to hurt her. What truly scared her were the feelings that he did stir in her.

She quickly concentrated on the treasures he'd brought her. Another rocking chair, a cedar trunk, a Tiffany lamp. But it was a small pedestal table that got her attention. She pulled back the tarp further and was rewarded with a leather top in nearly perfect condition.

"Where did you find all this?"

"Buried in the shed out back." He climbed up and stood next to her. "Why?"

Gina examined it more closely, pulling out the single drawer to see the name stamped inside. "It a Mersman pedestal table with a leather top." She ran her fingers over the camel-colored softness. "How is it in such perfect condition?"

"Like I said, it was protected by a tarp and buried under a lot of stuff. I think it belonged to my grandmother. Maybe after she died, Fletch just put her things away."

She gave him a questioning look. "Are you sure your grandfather is okay about selling these things?"

"I saw him yesterday. He agreed that the cabin needs to be cleared out. He gave me first pick on these things. Except his bed. He wants me to keep my hands off that bed."

She smiled. "Your grandfather seems to be quite a character."

"Joe Fletcher was a miner, which wasn't an easy life. He once lived in Destiny, but after my grandmother passed away, he moved up to the cabin to work his claim. My father didn't like the life there so he didn't hang around after he turned eighteen. He didn't come back here much, either." Only to drop his kid off so he didn't have to deal with him, he added silently.

Gina studied him. "But you like it here."

"Old Fletch wasn't so bad." Their gazes locked, and he found himself saying more than he'd planned. "I was sent to spend my summers here after my parents divorced."

"It's nice you had him, but it must have been hard…" Her face brightened, and he could hardly draw a breath. "I bet those times were fun."

Yeah, he loved the old guy. "No one taught me more." He glanced around at the mountain range. "I hiked this area a lot of summers."

"Must be some nice memories," she said and sighed. "I want that for Zack. I want him to be able to erase all the bad that has happened to him."

Grady studied her pretty face. He found the need to reach out and touch her, but he fought the attraction. Making any kind of connection was a bad idea. "You have a good start here."

"I hope so," she said. "And I bet Fletch is happy that you're back here."

Honestly, he'd always felt a connection to this place. "Since the army sent me packing, I need to make a living. So it's back to Texas and my business."

She nodded. "But you have family here. I learned it's not the structure that makes it a home, it's the people. My son and my sister are my family, and we added Jace and Cassie. I'm lucky to have all of them."

This discussion was getting far too involved. "Yes, you are. Look, I need to get going. Scout has been in the truck a long time."

"Oh, of course. Just tell me what you want me to do about the table. Do you want to sell it on consignment? I'm not sure I can afford to buy it outright."

He moved the table to the end of the truck bed, then jumped down. He needed to put some distance between them. "Whatever you decide. I just need to clear out things to make room for when Fletch comes home."

Gina nodded. "How about I clean it up for you?" she suggested. "You might want to keep it. After all, it belonged to your grandmother."

"Whatever. You can go ahead and sell the trunk and rocker."

They moved the items out of the truck bed, then he helped her down. He didn't want to make a big deal about touching her, but when he put his hands on her tiny waist, his reaction became one. As hard as he tried, they ended up too close. Then their eyes met and he saw she was just as affected as he was. Great.

He placed her on the ground and she stumbled. He reached out and pulled her to him before she fell. Her softness pressed against his body was torture, the best kind.

"Ah, sorry." She regained her balance and moved back. Way back. "If you help me get these things inside, then you can be on your way."

He didn't say a word, realizing it had been a bad idea to come here in the first place. He needed to stay away from Gina Williams.

As he lifted the table off the truck, Marie came out. She called to Gina, "The school called."

"Oh, no. Did something happen with Zack?"

The blonde smiled. "No, but it seems he has a visitor. His name is Bandit."

Ten minutes later Gina and Grady with Scout on a leash headed to the school office. He'd brought the dog along in case they needed some extra support to corral Bandit.

A middle-aged principal came outside to greet her. "Hello, Ms. Williams."

"Hello, Mr. Markham. This is Grady Fletcher.

"Mr. Fletcher." The principal nodded, then turned back to Gina. "It seems your son's dog came to school."

"I'm so sorry, Mr. Markham. The last I checked Bandit was in the backyard." She looked at Grady. "How could he find his way to the school?"

Grady answered, "Either he followed the scent, or the sound of the kids' voices. He has more potential than I thought."

Gina didn't care how the dog got there. Just that she had a problem if he kept getting out of the yard.

"Well according to Zack," Markham began, "Bandit is a very smart dog. Outside of a German shepherd named Scout, Bandit is the smartest dog in the whole world. And he was in the army."

"Meet Scout," Grady said and Gina noticed a hint of

a smile. "I'm the one who gave Bandit to Zack. Where is the dog now?"

"Zack is with him on the playground."

Together they all walked back to the area behind the building. "Mr. Fletcher," the principal began, "Zack has told me a lot about your dogs, Beau, Rowdy and Scout. He said you're training them to be search-and-rescue dogs."

"I've only been working with Scout so far." He glanced down at his obedient shepherd. "He's coming along. Bandit hasn't had as much training. But I'm thinking he should get a gold star for finding little boys now."

"We all hear that Scout found Zack when he was lost," the man said.

Grady nodded. "He played a big part in it."

The principal caught Gina's attention. "I know you and your son have been through a rough time this past week."

Gina hated that everyone knew what had happened. She'd hoped that she could leave her past behind in Colorado Springs. "Yes, we have. Thank you for understanding."

The man nodded. "I noticed how much Zack responded when his dog showed up today. Even though I can't have Bandit at school every day, maybe a little show-and-tell with the two dogs wouldn't hurt."

Grady hesitated, then said, "After today, I'm not sure Bandit is ready for prime time."

"Maybe in a few weeks then?"

"We'll see."

They reached the playground and found the boy and the dog along with Claire Keenan, an aid from the class.

Zack spotted her. "Mom!" he cried and came running to her. "Mom, look, Bandit found my school. He followed my scent. He came to my classroom door. He really did."

"I heard," she said, wondering how to fix this problem. She looked at Mrs. Keenan. "Claire, thank you so much for staying with them."

"Oh, I was happy to do it." She looked at Grady. "Hi, Grady. It's nice to see you again."

"Hello, ma'am."

The older woman smiled. "I just love how respectful these soldiers are. But you can just call me Claire."

He nodded then snapped a leash on Bandit. "Thanks, Claire."

Mrs. Keenan was starting to leave, then stopped. "We're having a little get-together Sunday afternoon at the inn, just family and friends. We would love it if you all would join us."

"Thank you, Claire," Gina said. "That would be nice."

The older woman looked at Grady. "You could bring Scout, and Zack can bring Bandit. There's a wooded area behind the inn—maybe you can work the dogs. The kids would love it."

Grady was barely able to keep from squirming. Great, the good citizens of Destiny were trying to bring him into the fold. "Thank you for the invitation."

"Any time. We want you to feel a part of this community."

That was the problem. He wasn't sure if he wanted to be part of anything. "I'll try and make it."

"It's an open invitation, Grady." Claire walked back into the classroom, with a promise from Gina that she'd bring Zack.

Zack's smile faded as he looked up at Grady. "Is Bandit in trouble?"

"He's your dog, son. But I suggest he has some re-inforcing discipline. It sounds harsh but you don't want Bandit to get hit by a car—which he might do if he's forever wandering about the town. So it looks like you'll need to work with him. Teach him his boundaries."

Gina watched as her son leaned against the dog in question. The two were already so close.

"Will you help me, Grady?" Zack asked. "I want Bandit to be as smart as Scout."

Grady went down to Zack's level. "Then he needs *you* to teach him. You need to show him who is the leader of the pack."

"I don't know what that means."

"It means you're the boss."

Gina watched the exchange between the two. Her son was hanging on to every word Grady said. Even with Lori's husband, Jace, it had taken Zack a long time to warm up to him. Not true with this man. She wasn't sure if that was a good thing.

"Hey, Mom, I'm the boss of Bandit."

"Well, right now, I'm the boss. And you need to go back to class. So say goodbye to Bandit."

Her son hugged the dog, then stopped in front of Grady. "Will you come to my house and teach me how to be the boss?"

Gina held her breath. She didn't want to step into this, even though she knew that Grady had done so much for them. More than she could ever repay.

"How about I make sure the backyard is secured?" he told the boy. "I'll give you some exercises to help show Bandit his boundaries. But you have to do the work."

That seemed to make her son happy. "Okay."

Gina saw the change in Grady from earlier when he'd opened up to her. Were they becoming too much of a burden? Of course they were. Grady was a single man who didn't need a kid hanging on him. She kissed her son goodbye and watched him head off to class.

The ride back to her house with Grady was a silent one. When she climbed out of the truck with Bandit in tow, she expected Grady to drive off. Instead he followed them to the backyard. He searched the area until he found the hole under the fence where the dog had escaped.

"Do you have any extra wood?"

"There's some in the garage."

When he started to walk off, she tied Bandit to the post and went after Grady. "You don't have to fix it. I can do it."

"Not a problem."

She unlocked the door to the structure, turned on the light and led him to the neatly stacked boards that Jace had left after doing some house repairs.

"This is only a temporary fix," he told her.

"Then let me help," she insisted.

"There's no need." He started past her, but she refused to be ignored as she followed him.

"There's every need. I'm not helpless," she argued, then suddenly ran into the back of the man's hard body.

With a gasp, she backed away.

The wood hit the ground as Grady cursed and turned around.

His gaze met hers. "You okay?"

She nodded. "I'm sorry, I didn't know you were going to stop."

He just stood there staring at her, those dark eyes piercing.

"I don't know why, but I've made you angry."

He glanced away, then back at her. "I'm not angry at you, Gina. I'm angry with myself."

"Why?"

He took a step closer to her. "Because I can't stop thinking about doing this." He leaned down and his mouth closed over hers.

CHAPTER SEVEN

GINA jumped back quickly. "Why'd you do that?" She fought to keep her composure.

Grady shrugged. "Hell if I know."

"Well, next time try to control yourself."

"I'll be sure I do that." He turned, grabbed the long piece of wood and stalked out of the garage.

Gina sagged against the workbench and tried to slow her breathing. She ran her tongue over her lips. Oh, God. She could still taste him. Stop. It was only a kiss.

No. She wasn't going to get involved with a man. Not again. Never again. She already had the life she wanted for her and Zack. She didn't need a man in it. Besides, who would want to deal with all her hang-ups? She was so afraid of being touched, she'd never have a normal relationship.

She thought back to her old life. Eric had never treated her like anything but an object. She'd met him as a teenager when she had been so eager for attention. At that time, she'd been willing to do anything to have someone love her. Problem was, she'd confused sex with love, and had let Eric talk her into whatever he wanted. He never cared about her, only the power he had over her. And then the control had begun.

Too late, she'd realized she'd never had a voice about

anything. At nearly nineteen, she'd become a bride and a mother. She knew nothing. When Eric had started pushing her around she was too ashamed to tell anyone. It had been Lori who had rescued her and Zack.

Even after counseling, she still had trouble with self-esteem, especially when it came to men. Could she handle a man's touch? She wondered if she'd ever be able to enjoy the physical part of a relationship. Could she hold the interest of a man like Grady Fletcher? As good looking as the man was, he had to be used to women's attention, experienced women. She was far from knowing how to please a man…how to keep a man.

Gina walked to the garage doorway and looked out. She saw Grady as he knelt down at the base of the fence and went to work at boarding up Bandit's escape route. Big and muscular, she had no doubt Grady was a take-charge guy. Yet, he'd never made her feel any fear. She touched her lips with her fingertips. The yearning was still there, making her want something she couldn't have. A normal relationship with a man.

Thirty minutes later Grady drove his truck along the dirt road to the cabin, still cursing his bad judgment. Damn! Why couldn't he just keep his hands off Gina? He didn't need this complication. He'd come back here to take some time to heal and rebuild his life. He didn't need Gina Williams distracting him, making him want things again. Especially not a woman with a child reminding him of everything he'd lost.

Grady parked the truck in front of the cabin and climbed out. He got Scout from the backseat and walked up to the porch. After unlocking the door, he went inside and glanced around at Gina's handiwork.

A woman's touch. Something he'd taken for granted

during his marriage. Even though he and Barbara had been together only four years, he'd got used to coming home to all the comforts. Even with the short time they'd had together as a couple, he'd missed the things that only a woman could give.

In the end, he hadn't been there enough. Okay, so she had signed on as a career army wife, but two tours of duty overseas during a marriage had taken a toll.

Although he'd warned her, Barbara still hadn't deserved the heartache. He'd given it a hundred percent when he was stateside, but that hadn't been enough to make it work. He'd learned too late—he was never the marrying kind. He should have saved them both the heartache.

He walked into the cabin's one bedroom and went to the scarred dresser, then opened the top drawer and took out a small box. The only thing he'd taken from his home after the divorce. He felt his heart begin to pound and his hands shook as he raised the lid on the treasure box he'd had since he'd been a kid. But it was what was inside that tore him apart. He looked down at the grainy photo. The only picture he had of his son.

A sonogram.

Grady sank onto the bed as he studied the image of a child that had never been born.

He took a shaky breath, wondering if this sad helpless feeling would ever leave him. The feeling that told him he'd served his country proudly, but couldn't get home to help his family. Of course, if he'd known that Barbara had been pregnant before volunteering, he might have thought twice about going back overseas. He remembered the weekly phone calls he'd made home and hearing about the pregnancy, then later when the commanding officer had given him the news that his wife was in the hospital. He'd managed to get on the first plane home. But it was too late. Worse, Barb blamed him for everything, but not nearly as much as he blamed himself.

He quickly shook away the memory.

His thoughts turned to Gina. No! He wasn't getting involved with her. She needed a man who would be there for her. A normal man without battle scars, who was able to give her what she needed. Treat her how she needed to be treated, special. Give her a home and a life of happiness.

Hell, he wasn't sure what his future would be. He had a grandfather who needed to be cared for. A cabin in the mountains that didn't even have a flushing toilet. He'd had no business kissing her. He needed to stay away from both mother and child.

Scout barked then raced out of the bedroom. Then Grady heard, "Hello, is anyone here?"

"Who the hell?" Grady quickly put the box back into the drawer and hurried through the cabin to find the intruder leaning down and petting the shepherd in the open doorway.

"Hey, Sarge, you shouldn't leave your door open," the man said.

Grady recognized the army corporal right away. Twenty-seven-year-old Josh Regan had served in his unit overseas. They'd both survived the explosion that day that had taken out two of their squad members. They'd spent time in the hospital where they'd been treated for wounds and burns. That was where they'd come up with the idea of training dogs.

"Hey, partner. What are you doing here?"

"Well, I figured I'd stop by and see how you're getting along with the dogs."

Grady couldn't help but smile. "Not too bad. I thought you were headed home to Georgia for a visit with your family and your girl."

The tall, lanky Southern boy straightened. "I've been home and discovered there isn't a girl waiting any longer." He sighed. "So after chowin' down enough of my mother's cooking, I thought I'd stop by here to see you and the dogs and firm up our plans before I headed back to Texas." Regan looked around. "So this is the place you talked about… Nice digs."

"Livable. The view is the best." He studied the kid. "I told you the last time we talked, Josh, I can't leave yet." They'd planned the partnership, but then that had been delayed when his grandfather had ended up in the hospital. "I'm not sure when I'll get back to Texas."

"I know that. I just thought I'd take a detour before heading back to Lackland. Maybe I can hang around for a few days and we can work with the dogs."

The idea was a good one. He could get some work done on the cabin and not neglect the dogs. "I should have thought about that. We could work here for now. The cabin is short on guest quarters, but you're welcome to bunk on the sofa."

Regan seemed to relax. "You sure?"

"Wouldn't offer if I wasn't. Besides, I could use a hand with the training here, and you're the expert handler."

A big boyish grin appeared. "I've got a sleeping bag in my truck. Then I'll go visit with Beau and Rowdy."

Josh followed Grady out to the porch. He pointed over his shoulder. "I have built some makeshift kennels for now, but we might need something sturdier if we're going to work on training."

The corporal stopped and looked around at the view. "I could get used to this great view."

It was a great view, but their training facility was in Texas. "Yeah, but it's still my grandfather's cabin and he's dead set on returning here once the doctor releases him."

Josh let out a long breath. "Too bad. I could get used to the cooler weather."

Grady couldn't help but smile, too. It was good to see a familiar face. Someone who had been through the same things and understood. "Well, you're not going to get the chance to sit around and enjoy it. We'll be working."

"That's why I'm here. To help out."

And Grady was glad. They could get some things done, and it would keep him from thinking about a pretty brunette who was too young and fragile for him. He glanced at his partner and realized Josh was better suited for Gina. Yet, he didn't want the man anywhere near her.

"Don't think I don't know what you're up to."

The next morning, Grady sat across from his grandfather at Shady Haven. "Okay, what am I up to?"

The older man glared. "You're cleaning up the cabin, then you're going to clear out as soon as I get out of this place."

Grady sighed. "You always knew I was headed back to Texas, but I'm not going to leave you until you can make it on your own. You still need rehab on your hip. That means you can't return to the cabin, especially with so much stuff crammed into the place."

"I did just fine before," Joe said, his dark eyes narrowed as he raised his large, veined hand. "I know where everything is."

"So you want me to put everything back? That might be hard to do since Gina Williams carted most of it off."

The old man frowned. "Who is Gina?"

"She runs the thrift store in town."

"You kept my bed, didn't you?"

"Didn't touch your bed. But Gina wants to know about some of Grandma's things."

Joe eyed him closely. "Seems you're spending a lot of time with this woman. Are you sweet on her?"

Grady wasn't sure how to handle this one. "No, I'm not. I don't have the time for a woman. Besides, you know I don't do so well in relationships."

"You would if you picked the right one." There was a hint of a smile. "Bring this Gina by here. And I'll tell you if she's good enough for you."

"Look, Fletch, don't you think I'm too old to have your approval on who I see."

"Ha, ha. So you are seeing her," he said, then he sobered. "Don't be too stubborn to see what's right in front of you, boy. Take it from one who knows. Time slips by fast. So make an old man happy, and bring your young lady by."

Grady knew it would be foolish if he did bring Gina here. "I'll see what I can do."

Sunday afternoon, the Keenan Inn was the place to be, especially if you liked to be around family, friends and good food.

Gina got out of the car followed by Zack just as another vehicle pulled up behind her. She immediately recognized Grady and it sent her heart racing. She'd known he was going to be here, but she still wasn't ready to see him again.

"They're here, Mom. Grady and Scout are here."

Before she could stop him, her eager son grabbed Bandit's leash and raced off toward the truck as Grady climbed out. It had been a few days since the incident in the garage, and their kiss. The feel of his firm mouth against hers, his scent stirring her emotions. It was still fresh in her mind.

The man was hard to forget. His mere size and presence demanded her attention. Yet, she'd never been frightened by him, even by those dark, piercing eyes. He looked good. She knew he was self-conscious about the scar along his neck, but she didn't even notice it anymore.

She inhaled a calming breath and walked over to him. His gaze caught hers and held, refusing to let her look away. Then finally he spoke. "Hello, Gina."

"Hi, Grady," she managed to say.

Zack caught her attention. "Mom, can I go hide some stuff so Scout and Bandit can find it?"

"In a minute," she said, noticing another man getting out of the passenger side of the truck. He was younger with dark hair that had the familiar military cut.

"Gina," Grady began, "this is Josh Regan. We served together. He's also partner in training the dogs. He's staying with me for a while."

The younger man said, "Hello, ma'am."

"It's nice to meet you, Josh. Please call me Gina. This is my son, Zack, and Bandit."

Josh smiled. "It's good to meet you both."

"Are you in the army, too?" Zack asked.

"I was. I served under Sgt. Fletcher. I was a dog handler."

"Wow! Cool."

Grady stood back and watched how Regan's attention remained on Gina. Okay, she was pretty enough to be stared at, but not as if she was his next meal.

"Hey, Josh." Grady handed him the dog leash. "Would you mind taking Scout out back and getting the kids organized on the exercise? I'll be there in a few."

"Sure." The younger guy didn't question the order and walked off with Zack and the dogs. Grady turned back to Gina. Oh, Lord, she looked good. "How have you been?"

"I'm fine."

He watched her, seeing her cheeks redden. Was she thinking about the kiss? He quickly asked, "I meant, how have you and Zack been?"

"He's back in his own bedroom."

"That's good." Enough small talk, he needed to clear the air. "Gina, about the other day… I was out of line. I promise it won't happen again."

"Let's just say we were both caught up in the situation…" She glanced away. "I just didn't want you to get any ideas. It's not that you're not attractive. I mean, any woman would want your attention." She shook her head. "It's just I'm not ready, nor do I want to get involved with anyone."

Grady heard her words of refusal, but that didn't change the fact that he was still drawn to her. "I can understand you feeling that way, but never is a long time. You're too young, Gina. There's a guy out there for you. Not all are jerks like your ex." He turned and headed toward the backyard of the inn.

Gina released a breath. The last thing she needed was Sgt. Fletcher telling her to date. She liked her life just fine as it was. She walked up the steps at the inn. She had her son and business to concentrate on. Grady had his own work, too. They should both be able to keep out of each other's way.

Resigned to keeping her distance from the man, Gina walked through the double doors with the glass oval panels, etched with the Keenan name. Inside, she stood in the entry with the antique desk used for registering guests at the historic bed-and-breakfast.

She glanced around at the high ceiling trimmed with crown moldings and wainscoting stained in a honey color. The walls were painted a light tan and the floors were covered in a burgundy carpet. The large polished oak staircase led to the second and third floors.

"Welcome."

Gina turned and found Tim Keenan. The handsome sixty-year-old offered her a ready smile that reached all the way to his clear blue eyes.

"Hi, Tim."

He walked up and hugged her. "Gina, so glad you could make it today. We don't see enough of you or your boy. Where is Zack?"

She stepped back. "He's headed out back with Grady and the dogs. I came in to see if I can help Claire."

"I think we have enough hands in that kitchen, but let's head back and ask them."

Tim and Gina walked through the dining room, which had several small tables for guests.

"How is Zack handling things these days?"

"Better," Gina told him. "He had a few sessions with a counselor." She smiled as they continued their journey through a butler's pantry. "I seem to be the one with the problem."

Gina was still a little overwhelmed by what had happened with the kidnapping and how close she'd come to losing her son. Yet Zack had seemed to fit right back into school and with the other kids. She was glad about that.

"I think as parents, Gina," Tim began, "we always worry about doing everything right for our kids. We can't. We just do our best and from what I see you are a great mom."

Gina felt the emotions building. "Not always. I made so many mistakes…with Eric. My son had to pay for that."

The big Irishman drew her into his arms again. "Oh, lass. You've got to forgive yourself and move on." In his tight embrace, she wondered if this was how girls felt having a father who cared about them. "You and Zack are safe here and Eric will never hurt either of you again."

"We're going to try." She pulled back, embarrassed by the tears in her eyes. "Sorry, I didn't mean to get so emotional on you."

He grinned. "Not at all. Now, our youngest, Leah, is the emotional one in the family. Always loved drama. Of course if you say anything, I'll deny it." He winked. "Come on, let's join the others."

They were greeted by the sound of voices first, then when the door opened, Gina saw several women working together in the huge kitchen, which was divided into two areas, a prep station for cooking and a dining area.

The Keenan daughters, Morgan, Paige and Leah, were helping their mother. There was a large picture window behind the table and she could see a group of kids running around the yard. The men were standing together talking as they watched the children.

Gina felt a different kind of emotion. Maybe a little

panic. She'd heard from Lori that Claire Keenan had played matchmaker more than once.

They were all paired off in couples. Except her and Grady. Of course Josh made it an odd number. Good.

"Grady should open a day care," Paige said as she nodded to the group of children. "Look how he's handling those kids. They aren't moving a muscle, just glued to his every word. Who knew all that military training would come in so handy?"

Morgan stepped in. "Maybe he can share some pointers on giving orders."

Gina turned her attention to Grady Fletcher. Okay so she was drawn to the man whether she liked it or not. Big and strong, he held your attention by his mere presence. The years of military training were engrained in the man. He demanded respect and he got it. From the kids and his dogs.

"Gina! You made it."

She turned to see Claire Keenan crossing the large kitchen to greet her. After a big hug, the older woman stepped back. "You look lovely."

Gina glanced down at her dark slacks and cream-colored sweater. "Thank you."

"Since I haven't seen Bandit at school again, I guess you fixed the escape route."

Gina nodded. "Grady repaired the fence. And he gave Zack some ideas on keeping the dog home."

Claire looked out at the yard. "That man seems to have a lot of talents. We just need to convince him to stay here." The older woman looked back at Gina. "We need another nice addition to our town, like you and Zack."

"Well, we sure love it here. And Second Best is doing great."

Claire smiled. "I hear you're doing some reupholstering."

Word spread fast in Destiny. "Grady was very generous and gave me a few items from his grandfather's cabin. I'm selling some other things for him, too."

"It's about time someone cleared out some of Joe's... treasures." Claire turned to the window. "I'm also glad that Fletch has his grandson around to help with his recovery." She nodded toward the window. "It also seems he's pretty good with the kids, too. That's something special in a man."

Gina had to agree. "Yes, he is." That was all she said as she walked outside. She leaned against the railing on the deck and watched as Grady talked with Zack. She saw the happiness and respect in her child's eyes. Except for Lori's new husband, Jace, her son had never had a man to look up to.

Then Eric had found them, tried to destroy their happiness. She'd worried that Zack would pull back again, but it looked like her boy had survived, and her ex-husband hadn't won.

Best of all, with numerous charges against him, kidnapping, attempted murder and resisting arrest, he would never be a threat again. Sheriff Larkin was going to make sure that he got everything he deserved. Maybe life was turning out to be something to look forward to.

Once again, her attention went to Grady. Darn if the man wasn't one big distraction. It was a good thing his visit was temporary. Now all she had to do was stay away from him until he left town. She could do that.

CHAPTER EIGHT

GRADY stood at the edge of the yard and watched as Josh took over exercising the dogs. The kids were so into it, and did exactly what they were told to do.

Scout didn't let them down after only one sniff of a small stuffed toy. Two of the older kids had been sent off to bury it, then using only their scent, Josh harnessed Scout and they went into the wooded area and soon returned with the correct items.

Morgan's husband, Justin Hilliard, came up to Grady. "I'm impressed," he told him.

Grady nodded. "Scout's been well trained."

"Does he work in snow?"

Grady continued to pet the shepherd. "Since we didn't arrive here until February, there's been limited opportunity to train, but we did a bit of tracking in the snow. I'm forever surprised how well these animals adapt to different climates."

Justin nodded. "I was surprised to hear that you're headed back to Texas."

"That's the plan." Grady glanced at Gina standing on the deck. It was tempting to stay, but a bad choice. "I'm only here until my grandfather is able to care for himself."

Hilliard let out a sigh. "I was hoping you'd think about training your dogs here."

Grady wonder what the man's point would be. "Why is that?"

"A couple of reasons. I run an extreme ski resort. People pay a hefty price to get the thrill of pushing it to the limit on the mountaintop. With that, there's always a threat of a possible avalanche. You know how critical time is in finding a buried skier and the mountain rescue squad here is one of the best. Call me a control freak if you will, but I like to have my own resources. My own qualified rescue team that I could airlift at a moment's notice."

Grady was surprised. "You want your own rescue dogs?"

Justin nodded. "Not just dogs, but I want a team with their handlers. And I'll pay well for it."

"Just for the winter?"

"Colorado has a long ski season." Hilliard went on to say, "I'm also developing mountain bike trails, with a training facility that will open in a few months. People go off the trail and get lost, even experienced hikers and bikers. I'd like to offer them that sense of security, especially since I'll be responsible for a lot of amateurs not used to the rough terrain."

Grady didn't want to be interested in the project, but he was. "You have a lot going on."

Justin nodded. "I do. I like living in a small town the size of Destiny. It's a great place to raise a family. Tourism is our main economy here." He glanced around. "This is all too beautiful to change. A lot of opportunity for someone with your talent." He handed him a business card. "If you have a chance, stop by my office at the Heritage Mountain Complex, and I'll show you my biking trails."

Grady took the card. "I can't promise anything."

"I understand, but I'd like a chance to show you what I could offer you and your partner."

Before Grady could say any more, Zack raced up to him. "Grady, look, Bandit found this." He waved the old T-shirt, but he held on to the leash with his other hand. "I buried it, and Josh took him out to search and he found it."

Justin excused himself and walked away.

Grady knelt and petted the boy's dog. "Hey, that's a good start."

The kids agreed. "And I want to train him more," Zack told him.

"It not something that's going to happen overnight, son. Scout took months and he was worked with every day."

"If you show me what to do, I'll work with Bandit every day. I promise. And my mom can bring Bandit out to you on the weekends so he can let Scout show him what to do, too."

That was the last thing Grady needed, more time with Gina. "Why don't you concentrate on Bandit being a good friend? You don't need him to be a rescue dog."

He saw the disappointment on the boy's face. Suddenly the memory of being a neglected kid with no one having time for him rushed back. "Okay, how about this?" Grady said. "What if I bring Scout into town a couple of afternoons and we'll spend time teaching Bandit a simple command?"

The boy's eyes rounded. "Really?"

"Zack, I'm willing to help, but I'm not going to be around very much longer."

The kid looked shocked and sad. "Why? Aren't you going to live in the cabin and train rescue dogs?"

"I'm only training here temporarily. I'll be going home to Texas." He hadn't had a home anywhere in a long time. "As soon as my granddad is better."

The boy's eyes lit up. "What if he doesn't get better for a long time? Can you still help me with Bandit?"

He found he would miss the boy, too. "Only if it's okay with your mother."

"If what's okay with me?"

Grady turned around to find Gina approaching them. He felt his mouth go dry, hating that she had that effect on him.

"Mom, Grady said he'll help me train Bandit. Please, can he?"

"Zack. We talked about this. You can't take up all Grady's time. He needs to work with his dogs, too."

Grady stepped in. "I wouldn't have offered if I didn't want to do it."

She didn't look convinced. "Zack… Why don't you go and get Bandit some water?"

Once the boy and dog were gone, she spoke. "Grady, you don't have to do this."

The sound of her saying his name did things to him. "It's really not a problem."

It was a problem for Gina. She didn't need to spend any more time with this man. "Still, your time is valuable."

"So is yours and you took the time to straighten up the cabin. Speaking of which, I need to ask you a favor."

What could he possibly need from her? "Sure. Whatever you need."

"My grandfather wants to talk to you about the furniture."

"Does he want it all back?" she asked. "Of course he does. I haven't sold any of it, so the sofas can go back."

She looked up to catch him smiling. "What?"

"You can't let Fletch intimidate you. That cabin was a disgrace. It's needed to be cleaned out for years. I only want you to check with him about a few of my grandmother's things."

"Of course. I'm sure you want them to stay in the family, something to hand down to the next generation."

He frowned. "That's something that isn't going to happen. The Fletcher line ends with me."

Gina watched as Grady walked off to care for the dogs. Okay, she'd said the wrong things again. Did he think he wouldn't ever marry, ever have children?

"Hey, sis," Lori called to her.

They hugged. "Hi, Lori. Glad you could make it." She glanced at her niece, Cassie, who was already playing with the others.

"Jace had a business call." Lori looked at the group with the dogs. "Seems you got here early enough to spend time with the popular dog trainer."

"Don't get any ideas," she warned. "It was Zack who wanted to bring Bandit. Besides, I'm doing business with Grady. He's cleaning out his grandfather's cabin and the furniture is filling up the shop."

"He's also a man who spends time with your child. I'd say that's a good quality. I take it he's going to help Zack train Bandit."

"I don't know, Lori. Why don't you ask him?"

Her sister looked taken aback by her attitude. "Are you okay?"

She released a breath. "Yes. Sorry, I'm just tired of everyone asking me about Grady. Don't get me wrong.

I'm so grateful the man found Zack, but that's as far as it goes. He's not my man. We're not together in any way." She took a shaky breath, unable to stop the awful memories from her marriage. "I'm not ready to be with a man, Lori…. I might never be."

"Shh. It's okay, Gina." Lori took her hand and walked away from the group for more privacy. "I'm sorry I said anything. And I promise I won't push you anymore. But be assured, when you find that right man, you'll be able to trust again."

Gina felt that familiar lonely ache that tore at her. She glanced at the good-looking ex-sergeant and a different kind of feeling washed over her.

She quickly averted her eyes away from temptation. "What if I'm never ready, Lori? What if I can't stand to ever let a man touch me again?"

She studied her. "Are you still going to your support group?"

"As much as I can. I've been focused on Zack lately."

"You need to focus on yourself, too." She smiled. "Who knows, you might start feeling secure enough you'd trust a nice man like Grady Fletcher."

Gina started to argue and her sister stopped her by saying, "Just don't rule the man out."

Gina knew she couldn't risk it. Besides, the man wouldn't be here long enough. He was headed back to Texas and out of her life.

Two mornings later Grady pulled up behind the Second Best Thrift Shop and parked. Maybe he should have called Gina first, but it had all been a bit last-minute. Then he'd got the call from Shady Haven. His grandfather had summoned him.

He might as well get this over with so he could get

back to work at the cabin. He climbed out of the truck and headed for the large back door. He opened it and peered inside. Marie was in the work area, stretching fabric over the arm of one of the sofas he'd given to Gina.

She saw him right away and stood. "Hello, Grady. What brings you here? You find more treasures?"

"What you call treasures, I call junk." He glanced around. "Is Gina here?"

Just then the woman in question walked through the door from the front showroom. She was dressed in her standard dark slacks, but today she had on a soft white-and-navy-striped blouse. It was fitted, showing off her narrow waist and nice curves. Her long dark hair was pulled back into a ponytail and hoop earrings hung from her ears.

She finally spotted him. "Oh, hi, Grady. What are you doing in town?"

He found he could easily get lost in her green eyes. "Ah, I got a call from my grandfather. He was wondering if you had time to see him today."

"I'm not sure…"

"I told him he couldn't order people around just to please himself."

Marie stood. "Gina, I can watch the shop. Sophie is here, so it's fine for me to stay."

Gina checked her watch. "Okay, but I'll have a sandwich sent over from the Silver Spoon. My treat."

"No, it'll be my treat," Grady insisted. "We'll take Fletch a piece of pie, too."

Gina couldn't think of any more excuses not to go. She went to get her purse and realized her heart was beating like a drum, hard and fast. She had to pull herself together and stop letting him get to her.

She followed him to the truck and let him help her in, and that meant he touched her. Oh, God. She felt his heat and his strength as he lifted her up into the vehicle. Once fastened in, she laid her head back and tried to relax. Grady didn't seem to be any more talkative than she. Thank goodness the trip to the restaurant was quick, then the ride outside of town only took about fifteen minutes.

Grady finally broke the silence when he announced, "We're here."

He parked in the Shady Haven lot, then they walked up to the entrance of the two-story building. "Just one thing before we go in. Don't let my grandfather get to you. He thinks because he's old he can say and do whatever he wants. If he gets too personal, tell him to back off."

"I'm sure he'll be perfectly nice," she said.

Grady wasn't sure what Joe Fletcher wanted with Gina. He figured it was because he hadn't been out for a few days, and the man was probably lonely.

They walked through the double doors of the facility. "Oh, Grady, it's lovely here."

He had to agree. "I tried to tell Fletch that he'd be more comfortable moving in here, but he misses the cabin." He went to the desk and asked the receptionist for his grandfather.

The young woman sent them into the recreation room. Grady guided her down the hall to a large area that had a huge flat-screen television. The walls were lined with bookshelves filled with books. There seemed to be a lot of activities going on, and a lot of interaction between the patients and other guests.

There were several small tables for games. That's

where he found his grandfather with three women. They were playing cards.

"There he is." He put his hand against Gina's back and guided her through the room.

"Well, well, Granddad," Grady said as he stopped at the card table. "Seems you're not so lonely anymore."

Joe Fletcher glared at him. "It's a shame I need to call you to come and see me."

"I was here two days ago."

"Oh, Joe, is this your grandson?" asked one of the gray-haired women at the table. "He's just as handsome as you said."

"Grady, meet Alice, Mary Lou and Bubbles."

He nodded as they seemed to be blushing at his attention. "Ladies and Granddad, this is Gina Williams."

She stepped forward. "It's nice to meet everyone." She looked at Joe. "And especially you, Mr. Fletcher."

Joe Fletcher smiled as he looked Gina over. "Well, well, you're mighty pretty, Miss Williams. I can see why my grandson has been distracted lately."

"Granddad," Grady said in warning.

Gina blushed. "Why, thank you, Mr. Fletcher, but I think Grady's been busy with training his dogs."

"That's probably true. Sad, but true," Joe said, then excused himself from the ladies at the table. Grady took charge of Fletch's wheelchair and they crossed the room to an empty table.

"Can't wait to get out of this contraption." Joe hit the arm of the wheelchair. "I can't even go to the bathroom by myself."

Grady sat. "Fletch, you know once you finish rehab, you'll be able to walk again. All the doctors said so."

"I could be dead by then."

Gina sat across from the older man. "Mr. Fletcher,

you should listen to your grandson. He's been trying to make the cabin ready for your return, but you have to do your part."

Grady bit back a grin.

Fletch finally smiled. "I like you, Gina Williams. Besides being pretty as a new spotted pup, you seem to have a head on your shoulders."

"Sometimes we learn from our mistakes." She handed him the container with the pie. "Here, Grady brought this for you."

He took the offered dessert. "Do you have a man in your life?"

Gina wasn't going to fall into this trap. "Yes, I do, as a matter of fact. And I love him to death. In fact, he and Grady are very good friends."

The thin man raised a bushy gray eyebrow. "Then he must be a good guy if Grady likes him."

"Of course. Grady even got him a dog, Bandit, and is going to help train him. Of course, we both got worried when the dog took off and followed Zack to school."

"School?" Joe wasn't dumb by any means. "Just how old is this man?"

"He's nearly eight." She glanced at Grady and felt a rush of admiration, something she didn't want to admit. "Your Grady and Scout saved my son's life." She swallowed back the emotion. "I will always be grateful."

Fletch smiled. "So it was your boy who got lost?"

"Yes. That's why I want to help to fix up the cabin. You had a lot of furniture, Mr. Fletcher. But if there's a question about anything I have in my store, of course I will return it."

The old man shrugged. "There's not much I care to save. My wife had a bunch of frilly stuff——" he glanced at Grady "—I'm sure my grandson could care less about."

Gina asked, "Is there anything you care about, Mr. Fletcher?"

He gave her a big grin. "Just my bed. I love my big brass bed."

She smiled. "Oh, I've seen it. It's lovely."

"Glad you like it. Someday Grady is going to inherit that bed."

An hour later, filled with several long stories of the past, Grady and Gina said goodbye to Fletch and walked out of Shady Haven.

Gina was quiet as she thought about Grady and his grandfather reminiscing about their past summers together. She got a sneak peak of a side to Grady she hadn't seen before, a more relaxed, a more outgoing side. She doubted that Grady had revealed it to many, and she felt lucky to get a glimpse of this man.

What she quickly discovered was that she'd like to know more about Grady. Spend more time with him, find out if he wanted more from her than just a spontaneous kiss in the garage.

She glanced at the handsome man beside her. There was a sudden tingling in her stomach, something she hadn't felt in a long time.

Was Lori right? Maybe she was ready to move on.

They reached the truck and Grady turned to her and said, "I'm sorry Fletch bored you going on and on with those stories, and the questions. You should have told him to mind his own business."

Gina smiled up at him. "Fletch is a wonderful old man. And you're pretty wonderful, too."

Grady didn't have time to react as Gina rose up,

locked her hands around his neck, pulled him down and covered his mouth with a kiss. Caught off balance, he gripped the sides of her waist and just managed to hold on. As kisses went, what she lacked in experience, she made up for in enthusiasm. He could get into this. Then she quickly released him, looking shocked at her actions.

"Not that I'm complaining, but didn't I just get into trouble for doing the same thing last week?"

Her cheeks were rosy with embarrassment. "You act so big and tough. Then I see how sweet you are with kids…and how much you care for your grandfather."

He leaned against the truck and couldn't help but smile. This woman was so appealing, and so much trouble. That meant he should stay far away from her.

"Hell, if I'd known that would earn me a kiss from you, I'd have brought you here to see Fletch sooner."

"Oh, maybe I shouldn't have done that." Her face flamed even more and her gaze darted away.

He touched her chin and made her look at him. "Did you hear me complain?"

She only shook her head.

He wanted nothing more than to continue kissing her, but knew better than to go any further. That still didn't stop him from asking, "How would you like to get some lunch?"

She looked surprised at his offer. "I shouldn't. I mean, Marie is already staying later." She hesitated. "I guess I could call her."

He pulled out his phone. "What's the number?"

CHAPTER NINE

TWENTY minutes later Grady escorted Gina into the Silver Spoon Restaurant. They walked through the glass-paneled door and were greeted by a surprised Helen Turner. The middle-aged owner was wearing jeans and a white blouse, covered by a starched apron. She also had on a big smile.

"Well, well, isn't this nice." She set down two glasses of water as they slid into a booth in front of the window. "Twice in one day."

Grady spoke up. "We took the pie out to my grand-dad and realized we hadn't eaten."

"How is Joe?" Helen asked. "Did he enjoy the pie?"

"Yes, he did. He told me to tell you it was delicious."

Helen grinned. "Well if that just doesn't make my day." She handed out the menus. "I may have to go see that old man."

After the woman walked off, Grady leaned forward. "No doubt by tonight the town will be buzzing about us being together." He looked around the room, seeing glances from the curious patrons. "They're probably wondering what an old guy like me is doing with someone as pretty as you."

"You aren't old, and thank you for saying I'm pretty."

He leaned back in the booth. "He sure did a job on you, didn't he?"

Gina didn't want to talk about her past, or her ex. "It's not something I'm proud of."

Grady wanted to set her straight, but Helen reappeared and took their order. After she left he said, "That's what you have to change, Gina. Your way of thinking that anything that bastard did was your fault." He leaned closer again, his eyes locked on hers as his voice lowered. "It wasn't, Gina. You found the courage to take your son and leave him. I'd say you're a pretty amazing woman."

Gina's heart was pounding at Grady's words. "Thank you."

"I'm speaking the truth. You're making a fresh start for yourself and Zack. You're building a business that seems to be doing well. Soon there'll be men lining up to spend time with you."

She quickly shook her head. She couldn't stop the panic she felt building up inside. "I'm not sure I can get involved with a man again."

"Why not? You managed to kiss me."

She didn't want to rehash her sudden impulsiveness. It had been so unlike her. "You're different."

He frowned. "I don't know if I like the sound of that."

She shrugged. "I've got to know you. I trust you." And she was attracted to him, she added silently. "Too bad I can't practice on you."

Grady hadn't been surprised after Gina's admission that lunch was eaten quickly and the subject had been changed to work. Twenty minutes later Grady drove Gina back to her store. He parked out back and she thanked him, then couldn't get out of the truck fast enough.

He sat there a few minutes, telling himself what Gina had said at the Silver Spoon was just joking around. He needed to let it go. So why couldn't he?

Grady climbed out of the driver's side and walked to the back door of the store. He said hi to Marie as she pushed a baby stroller out the door.

He moved into the work area and stopped, amazed to see that the old sofas were nearly finished. One was covered in a gray-and-white stripe, and the other was in a camel color. He smiled as he imagined all the work Gina and Marie had put into them.

He went down a hall past an office, then a small bathroom. He continued his journey into the main room where there was furniture arranged in groups. Against the far wall were lamps and several dining room tables and chairs. He moved toward the front and discovered a high counter. Gina stood behind it with her back to him, talking on the phone.

"Yes, Mrs. Browning, I can be out tomorrow morning." She paused. "Of course, I'll give you my price before I take anything. Okay, goodbye." She hung up and turned around.

That was when she saw him. "Grady. I thought you left."

He should have. He was crazy to be here to pursue any part of this woman. "What did you mean by saying you want to practice on me?"

Gina groaned. She was so embarrassed. "Oh, that. I was just kidding around."

He came behind the desk. "Were you joking around when you planted that kiss on me at Shady Haven?"

He wasn't going to let this go, she realized. "Gosh,

you caught me. I was impulsive and talkative all in one day." She waved him off. "Just forget it happened."

He moved closer as he pushed his cowboy hat back off his forehead. "What if I don't want to forget it? What if I want to hear what you're thinking?"

Gina brushed back her hair, feeling her heart racing with him standing so close. "You've got to have better things to do than—"

"Than what?" he asked. "Show you how to kiss properly? How to feel comfortable around a man?"

She swallowed. Her throat was bone-dry. "It sounds silly to hear you say it. Besides I don't have time to date anyway. Zack needs my attention." She sighed, trying to push away the endless loneliness she always felt. "But there are times when I don't want to be alone."

"Like in the middle of the night?"

She wasn't ready to admit that yet. "More like when you get invited places and you're the fifth wheel, or everyone wants to fix you up with someone. I'm tired of the pity. The poor girl whose husband was abusive… the poor girl who had it so rough."

He reached out and touched her cheek. "First of all, you aren't a girl anymore, Gina. You're definitely a woman. A strong woman who has started a new life and is doing a good job of raising her son. Those who think differently, to hell with them."

He lowered his head and her heart began to race. "Now, as for the amount of instruction you'll need, first I'll need to sample you again."

Before she could say anything, his mouth closed over hers. It was soft, a whisper of a kiss, teasing her, making her want more.

Before she could react, Grady pulled back a little, enough for her to see his dark gaze. "Open just a little,

Gina." It wasn't a demand, but a request as his thumb caressed her lower lip. "Perfect," he breathed, then went back for more. This time he added some pressure, then his hands went to her face and held her tenderly. His mouth moved over hers, tasting and caressing until she lost all track of everything except this man. *Oh, my,* she sighed in a moan as her hands came up to his chest. His tongue teased along the seam of her lips, then darted inside when she opened wider. And her own body's re-action caused an ache she'd never felt before.

He pulled back and looked down at her. She couldn't miss the desire she saw in his eyes.

She managed to speak. "How was I?"

"I think you know the answer already. I want you, Gina." He released a breath. "Does that frighten you?"

She was thrilled at his declaration, but scared to death. But knowing how much she wanted to move on, to take a chance on finding happiness. "Yes! No! I don't know, but I do trust you."

Those words seemed to bring him back to reality. He took a step back. "Don't make that mistake. You need to find a man who wants to settle down and have a family. Someone closer to your age."

She didn't remove her hands from Grady's chest. She didn't want to break the contact with him. "You have this thing about your age. You're not that much older than I am." She moved closer to him. "It didn't feel like an old man kissing me."

"You're asking for trouble."

She raised an eyebrow, going after what she wanted. To stop letting the past dictate the future. "Seems you are, too. Isn't that the reason you walked in here?"

She saw the confusion in his eyes. She forced herself to stand her ground.

"I need to go," he said, and she was a little relieved and a little disappointed when Grady turned and walked out.

It was Tuesday and Grady had promised Zack that he'd work with him after school. Since he'd walked out of Second Best four days ago he hadn't contacted Gina. He hadn't even called her, and that was for the best.

He needed time to think, needed to come to his senses. It hadn't done any good, though. The bottom line was he wanted to be with Gina Williams. And yet, he wanted more than just to spend time with her. He wanted to get her naked, to make love to her until they both couldn't think about anything else.

He released a breath. He hadn't been with any woman since his divorce. And not since he'd been burned. He touched the scar above his shirt collar and recalled Gina's hands on his chest. A portion of his upper body had been burned, too. Would the scar repulse her?

He turned down Cherry Street and found Zack was waiting for him at the curb as he got out of the vehicle.

"Hi, Grady. I've been working with Bandit every day. He's been behaving really well, too."

He retrieved Scout from the back. "Glad to hear it. Let's go see how he works today."

Grady placed his hand on the boy's shoulder as they headed to the side gate and into the backyard. Gina came out of the sliding door off the deck. He stopped cold seeing her in snug jeans and a T-shirt. Her legs might not be that long, but they were toned and shapely. Her hair was pulled back into a ponytail.

She smiled. "Hi, Grady."

"Gina."

She came down the steps and he had to stop himself

from reaching for her and giving her the proper greeting he'd been aching to do since he'd left her four long days ago.

"How have you been?" he asked.

"Good." She beamed and her eyes brightened. "I sold the camelback sofa today." She giggled. "I got six hundred dollars for it."

He blinked. "Hey, that's a good profit."

"I'm glad I could give Marie a nice bonus, too. She and her husband could use the money. I feel like I should give you some, too."

He shook his head. "You did me a favor and hauled it out. I should have paid you."

"Okay, we'll call it even."

Zack came up to him. "Grady, can we start now?"

Okay, so now she was distracting him from his job. "Sure."

He walked off with Zack and for the next hour they worked Scout, all the time hoping that Bandit would follow the boy's commands, too.

Grady observed the boy and his dog. He was impressed at how well the kid handled the large animal. "Okay, tell Bandit to heel."

Zack had his dog on the leash at his left side. The twosome began walking, then Zack gave the command and Bandit obeyed. Both dogs were rewarded with some play time. They tossed tennis balls so the animals could retrieve them.

Zack came up to him. "Grady, can I ask you a question?"

He was surprised the see the serious look on the boy's face. "Sure, I'm not guaranteeing I'll have an answer."

"Does the scar on your neck hurt?"

Grady knelt and the animals came up to him. He had them sit and gave his full attention to the boy. "It used to hurt a lot," he answered honestly. "Not so much anymore."

"Did you get it when you were fighting the bad guys?"

He wasn't sure he could explain it to a seven-year-old. "Yes. There are a lot of us over there fighting."

"My teacher says you're making it safe for all of us so we can live free. And we should always thank you."

Grady nodded. "There were many soldiers who gave their lives for that freedom, too." He couldn't help but think of the men he'd lost that day. "Honor them for their sacrifice."

"I will," Zack promised. "I'm glad you came home, Grady. Really glad."

Zack smiled. "I'm glad you live in Destiny, too."

Before Grady could contradict the boy, Gina called out, "Supper's ready."

Grady glanced up, not surprised to see her curious look. He stood. "I've got to be going."

"No, please stay," Gina coaxed. "Unless you have plans."

He could lie, but Josh had gone out tonight, so he was just going to pick up a sandwich in town before heading back to the cabin. "No plans."

She smiled. "Good. I hope you like meat loaf."

What does one meal hurt? "You're talking to a man who spent twenty years in the military. We appreciate any home cooking we can get."

Leaving Scout out on the deck with Bandit, he walked into the homey kitchen. Not the most updated appliances, and the countertops were chipped, but Gina had painted the walls a soft green and added those womanly touches.

"We've got to wash up," Zack said, and took him down the hall. There was a detour into the kid's bedroom. It was blue with a lot of baseball posters on the walls.

Grady said, "I guess you like the game."

"I get to play Little League next month, but I'm not very good. Uncle Jace has been practicing with me, but I still have trouble catching."

"You'll get better with practice."

"But the other boys have been playing for two years." Zack moved his gaze away. "I didn't get to play when I lived with my dad. He didn't like me playing 'cause I couldn't do anything right."

Grady knelt down to be eye level with the sad boy. He worked to hide the anger he felt toward Lowell. "You have to know that your dad didn't treat you right. It had nothing to do with you. None of it was your fault. You can do anything you want to do. Look how much you've accomplished with Bandit."

The boy's head bobbed up and down. "And now Mommy and me don't have to be scared. I'm glad my dad went away."

So was Grady. "And he's never going to hurt either you or your mom again. Sheriff Larkin will make sure of that."

Zack threw his arms around Grady's neck. "Thanks, Grady. And I'm glad you're around, too."

There was a sudden constriction in his chest as he felt those tiny arms around him. He couldn't help but wonder if his son had survived, how close they would have been. Would they have had moments like this?

"You're welcome, kid." He stood.

After washing their hands, they went back into the hall and walked past another bedroom. No doubt it was Gina's. The walls were painted a soft yellow. It had a queen-size bed with a solid pale blue comforter, adorned with several pillows. As much as he tried to fight it, he could picture her in that big bed, with all that pretty dark hair spread out on the pillow.

He blinked away the daydream and caught up with Zack as they entered the kitchen where the food was on the table. Zack took his seat, then Gina sat. An ache filled him as he took the empty seat.

Okay, maybe he did want this. As a kid, he'd never been part of a family. The army had been the family he'd shared his life with. He looked at Gina. Why now? What was it about her that made him want something he'd already failed at miserably?

Two hours later Gina was surprised that Grady was still there. He'd insisted that he and Zack would do the dishes, then the next thing she knew, he was helping her son with his homework.

Once Zack was tucked into bed, she went in and kissed her son good-night. When she came back out to the living room she found Grady waiting by the front door, hat in hand.

"I've got to go."

She nodded. "Of course. I'm sorry, I didn't mean to take up so much of your evening."

He reached for the doorknob and stopped. "I'm not good at this, Gina. I've tried before and I made a lot of mistakes."

He must be talking about his marriage.

"I didn't mean to bring back bad memories. I'm sorry, Grady." She glanced away, feeling foolish about all those kisses they'd shared the other day. "Thank you for all your help with Zack."

She heard his curse, then he reached for her. She gasped, not from fear, but from surprise when his mouth closed over hers. She was hungry for him, praying all evening that he'd kiss her again.

He broke off the kiss. "Damn. I shouldn't have done that." His dark brooding gaze searched her face. "It's not you, Gina."

That made her angry. "Even I have heard that line before. If you don't want to get involved with me, that's okay, but don't make up excuses."

"Dammit, I'm not a good bet." He glanced around. "My marriage was a disaster."

She wasn't sure if she wanted to know that he had loved another woman. "How long were you married?"

"Five years." He laughed. "On paper, but in reality, we weren't together much of that time. I was overseas twice. The second time was the clincher. Barbara left me."

"I'm sorry, Grady. I know that must have hurt you."

"Not as badly as I hurt her. I was never there for her. I can't blame her for ending it."

"If you were in the army when you got married, she had to know that you'd be away a lot."

"That's easier said than done. Barb asked me not to go, but I chose a unit that was going to be deployed. I chose 'the cause' over her." His pained gaze met hers. "I realized then that I could never be a permanent kind of guy. And that's exactly the type you and Zack need, a family man."

She nodded, understanding what he was trying to tell her. "Someday I want to give my son the security of a family." She hesitated, feeling her fears and emotion surface. "That's what I'm afraid of, Grady, that I never will be able to. I'd been with Eric since I was a teenager. He's been the only man I've…known. I'd never even kissed another man until you."

Grady was shocked at her confession. "Hell, Gina, there's a hell of a lot of men out there who would love the chance."

She stepped away, and he missed her closeness. "I lost so much of my adolescence, and with my abusive marriage, I'm frightened to try another relationship." Her rich green eyes met his. "I don't know if I can ever be with a man again." Her voice lowered to a whisper. "Not intimately anyway."

He fought going to her and proving her wrong. "It'll take time, but I'm sure you'll find someone."

He watched her swallow, square her shoulders, then she asked, "Would you help me, Grady?"

Not what he expected her to say. Of course nothing had been what he'd expected since he'd met this woman. Common sense told him to leave, but that didn't stop his ache for her. His head said to run away. He didn't want to know what his heart said.

"That's the worst idea I ever heard."

"Why? I trust you."

"That's your first mistake. You shouldn't." He started to pace. "You don't want a man who will take what he wants from you then leave. And I am leaving, Gina. As soon as Fletch is well enough, I'm gone."

She nodded. "I know. That's what makes this work. You can show me how a man is supposed to treat a woman, and when it comes time for you to leave, I won't try and stop you."

"It isn't always a clean break. You could get hurt."

"I'll be sad when you leave, but if I know that it's

coming, I can deal with it." She walked toward him. "I just want to know what it's like to be in a normal, healthy relationship. One where I get to be an equal partner. One where a man doesn't control me, make me do things that I don't want to do."

She blinked and glanced away. He went to her and turned her face toward him. He saw the pain and hurt. He wanted to erase all of it.

"Hey. Shh." He bent down and brushed his mouth over hers, once, then twice, listening to her soft moans of wanting.

"You said the other day you wanted me," she said. "Have you changed your mind?"

He answered as his mouth captured hers in a hungry kiss. He drew her close, careful not to be too rough. He pressed her body against his, letting her feel his desire. "Does that answer your question?"

She was breathing hard. "Oh, yes. I want you, too, Grady Fletcher."

CHAPTER TEN

HE WAS nothing but a coward.

Later the next morning Grady pulled into Shady Haven's parking lot, unable to forget how twelve hours ago, he'd run out on Gina. Facing the enemy in a foreign country had been easier than dealing with this 110-pound woman.

All night Gina had invaded his sleep, along with his peace of mind. Any rational thinking on his part had disappeared because he was actually considering her crazy idea.

Worse, it was affecting his concentration with the dogs this morning. Even Josh had noticed he'd been distracted. Finally, Grady had ended the struggle and decided to go visit his grandfather. But if the old guy brought up Gina Williams, he wasn't going to be held responsible for his actions.

Grady walked inside and the receptionist looked up and smiled, then she pointed toward the recreation room. There was no doubt his grandfather was the social one in the family. Grady headed down the hall and found Fletch sitting at his usual table with a younger woman. Lori Hutchinson Yeager.

What was she doing here?

He walked over and his grandfather smiled at him. "Hey, son, I didn't expect to see you this morning."

"Here I thought you might be lonely. I'm glad to see you're not." Grady turned his attention to Gina's pretty blond sister. "Hello, Lori."

She nodded. "Hi, Grady. I didn't mean to take up all your grandfather's time. It was important that I clear up something with Joe." She smiled at his grandfather. "We've just finished with our business."

Grady sat and asked, "And exactly what business would that be?"

His grandfather spoke up. "Watch your manners, son. Miss Lori is nice enough to come out here and correct a grave mistake she found." He nodded to Lori. "Tell my grandson, Miss Lori."

"Of course," Lori said. "Grady, I can understand your concern, but this is good. I mentioned something to you a few weeks ago about a questionable parcel of land of my great-grandfather Billy had the papers for. We discovered that he didn't really own it, at least not legally. He took it from your grandfather saying he hadn't paid the taxes. Since I took over running the bank this past year, I discovered the taxes assessed on the property were three times the normal rate." She sighed. "I'm not proud of what Billy did. So I hope after today, I've corrected the issue about the land. It will be returned to Joe."

Grady wasn't sure what was going on. "Fletch doesn't need another old abandoned mine."

"That's what is great about this, Grady," Fletch began, "It isn't a worthless mine. It's prime land just outside of Destiny. It belonged to your grandmother and now, thanks to Miss Lori, we have it back." His grandfather grinned. "And I'm going to deed it over to you."

Grady was skeptical of all this, but the look on his grandfather's face was priceless.

Lori smiled. "Well, I should get back to the bank. If

it's all right with you, I'll have Paige Larkin start the paperwork."

Joe looked at his grandson. Grady nodded.

"Okay, then," Lori said. "In a few days the papers will be ready to sign."

She stood and so did Grady. That was when he noticed the roundness of her stomach. Gina's sister was expecting? "I'll walk you out," he offered.

"I'll be right back," he told Fletch, then he escorted Lori down the hall.

"I hope you'll accept my apology for the actions of my great-grandfather," Lori said. "As I told your grandfather, I've been trying to correct a lot of Billy's mistakes. Thank goodness, I'm nearly at the end of the list."

"I appreciate your efforts," Grady told her. "You've made Fletch happy. He needs something to look forward to."

Lori stopped at the building entry. "I'm glad." She hesitated. "I can't thank you for all the help you've given to my sister and nephew."

"Not a problem."

"It's still nice that you've been helping Zack with Bandit."

"And if I want to spend time with Zack's mother?"

That brought a smile to her lovely face, reminding him of Gina. "You don't strike me as the type of man who asks for permission."

Maybe he'd changed. "How about if I ask if you'll watch Zack one evening?"

"Of course I would." She grinned and headed to the door, then looked back. "He loves to sleep over at Aunt Lori's house."

* * *

It was a date. She had a date with Grady.

That was all, Gina told herself as she kept changing her outfit. She didn't exactly have many choices of what to wear.

"Here, put on these," Lori offered. She held up a pair of expensive jeans. "They'll look great with your teal sweater."

"I can't wear your pants. What if I spill something on them?"

"Come on, sis. They're a pair of jeans. I'll buy more after the baby comes." She rubbed her bottom. "That is if I ever lose the weight."

"You look great. And more importantly, your loving husband thinks so."

She held out the pair of denims to her. "Then wear them."

Gina relented and stepped into the jeans. Thank goodness the fabric had stretch in it, or she would never get them zipped. She turned from side to side to get a look. Not bad. She slipped on the sweater and put on another loan from sis, a pair of high-heeled sandals. She stood. Okay, she looked taller. What would Grady think?

Just then the doorbell sounded and her heart began to pound. "Oh, he's here."

"Slow down," her sister coaxed. "It won't hurt him to wait a few minutes. You're worth it."

Gina agreed, knowing she had to reprogram her way of thinking. From now on men were going to treat her right.

After applying lipstick, she grabbed her purse and walked out to the living room to find Grady talking with Zack.

Oh, my. He looked so...wonderful. Dressed in a burgundy Western shirt that was fitted over those broad shoulders and tucked neatly into a pair of killer black jeans.

Her son turned around. "Oh, Mom," he called. "You look so pretty."

"Thank you, Zack." She felt the heat rush to her face as she glanced at Grady. "Hello, Grady."

"Hi, Gina." His gaze was dark and intense, then he smiled as he made his way to her. "Your son's right, you do look pretty."

More heat shot to her face. "Thank you."

She managed to kiss her son goodbye before he walked out the front door with Aunt Lori.

The room grew silent as Grady stood at the closed door, his gaze moving over her body. "What you do to a pair of jeans should be outlawed."

She found she was a little breathless. "You should be happy. I can't eat much in these."

He walked to her, leaned down and brushed a soft kiss against her lips. "We'd better get out of here, or I might just decide to skip food all together."

She swallowed. "Oh, no you don't, Grady Fletcher, you promised me dinner." She grabbed his hand and hauled him toward the door and they laughed all the way to the truck.

The trip to Durango took about forty minutes. It wasn't that Grady didn't want to take Gina to dinner in Destiny. He just didn't want everyone watching them, speculating on their relationship. What they were doing or not doing was no one's business.

Damn. What was he doing? He was too old to start the dating game.

Grady parked in the public lot and escorted Gina the

two blocks to Main Street and Francisco's Restaurant. Although he'd made a reservation, he took her into the bar and sat. "Would you like something to drink?"

At first she turned him down, but when the waitress suggested their famous margarita, Gina agreed to try it. Once the large glass arrived, she looked intimidated, but took a sip. "This is good."

Grady took a drink of his beer. "Just be careful. Tequila has been known to sneak up on you."

"Are you talking from experience?"

He couldn't help but smile. "Could be. In my younger and not-so-wiser days."

"I never had the chance to do much of anything. I got married when I was barely out of high school. I never went out much, or had girlfriends." She took another sip, then said, "I guess I'm overdue some experience…life."

They exchanged a glance that told him she wasn't talking just about the alcohol and his gut tightened. There was so much he wanted to share with this woman.

Finally the waitress took them to their table in a quiet corner. It was next to the fireplace and the sound of soft music filled the room. Gina sat at an angle to him. He found he liked her close, close enough to touch.

"This is lovely, Grady," she said. "Thank you for bringing me here."

It was hard to believe that she'd never been taken out to a nice meal. "You're welcome." He had to stop thinking about all the "firsts" he wanted to share with her. The waitress handed them menus and Grady opened his. "I hear the seafood is good."

Gina started to look hers over. "Oh, there's so much. Will you order for me?" she asked.

He shook his head. "Tonight, Gina, you're making your own choices."

She looked at him, her green eyes leery. She glanced over the list again. "Well, then, I'm going to have…the penne pasta and scallops." She closed the menu and handed it to the waitress.

"I'm a pretty basic meat-and-potatoes kind of guy. I'll have the rib-eye steak, medium rare."

The waitress smiled then walked away.

Gina liked that she wasn't nervous with Grady. Maybe it was the margarita that helped her relax, but she found herself at ease with him. "There's nothing basic about you, Sarge."

He gave her a stern look, then his expression softened. He reached for her hand. "I'm sure you're going to tell me why you think that."

She took another sip of her drink and said, "Maybe later. I don't think I need to inflate your ego any more."

"Wait a minute. I have an inflated ego?"

She laughed. "I was teasing. It's that you've accomplished so many things, and you've probably done everything very well."

He took a drink of his beer. "You just don't know my failures."

She studied his handsome face. "There can't be many. You had a long career in the army. I can see the respect you get from Josh. I suspect all the men in your unit felt the same about you."

It was endearing to see him blush. "Aren't you the wise one?"

Gina felt the warmth of his hand caressing hers. It sent shivers up her arm, making her aware that she was female. She glanced away and took a breath for courage before she turned back to him. She caught his gaze on her. The things this man could do to her with only a look.

She sobered. "I know a lot has changed with your accident and retiring from the military… But, Grady, you've already started a new career that you love. I'd say, all in all, you're a pretty lucky guy."

Grady didn't want to get into his past or his future. This was only about tonight. He squeezed her hand. "I feel lucky that I'm with the prettiest woman here."

She smiled at him and his gut tightened. "Thank you for saying that."

"Someone should be telling you that all the time." He just couldn't be that guy, he added silently. "You're special, Gina."

"I guess we should start each other's fan clubs." She giggled and he found he liked the sound. That was the problem. He liked too many things about this woman.

About two hours later Grady pulled up in front of her house. He turned off the engine and sat back wondering what was going to happen next. He knew he didn't want the evening to end, but it also wouldn't be wise to stay. No matter how much he wanted Gina, he wouldn't take advantage of her. If he did take things further, it wouldn't change anything between them. In the end, he'd be leaving town.

He walked around the truck, opened the passenger-side door and helped Gina out. They made their way along the walkway and up the steps. She put the key into the lock and opened the door.

She turned back to him. "Would you like to come in for some coffee?"

With any other woman that would be a signal for something else, but with Gina, she was most likely going to fix him coffee. "Sure."

He followed her inside the dark house as she dropped

her purse on the table. He stood close enough to catch her intoxicating scent, and had to fight to resist her as he followed her into the kitchen. Turning on only the under-counter lights, she busied herself filling the coffeemaker. Once finished, she turned around and looked up at him. "It'll take a few minutes to brew." She seemed nervous. "I had a good time tonight. The food was delicious."

Hell, she sounded about as unsure of this as he did. "I'm glad you enjoyed yourself."

She stepped closer. "I have you to thank for that. You made me feel…special."

"God, Gina. You have no idea how special you are." He couldn't stop himself—he pulled her into his arms and lowered his head. "Let me show you."

His lips brushed over hers and when he heard her gasp, he went back and captured her mouth. With her sweet body pressed against him, he lost any rational thoughts of going slow.

Gina followed his lead. Her arms circled his neck and she opened her mouth, allowing him to deepen the kiss. And he did. His tongue dove inside, brushing against hers, tasting and caressing. That only made him want more.

He finally tore his mouth away. "I've wanted to do that all night," he breathed, then continued the contact as he placed openmouthed kisses along her jaw, working his way to her graceful neck.

She sucked in a breath when he touched a sensitive spot. "Oh, Grady. I wanted you to kiss me, too."

"Let's see if we can keep agreeing."

He dipped his head and took her mouth again. She whimpered as he pulled her closer. The things this woman did to him made him forget everything.

Suddenly the sound of a phone startled them back to reality.

"I've got to get that." Gina pulled away and reached for the phone on the counter. "Hello?" She paused and said, "Lori, is something wrong with Zack?" She paused. "It's okay. I know you wouldn't call if it wasn't important."

Grady stepped away, trying to regain some control. Maybe letting things get this far wasn't a good idea. Gina wasn't ready.

He turned around when she ended the call. "I'm sorry, Grady. I've got to go get Zack. He's sick."

"I'll take you."

"You don't have to do that," she told him as they walked out the door. "Zack is my responsibility."

"If I drive you, then you can sit with him in the backseat."

She paused.

"Come on, Gina. You're wasting time." He guided her to his truck, realizing that the wind had picked up. There was rain in the air. "I'm a friend who wants to help you get your sick son home."

She finally smiled. "I hope you're not sorry that you volunteered."

Grady had a long list of things he was sorry about, but getting to spend more time with Gina Williams wasn't one of them.

Thirty minutes later Grady pulled up in front of Gina's house again. He got out and hurried around to the back door and opened it.

"Gina, go unlock the front door and I'll carry Zack inside."

She didn't argue and hurried up the walkway.

"Hey, Zack. Put your arms around my neck, and I'll carry you inside."

The boy groaned. "Grady, my stomach really hurts."

"It's going to be better, son. You'll be in your own bed."

No sooner had he lifted the boy out of the truck than Zack groaned, alerting Grady to what was about to happen. In a flash, Grady turned the child away as everything in his stomach came up and went all over the side of the truck and into the gutter.

"Well, that should make you feel better," he said.

Gina came running. "Grady, I'm sorry. Here, I'll take him."

"No, I got him." He took the handkerchief from his pocket, and gave it to the boy. "You finished?"

Zack managed a weak nod. "Yeah, I want to go to bed."

"You got it." Grady picked up his bundle and headed for the house. He carried him down the hall and into his bedroom. Placing him on the bunk bed, he stepped away and let Gina tend to her son.

Gina managed to help Zack into clean pajamas, get his mouth washed out and put him back into the bunk. She checked the window as she'd done every night since the kidnapping. It was starting to rain. A flash of lightning lit up the sky, reminding her that it was spring in Colorado.

"Are you going to be okay?" she asked her son.

He nodded. "I think I ate too much stuff at Aunt Lori's house."

She brushed back his hair. "Well, I'll be close by."

He snuggled under the blanket as the rain outside grew more intense, pounding against the roof. She kissed her son's head and realized he was already asleep.

She walked down the hall and into the kitchen, stopping suddenly when she saw Grady standing at the sink with his broad back to her as he washed up. In only his white T-shirt, she watched his toned muscles work across his broad shoulders and back as he washed up. Her gaze lowered to those killer black jeans that emphasized his narrow waist and hips.

She released a breath to calm her heart rate, glanced at his nice burgundy Western shirt wadded up on the table.

"I'm sorry. Is your shirt ruined?"

He turned around. "No, it just needs to be laundered."

She walked up to him. "Then I'll do it. That and apologize for Zack getting sick all over you."

"Believe me this hasn't been the first time. Through the years, I've held many a recruit's head over a latrine. Listening to them bellyache was a lot worse."

She couldn't get over this man. He took everything in his stride. "Well, as Zack's mother, I thank you for all your help."

The tension in the room was evident. Was he remembering earlier? Their kiss?

"I checked on Bandit, too," Grady told her. "He's fine, but I didn't know if he should stay in the utility room, or go to Zack's room."

"I've been trying to keep him on the porch."

"Good idea." He leaned back against the sink. "I should leave."

"But it's raining so hard."

His gaze remained on her. "If I don't, Gina—"

Suddenly lightning flashed and a loud crash of thunder sounded, then the lights flickered and went out.

"Oh, no." Instinctively, Gina started to go check on her child, but Grady stopped her.

"Bad idea to go running off without a flashlight." He felt his breath against her ear. "You have one?"

She couldn't think momentarily with him close, and touching her. "There's one in the drawer, the top one on the left."

He reached over her and his warmth seeped into her. It felt so good. Really good.

He pulled out the flashlight and turned it on. "I'll check on the boy. You stay put."

Once Grady left, Gina pulled herself together and found candles and matches. She lit them and had several arranged around the kitchen by the time Grady came back.

"Zack's sound asleep." He paused. "Looks like you're prepared."

For some things. She wasn't prepared for her feelings for him. "It's hard to tell how long the electricity will be out." She was chattering away aimlessly.

"Good idea," he told her as he made his way across the room.

Her pulse pounded in her ears, drowning out even the sound of the hard rain. She saw the smile he offered and it made her heart soar. So many emotions, she wanted to run, but she also wanted this man. "I know they might not be safe, but as long as we watch them, it should be okay."

"I'm afraid I'll be distracted," he said just as his head descended, then his lips touched hers. She sighed as the kiss deepened. She melted into him and let the sensations take over.

Grady felt an overwhelming desire as Gina moved against him. He couldn't stop feasting on her delicious mouth if his life depended on it. One kiss, two kisses weren't enough.

He tore his mouth away, then bent down and lifted Gina onto the counter. The soft glow of the candlelight only added to the intimacy.

He began raining kissing along her face to her ear. "You know where this is leading, don't you?"

She looked into his eyes and gave a nod.

"We need to *slow down*, Gina." He blew out a breath, not wanting to do anything to frighten her. "This is going too fast."

Gina wasn't sure if she knew what she was doing. She only knew that she wanted this man. "You make me feel things, Grady. Things I've never felt before."

Her hands moved up his chest over his T-shirt. She wanted so badly to touch his skin. She went to the hem of the shirt and slipped her hands underneath. The heat nearly burned through her as her fingertips made contact with his flat stomach.

For the first time she wasn't afraid of taking this next step…not with Grady. She tugged the shirt higher and leaned down to place a kiss against his skin. She felt the shiver along with his groan.

"Damn, Gina. If you are planning to drive me over the edge…"

Her own hands were trembling as she cupped his face. She leaned forward and placed a kiss against his lips. "I thought that was the point."

She went back for another kiss. She pulled the shirt higher and went for the center of his chest. Even in the candlelight, she could see the long puckered scar on his left side. It had to run from under his arm nearly to his waist.

"Oh, Grady," she cried on a whisper, feeling tears fill her eyes.

He quickly jerked down his shirt and stepped back. "Sorry, I should have warned you. It's pretty ugly."

"I'm not upset about what it looks like. Just the pain you must have endured."

He shook his head. She could see he was shutting down. "It was a long time ago." He released a breath and stepped back from her. She missed his warmth.

She got off the counter. "Grady…"

He didn't react to his name as he stood at the window. His broad shoulders were stiff, his back straight. She started toward him, but stopped, knowing the mood had changed. "Grady, I didn't mean to bring up bad memories."

"I don't have to look very far to be reminded of what happened that day."

She didn't know what to say to that, but she didn't have to—he made the choice for her.

"The rain has let up. I need to go."

She followed after him. "Grady, don't go."

He stopped at the door, but didn't turn around. "Gina, I'm not the man you need to teach you about anything. You'll need to find someone else for your next lesson."

CHAPTER ELEVEN

THE next day was Saturday and with Zack in tow, Gina went into the shop. While she'd felt lousy about how the date had turned out, something good had happened. Her son woke up this morning feeling great. He was also talking nonstop about Grady.

Since she hadn't slept much last night, she didn't feel much like conversing at all. She just wished she understood what had happened between her and Grady.

"Mom," Zack called to her. "Can I take Bandit for a walk?"

"Yes, but don't leave the block. Check back in twenty minutes." Old habits die hard. There was a time she wouldn't have let Zack out of her sight. Now, with Eric in jail, she knew they were safe. Plus she knew the town was filled with people who looked out for one another.

She closed the front door and turned her Open sign around and walked to the counter. Once again, her thoughts wandered back to Grady. After he had pulled back and walked out her door last night, she should have come to her senses. Besides, he wasn't going to be around much longer. How many times had he told her that? So maybe ending her crazy idea was for the best. Problem was, she wasn't interested in any man but Grady Fletcher.

The door of the shop opened and Lori walked in. "Hey, Gina," she called.

Her older sister was wearing a pair of black stretchy pants and a long pink polo shirt that showed off her blossoming pregnancy.

Gina went to greet her. "Lori. What brings you in?"

She hugged her. "I wanted to check on Zack. If he still wasn't feeling good, I'd take him off your hands. But since I ran into that happy kid outside, I see there's no reason. Cassie's helping him walk Bandit." She smiled. "Now we can talk." Her sister placed her hands on her hips. "So spill it. Is Grady Fletcher a good kisser?"

Gina felt her emotions churning inside. She shrugged as the bell over the shop door jingled and a woman walked in. Gina started to go to her, but Marie stopped her as she came in from the back and went to greet the customer.

"Come on." Lori took Gina by the arm and they headed toward the back for privacy. "You're not getting away with not telling me about your date."

Gina shrugged. "There's not much to tell. We had a nice dinner in Durango at Francisco's. He had steak and I had—"

"Stop," her sister said. "I don't need to know the menu. I saw how the man looked at you when you both came by the house to pick up Zack. So you can't tell me that he didn't kiss you once all night?"

"I didn't say that." Tears welled in her eyes. "I just don't think he wants to kiss me again. Ever."

Gina told her sister about what happened when they got back to the house.

"He might be insecure about the scar," Lori tried to assure her. "Does it bother you?"

Gina shook her head. "Of course not. We all have our scars." Gina couldn't stop the flood of awful memories of her marriage. Would she ever forget the things that Eric had done to her? Probably not, but she wanted to replace bad times with new, happy ones.

Lori drew her attention back. "Oh, honey, I wish I could have been there to help you more. To stop Eric."

"You were there for me, Lori."

Lori hugged her sister. "Well, I'm so proud of you. And thanks to your support group you're doing a lot better. If you ever need help getting to your meetings, just call me."

Gina smiled. "Thank you. You've always been there for me. It's time I do things for myself."

"Yes, it is. And I think Grady Fletcher is just the man who can be a positive force in your life."

"I think Grady has his own demons." She released a breath, knowing it was more than his physical scars. She'd seen the pain in his eyes.

Lori studied her. "You care about him a lot, don't you?"

She sighed. "I never planned to let it happen, but I can't seem to get him out of my head. He could break my heart, Lori."

"There's always that risk, sis. But if you don't go after what you want then you'll never know how wonderful it could be."

"Spoken like a happily married woman."

Lori grinned. "Yeah, I am. And I want you to find happiness, too. You and Zack deserve that."

Yes, they did. She thought about the mess she'd made of everything last night. "I'm not very good at this dating."

"While you're figuring it out, how about if I take

Zack home with me this afternoon while you work, then you can come by the house for supper?"

Gina had a funny feeling her sister was cooking up more than food. "You don't need to do that."

"I do, since I need a favor from you." She reached inside her oversize bag and pulled out a manila envelope. "These are papers for Joe Fletcher to sign. Would you give them to Grady so he can take them to him?"

Gina froze. *Go see Grady?* "Why don't you just take them to Shady Haven?"

"Because Joe asked me to give them to Grady first, so he can look them over."

"Why don't you have one of the bank employees do it?"

"I thought you were a bank employee."

"Come on, Lori. I've only staged a few bank-owned houses to sell."

Her sister shrugged. "Close enough." She walked to the door. "I'll go round up the kids and the dog. See you later." She paused at the door. "And take your time."

Great. Gina watched her sister leave. What was she going to do now? It would be a little too obvious when she showed up on Grady's doorstep.

Her assistant called to her. Marie walked over with a smile as the customer walked out the door. "You won't believe this. I just sold the Mersman pedestal table and the sideboard cabinet." She held up the credit card receipt so Gina could see the large amount charged. "Full price. She's even paying for us to deliver to Durango."

Gina glanced over the amount. "That's like two weeks' worth of sales."

"I know," Marie agreed.

Gina hated that Grady's things were disappearing

from the store. "Maybe you should call Grady and let him know."

Marie shook her head. "I think for half of this amount, you need to give the news to him in person."

"Where's that pretty Gina?" Joe Fletcher asked when Grady sat at the table at Shady Haven. The day was turning out to be nice so he'd wheeled his grandfather outside into the sunshine.

"I guess she's at her store, working."

The old man studied him and leaned down to give some attention to Scout. "You'd be wise to spend a lot of time with her before another man steals your claim."

Here we go again. "I have no claim on Gina."

"But you should, son. She's a keeper. I heard she's got a boy about eight."

Grady nodded. "His name is Zack. I found him in your mine, remember?"

"That's what I mean." Fletch raised an arthritic hand. "That young boy needs someone like you in his life."

Grady already knew the kid could use a father figure. "I'm not a family man."

"Says who? That ex-wife of yours? Look, Grady, I'm not an expert by any means, but—"

Grady interrupted. "But you're going to tell me anyway."

His grandfather glared at him. "Like I was sayin', I think you've had to take the blame for a lot of things that weren't your fault. Good Lord, son, you were off fighting a war, defending our freedom."

Grady had known before he'd left on his last deployment his marriage had been on shaky ground. So the pregnancy had been a shock, but he still had wanted to be there for his child. That was what he had trouble dealing with. "Look, Granddad, could we change the subject? Talking about it isn't going to change anything."

The old man studied him for a long time, then said, "Maybe it will. I've decided to stay here to live."

"At Shady Haven?" Grady asked.

His grandfather nodded. "They have apartments for seniors."

"Why? Isn't your hip healing correctly?"

"My hip is better than ever, and I've started therapy. It's not a walk in the park, but I'm handling it."

Grady was relieved.

"Once I'm on my feet, I'll be able to take care of myself. And here there are plenty of people my own age to keep me company."

Grady still wasn't buying this. "Are you sure this is what you want?"

Fletch nodded. "Yep, I'm too old to live up on that damn mountain."

"But you love it there."

A tired-looking Fletch turned to him. "I realized something, son. I was damn lonely."

That suddenly made Grady realize he'd neglected the one person who cared about him. "Granddad, I had no idea."

"No, son. I didn't even realize it myself until I came here and made some friends. We have a lot in common." He blew out a breath. "Besides, you'll be leaving soon, right?"

Now that his grandfather wouldn't be alone or lonely anymore, that would make his decision easier. Grady thought about Gina. How much he wanted her, but he knew in his heart, he wasn't the right man for her.

He nodded slowly. "What do you plan to do with the cabin and your properties?"

Fletch shrugged. "That's not my worry anymore. I've signed most everything over to you."

Gina wanted to turn around several times during her drive up the mountain. Once she saw Grady's truck, she knew there was no going back, especially when the man came walking out from behind the cabin. He was in his usual uniform, jeans and a black Henley T-shirt that made his shoulders look massive and his arms incredibly large. He had a towel draped over his shoulder, his hair was slicked back. He must have been in the shower. God help her, she thought as she got out of her car and walked up the path.

He looked concerned. "Gina, is there something wrong?"

"No." She put on a smile, seeing the droplets of water in his hair. "Sorry, didn't mean to disturb you."

He shrugged. "Since my shower is outside, I grab it during the warmest part of the day.

The picture of Grady with water sliding over his naked body flashed in her head. Her breathing grew labored.

"Gina, what brings you out here?"

She shook away the thought. "Marie sold the pedestal table and sideboard." She reached into her purse and realized her hands were a little shaky. She managed to take out the envelope with the check inside. "Here's your share of the sale."

Grady didn't take what she offered, but instead said, "Please, come in."

She walked up the steps and into the cabin, noticing right away how he'd kept the place clean and organized. She set her purse down on the kitchen table. She needed to make this quick and leave. "We got full price for both items."

He pulled the towel from his shoulder and took the check. "This is a nice profit."

"Yes, I appreciate you letting me sell them for you."

She locked on his deep-set brown gaze and it stole her breath. Why this man? She also noticed that he looked tired. Maybe he hadn't slept any better than she had. He caught her staring and frowned. She glanced away and pulled out the manila envelope from her large purse.

"Lori asked me to give you this," she said. "It's the legal papers on your grandfather's property." She hated feeling the tension between them. "She said you needed to have Joe sign them. But he wanted you to look them over."

"All right." He didn't open it. "The next time I visit."

"Okay. I should go." She nodded and turned toward the door, but never reached her destination.

Before she got there, Grady reached for her. "Gina."

She loved his hands on her, but had to resist. "Don't, Grady." She couldn't look at him. "Please, don't say anything. I'm sorry that I upset you last night. I never meant to." She ached inside as tears gathered in her eyes. Please, she couldn't cry in front of this man.

"You didn't upset me. I did that all by myself. You did everything right. That's the problem, Gina. I keep thinking that it would be so easy to let things happen between us." He turned her around to face him. "I want you, Gina Williams. That hasn't changed, but neither has the reality that I'm leaving here."

She felt brave. "Did I ask you to stay?"

Grady released her. "No, you didn't."

"I know your life is in Texas. Mine is here with my son." She wanted him to be a part of that family, too. "For the first time in a very long time, I'm making my own decisions on what I want to do." She took a step closer. "And I wanted you to show me what it's like to make love."

Grady was a little stunned by her declaration. "Gina, you're not thinking this through."

"Oh, but I have. You've been honest with me in saying you wanted me, and I'm saying that I want you to make love to me. To show me what it's like to feel tenderness, to be cherished by a man—"

Grady stopped her words when he reached for her and his mouth closed over hers. She could only manage a weak protest as he drew her into a tight embrace.

In no time at all, she became a willing participant, slipping her arms around his neck. His tongue ran along the seam of her lips and she parted them, allowing him to delve inside to taste her.

He finally tore his mouth away. His breathing labored. "God, Gina, this isn't a good idea. You deserve to be cherished and more." Grady searched her pretty face and her thoroughly kissed mouth, wishing he could give her the world.

"Damn, you're so sweet," he breathed, then went back for more because he couldn't seem to avoid the temptation. He pulled her against him, feeling all her curves, and backed up against the table. He lifted her and sat on the edge, then pulled her between his legs.

She whimpered and he immediately pulled away. "Did I do something wrong?"

Her pretty green eyes were glassy with desire. "No, it's just I've never felt like this before." She smiled shyly. "I like your hands on me. I like it when you touch me."

She took his large hand and brought it to the front of her sweater and placed it on her breast.

He cupped her weight in his palm and watched her eyes close, but not before he saw them darken with desire. "Oh, Grady."

He kissed her again, bringing her body against him. This was quickly getting out of hand.

"Gina, we're reaching the dangerous area here. My control is only so strong."

He found himself smiling at the fact that Josh wasn't going to be home until tomorrow. Cupping her face, he zeroed in on her big green eyes. "Gina, this is your decision. If you want this to go any further, it's your choice."

She leaned forward and placed a soft kiss on the scar on his neck. "I choose you, Grady Fletcher."

He shivered at her tender gesture, causing him only to want her more. "Then I suggest we move this off the table and into the bedroom."

He captured her mouth again in a hungry kiss, then scooped her up into his arms and carried her into the bedroom. The curtains were closed, leaving the room in shadows.

"I've been aching for you since that first night you slept out on the sofa."

He set her down next to the big brass bed.

"I didn't know," she said, sounding a little breathless.

He kissed her again. "It's a good thing."

Reaching for the hem of her sweater, he swept it off over her head, revealing her ivory lacy bra that barely hid the full breasts. His heart raced as he unfastened her jeans and slid them down to display the matching scrap of material that served as panties.

"Oh, darlin', you're lucky I didn't know what you had on underneath your clothes."

"You like?"

He gave her the once-over from her shapely legs up over her trim waist and flat stomach, then to her full breasts.

He wasn't going to survive this. "You have no idea."

She smiled shyly. "I was thinking about you when I bought them."

Grady took a steadying breath. He'd never felt desire like this before. He fought to keep it light. "Why, Miss Williams, are you trying to seduce me?"

"I have no idea what I'm doing." Her voice was husky. She reached for the three buttons at his neck and managed to open them. She looked up at him. "I don't want to do anything that bothers you, Grady." Her palms rested on his chest as her emerald gaze met his. "I have scars, too. Maybe not as visible as yours, but they're there just the same. Your scars were honorably earned, Grady. They could never change how I feel about you."

He remained silent as Gina took over and tugged the shirt from his jeans, then slipped her hands underneath. He sucked in a breath as her touch began to work magic. Then she took it further as she raised the shirt and placed her lips against his hot skin.

Once, twice… Oh, God. He was barely holding on to the last of his control when he jerked off the shirt, exposing the damages of war.

She looked at the puckered skin that ran from his shoulder to nearly his waist, then up at him. He saw the tears in her eyes. "Oh, Grady." She then leaned in and kissed the puckered skin. "How you suffered."

He didn't want to think about the past. Only now, with her. "You're making it feel a lot better." He lifted her onto the bed. "But right now that's not the area of my discomfort."

She smiled up at him. "Then maybe we should redirect our efforts."

His mouth covered hers and he kissed her as he continued to show her how much he desired her. How much he would always desire her. That was the problem. Being with her like this was only going to make it harder to walk away.

CHAPTER TWELVE

THREE hours later Gina opened her eyes and discovered the sun was going down. She glanced at the clock beside the bed and saw that it was after six. And here she lay naked in bed, Grady Fletcher's arms wrapped around her waist, holding her close. She smiled, knowing she should be heading back to Destiny and dinner with Lori.

"Getting restless again?" Grady raised his head from the pillow, but didn't release her. "I thought the last time would keep you satisfied for a while."

She blushed, recalling they'd made love twice. Never had she been treated as if she were so special, so treasured. She rolled over and smiled at the sexy man.

"It was wonderful. But…I do have to pick up Zack. He's with Lori and Jace."

He frowned. "What if I won't let you go?" He pulled her close, letting her know he still desired her.

"I didn't say I wanted to leave." She cupped his face and pulled him down to meet her lips. And within seconds she let him know how much she meant those words.

He rose over her, bracing his arms on either side of her head. "That's some serious seduction tactics."

"So, Sarge, what are you going to do about it?"

Truthfully, Grady had no idea what he was going to

do with her, but at this moment, he wasn't going anywhere. "My best, ma'am."

He lowered his head and kissed her, once, twice, then his mouth began to move, trailing kisses, tasting her soft skin. He worked his way down over her breasts, lower to her flat stomach. That was when he caught the nearly invisible tiny white lines. Stretch marks. The proof she'd carried a baby in her womb. He closed his eyes and tried to push away the recurring memory about his own child. He paused and Gina's hands moved to his back.

"Grady?"

He raised his head. "Sorry." He rolled away, grabbed his jeans from the floor and slipped them on. "I guess you can call it a flashback."

He turned back to see she'd covered her body with the sheet. "It's okay, Grady."

He watched her eyes shift away from his gaze. "Oh, hell." He went back to her and sat on the bed. "It's not you, Gina. I know that sounds like a line, but it isn't. I carry around a lot of baggage."

She touched the side of his face. "Is there anything I can do to help you?"

"I just need some time." That was a lie. He hadn't been able to forget the pain or the guilt over the last few years. "I'm working through some things." He got up, grabbed his shirt off the floor and walked to the doorway. "I should go check on the dogs." Then he left.

Gina sat there stunned. What had happened? Okay, she wasn't so experienced that she could drive a man wild, but she thought together they'd been pretty incredible. She climbed out of the big bed and started pulling on her underwear. After she fastened her bra, she quickly dressed in her jeans and sweater. She should be getting home anyway. Her thoughts turned to Zack.

The safe way would be to forget about a relationship and focus on her life with her son. Grady Fletcher wasn't going to commit to her. She'd thought that was what she wanted until she realized how much she cared about him.

She passed the dresser and saw Grady's keys and coins tossed on the scarred surface. She also noticed the carved box and the corner of a photo hanging out. Okay, she was curious. She opened the lid and took hold of the grainy picture. A sonogram?

She looked closer and smiled seeing the familiar details of the baby. Who was this? She turned the photo over to the back and read, "Boy Fletcher" and the date. Several years ago.

She gasped. Grady had a child? She suddenly realized she wasn't alone in the room and glanced toward the doorway to find Grady.

"I'm sorry. I had no right." She put the picture back. "I should leave."

Grady came inside the room and took the picture. He wasn't sure why he was so angry. "Come on, Gina. Don't stop now. Don't you want to know who this is?"

She swallowed. "Only if you want to tell me."

His chest tightened, but he got the words out. "That's my son."

"You have a child?"

"*Had.* That's the operative word, Gina. Had."

"What happened to him?"

Here came the hard part. "My wife went into early labor…he was stillborn."

She gasped. "I'm so sorry."

"So am I. I was told that no one was to blame for what happened."

Grady remembered the two days it had taken him to get across the globe, to be there for Barb, for his son.

He couldn't look at Gina. "That's what the doctor told me once I got there two days later. I was overseas when my wife was delivering our baby."

He closed his eyes, and could see the long hospital corridors as his footsteps echoed when he ran from the elevator to the nursery, but there wasn't a Fletcher baby behind the glass. Finally the nurse sent him to see his wife in her room. He found her, all right. She was packing her clothes and about to go home with her parents. When he went to her, she pushed him away.

"You're too late, Grady," she cried. "Too late for your son. And too late for us." She'd walked out the door.

He opened his eyes and met Gina's gaze. "Don't make that mistake, Gina. Don't depend on me. I'll let you down."

"How could you know your wife was going into labor early?"

He shook his head.

"Did she keep the pregnancy from you?" she asked.

"No, but it wasn't planned, either." He sighed. "When things started to turn bad in the marriage, I chose another deployment, instead of staying and trying to work through our problems."

"The army was your job. Surely your wife knew that when she married you."

Gina went to Grady, wondering who'd been there for him to help him grieve over his child. She reached for him and felt him tense, but she ignored his resistance. She wrapped her arms around his waist and laid her head against his chest. She shed tears for the father and the child.

"I'm sorry that you never got to hold your son. That

you never got to say goodbye." His grip tightened around her and she felt his tears drop against her cheek. She never dreamed she could love a man as much as she loved Grady Fletcher. She held on to him a few minutes until he finally loosened his grip and moved away.

Once he composed himself, he turned back to her. "Thank you."

"Any time."

He started to say more when his cell phone rang. He pulled it out. "Hey, Josh." He answered it as he walked away.

Gina put the treasured picture back in its special place, then pulled the bed together before she walked back into the main room.

"Okay, I'll see you back here tomorrow," Grady said into his phone. "Goodbye." He hung up.

Embarrassed that she hadn't given a thought to Grady's housemate, she blurted, "Oh, I forgot all about Josh."

"I didn't. He went to Texas to check out places for our kennel."

Suddenly reality hit her. Grady was still leaving.

He noticed her surprise, too. "I told you from the beginning, I was opening our business in Texas."

"I know, but a girl can always hope."

He came to her. "Gina. I can't tell you how special you've become to me, but… I've tried to make a go of settling down before."

She hurt a lot. "Can't say you didn't warn me." She forced a smile. "Hey, it was fun." She worked hard to hide her blush. "And this afternoon…was incredible." She glanced around for her purse and grabbed it to make her escape. "I've got to go. Maybe before you leave town you'll stop by and say goodbye."

He took her arm and stopped her. "Gina. Don't do this. You mean too much to me—"

She stopped his words of regret. "Just not enough to stay around."

"I told you before—"

"Believe me, I heard everything you said." She released a breath. "Too bad for you, Master Sergeant Fletcher, because there's a guy out there who's going to want to stick around for me."

"And that's what you deserve."

"It's something we all deserve, Grady, but first, you have to forgive yourself, realize you deserve happiness, too."

She swung around and walked out praying she could make it to her car. Once down the road, she pulled off and burst into tears. She'd lost everything she'd ever wanted in a man.

By the next morning Grady's bad mood hadn't improved at all. Even the dogs wanted no part of him. Add in no sleep and too much coffee, there was no hope that things would change anytime soon.

"Break time, boys," he called to the dogs. "Get your toys."

The shepherds took off and Scout was the first back with the yellow tennis ball. The animal dropped it on the ground and Grady threw it to the far end of the pen while he kept telling himself he'd done the right thing by letting Gina go yesterday.

He felt his chest constrict as he continued to toss the ball. She had no idea how hard it had been to lie to her, to tell her he didn't want her or her kid.

Hell, he was already involved whether he liked it

or not, but she'd already had one jerk in her life—she didn't need another.

He closed his eyes and could still picture her in that big bed. Her sweetness nearly drove him over the edge. Yet, everything she did pleased him. He'd never... He shook away the wondering thought.

Damn, he had to get out of here and back to Texas.

He called to Scout, Beau and Rowdy. "Time to get to work," he told them.

He'd only been at it for about ten minutes when he saw an SUV pull up and Justin Hilliard got out.

The businessman was dressed in dark pleated trousers, a white shirt and striped tie. He walked through the rough terrain as if he had on boots instead of expensive Italian loafers.

Grady shook his hand. "Hey, Hilliard. What brings you out to my neighborhood? Come to see how the other half lives?"

The sarcasm didn't seem to bother the visitor. "I came by to see you, Grady," he said as he stopped beside the waist-high gate. "I just finished a meeting down in Durango with my new mountain bike instructor, Brian Connelly. He's retired now from the pro circuit, so running my school is perfect for him." The man grinned. "Also he'll be designing mountain bikes which I'll be manufacturing right here in Destiny."

Grady felt extreme envy for the man who just about had everything, not his money as much as his pretty wife and children. "Seems all your dreams are coming true."

"Yeah, I've been a lucky guy. That's why I can afford to spread my good fortune around."

That piqued his interest and Hilliard saw it. "You haven't stopped by to see me, Grady."

"I've been busy. Mostly I'm not interested."

"I'm not going to let you off the hook, not until you hear me out."

Did this man ever give up? "I've already heard your spiel."

"A lot has changed since we last talked. Seems your grandfather owns some of the property I want."

Grady sent the dogs off to play as he walked out the gate to the pen. "You want this property?"

Hilliard shook his head. "The three acres just north of town. I'd planned to buy that section when Billy Hutchinson's name was on the deed, but Lorelei Yeager discovered that Joe Fletcher is the true owner. Now it seems he's transferred the title to you."

This was getting interesting. "Is that so?"

Justin nodded. "I already own the adjoining land, but I'd like to extend my trails. I want to buy your property. Question is, what's it going to cost me?"

"I haven't even had a chance to look over the land in question."

"It's definitely a prime area. I don't want to develop it, if you're worried," Justin insisted. "I want to keep the land in its natural state, except for bike trails. Do you think we could work out some kind of deal?"

A dozen things rushed though Grady's head. The sale would cut the ties here in Destiny. He could take the money for his project in Texas.

"I have another idea, Grady," Justin told him. "Since the land is a heavily wooded area, it could work for other things, too. Like training rescue dogs." He glanced around the temporary structures Grady had built. "You could build a real kennel there, too."

"That could take a lot of money."

"It's going to take money in Texas, too. It's hotter

there and doesn't have these mountain views, or my offer of leasing your dogs for the winter months."

Or Gina. Grady hated that the man had him thinking of changing his plans.

Hilliard checked his watch. "Look, I've got to go now—my son has baseball tryouts." He smiled. "I can't miss it."

Another dose of envy hit Grady. "Then you should go."

"I still want to talk to you about this some more. Could you meet up later with me and Jace Yeager? Say about eight o'clock at the Rocky Top Saloon in town? We can talk over a few beers. I'm buying."

"Look, I can't promise you anything. I have a partner."

"I know." Justin began backing away. "Bring Josh along, and we'll all talk."

"Good luck to your son," Grady called.

"Thanks, I appreciate it."

Grady watched the man leave and he thought about Zack. How would he do today? He found himself putting the dogs into the kennels and heading down to town. What would it hurt just to check on the boy?

Gina walked around her empty house that evening, restless. Zack was spending the night with Ryan Hilliard. They'd been picked to be on the same baseball team today, so they were best friends now. She smiled, feeling so blessed that Tim Keenan had volunteered to be the team's coach.

She might be Zack's mother, but she had no idea how to encourage her nearly eight-year-old's new love for the game. She'd tried to help, but Zack hadn't wanted her to go, and Uncle Jace was working. She thought about

Grady, but she couldn't impose on him any longer, not after yesterday. All her worries had been unfounded, though, when Zack came home beaming with news of his day. Her son's life seemed to be perfect now.

Hers was a mess. She recalled how Grady had made it clear that he didn't want her in his life. She could survive the rejection, but if he stayed in town… She blinked away threatening tears. She didn't want him to leave at all. She loved the man, and she probably would for a long, long time.

There was a knock on the door and she looked out the peephole to see her sister. She quickly let her inside.

"Lori, what are you doing here?"

"We both have the night off from kids. Zack's at a sleepover, Jace has a business meeting, and Cassie is staying with Maggie."

Gina smiled, remembering the housekeeper from Hutchinson House who'd helped raise Lori when she was a child. "How is Maggie adjusting to her new apartment?"

"She's doing fine, but I had to insist that she hire more help when the mansion is rented out for functions." Lori waved her off. "Hey, I just got a call from Paige to meet her and Morgan at the Rocky Top Saloon. You wanna come with us?"

Gina wasn't in the mood to go anywhere. "I think I'll pass."

"Why?" Her sister placed her hands on her hips. "You aren't moping around over a man, are you?"

Gina started to deny that Grady was the reason for her misery. Her sister wouldn't buy it anyway.

"Okay, give me five minutes to change."

At eight o'clock Grady and Josh walked into the Rocky Top Saloon. There was a large entry with a bar on one side and the dining room on the other. The entire place had the look of a hunting lodge with hardwood floors and open beamed ceilings, not to mention the elk and deer heads mounted on the knotty-pine-paneled walls. Country music poured out of the jukebox, but he managed to hear his name called out.

Justin stood across the room past the small dance floor toward the back. He nudged Josh and they walked over.

"Hey, glad you two could make it," Justin said.

Grady nodded as he introduced Josh.

Hilliard did more introductions. "Grady and Josh, you remember Jace, and of course, Reed. And this is Brian Connelly."

Grady shook hands all around. "Good to meet you," he said to the new guy.

Hilliard ordered another pitcher of beer as Grady sat. It was Connelly who began the conversation.

"I hear you're retired army."

Grady nodded. "Got out in December."

Josh added his similar résumé.

"Well, all I can say is thank you both for your service."

Grady nodded and took a sip of the beer that had been placed in front of him while Hilliard filled Josh in on his ideas for a kennel in Destiny.

Brian cornered Grady. "Justin told me about your dogs."

For the next twenty minutes every guy at the table was talking up all the good qualities of the town. Grady couldn't deny that Hilliard had a well-crafted plan for his biking school, riding trail and snow adventures. He put down some numbers for the property that were also impressive.

Grady leaned back in his chair. Okay, he couldn't help but think about it. Damn, it looked profitable on paper, and then he was surprised when Hilliard offered to be a silent partner in the rescue dog business.

Grady exchanged a glance with Josh. He looked curious, and Grady was once again thinking about the deal. There was only one person keeping him from signing. Gina. Could he live in this town and be around her all the time?

"Hey, Reed?" Jace called. "Did you tell our wives where we were meeting?"

Grady and all the men turned toward the door. That's where they saw four of the prettiest women in town. Morgan Hilliard, Paige Larkin, Lori Yeager and Gina.

CHAPTER THIRTEEN

GINA felt a warmth pulse through her as Grady's hand pressed against her waist as he escorted her to the dance floor. Silently he took her into his arms and began to move to the music. She couldn't resist and leaned into him, inhaling his scent, a mixture of soap and what she knew to be pure Grady.

She also liked the familiar feel of his body molded against hers. The heat of his skin, and the strength of his hands, hands that had touched every inch of her flesh just days ago…

She shivered.

"Are you okay?" he asked against her ear.

No! "Yes, I'm fine."

She closed her eyes, recalling the look on his face when she'd walked up to the table. He didn't want to see her here tonight. That hurt. She knew he was only her dance partner out of obligation. He hadn't been given a choice when all the other couples had got up.

"You don't have to do this, Grady." Okay, so she wanted to be in his arms, just not this way.

He pulled back. "Since I left the army, I've been pretty much making my own decisions."

She nodded, then glanced away.

He touched her chin, making her look at him. "Believe me, Gina, holding you in my arms has never been a hardship."

To prove the point, he pulled her close as George Strait sang about getting to "Amarillo by Morning." She didn't want to listen to the lyrics. Grady was leaving soon. That she had to accept, but it didn't stop the hurt.

She felt his arm tighten around her waist as he pulled her closer against him, his strength making her remember how gentle his touch could be, how loving.

The song changed to Lady Antebellum singing "Need You Now." Grady's hold tightened as their feet shuffled back and forth in the crowd of dancers. Then she felt his mouth against her ear. His warm breath caused her to shiver. Why was he doing this? Why couldn't he leave her alone?

Gina pulled back. "I can't… I've got to go." She moved through the couples dancing on the floor. Once at the table, she grabbed her purse and headed for the door.

Grady cursed, then made his way through the crowd, finally catching up with Gina at the door. With several couples nearly blocking the area, he escorted her outside and to a private spot.

"Gina, I'm sorry. I didn't know you'd be here."

She finally looked up at him. "I know. I'm sorry I spoiled your fun."

He ran fingers through his hair. "Dammit, Gina. It wasn't supposed to be fun. Justin said it was a relaxed business meeting, and then we looked up to see their wives." He met her gaze. "And you…"

"Well, I'm going home so you can go back and finish the meeting. Enjoy the evening." She took off down the street.

Grady hurried after her. "Gina, let me drive you."

She shook her head. "No, I'm not your responsibility. Besides, I can handle the short walk."

Damn stubborn woman. "I have no doubt you can, but at least let your sister know that you're going home."

He was rewarded with a furious look. "I'm not going back inside." She took out her phone and punched in the number. "Lori, I'm going home." There was a pause. "No, you stay. Grady's taking me." She ended the call and dropped it back into her purse. "Okay, you're relieved of duty," she told him and marched off.

What the hell? He went after her. "What do you think you're doing?"

"I'm walking up Main Street, then making a right on Maple, then a left on Cherry Street."

He ignored her smart answer. "So you lied to your sister."

"I don't want her to worry." They stepped off the curb and started down the next block, passing the town square and the sheriff's office. The parking lot was well lit, so was the street.

"What if something happened to you?"

She stopped and faced him. "Look, Grady, you have to quit doing this. Stop playing hero. Stop thinking you have to rescue me. I'm trying really hard to take control of my life. Do things on my own, to be independent."

He arched an eyebrow. "And I'm interfering with that?"

"Yes. You are."

"What if I just want to do the gentlemanly thing and walk a lady home?"

She threw up her arms in exasperation. "I give up."

Well, he wasn't going to and he followed her as she walked on.

Ten minutes later they ended up on her porch. "Okay,

I'm home safe and sound." She slipped her key into the lock. "Good night, Grady."

"Gina," he whispered her name, hoping to get her to turn around and look at him. No such luck.

Still she faced the door. "What, Grady?"

"I'm headed for Texas in a few days."

In the soft glow of the porch light, he saw her tense. "Have a safe trip."

"Gina, it's for the best."

She swung around. "You call running away the best solution? Well then, go for it. But I think what you're doing is giving up. A second chance at a home, a family with a grandfather who loves you. But go. I hope whatever you're looking for makes you happy."

She stared at him for what seemed to be an eternity, and he couldn't stand it anymore.

He pulled her into his arms and held her. She felt so good, too good. He kissed the side of her face and quickly worked to her tempting lips.

"Grady…"

He ignored her as he covered her mouth in a heated kiss. He just needed one more taste of what he had to give up. She gave the soft moan he knew so well, but he resisted taking any more. He tore his mouth away. "Goodbye, Gina."

"Goodbye, Grady." She turned and walked inside. He just stood there, aching to go after her. Instead he started down the steps when he heard something. Moving back to the door, he recognized the sound of her crying. His chest tightened. Oh, God, he'd never wanted to hurt her. He started to knock, but paused, knowing he had too many things he had to deal with first. Instead he turned and walked away. Again.

* * *

It was a beautiful spot.

The next day Grady walked along the edge of his grandfather's property and glanced up at the picturesque San Juan Mountains. The sky was so blue it took your breath away. He also liked that so much of the area was densely wooded. He glanced at Josh and he seemed just as intrigued with it, too.

Justin caught up to them. "I can't believe you want to leave all this." The businessman shook his head. "Seems you two could have it all." He pointed off toward the woods. "What a training ground. And you can put your kennels at the base, right off the highway. You're far enough away your dogs wouldn't bother my training facility, or the guests. And we wouldn't bother your dogs."

Grady was thinking about it. "It's beautiful."

"I agree. You've got a sweet parcel of land, Grady," Hilliard told him. "Look at the spot over there." He pointed to the crest of the hill. "You could build a house there and have views all around."

With the idea of a home came thoughts of Gina. How would she like it here?

No, he had to push any thoughts of her aside, not think about what he couldn't have.

He turned to Josh. "What about you?"

"I think this is a great place," Josh said, and looked at Grady. "And it seems to me that owning the land already eliminates a big expense, and frees up more money for dogs. Maybe hire an employee to help with the upkeep. We can concentrate on the training. Whatever you decide, Sarge, I'll go along with it."

That was the lead-in Justin needed. "Look, if you're reluctant about selling any of your land to me for my training facility, how about we lease the section from you?" His hand made a sweeping motion. "And you don't lose any of this."

So tempting, Grady thought. "I need to think about it. Can you give me a few days?"

Justin nodded and walked away with Josh, leaving Grady alone with his thoughts, his dreams and what he couldn't have that kept it all from being perfect.

Little League practice was the next afternoon, and Grady found he couldn't stay away. Despite him leaving for Texas in the morning, he wanted to see how Zack was doing.

He parked on the far side of the baseball field and got out to watch the last of the practice. Tim Keenan and Jace Yeager were the coaches, but when he saw Gina's brother-in-law, he thought he'd better leave.

He headed back to the truck when he heard someone call him. He turned to see Zack running toward him.

"Grady, aren't you going to help me today?"

"Well, it looks like you have enough help already."

Tim came up to him. "We can always use another hand."

Grady looked at Jace. After a few seconds he motioned for him to join them. "Okay, what do you want me to help with?"

Tim smiled. "Jace has fielding, and I'm working with them on running the bases. So how about hitting?"

Thirty minutes later, Grady finally thought Zack was making some progress. He was a quick study.

"That's it son, keep your eye on the ball." He pitched a ball to Zack. The first one he missed, but he made contact with the second and the third. "That was great." They exchanged high fives.

The kid beamed. "You showed me real good, Grady."

He felt the pride for the boy's achievements. Finally, Tim called a halt to the practice and they finished with drinking bottles of cold water. Soon the kids went off with their parents. Zack turned to him. "I'm having my birthday party next Saturday. Will you come, Grady?"

"Oh, Zack. I'm not sure I'll be here. I have to leave town for a few days."

The boy's face dropped. "Oh, I wanted to show you some tricks I taught Bandit."

Grady knew he didn't want to encourage the boy, then have to disappoint him. "I bet they're good tricks, too. Maybe I'll stop by the house when I get back."

"So you are coming back."

With his nod, the boy said, "Okay."

Hearing Zack's name called, Grady turned to see Gina. She was walking across the field, but when she spotted him, she stopped. His gaze surveyed the petite woman in jeans and a sweater. Just like every time other time he looked at her she affected him like no other woman. How long would it take to stop wanting her? Never.

Gina raised a hand and waved to her son. "Come on, Zack," she called. "We need to get home."

"I got to go." Zack went to him and threw his arms around his waist. "Thanks for helping me today. Bye, Grady."

The boy ran off to his mother. When he reached her, Gina put her arm around her son and they walked off together. Grady had to resist running after them both. The pain in his chest spread to his heart as the two most important people walked out of his life.

"Those two are really special."

He glanced at Tim Keenan. "Yeah, they are. I need to go."

"I'll walk with you to the parking lot," Tim said. "I couldn't help but overhear you tell the boy you're leaving town."

Grady nodded. "I'm going to look at some property in San Antonio." Although he knew staying here would be better all around, he needed to make a clean break from Gina. "It's close to the base where we can get more dogs."

Tim nodded. "I guess a convenient location is important." There was a pause. "I would think staying here would be even more convenient, especially with your grandfather here and other special…friends."

Grady stopped. "Look, Tim, I know you're trying to help, but this is best for everyone."

Tim nodded toward Gina's car as it drove out of the lot. "I know there are at least two people who don't feel that way."

Later that evening Grady sat in his grandfather's room at Shady Haven.

"So you're really gonna go?" Fletch asked, not looking happy.

This wasn't getting any easier. "You knew I was leaving eventually."

"Hell, son, an old man can hope."

Grady noticed the sadness in his eyes. "I'm sorry, Granddad."

"I can deal with you leaving again, Grady, if it's for the right reasons. And if it makes you happy."

"It's for my business." God, he was a lousy liar.

"Let's at least be honest, son. My eyesight isn't so bad that I can't see you care about that pretty Gina Williams."

Damn, he didn't want to do this. "Look, Fletch, I

know you want me to stay here, but…" Grady wasn't sure if he could be around Gina and Zack. "I'm not sure I fit in to all this family stuff."

Fletch looked sad as he shook his head. "I blame your parents for that. After their divorce, I wanted you to live with me permanently, not just those summers when your dad didn't have time for you."

Grady swallowed back the emotions clogging his throat. "I know."

"You always tried so hard to keep your distance, son. You wouldn't let anyone get close." He paused. "Not all people are out to hurt you like your parents, or your ex-wife."

Grady tensed. He didn't want to rehash any of this. "I tried to play the family man before—it didn't work."

His grandfather watched him, then said, "I wish I was wise enough to give you all the right answers, son, but I can't. I lost your grandmother too soon. I didn't want to try to find someone again." Those kind hazel eyes stared at him. "That was a mistake. I was a lonely man for a lot of years."

"At least your marriage wasn't a failure. I've done so many things wrong."

"People make mistakes, son."

The pain was nearly overwhelming. "I was never home…not even when my son was born." He felt his throat closing up. "He didn't survive."

Fletch leaned forward and gripped his grandson's hand. "Oh, Grady, I'm so sorry." The old man was silent for a long time then said, "As tragic as it was to lose a child, you can't blame yourself for what you have no control over."

Grady didn't want to hear excuses. "I should have been there."

"Of course you should have been there for your wife. But, son, would it have changed the outcome?" Fletch asked.

He shook his head, unable to say the words.

"We can't live on what-ifs, son." His grip tightened. "You'll always grieve for your child, but it's time to forgive yourself, too. Let people help you," Fletch told him. "Maybe that special someone."

"Gina."

Fletcher shrugged. "I just thought that she would be someone you could build a future with. And what's not to like about a seven-year-old kid? Seems to me, that boy could use a good male role model in his life."

His heart ached. He couldn't stop himself from wanting the same thing. "I failed before."

"You weren't alone in your first marriage, so don't take all the blame." There was a long pause, then his grandfather said, "Gina's marriage was a tragic one, but she trusts you. That's because she sees what I see, a good man. Love with the right person can heal a lot of wounds," the old man added.

Grady felt a glimmer of hope. He'd never planned on another relationship, and then along came Gina and he couldn't get her out of his head, out of his heart. And she made him want to reach for that dream.

Grady thought back to the afternoon Gina had held him and cried with him for his child. How her touch had comforted him, how it had soothed his scarred body. How she had made him feel…loved. He closed his eyes and took a shaky breath. God, he loved her, and all he did was reject her. Would she ever forgive him for that? Take a chance on him?

He had to convince her. He suddenly realized how

badly he wanted to make a life with her and Zack. How badly he wanted to stay right here in Destiny.

He stood and smiled at Fletch. "Do you think you could put up with me hanging around?"

The old man grinned. "Maybe if you bring Gina around to see me once in a while, and I wouldn't mind getting a great-grandkid or two out of it." He arched an eyebrow. "You need me to put in a good word for you?"

"No, I think I can handle that part," he said, though deep down he wasn't so sure. He had to repair a lot of damage.

Two days later Gina had been at work for an hour at the thrift shop. Since 7:00 a.m. She'd managed to get a lot done, too, including moving another reupholstered sofa to the display window.

"Marie, your work is incredible," Gina told her as they stood back and enjoyed the view.

"What are you talking about? You redesigned it. The sofa looks totally different."

"Well, you did most of the sewing. So why don't you take the rest of the day off?"

"Oh, no. I'm fine, really. I have a ton of work to do here."

"Not today. Take the baby to the park. You need some sunshine. Go."

The woman didn't argue, and within ten minutes Gina was alone. Oh, boy. Maybe that wasn't such a good idea. She had too much time to think.

"Do some paperwork." She went behind the counter and picked up the receipts from yesterday and started to head back to the office when the bell signaled over the front door. She glanced up to see Grady Fletcher.

Her breath caught as the tall man dressed in jeans and a collared shirt walked in.

Oh, God. What was he doing here?

He looked as nervous as she felt. "Hello, Gina."

"Grady."

He shut the door and flipped the Open sign to Closed. Then he locked it before he walked over to her.

"What are you doing?"

"I'd like to talk to you. So I need a few minutes of uninterrupted time."

"And I have a business to run." She started to walk past him when he reached for her.

"Please, Gina. It's important."

Those dark eyes bored into hers. "Funny, you didn't have time for me when you needed to leave town."

"I didn't leave," he said.

She froze. "Why not?"

"I had things to do here. To settle."

She felt the imprint of his hand on her arm. She pulled away. "So when do you leave?"

"I'm not going to Texas."

Those words got her attention.

He glanced around. "Could Marie watch the shop for an hour or so? I want to show you something."

"Marie isn't here."

Then she heard the voice from the back room. "I'm here, Gina." She walked in from the back, pushing the stroller. "I returned to get my purse." She looked at Grady. "If it's for a good cause, I don't have a problem staying a few hours."

"A very good cause."

Grady turned back to Gina. She looked so pretty it took his breath away. Stay focused. He glanced over her jeans and pink blouse and tennis shoes.

"Good, you're dressed for where I have to take you."

She still resisted. "Who said I'm going anywhere?"

He stopped. "I'll make it worth your while. You can have all the furniture in the cabin." When she still didn't move, he added, "Please, Gina. If it wasn't important, I wouldn't ask you."

"You have no idea what you're asking of me."

"I do. I'm hoping you still trust me enough to give me this chance."

She sighed. "Okay, I'll go." She glanced at Marie. "But I won't be gone long."

To Grady she said, "This had better be important."

He nodded, staring into those mesmerizing green eyes. "It's the most important thing I've ever done."

CHAPTER FOURTEEN

TEN minutes later they were going out of town, and at first Gina wondered if they were headed to the cabin.

No! She couldn't go back there. There were too many memories. Before she could protest, Grady drove by the turnoff. Instead they passed the new construction site that was Jace's new project.

"Isn't that the new mountain bike training center?"

"Yes. They're moving fast to complete it by mid June. Justin already has twenty students enrolled."

Gina studied the man behind the wheel. With the cowboy hat pulled low, she had trouble reading him. Why did he want her to come along? Better question, why had she consented to go with him?

He pulled off the road and into a clearing, then parked. "We're here," he announced as he climbed out and hurried around to her side. She had no choice but to take his offered hand to help her out of the truck.

"Come on." He didn't release his hold as he walked her to the edge of the hill.

She didn't want to think about the warmth of his large hand engulfing hers. How safe and utterly feminine he made her feel.

She concentrated on the beauty before her. Miles of

pine and cedar trees covered the mountain range—the peaks looked as if they could touch the rich blue sky.

"It's breathtaking." That wasn't a lie, but why was she here?

He turned to her. "You really like it?"

"What's not to like?"

"This is where I'm building Sarge's Rescue Dogs and Kennel." He pointed off in the distance. "Well, it's actually going to be over there."

Her heart raced as she fought to contain her excitement. "So you decided against Texas."

"I weighed the options." His dark gaze locked on hers and held for a long time. "This is my grandfather's land. He gave it to me. Then Justin offered me a good deal to help my business—even Josh encouraged me. It seemed impractical to leave."

Well, that was just great. "Good for you. It's a lovely spot." How would she deal with Grady staying, running into him around town?

"I'm happy for you, Grady. Now, could you please take me back?" She started to leave when he stopped her.

"Not so fast. I haven't finished telling you everything."

He'd said enough. She didn't want to hear about his new life here. How he'd moved on and didn't need her in his life. "Grady. Please." She turned and marched back to the truck.

"Gina, wait," he called.

She ignored him as she reached for the passenger door, when he caught up and stopped her from opening it. He stood so close that Gina couldn't move. His breath was warm against her neck.

"You aren't even going to hear what else I have to say?"

She didn't turn around to look at him, just shook her head.

"You don't want to hear that I plan to build a place on the crest over there. How I want the whole back side of the house to be glass so you can see that view from every room."

"Sounds lovely. Can I leave now?"

"Not before I tell you—"

"Stop." Gina swung around. "I'm glad you've moved on, Grady. Okay." She hated that tears filled her eyes. "I just don't need to hear—"

Her words were smothered when his mouth closed over hers. She moaned and gripped the front of his shirt, and in her weakened state, allowed Grady to have his way. She'd missed him so much. The feelings he created in her.

He broke off the kiss. "I've missed you, Gina. God knows, I tried to stay away, tried to let you find someone who would be better for you than a set-in-his-ways ex-army guy. But I discovered that I want you, only you."

Even though his confession thrilled her, it wasn't enough. "Grady. I can't deny I want you, too." She couldn't help but think about their little time together. "But I want more than some stolen hours."

He pulled back and his hard gaze locked on hers, then he stepped back.

"I want more, too, Gina." He still looked uneasy. "I know it's hard for you because of your bad marriage. And my track record in that department was lousy."

She frowned when he backed away. She watched as he pulled off his hat, raking fingers through his hair.

"Grady," she called to him. "Tell me why you brought me here."

He turned back to her. "I'm not good at this, Gina. In the army, you're given orders and you carry them out."

"Then consider this an order and tell me what you have to say."

Grady felt his palms sweat, his heart race. Hell, he felt like a teenager.

"I want to stay in Destiny, be close to my grandfather. Build my business here." His gaze met hers. "But most importantly, Gina, I want to build a life with you."

"But I thought you wanted to leave so badly," she finally said. "That you weren't the man for me. You couldn't give me what I needed."

He blew out a breath. So she wasn't going to make this easy. He thought about Tim Keenan's advice. He straightened and walked toward her. "That was before I realized that I could give you more than any man." His throat suddenly went dry. "Because no one could love you as much as I do."

Gina blinked, then he saw the tears in her eyes. "Oh, Grady."

He stepped closer. "Is that a good 'Oh, Grady' or a bad 'Oh, Grady'?"

She smiled. "It's good." She rushed into his arms. "I love you, too, Grady Fletcher."

He tossed his cowboy hat into the back of the truck, then reached for her. "Those are the sweetest words I ever heard," he whispered right before his mouth captured hers.

There was no way he could ever express the depth of his feelings for her, but he was going to try. He pulled her tighter against him, letting her know how much he desired her, wanted to cherish her for a lifetime.

He pulled back, but didn't let her go. He cupped her face tenderly. "I meant what I said, Gina. I want a future with you and Zack. I know you've gone through a lot. You can have all the space you need to heal, just know I'll be there. I want you to trust me that I'll never hurt you intentionally."

She kissed him sweetly. "I know that, Grady. I've known that from the first." She reached up and touched the scar on the side of his neck. "That afternoon when we made love, everything you shared with me, I know it was painful for you, both physically and emotionally." Her gaze met his, but he felt the connection deep down into his soul. "I've never felt that way...ever. Being with you was so special."

"I want to make you feel that way always," he said. "I want to marry you, Gina." He saw her surprised look. "Okay, maybe it's too early for that step. But I want to be your husband, your partner and Zack's father."

This time the tears did fall. "Oh, Grady."

He searched her face. "Again, is that good or bad?"

She nodded. "Oh, definitely good." She cupped his face. "You'll be a wonderful father... One any child would be proud of." She knew he was thinking about the son he'd lost. "Zack is going to be so lucky to have you."

"No, I'm the one who's lucky to have you both." He took a steady breath, then knelt on the ground in front of her. "Gina Williams, I love you more than I ever thought possible. Would you do me the honor to marry this old soldier? I promise to love and cherish you forever."

Her eyes widened at his proposal. "Oh, yes, Grady, I'll marry you." She leaned down and placed her mouth against his. With a groan, he stood, wrapping her in his arms and kissed her until they were both breathless.

"Oh, Grady, I'm so happy."

"Enough to play hooky with me for the rest of the day?"

Gina looked up at the handsome man who was going to be her husband. "Sounds tempting." She hesitated. "I guess I could call Marie and have her close the shop. So what do you have in mind?"

"I could lie and say we have a lot to discuss, but I have a feeling we'll get distracted the second we're alone." He grinned at her and she couldn't resist.

"So you're saying you can make it worth my while?"

"I'm a soldier, I don't back down from a challenge. Especially someone as tempting as you."

She gave him a soft kiss and turned in his arms. Together they looked at the view as she pointed toward the ridge. "You said you're building a house there?"

"Our house," he corrected. "First, though, I need to finish the kennel for the dogs, which Jace said would be complete by summer's end." Grady smiled. "Then we can break ground on our home. We want to get as much done as we can before winter." He leaned down and kissed the side of her neck. "I want to do everything quickly so it's ready for you and Zack."

"How soon do you want to get married?"

"If it was up to me, I'd marry you this minute." He turned her around to face him. "I know you need time, Gina. I'm willing to wait until you're ready."

She felt the rush. Oh, she was so ready for this man. "Okay. We can talk about it. We need to talk to Zack, too. And your grandfather."

Grady grinned. "I can tell you Fletch wholeheartedly approves of us."

Gina smiled, too. "I love that man. Mainly because he raised you. He helped make you the man you are. The man I love."

"And you're the woman I love. The woman who saved me from loneliness. You were there for me when I didn't think I needed anyone. Gina, I need you in my life."

He paused and she knew he was thinking about his son.

"Oh, Grady. You've helped me through a lot of things, too. Mainly, I learned to trust." She slipped her arms around his waist. "How wonderful it is to be loved by a man who cherishes me. And you love my son." She smiled, realizing how lucky she was to find this man. "Zack's going to be so happy."

"I bet he's not nearly as happy as I am right now."

She nodded. "I think there's enough happiness to go around for all of us."

With Grady's arms wrapped around her, they looked out at the beautiful view, the site of their future home. Their new life. Together.

EPILOGUE

Two days later Saturday arrived, sunny and warm and perfect for an eight-year-old boy's birthday party. Also a great day for family, new and old. Gina felt almost giddy. Grady should be here soon and then they could announce their big news.

"Mom!" Zack came running into the house. "Did you get my cake?"

"No, Aunt Lori is bringing it," she reminded him, knowing in about thirty minutes half the town would be in her backyard for the party. They'd been lucky to find so many friends since coming to Destiny.

"Oh, I forgot," Zack said.

She hugged the little boy who suddenly looked so much older. Where had her baby gone? She got a strange feeling again, thinking about Grady and starting their new life together. Having another child. She was giddy at the thought of having Grady's baby.

"Mom. When is Grady getting here?"

She brushed his dark hair from his forehead. "Soon, he's picking someone up."

She knew Zack was eager to show off Bandit's tricks. "Come on," she said. "Let's check the tables before everyone gets here."

They walked out onto the deck to view the large

yard that had been decorated for the party. Several arrangements of balloons were tied to each fence post, and toward the back an obstacle course had been constructed late yesterday by one special man. Grady. She recalled last night, how she'd relayed her thanks to her man after Zack had gone to bed.

She could see Zack's excitement. "The obstacle course is so cool."

"Yes, it is. You're a lucky little boy, Zack Williams."

Gina twisted the large shiny pear-shaped diamond on her left hand. Grady had also surprised her when he'd slipped the engagement ring on her finger. In those stolen moments, her future husband had also proceeded to show her how much he loved her. Today was special for another reason. Grady wanted to ask Zack officially for his mother's hand before they made the announcement.

The yard gate opened and Grady walked in with Scout. Her breath caught at the sight of the tall man who was dressed in black jeans and a tan collared shirt. When he smiled at her, she saw the love shining in his eyes and nearly melted on the spot.

Zack spotted him, too. "Grady!" He went running off to him and greeted Scout. "I'm so glad you're here."

"I told you I'd come early." Grady smiled. "I brought another surprise. Someone who wants to meet you."

Grady winked at Gina and went outside the gate again, but soon returned pushing his grandfather in a wheelchair. "Zack, this is Joe Fletcher. Granddad, this is the special boy I've been telling you about."

Grady stood back and watched the two together. It was his grandfather who spoke first. "I hear you got lost in my old mine."

Zack nodded. "Yeah, but Scout found me."

"Maybe it's time I boarded that place up. Wouldn't want anyone else to get hurt."

"I think it's a cool place."

Fletch pursed his lips. "Maybe when I get out of this chair we can go up there together. I can show you where there's still some gold."

Zack's dark eyes lit up. "Really?"

Fletch nodded. "Say, I hear it's your birthday today. I got you something." He handed him the small box. "But you're gonna have to wait a little while to open it."

"Thank you. I'll put it with the other presents." He took off toward the table as Gina walked over and kissed Fletch on the cheek.

"Hello, Granddad Joe."

The older man grinned as they hugged. "There's my girl."

Grady raised an eyebrow. "Don't get any ideas, old man. She's spoken for."

Fletch waved him off and turned back to Gina. "Thanks for inviting me today."

"You're always included. You're family."

One of the many reasons Grady loved this woman— her big heart. He was one lucky man. He reached down and brushed a kiss across her lips. He couldn't help but recall their time together last night. "Hello, pretty lady." He leaned close to her ear and whispered, "I can't tell you how much I hated leaving you last night."

She looked up at him with those green eyes. "Maybe we can change that…and soon."

Before he could say any more, the boy returned with Scout. Grady stepped back from temptation. "Hey, Zack, how about we run the dogs through the obstacle course for practice?"

"Okay." Zack went to get Bandit out of the kennel.

Grady gripped Gina's hand, feeling the diamond, feeling her love, feeling her commitment to him. "Wish me luck."

"Always, but you don't need it. Zack already loves you as much as I do."

Grady looked down at his grandfather to see his smile. "I told you she was a keeper," Fletch said.

Grady motioned to Scout and together they walked off toward the edge of the yard where the course started. The boy met him there and gave the command for Bandit to sit, and then he unleashed him. Grady had Scout sit, too. "Could I talk to you, Zack, before we start?"

The boy looked worried, but nodded.

Grady knelt to be eye level. "I want to talk you about your mom." He released a breath. "You know I care about her."

Zack petted Bandit. "Yeah, I saw you kiss her."

"Does that bother you?"

The boy shook his head. "I just don't want you to hurt her like my daddy did. He was mean."

"No, Zack. That's a cowardly thing to do, especially to a woman or a child. There might be times when we disagree, but I'll never raise my hand to you or your mother. You have my word."

"I'm glad, 'cause Mom's happy now."

"And I want to make her even happier." This was harder than he thought. "I love your mother, and I want to marry her."

The boy's eyes lit up. "Really? You mean like Aunt Lori and Uncle Jace? We'd live together all the time?"

Grady smiled. "Yes. I'm building a big house so that will happen."

Zack's eyes grew larger.

Grady grew serious again. "Not only that, Zack. I want you to be my son."

"Really? You'll be my dad?"

He nodded, fighting for the right words. "As much as I love your mother, I also love you, too."

Before he could finish making his pitch, Zack had launched himself into his arms, nearly knocking him over. "I love you, too, Grady."

He hugged the boy, letting those sweet words sink in. That was when he saw Gina walk toward them. She hugged him, then her son. "So what do you think about us being a family?"

"It's cool!" Zack said. "Grady wants to be my dad." He petted Scout. "And we get to live with Scout and Bandit, too."

Grady suddenly realized how much he loved these two. "I think it's pretty cool, too." He hugged Gina to his side. "I get a wife and a son."

Zack grinned and looked up expectantly at his mother. "Mom, does that mean you're going to have a baby like Aunt Lori?"

A blush crossed Gina's face as her gaze rose to his; the love shining in their depths caused his chest to tighten with longing. He could picture Gina pregnant with his child.

She smiled. "I think that's something your new dad and I need to discuss. Alone."

Grady wished they were alone right now. "Hey, I think today is someone's birthday."

With their arms intertwined and two dogs with them, they turned back toward the house and noticed the party crowd. There was Claire and Tim Keenan, Lori, Jace and their daughter, Cassie, Justin and Morgan Hilliard and their kids. So many more gathered on the deck, but they had been giving them space. Privacy.

"I think everyone's a little curious about what's going on," Gina told him. "Maybe we should tell them."

Grady smiled. "It would be my pleasure, ma'am."

Before he could make any announcement, Zack spoke up. "Mom and Grady are getting married. And he's going to be my new dad." The boy beamed up at his parents. "This is the best birthday ever."

The crowd erupted in a round of cheers. Grady looked down at Gina and saw the love in her eyes. "How did I get so lucky?"

"Me, too."

They both had to be remembering that awful day when Zack had been kidnapped. The day one strong woman had climbed into his truck and announced she was going to get her child back. "You saved my son that day," she said.

He leaned back and brushed his mouth across hers. "No, you both saved me. I'm one lucky guy."

She smiled and his heart sang. This was their new beginning, and it was only going to get better. How could it not? He finally had everything he'd ever wanted—a home here in Destiny. And his family.

* * * * *

THE LARKVILLE LEGACY

A secret letter...two families changed for ever

Welcome to the small town of Larkville, Texas, where the Calhoun family has been ranching for generations.

Meanwhile, in New York, the Patterson family rules America's highest echelons of society.

Both families are totally unprepared for the news that they are linked by a shocking secret.

For hidden on the Calhoun ranch is a letter that's been lying unopened and unread—until now!

Meet the two families in all eight books of this brand-new series:

THE SOLDIER'S
SWEETHEART

BY
SORAYA LANE

First published in Great Britain 2013
by Mills & Boon, an imprint of Harlequin (UK) Limited,
Eton House, 18-24 Paradise Road, Richmond, Surrey TW9 1SR

© Harlequin Books S.A. 2013

Special thanks and acknowledgment are given to Soraya Lane for her contribution to The Larkville Legacy series.

ISBN: 978 0 263 90091 0
ebook ISBN: 978 1 472 00452 9

23-0313

Harlequin (UK) policy is to use papers that are natural, renewable and recyclable products and made from wood grown in sustainable forests. The logging and manufacturing processes conform to the legal environmental regulations of the country of origin.

Printed and bound in Spain
by Blackprint CPI, Barcelona

Writing for Mills & Boon® Cherish™ is truly a dream come true for **Soraya Lane.** An avid book reader and writer since her childhood, Soraya describes becoming a published author as "the best job in the world," and hopes to be writing heartwarming, emotional romances for many years to come.

Soraya lives with her own real-life hero on a small farm in New Zealand, surrounded by animals and with an office overlooking a field where their horses graze.

For more information about Soraya and her upcoming releases, visit her at her website, www.sorayalane.com, her blog, www.sorayalane.blogspot.com, or follow her at www.facebook.com/SorayaLaneAuthor.

For Natalie & Nicola.

Thank you so much for your encouragement,
support and friendship.

I don't know what I'd do without our daily email chats!

CHAPTER ONE

NATE CALHOUN held up one hand to shield his face from the sun. He'd forgotten what it was like to look out over the land, to see grass stretching so far into the distance that he couldn't tell where their ranch ended and the next one began.

Sand he was used to, but not grass.

He pulled the door shut behind him and stretched out his right leg, trying not to grimace. His damn calf wouldn't stop throbbing, and no matter how much he tried to ignore it, walking wasn't as easy as it used to be.

Nate glanced up at the main house, knew exactly what he'd find if he walked over. Nancy, their long-time housekeeper, would be clearing the breakfast dishes; there'd still be the smell of strong coffee lingering in the air, and there'd probably be some leftovers waiting to be eaten. But he wasn't ready to be part of that life again, didn't know when he'd be able to answer the questions his family seemed so intent on asking him whenever he spent time with them.

It was why he'd walked away from them all on his first night back and taken over the unused guesthouse.

Nate turned and walked a track that was still oddly

familiar to him. As a boy, right up until he'd left the ranch to join the army, he'd wandered to a massive tree tucked far enough away from the house to be private. Where a weathered timber swing had tilted back and forth in the breeze. Somewhere that he'd never shared with anyone except for...

Who the hell was that?

Nate stopped and squinted. He was close enough to see the tree but not close enough to figure out who was sitting on a swing that he'd expected to be long gone by now.

He straightened and tried his hardest not to limp, even though he knew that disguising his injury was impossible.

Then the mystery figure on the swing turned his way.

Nate gulped. Hard. Before grinding his teeth together and walking toward her.

It was Sarah. After all these years, he'd managed to find Sarah Anderson under his tree.

Some things would never change.

She stood as he approached, a shy smile making her lips tilt ever so slightly in the corners, a faint blush creeping across her cheeks.

"Hey, Nate."

He did his best to return the smile, but the truth was that simple things like grinning at a friend didn't come so easy to him anymore. And besides, he didn't even know if he could call Sarah a friend these days, not after what had happened between them.

"Sarah," he managed, stopping a few paces from her.

She hesitated, flushed all over again, before leaning awkwardly into him and giving him a hug.

Nate stiffened, tried to relax and found it impossible. Even with Sarah's gentle embrace, her arms so softly around him, her long hair brushing against his cheek. Once, he'd thought he'd never want to leave the comfort of Sarah's arms. Now it only made him want to run.

"You look good, Nate," Sarah told him as she pulled away and sat back down. "It's so nice to see you back here. I can't believe you're home."

Nate nodded, thrust his hands into his back pockets. "It's—" he couldn't lie to her, not to Sarah "—different being back."

"I'm so sorry about your father." Sarah's eyes flooded with tears as she reached for him, her fingers curling around his forearm as she leaned forward again. "He was always so nice to me when I was here with you."

Nate smiled. He didn't even have to force it. "Yeah, he was pretty fond of you, too." Back in the days when he and Sarah were joined at the hip, his dad had loved him having Sarah over all the time. Everyone had, because there wasn't a person in Larkville who didn't like Sarah Anderson.

He looked up as she removed her hand from his arm and immediately wished he hadn't. Because he'd never forgotten the warm amber color of her eyes or the way she seemed to be able to look straight through him, to see what he was thinking, what he was feeling.

Only there was no way that even Sarah could know what was going on inside of him, not now.

Sarah sighed like she wasn't sure what to say, before turning a sunny smile his way. "Have you heard that I've been roped into organizing the Fall Festival?" Sarah shook her head. "I mean, I'm looking forward to the tribute for your dad, but trying to get everyone in this town into line is harder than it looks, I tell you!"

Nate couldn't help but smile back at her, and for once it was genuine, not him trying to act happy to get the people around him off his back. "I bet you're loving it."

Sarah glared at him, a playfulness there that had been missing in his life for so long he'd forgotten it had ever even existed. A spark of happiness that for a moment, the briefest of moments, made him feel like he'd never left the farm, never seen what he wished he could forget, never... Nate swallowed hard and tried to focus on Sarah's pretty face instead of the memories that haunted him.

"Are you home for good, Nate?"

Her question surprised him, made him crash back to reality. "Yeah." He grunted out the word, still unable to believe that after all these years his career in the army was over for good. That he was back home, and in such a short time he'd lost both his mom and his dad, too. Home sure wasn't what it used to be.

"You're certain?"

Nate braved making eye contact with the girl who had stolen his heart when he was a teenager. "Yeah, I'm sure." He wished he hadn't snapped at her, but he couldn't help it. What did she want to hear? The truth of why he wasn't going back? Because not even Sarah could get details of *that* story out of him.

"I'm sorry, I know better than to pry." Sarah sighed again and looked away. "Moose!" she called.

Moose? Nate was about to ask her who the heck she was calling when… "What the hell?" Nate spun, ready to fight, body alert even though his leg was starting to throb.

"Moose!" Sarah called again, crouching toward the long grass where the noise was coming from.

A massive dog appeared, launching from his hiding place and landing in front of Sarah. Nate could have sworn his heart was about to beat straight from his chest and thump to his feet.

"Since when do you have a dog named Moose?" he asked.

The dog glared at him, sitting protectively beside Sarah.

"You know me, sucker for animals in need," she replied, stroking the dog's head lovingly. "Your brother found him one day and nicknamed him, because he looked like a gangly baby moose. No one knows how he ended up around here, but he's been with me ever since."

Nate eyed the German Shepherd, not liking the way he was being watched in response. The canine was acting like he was challenging his authority and Nate wasn't used to being the one on the back foot. "Is he as staunch with Todd as he's being with me right now?"

The smile fell from Sarah's face like water thrown over a flame at the mention of her husband.

"It was really nice seeing you, Nate, but we'd better be off."

He watched as she moved past him, her eyes damp

again like she was about to cry. "Yeah, nice seeing you, too."

He should have asked her to stay. Should have patted the damn dog instead of acting like his territory was at stake. Because Nate was alone and seeing Sarah hadn't been half-bad. At least she hadn't quizzed him like his family had the moment he'd stepped foot on the family ranch again.

After so many years surrounded by other men, of living and working with other soldiers at his side, he was alone. His family were like strangers to him; he had no one to talk to, *no one he wanted to talk to,* and seeing Sarah had been the first time he'd cracked a smile in what seemed like forever.

But instead of calling her back, he watched her walk away. And it felt like they'd just gone back in time six years, when he'd told her that he was staying with the army instead of coming home. When he'd ended their relationship for good.

Sarah touched the top of her dog's head before sending him away in front of her. She tried to focus on him bounding ahead, tail wagging back and forth. But the only thing she could feel, the only thing she could think about, was the man standing behind her.

Nate Calhoun.

After all these years, seeing him for more than a fleeting moment was… Sarah dug her fingernails into her palm. Refused to turn around to see if he was still standing where she'd left him. Nate had been the love of her life, and no matter how hard she tried to pretend that there was nothing between them anymore, she was still drawn to him like a magnet to metal.

Why after so many years, after he'd left her, could she still not push the man from her mind? When he'd left her brokenhearted, discarded like their romance had been nothing more than a holiday fling.

"Sarah, what are you doing here so early?"

She looked up, forgetting how close she was to the homestead. The ranch house never failed to impress her, had always had a warmth and homeliness about it that she admired, even though it was easily one of the largest homes in Larkville.

"I came to check up on my new horse, but Moose ran after something and I ended up following him."

Kathryn Calhoun leaned against the doorframe, eyebrows drawn together. "What's wrong?"

Sarah sighed. It didn't matter how hard she tried to keep something to herself, she always seemed to wear her emotions all over her face. "I saw Nate."

Kathryn frowned. "Did you talk to him?"

"Yeah, but…" What did she say? That she still felt a flutter of something for him, even though she could see from the darkness in his gaze, from the drawn expression on his face, that the old Nate wasn't even in residence anymore? Twenty minutes ago she hadn't even known Nate was home and now…

"You don't have to tell me, I know," Kathryn told her.

Sarah's face flushed hot, but she bit her tongue, waiting for Kathryn to continue. She liked Kathryn a lot, but it didn't mean she wanted to talk to her about her former flame, especially given she was married to Nate's brother, Holt.

"Sarah, he's changed. He's not the Nate his family knew, and he's not the happy-go-lucky town charmer that everyone seems to remember, either," Kathryn confessed.

Sarah was overcome with a burst of anger, wanting to defend him. "He's been through a lot, so don't we owe it to him to be patient? To give him some space to deal with being back here?"

Kathryn smiled at her, but there was a sadness there that Sarah couldn't miss. "I hope you're right, Sarah. I do. But Holt's not so sure that Nate's ever going to be the same again."

A wet nose thrust into Sarah's hand reminded her that she wasn't alone. "I think that's my cue to go," she told Kathryn. "I'm meeting Johnny to see how he's gotten on with my mare. He started her under saddle for me a few weeks ago."

Sarah waved to Kathryn as she turned, but the smile fled her face as soon as she walked away. *Nate was hurting.* It might have been years since they'd been together, but she still remembered every expression his face had ever worn, how much pain he must be experiencing to hide away in the guesthouse, away from the family he was once so close to.

She threw a stick her dog had dropped at her feet and tried to focus on where she was walking, rather than the man she could see in her mind.

Nate had left her. Nate had walked away and de-

*cided not to come home. He wasn't her responsibility
and he'd already made that perfectly clear.*

So why was her heart racing like it was in a speed-
way competition, and her mouth so dry it felt like she
hadn't consumed water in days?

*Because it was Nate Calhoun, and for as long as she
was alive she'd never, ever forget him.*

CHAPTER TWO

NATE stretched his leg out and practiced some of the exercises he was supposed to be doing, in an attempt to relieve some of the pressure in his head. It didn't work. Instead, he ended up with a throbbing leg and his head pounded harder than before.

He needed to find something else to do, something to focus on, but right now it was too easy to sit under the tree in the shade and think. *And the fact he could see Sarah in the distance wasn't motivating him to move, either.*

He could see her talking to his sister Jess's husband. Johnny was clearly gifted with horses; he could tell that from watching him for only a few minutes. Sarah was leaning against the rail of the corral, one hand on the head of her dog, the other keeping her balanced. He was waiting to see her mount the young horse, to see if she was still as talented in the saddle as she'd been when they were younger. Back then, she'd been easily as good as any of the boys.

"Nate." A gruff voice commanded his attention.

He turned and looked up to see his brother standing behind him, fingers rammed through the loops of his jeans.

"Holt," he replied.

His brother stared off into the distance. It was obvious that he'd been caught out looking at Sarah.

"We see more of Sarah these days than we did for a long while," Holt told him.

Nate tried to act disinterested, but the reality was that he was anything *but* disinterested. Seeing Sarah again had made something within him, something he hadn't felt in a long time, stir to life again. No matter how hard he was trying to force it back down.

"She having her horse broken in here?" Nate asked. He knew from the letters Jess had sent him that her new husband was something of a horse whisperer, but he'd never had the chance to get to know him.

Holt dropped to his haunches, plucking at a blade of grass and avoiding eye contact. Suited Nate fine. The last thing he wanted was to be interrogated again.

"Johnny's giving her a hand. It's nice to see her smiling again."

Nate raised an eyebrow in question, met his brother's gaze when he looked up.

"You don't know about her and Todd, do you?" Holt asked.

Nate shook his head, slowly. "What do I need to know about her and Todd?" He hated the guy, even though he couldn't blame him. Sarah had married one of his best friends, and he'd never forgiven either of them.

"Look, Nate," Holt began, standing up again and fidgeting like the last thing he wanted was to have a conversation about Sarah and her husband. "Todd's out of the picture, that's all I'm saying. I thought you'd want to know, but if you want details, then I think you should ask Sarah. It's her story to tell."

Nate couldn't help the frown that took over his mouth. "So you're fine with telling me her marriage is over but you're not going to tell me what happened and why?"

Holt sighed. It wasn't something he remembered his brother doing often. "Nate, there's no reason to go jumping down my throat. I just don't think it's my place to tell you, okay?"

He swallowed what felt like a rock. Tried to channel his focus into the dull thud in his leg, anything other than ripping into his brother again.

"I'm sorry." Nate choked out the apology, knowing he'd been a jerk.

Holt held up his hands. "Yeah, I'm sorry, too. I just thought that if there was any unfinished business between you—"

"There's not," Nate interrupted, hearing the sharpness of his own tone.

He watched the expression change on his brother's face and hated that they were acting like strangers. Or maybe Holt wasn't doing anything out of the ordinary, but *he* sure was. They'd been as close as brothers could be once, had spent day after day together, been inseparable. Like his buddies in the army, Holt had always been there for him no matter what, and vice versa.

But now Nate had changed so much he didn't know

if he'd ever be that brother to any of his siblings. Not ever again.

Holt walked backward, but he'd turned before Nate could apologize again, and he didn't even know where to begin, anyway.

So Sarah and Todd were over. He looked down and watched her, realizing it was she who was on the horse's back now. Elegant as ever, sitting straight and comfortable in the saddle, at ease with what she was doing.

He didn't need to know that Sarah wasn't spoken for any longer. He didn't need to watch her, or talk to her, or *anything* her now that he was back home. He had his family to deal with, twin siblings that he hadn't even met yet and a bunch of memories that kept him from slumber night after night after night.

Yet his legs were throbbing not from the pain right now, but from a desperate need to cross the field and seek out Sarah.

Just like he had as a lovesick teenager twelve years ago when he'd first seen her taking a riding lesson in the same corral she was in now.

Sarah nudged the young mare on. It was her first solo ride on Maddie, but she was responding beautifully, even leading the other horse beside them.

She gulped, trying not to think too hard about what she was doing. The last thing she needed was for Maddie to feel her nervousness and think it had something to do with their ride.

He was still there. The young man she'd known to never stand still for more than a moment, not able to stay in the same place because there was always something to do, was sitting where she'd left him, leaning against the tree like he had no purpose.

Sarah didn't bother calling out to him, because even though his head was down she knew he'd have heard her. Instead, she walked the horses straight over to him, never taking her eyes from his lone figure.

She'd been wallowing in her own self-pity, thinking she'd been hard done by. Seeing Nate and the change in him told her what she'd been through was nothing in comparison.

"Let's go, cowboy," Sarah ordered once she reached him, in a voice far more confident than she felt inside.

Nate's gaze made her smile wobble. It was as if a storm had brewed within him and was searching to exit through his eyes—eyes that had once been soft and loving now tumultuous and dangerous.

"You want me to ride?"

She held out the reins to the horse. It was one of Johnny's own, and he'd promised she'd be nice and quiet. Sarah had no idea how long it had been since Nate had ridden.

"It'll do us both good," she assured him.

Nate shook his head, before pulling his hat back over his short crop of hair, stretching and standing. "In case you haven't noticed," he said in a voice laced with ice, "I'm not exactly capable these days."

Sarah forced herself to look into his eyes, to not be scared off by his behavior. If he was trying to push her away, to make her scurry back to where she'd come from, then he was doing a darn good job. Except for the fact he was forgetting how determined she had to be with the kids in her classroom. Bullying and bad behavior didn't get her pupils anywhere, and just because he was a wounded soldier didn't mean he was going to get any special treatment.

"So you limp? I can see that for myself without you pointing it out, but I wouldn't have thought you'd let it stop you." Sarah's hands were shaking but she wasn't backing down. *This was Nate, for goodness' sake!*

"Sarah…"

"No, Nate, no," she insisted. "You can ride without stirrups, whatever, but I think it'll do you good."

He squinted up at her, his face showing the full force of his anger. "You been talking to my family?"

She thrust the reins down into his hands now he was closer. "Why, you been as rude to them as you're being to me right now?"

Nate's face crumpled, like a hard shell that had just been shattered, a snail dropped to the concrete from a bird's beak. "Damn it, Sarah, I'm sorry. I—"

She held up her hand to silence him. "There's time for apologies later, Nate, from both of us, but right now I just want you to get back in the saddle."

Nate looked at her, stayed still for a heartbeat, before throwing the reins over the horse's neck and positioning himself on the left-hand side. She couldn't help thinking that he was lucky he'd injured his right leg, otherwise he'd have found it hard to mount, but she turned away before he caught her watching. Gave him a moment to right himself before she faced him again.

"No stirrups, you reckon?" he asked, a glimmer of the old Nate flickering in his voice.

Sarah shrugged. "Whatever's most comfortable. I thought we'd just go for a nice long walk, give this one a bit of mileage."

Nate's focus turned to the horse she was riding. "Young?"

"Yep, just started under saddle a few weeks ago, so she's doing pretty well," she told him. "I've had her since she was a baby, and now it's time to see if she's too much of a handful for me or not."

Nate pushed his foot into the stirrup on her side. She imagined he did the same on the other side or tried to from the grimace on his face, but he didn't say anything. Pushing his heel down would no doubt be painful, but until he was ready to talk, she wasn't going to ask. *Anything.* He'd tell her what had happened to his leg when he was good and ready.

"Tell me what you've been up to?" Nate was obviously trying to make an effort.

Sarah didn't want to talk about herself, had liked the neutral territory of horses. "Oh, you know, nothing out of the ordinary."

Nate looked sideways but his focus was clearly on the horse now.

"Have you ridden since you left?"

"Nope." Nate stroked one hand down the animal's neck. "I guess it's one of those things that you never forget how to do, though, right?"

"So I hear you're—"

"What do you—"

They both laughed. "Sorry," Sarah said with a laugh as they spoke at the same time. "You go first."

Nate looked like he was about to object, to tell her to go first, when his face visibly softened. Almost looked pained before he spoke.

"I hear you're no longer with Todd."

Sarah focused on the inhale and exhale of air as it whooshed through her lungs. She hadn't expected him to know. "You found that out between us talking earlier and now?" She had no idea who would have told him. "And here I was thinking you'd been sitting under that tree minding your own business all morning."

Nate's body visibly stiffened and he looked off into the distance. "It's none of my business, Sarah, you're right. I just wanted to tell you I was sorry."

Sorry that her marriage was over or sorry that he'd walked off and left her to marry Todd in the first place?

"It's fine," she lied, fixing a sunny smile on her face, not wanting to be drawn back into the past. "Todd and I weren't meant to be, that's all." She omitted the part about him running off with another woman who was already carrying his baby, about how he'd ripped her heart out with his lies and left her without a backward glance as if their marriage had meant nothing.

"So nothing else happening around here I should know about?" Nate asked her, clearly trying to change the subject.

"Other than the Fall Festival?" she mused. "Well, there's a few new people in town, but other than that, we're just the same as usual here in Larkville, I guess."

They rode side by side, far enough apart that there

was no danger of them bumping knees, but close enough that it made talking easy. She noticed his foot was dangling from the stirrups now and she wondered if he'd done the same on the other side.

"Who knows about my twin siblings?"

Sarah bit down on the inside of her mouth, needing a moment to consider her reply. *Jess, Nate's sister, had told her about the secret Calhoun children and what had happened, but she hadn't expected Nate to bring it up out of the blue.*

"You haven't long found out, have you?" she asked him gently.

Nate glanced her way, made brief eye contact before fixing his stare forward again. "I wasn't contactable for a while, so I won't lie and say the news didn't come as a shock when they finally tracked me down and told me."

Sarah swallowed, uncomfortable. "Not everyone knows, but I've seen a lot of your family lately, and Ellie and I have become great friends. She's wonderful, Nate. I think if you gave her a chance you'd really enjoy her company. Maybe not as your sister straightaway, but as a nice friend at least."

He laughed. A cruel laugh that she didn't recognize. "Right now I can't even spend time with the siblings I grew up with, so what makes you think I'd do any better with a stranger?"

"Don't talk like that, Nate. Just don't." Tears flooded Sarah's eyes but she refused to let them spill over. She'd promised herself years ago that she'd never shed a tear over Nate Calhoun ever again, and just because the circumstances were different didn't change anything.

"I think we should head back," he announced, turning his horse in the direction they'd come in.

Sarah halted her horse and paused a moment before following him, whistled to her dog to call him over. This wasn't the Nate she'd known, and it sure as hell wasn't a Nate she could ever have imagined returning home. Sarah tried to quell the anger rising within her, anger toward Nate that she'd long held in check.

If she wasn't on a newly broken horse she would have cantered off with her head held high and left him, but with the way her mount was starting to dance on the spot beneath her, she wasn't going to push her luck. Not on her first ride.

Sarah trotted after Nate's retreating figure and contemplated pushing him clean out of the saddle. A smile played across her lips. *Returned wounded soldier or not, a slap across the cheek and a shove off his horse was probably exactly what Nate needed. Not that she'd ever be that game.*

"Nate, wait up!" she called.

He didn't stop, but she could see the slight turn of his head telling her he'd heard her.

"This is stupid," she told him.

"What is?" he asked, a scowl crossing his face. A face that even with a more weathered appearance, with soft crinkles alongside his eyes and faint dark marks beneath his bottom lashes, was still ridiculously handsome.

"You behaving like this, us acting like nothing has happened one minute, then you clamming up the next."

She could see the tautness in his jaw, that he was

probably grinding down on his teeth, a hollowness in his eyes that she wished wasn't there. "I'm not the man I used to be, Sarah. That's the truth of it, and there's nothing I can do to change that."

Sarah shook her head, sadness flooding her again. "I don't believe you, Nate," she told him. "I know you've seen awful things, that you're struggling with something right now and that you've been injured, but I believe the old Nate is still in there. Somewhere." She sighed, forcing herself to continue. "I don't know what happened to you over there, Nate, but don't give up on yourself yet. Okay?"

Nate didn't respond and she was too choked up to say anything else. So they rode in silence. Him on his borrowed mount, her trying to keep up, and her dog running along beside them without a care in the world.

Nate knew he'd been rude to Sarah, and she didn't deserve it. But he was all out of apologies, of trying to figure out the right thing to say. When all he wanted was to be left the hell alone.

He cleared his throat, knowing he needed to say *something* before he lost his chance and she walked from the barn and out of his life again for good. He'd already pushed her away once, and he didn't need another black mark on his conscience.

"Sarah," he started, running a hand through his longer than usual hair.

She stopped and turned to him, her face tilted up to look him in the eye. Next to him she seemed tiny, fragile. In reality she was tall and willowy, but in flat boots she seemed much shorter than he remembered.

"I, well, I'm not myself right now, Sarah. I didn't mean to snap at you before, but I can't deal with any of this. Okay?" Nate knew it was a terrible apology, but it was the best he could come up with right now.

"I know you're hurting, Nate," she responded, closing the distance between them to touch his arm, to tighten her fingers against his skin.

He looked into her eyes, into deep amber eyes that had haunted him for years…in his sleep, while he was awake, when he had nothing else to do but think about what he'd left behind in his determination to fight for a greater cause, to serve his country in the absolute best way he could.

If only it was someone as sweet as Sarah who haunted his nights now. No longer dreams, but nightmares that relentlessly kept him awake night after long night.

"Nate?" Sarah was still touching him, her grip heating his skin.

He untangled himself. He had no other choice. Sarah touching him was too real; he didn't want to feel human again, preferred the dull deadness he'd become used to. He didn't want to acknowledge how kind she was being to him when he knew how badly he must have hurt her.

"I'm here for you, Nate. If you want to talk, if you need anything, don't be a stranger."

Sarah's eyes were kind, the smile kicking up her lips so pure that he wished he had the guts to grab hold of her and not let her go. To fold her slender body against his and cradle her, to remember what they used to have, the man he used to be. To make him feel less like damaged goods and more like a human being again.

"Thanks," he managed, his voice a husky octave lower than usual.

Sarah's fingers skipped across his upper arm and she left, walked from the barn leading her young mare, ready to turn her out in the field again.

Nate stared after her until she disappeared, eyes caught by the softness of her silhouette. Slim-fitting T-shirt, worn jeans that she obviously found comfortable to ride in and that darn dog sticking close to her like he viewed Nate as an imminent danger.

Would she still use her maiden name? Nate forced the question from his mind, trying to refocus on the horse he was supposed to be brushing down.

So she was single again? What difference did it make to him? Nate had made a choice six years ago, and as far as he could tell, there was no going back from that.

Not now and not ever.

Sarah pulled out a chair from the table and dragged it across the room. She stood on it, rummaged around in the high cupboard and yanked out what she'd known to be hidden there.

She shouldn't be looking at it, not after all these years, but seeing Nate had brought back a flood of memories that she couldn't help but want to revisit. When she was married to Todd, she'd done her best to put the past behind her, but now...

Sarah smiled as she flicked to the first page. Hearts

doodled in pink pen, Nate's name written in curly letters that she'd thought were fancy at the time. There were pictures of them on the ranch and hanging out with friends, notes he'd written her back when they'd been in class. *She'd kept them all,* even after she'd married Todd and they'd moved in together, when she'd known they should have been forgotten about.

She turned to the last page, needing to wipe the smile off her face by reminding herself why they'd broken up.

Nate had looked so handsome that day, dressed in his uniform, cheeky smile on his face as he'd turned toward the camera.

They'd made promises the day he'd left to each other, promised that they'd find a way to stay together no matter what. She'd never wanted to hold him back, *but then he'd always promised he'd come home.* That they'd do whatever it took. Instead, he'd broken her heart, and made her realize that waiting for him had been a big mistake.

Sarah flipped the tattered book shut and left it on the table. Maybe she'd show it to Nate, maybe she wouldn't, but now he was back there was no use trying to run from the past. She'd loved Nate with all her heart, and maybe, just maybe, she'd never stopped.

Sarah walked into the kitchen and made straight for the cake she'd made earlier. She had planned on giving it to Johnny for helping her out with her horse, but she needed a sugar fix and fast.

And not for the first time, she wished she wasn't such

good friends with the Calhoun family. It wasn't like she could talk to them about Nate, not when it sounded like he wasn't even on speaking terms with them himself.

CHAPTER THREE

NATE took a deep breath. He wasn't used to being nervous, had spent years being the brave one no matter what the situation, but right now he was knee-shakingly worried.

He raised one hand and knocked lightly on the door, not wanting to alarm his sister or her new husband.

The door opened, only halfway, and Nate looked down to see a little boy with messy blond hair. *His nephew.* For some reason he hadn't expected the boy to answer.

"Hey, Brady." Nate could almost feel his blood pressure dropping from being confronted by a child instead of his little sister. She might be younger than him, but she could be darn bossy, and he was still wondering if he'd done the right thing in turning up. But he couldn't hide away forever, and he was lonely. After so many years in the army, he was equal parts miserable about being alone and relieved not to have to pretend like he was okay to his buddies.

"Tell Holt that he can't keep sneaking in the front door and stealing my chutney!" Jess called out.

Nate smiled. So Holt was still taking Jess's things

without asking. Some things never changed. Maybe he *had* missed them.

"Mom, it's not Uncle Holt," Brady called back, grinning as he grabbed Nate's hand and tugged him into the kitchen. "It's—"

The kid didn't have a moment to get the word out.

"Nate!" Jess dropped what she was doing and rushed around the counter to him. "Johnny, turn the television off."

Nate shook his head. "No, don't make a fuss. I just thought I'd take you up on that offer of dinner. If you have enough to spare, that is?"

"Enough to spare?" Jess gave him a hug, her slender arms wrapping right around him, before she pulled back and kissed his cheek. "We always have more than enough to share, especially for my favorite brother."

Nate gulped, pushing away the feeling that he should have stayed home alone. But he couldn't stay there forever, and if he was going to try to make amends, then Jess was the person he wanted to start with. She was his youngest sister, and even though she liked trying to fix other people's problems, for some reason he'd come to her instead of going up to the main house.

"So I'm your favorite brother now?" he joked.

Jess responded with a slap to his arm, followed by a tight, impromptu hug.

One step at a time, or at least that's what he was trying to keep telling himself.

"Nate."

He clasped hands with his brother-in-law, forcing a smile. Nate had nothing against the man, was pleased his sister had found happiness, and he seemed like a good guy; it was just that he wasn't ready for small talk again yet. Especially not with someone he didn't know.

"I hope you don't mind me dropping in like this?" Nate asked Johnny, releasing his palm and stepping back, shoving his hands into his pockets.

"I know all about wanting to be alone, so you can come here whenever you want," Johnny told him, slinging an arm around Jess's shoulders. "This one here might try to talk your ear off, but—"

There was a soft tap at the door followed by the creak of it opening. Before Nate could raise an eyebrow at his sister, ask who they were expecting, or even turn, he caught sight of the grimace on Jess's face.

"Are you…?" Nate didn't even get to finish his sentence.

"Sarah," Jess said with a smile, nudging him on the way past. "I was just about to tell Nate that we were expecting company for dinner, and here you are."

Nate looked at Sarah, at the frozen expression on her face, and then surveyed the room. He should have realized when he'd arrived that something was up. The table was set with pretty napkins that he was certain wouldn't be used on a nightly basis, and even Brady was dressed nice, not in clothes dirty from an afternoon playing outside.

"Nice to see you again, Nate."

Sarah's soft voice pulled him from his thoughts. He had no place being rude to her, giving her the silent treatment, so this was going to have to be his chance to redeem himself.

"You've already seen Sarah since you've been back?" Jess asked.

"I found Sarah under my tree this morning," he told his sister, still not taking his eyes from the woman standing in the entrance to the room, cake held out awkwardly in one hand, bottle of wine clutched in the other.

"Nate, please don't tell me you've forgotten your manners."

Nate laughed. Jess sounded just like their mom. Bossy but saying her words with a smile so it sounded less like an order than it was. He crossed the room and took the plate from Sarah, giving her what he hoped was a warm smile. "Sorry," he muttered.

Sarah looked up, her amber eyes lighter than he'd remembered, her cheeks pink like she was as embarrassed as he was. Nate turned before he stared at her any longer, trying to ignore the way her dark auburn curls brushed her shoulders, or the low scoop-cut of her T-shirt.

"The cake looks, ah, great."

Sarah laughed. "It should do! It's the second one I've made today."

Nate looked over his shoulder to see his sister take the bottle of wine and follow him into the kitchen. Brady was talking flat-stick to Sarah, already dragging her by the hand to the sofa.

Jess prodded him in the back.

"Ow!"

He got a soft kick to the calf in response. Clearly his sister didn't care about him being injured. "It seems a little convenient that you've only just come home and yet you managed to find Sarah sitting under your tree already. Is that why you showed up here tonight?"

Nate crossed his arms over his chest as Jess moved around to stand in front of him. "Give me a break, Jess. Maybe I should have just stayed home." He was tempted to wave them all good-night right now and leave them to their dinner, and that was before his sister had started to interrogate him.

"All I'm saying is that Sarah's been hurt enough this past year without you coming here and doing the same. Again."

Nate closed his eyes and took a deep breath. He wasn't ready for dealing with this kind of thing, not yet. He didn't have the thoughts inside his head in order, hadn't dealt with what was troubling him, so he couldn't take on anyone else's troubles.

Besides, it was she who'd been sitting under his damn tree!

"I would never hurt Sarah, you know that. And I'm not interested in her that way, not anymore."

Jess shook her head. "You've hurt her before, Nate, and anyone can see the way you two still look at each other."

She was wrong. Jess was way off the mark with that comment. "Do you want me to go?" he asked.

Jess set down the bottle of wine she was still carrying and marched him into the living room. "You're not going anywhere, Nate. It's about time you came back to your family."

Nate groaned. Maybe he should have gone up to the main house, after all. If he was going to make an effort, Holt might have been easier to spend an evening with, and his new wife would surely have been easier on him than Jess was.

Sarah was struggling to engage in conversation. Heck, she was struggling to breathe, so it was no wonder she couldn't speak! Nate was sitting quietly on the other side of the table, his eyes still stormy but without the anger she'd seen flashing there earlier.

"Sarah, would you like some more?"

She locked eyes with Jess, who was staring at her with a smile on her face. Sarah tried hard not to blush, but she'd been caught out watching Nate and now everyone was looking at her. Even little Brady had stopped his chatter.

"Maybe just a little," she murmured, focusing on spooning more of the chicken and rice dish onto her plate. "It really is great, Jess. I'll have to get the recipe from you one day."

Nate chuckled. "I think you'll find that there's not a recipe as such."

Sarah relaxed as the burning heat receded and left her cheeks at a more comfortable temperature. "Sounds like there's a story behind this dish, then?"

Nate straightened and leaned forward slightly, the first time he'd actively engaged without his sister prompting him. Everyone else was silent.

"Mom made this for us when we were young, even though she always moaned about how many chickens she needed to fill us all."

His smile made Sarah grin straight back at him. It

was so nice to see that flicker of…*Nate*. Him being like this reminded her of how he'd been years ago. Before everything had changed.

"We used to beg her for this every birthday, special occasion, you name it, even when we were growing up," Jess continued, rising and dropping a kiss to her brother's head as she passed him. "She never did have a recipe for it, because she'd tasted something similar in a Chinese restaurant and this was her trying to replicate it."

Sarah looked at Nate again. There was a frown starting to drag the corners of his mouth down, but she could see he was trying hard not to pull away from them.

"When Mom died, when I could have thought of so many things, I thought about this," Nate told them, shaking his head as he pushed his fork around his plate. "One of the first things I thought was that I'd never eat her chicken and rice again. Stupid, I know, but I was so damn hungry at the time, sick of eating crap food where I was posted, that I could almost smell the chickens roasting in her oven. Could see myself sitting in her kitchen as she cooked up a storm around me."

Sarah couldn't help it, she reached across the table for Nate's hand. He didn't resist, and she needed to touch him. Needed to comfort him when he was so clearly lost. She should have been angry with him, but right now all she could feel was his pain.

"When she confessed to not having an actual recipe, I started to watch her every time she made it," Jess said, taking over the storytelling. "I used to cook it for

Dad sometimes, to remind him of her, and now I can cook it for all of you when we need a little pick-me-up."

Sarah had no idea how she'd ended up sharing a meal with Nate after all these years, being part of his family again. She moved her hand away from his, but not before squeezing gently.

The look he gave her, the powerful way he seemed to stare straight through her, sent a soft tickle down her back, and she didn't look away.

Right now, it was like a glimpse of what could have been. *If Nate had come home, if he'd never left, they could have been sitting around this table every week. But the one thing that wouldn't change was that there'd be no little Nates sitting with them....*

Sarah glanced at the food on her plate, the extra spoonful she'd only just added, and knew she couldn't eat it. She stood to help Jess clear the table instead, needing a moment away from Nate. Away from the happy family scene that she'd been enjoying so much until her silly fantasy had taken over her thoughts.

It didn't matter that Nate was home, and there was no point even thinking about what could have been. Because the truth was he'd made the decision that he didn't want to be with her when he chose not to come home. And the perfect little family they'd often talked about when they were together? It wasn't even possible.

No matter how badly she wanted children of her own, that wasn't in her future any longer. There was nothing she could do to change that, and she sure didn't want Nate to know about it, either.

"Do you want to cut the cake or shall I?" Jess called out.

Sarah hurried into the kitchen and took a deep breath, relieved to be away from the table even for a moment, before taking the knife and starting to slice into it. "I'm fine doing this, you go and sit down," she told her friend.

She'd already eaten enough cake to make her stomach ache earlier in the day, yet her brain was trying to tell her she was ready for more comfort food already.

Sarah spun around with a plate in each hand before dropping one with a smash to the floor.

"Nate!" She'd run smack-bang into him, the plates bumping straight into his chest.

He bent to scoop up the fallen slice of cake with one hand, the other collecting what was left of the broken plate.

"I'm sorry, I…" Sarah didn't know what to say, so she put the other plate on the counter and bent down, too, picking up the smaller fragments.

Nate's hand hovered close to hers, so close she wished he'd touch her, to feel his fingers against her skin. Like a drug she'd long given up but was so overwhelmingly tempted to consume again.

"Everything okay in there?"

"Fine," Nate called back to his sister.

Only Sarah wasn't so sure things were fine. Her heart was beating hard and fast, and her stomach was flipping at a rapid rate. She held the broken pieces of plate in her hands before braving a glance at Nate, and finding him looking straight back at her. His blue eyes icy as he stared.

"Sarah." He stated her name, like he wanted to say something else but couldn't figure out what or how to go about it.

"Do you want to go for a walk?" Sarah's question came out as a whisper.

"Now?"

She nodded. Nate plopped the cake on the remainder of the plate he held and offered her his arm, careful to keep his sticky cake fingers away from her. Sarah accepted his help but didn't look him in the eye again. Didn't connect with him or touch him in any other way, because she was starting to feel so out of her depths, so weak, that she was terrified.

They both rinsed and dried their hands in silence.

"Jess, we're going for a walk," Nate told his sister, calling out but not moving. "Be back soon."

Sarah followed his lead, heading out the back door. And when his fingers brushed hers, the most gentle of touches as they walked together, hands hanging at their sides, she didn't pull away. They curled against her own, fingers so close to interlinking they were halfway to holding hands, before the moment was over and she was left with a shiver crossing her shoulders as the wind touched her bare skin instead.

CHAPTER FOUR

NATE buried his hands deep in his pockets to avoid doing anything with them he'd regret. What was he thinking, reaching out to Sarah like that? He hadn't just come home to his sweetheart and he needed to remember it. But the pull toward the woman beside him was almost impossible to ignore.

"I'm sorry if I ruined your night."

Sarah's softly spoken words made Nate stop walking. "What's that supposed to mean?"

She wrapped her arms around herself, like she was trying to shield her body from danger. "When I arrived and saw you there, I don't know…it just felt like I was intruding. And I know you haven't seen much of your family since you've been home."

Nate started to walk again. He didn't want to do this. Didn't want to talk about his feelings, or why he was so distant with his family, or how conflicted he felt being here with her right now. *Or why it somehow felt right, either.*

Because the truth was he was still angry with Sarah. Even though he knew he'd played his part in what had happened, that he'd been the one to end things, she'd taken a piece of him when she'd married Todd.

Just like Jimmy's death had taken a piece of him, and his parents' dying had smashed away another chunk that would never grow back.

He was a broken man and he knew it.

"No one seems to realize what I've been through, Sarah, and that makes it kind of hard to relax around here." Nate looked away, wondering if he shouldn't have been quite so honest. "I don't feel like I fit in anymore, that I'm part of anything that's happening here now."

Sarah didn't give him time to think about it. She was at his side, hand clasped around his wrist, tugging him around. Not letting him continue.

"How can they know anything about what you've been through if you don't explain that to them?" she asked, her voice low.

He wished he wasn't staring into her eyes, wished he could ignore what she was saying and walk away, but he couldn't.

"Sarah, I can't go there," he told her, his voice rough with the honesty of his words.

She didn't break eye contact with him. "Can't or won't, Nate?"

Nate faltered, a lump of emotion forming in his throat and threatening to choke him. "What happened over there, what I've…" He stopped talking as abruptly as he'd started. "I'm sorry."

Nate walked away, because he didn't need anyone seeing him like this, seeing the way he couldn't deal with what was going on in his own head. Didn't need to relive what had happened, not again. *He already did that every time he shut his eyes.*

"Nate." Sarah was in front of him again, blocking his path, the gentle way she said his name making him turn.

Then she did something he really hadn't seen coming. She thrust her arms around his neck, pulling him in tight for an embrace he was powerless to evade. Held him like he hadn't been held since the last time he'd seen his mom, the kind of hug that forced his body to relax and be comforted. The kind of hug that would once have made him feel loved.

"You're home, Nate," she whispered in his ear. "You're home and you need to remember that. Home is where the heart is, and that's right here on this ranch with your family."

He didn't know if it was the smell or feel of Sarah in his arms, the safeness of being cocooned by her, or just being held by another human being, but Nate was fighting a losing battle.

When she tipped back, looked up at him for the briefest of moments before pulling away, he did something he'd thought about for longer than he could remember. Something that he'd never forgotten, a memory he'd never let go.

Nate reached out to stop her, his palm tucked to the back of her head, holding her in place. *And then he kissed her.* Brought his mouth toward hers before she had a second to see it coming, to resist him, and touched his lips to hers.

Sarah sighed into his mouth, slipped her hands around his waist, pillowy lips brushing like the softest of feathers against his. Mouths grazing together in the most gentle, intimate of dances. Until she pulled back like she'd only just realized what had happened.

"This doesn't mean I forgive you," Sarah said in a low voice, slowly removing her hands from his waist and crossing her arms across her chest instead.

Nate swallowed hard and looked down at Sarah. She looked tiny yet brave at the same time, stronger than he'd probably ever given her credit for. He wished he could snatch her hands back and plant them on his hips again, but he fisted his own hands at his sides instead.

"For the record, I don't forgive you, either." And he didn't, it was true. Forgiving her or not had nothing to do with kissing her. That was something he'd *needed* to do, and it had sure taken his mind off everything else that had been troubling him.

"I think we should head back," Sarah told him, angling with her head over at Jess's house. They had walked a short distance away, but even in the pitch-black the house was clearly visible. Lights illuminating every window, glowing as if inviting them to enter.

It was the sort of homely scene that should have tugged him back into the life he'd once yearned for. The life that he'd imagined going back to once he'd served his country, before everything had changed forever.

Nate tried not to let his pain show as he walked beside Sarah. Sometimes it was the pain within him, the pressure in his head, the stabbing betrayal and loneliness that constantly hurt him, far worse than the physical pain in his leg.

"So are you here riding again tomorrow?" Nate asked

Sarah, needing to break the silence more to get away from his own thoughts than to fill the air around them with words.

Sarah smiled, shyly, and he knew she'd be blushing if only he could see her cheeks. It was dark now, but still light enough that he could make out her features.

"It's summer vacation for me, so I'll be riding as much as I can over the next month."

Nate nodded. "You love being a teacher as much as you always thought you would?" He'd always remember how much Sarah loved children, how she'd always wanted to be a teacher in their small town, taking all the younger ones under her wing. Children had always flocked to her like a honeybee to pollen.

"It can be hard work, probably harder than I ever thought it would be, but there's nothing more rewarding that I could imagine doing," she told him, walking faster than before.

Nate laughed, finally starting to relax in her company. "All you're missing are the four kids of your own, right?"

The smile fell from his face as Sarah's arms wrapped around herself again. She didn't make eye contact, acted like she hadn't even heard what he'd said, or like he'd said something he should have kept to himself.

"I'm sorry," he said, running a hand back and forth through his hair. What the hell had he been thinking, saying something like that? "Just because Todd wasn't the one doesn't mean you won't have everything you dreamed of one day, Sarah."

She faced him, stopping just ahead of him, a tight

smile greeting him as he watched her face. "Not everything turns out the way we want, Nate. We both know that."

Nate tried not to grind his teeth, tried to ignore the discomfort of what they were suddenly talking about even as it drilled through his body. *Once, there were so many things he'd have said to Sarah. So many things he would have apologized for, promises he could have made. But not now. Once, he'd have known why his words had stung her like they so obviously had, too.*

"You're right," he said, instead of any of the other thoughts going through his mind. "It was nice seeing you again, Sarah. If you wouldn't mind telling Jess for me that I've called it a night, I'd really appreciate it."

He continued to stare at her face, seeing the hurt that he was powerless to do anything about.

"Goodbye, Nate." Sarah shook her head, just the barest of motions, but she didn't turn away.

But he did. Before she told him something he didn't want to hear, or he said something he'd only regret later. Nate walked away, knowing that he needed to get back to the guesthouse, to be alone to deal with what he needed to think through.

Alone.

He repeated the word in his mind until he heard Sarah walk away, too.

Sarah fiddled with her keys. She'd been jangling them in her palm since she'd left the house, and now she was standing beside her car trying to make a decision she shouldn't even be considering.

What was it about Nate Calhoun that still made her twist up in knots like this?

Sarah sighed and decided to drive as close as she could to his place and walk the rest of the way. She had a piece of cake wrapped up that she wanted to give him, since he'd missed dessert, and for some reason she wasn't sure that he was in the right frame of mind to be left alone.

He wasn't her problem anymore, but she still wanted to help. Because she knew what it was like to be left, to deal with secrets and feel like there was no one in the world who would understand. She needed to keep swallowing her anger, wait until the right time to confront him with her pain, with her questions. *And that time wasn't now.*

Sarah parked her car less than a minute's drive away from Jess's place, and walked quickly toward the small house Nate was staying in. There was only one room illuminated in the dark, the window coverings pulled to mute the light, but still enough for her to see the way.

What would he be doing? Watching television, reading a book, staring into space?

Sarah summoned all the courage she could muster and raised her hand to knock on the door. There was no answer. She tapped again, harder this time, wishing the door wasn't made of solid timber so she could look in and see if he was there. Peer in and make sure she'd made the right decision in coming here instead of driving to the safety of home. As far away from Nate as possible.

She went to knock again before the door was flung

back, nearly sending her spiraling forward into the house.

"What do you...?" Nate's angry question trailed off when he saw her.

Sarah stared at him, unsure what to say. He'd been crying. *Nate had been crying.* The same Nate who she'd never seen cry in all the years she'd known him. His eyes were bloodshot as he swiped his face with the back of his hand, trying to remove any evidence of the tears she'd seen sticking to his skin.

"Nate, if this is a bad time..." she managed.

His dark laugh sent shivers across her skin. "It's always a bad time for me lately."

She wondered who he'd thought it was when he'd opened the door as angry as a disturbed, hibernating bear. But she knew that if he truly wanted to be left alone, if he enjoyed being locked away from the world as much as he was pretending to, then he never would have answered the door.

Sarah held out the piece of cake. "I just came past to give you this on my way home."

Nate took the dessert, raised his eyes and stood back from the door. "Good night, Sarah. Thanks."

She walked backward and jumped slightly as the door shut. *What the hell was she doing? Nate was crying and she hadn't even tried to comfort him.*

Sarah marched back up to the house with a determination she'd thought had long departed. She went to knock, changed her mind and swung the door open instead.

It was warm inside, that was the first thing she noticed when she stepped in, until...*oh, my.*

Nate's head was in his hands, his shoulders hunched, body crumpled like it was broken. Sarah took a deep breath and crossed the room, falling gently into the sofa beside him. She tucked one arm around his shoulders, hugging him tight.

"Go away, Sarah." His voice was muffled, strained, as he tried to push her away.

"I'm not leaving you, Nate," she told him, pulling him tighter.

He shook his head, face still hidden by his hands. "I don't want you to see me like this. I don't want anyone to see me like this," he mumbled.

Sarah resisted the urge to touch his hair, to run her fingers through it or trace the edge of his face and pull his hands away. Instead, she stayed still and took a deep breath.

"Nate, you can't keep doing this alone."

"After what I did to you, why do you even care?" He raised his face, straightened his shoulders and looked at her. He'd cried so much that she could see a damp line across the top of his T-shirt, his eyes still full of tears she'd interrupted, waiting to fall but instead left in residence against his dark lashes.

"Just because I care doesn't mean I have any interest in you romantically," Sarah told him, trying her hardest to keep her voice even. Technically, her response to their kiss earlier would prove her a liar, but she wasn't ever going to admit how good it had been to get up close and personal to her former flame again. "Yeah,

I'm still angry with you, Nate, but right now that's not what's important."

Nate stared at her, like he was questioning her without saying anything.

"I need you to leave."

"No," she replied defiantly.

He fell back into the sofa. "Why? Why won't you just leave me the hell alone?"

Sarah bent forward and wrapped her arms around the man she'd once thought she'd marry. "Because you're stubborn and you need a hug and someone to talk to."

Nate laughed. Despite the terror and heartache she'd seen in his eyes when she'd first walked in, and the pain she could see within him still, he laughed at her.

"Can we skip the talking and just drink coffee instead?"

Sarah let go of him and edged her bottom backward, her fingers curling against the edge of the fabric beneath her. "How about I get that coffee brewing?" she suggested.

Nate looked as unsure as she felt, although she doubted his insides were flipping as fast as hers were. Like her stomach was a pancake being turned constantly in a frying pan.

She had no idea why she was here, why she was torturing herself with Nate's company. Because they were never going to have a second chance, and she was never going to have the future she'd dreamed of, with or without him.

"Nate?" Sarah asked as she rose.

"Yeah?"

"You can still tell me to leave if you don't want me here." Sarah kept her eyes down, not looking up until his fingers hooked under her chin, forcing her to look at him. At the man she'd thought only moments earlier was broken but who now looked like life was slowly seeping back into him, his gaze brooding and fierce.

"Maybe I was wrong. Maybe you're exactly what I need right now."

Sarah jumped up, broke the contact before she had the chance to relax into his hold.

"Good, then I'll get that coffee we talked about."

Nate watched as Sarah crossed the small living area and stepped into his kitchen. *She still took his breath away.* Even a war-hardened cynic like him couldn't deny how beautiful she was. *But he needed to block out any thoughts of why he found Sarah so attractive, because that kind of thinking was going to get him nowhere fast.*

"Where's your dog tonight?" Nate had no idea why he was thinking about her animal, but he didn't want her neglecting her dog for his sake.

"In the car," she called back.

He watched her move the coffee cups closer to the fridge, before reaching in and pouring milk into each one.

"I guess you better go get him, then."

Sarah laughed at him, her entire face changing as she clearly tried to stop herself from making fun of him. "Are you sure about that? I'm not convinced you two got off to the best start this morning."

Nate glared at her, but the plain simple truth was that her being here was already helping. Had somehow pulled him clear of the darkness he'd been falling head-first into when she'd opened his door.

"How about you go get him, then? Have some bonding time together, work out your issues," she suggested, still grinning.

Nate headed for the door, wishing he could think of something to say back, a joke even, but struggling. He felt better, but still not himself, if he even knew who *he* was anymore. Sarah had just seen him at rock bottom, *or maybe not true rock bottom when he considered where he'd been these past few months, but bad enough for him to feel embarrassed about what she'd witnessed before.*

He'd never let anyone see him cry before, not like that. *Not ever.* But maybe the only way he was going to get better *was* to let someone in.

Nate kept walking, spotted her car as his eyes adjusted to the dark. But with his head full of thoughts about the woman in his house, about what he could talk to her about and what he couldn't, he didn't hear the person creeping up on him until it was too late.

The crunch of a footfall, too close for him to avoid, made his body tense. His muscles screamed, senses heightened as he switched from hunted to predator.

Nate spun in a deadly turn and grabbed his attacker, all in one swift motion. He was blinded by desperation, not prepared for the neck he clasped in one hand to feel so smooth, for the body to be so light as he swung it to the ground and landed astride his attacker.

Damn!

"Sarah, I'm sorry. Oh, my God, oh, no, Sarah…" Nate removed his hand from her neck like a snake had bitten him. *What the hell had he done?* Tear-filled eyes looked up at him, the terror on her face so obvious Nate could hardly breathe. "Sarah, Sarah…" he choked out her name.

"Nate," she whispered. "I'm sorry." It didn't sound like her voice, was so meek he wouldn't have recognized it if he hadn't been staring straight into her eyes.

"*You're* sorry?" he whispered back, forcing his legs from either side of her, before crouching and collecting her to him like she was the most precious of dolls. "I could have killed you, Sarah. I'm…" He kept all the expletives locked in his mouth.

"It's okay, Nate. I shouldn't have snuck up on you like that."

He could feel her body shaking, like a leaf trembling in the worst of a winter's storm. "Please don't tell me what I did to you just now is anything close to *okay.*" He took a deep breath, forcing himself to keep his feet planted in the soil beneath him. Nate gently, *so gently,* touched her throat with his thumb, stroking it. "How bad does it hurt?"

She wrapped her palm around the delicate skin at her neck, forcing his hand to drop away. "It'll be fine. Honestly, Nate, I'll be fine. You let go pretty quickly."

Nate was listening but he wasn't. There was no way any part of this was fine, or that she wouldn't be traumatized by what he could have, what he *had,* done to her just now. She was brave, he'd give her that, but she was also stupid not to be angry with him.

Nate turned away and took another deep breath, trying to deal with the situation as a soldier, not as a messed-up guy who'd just flattened an innocent woman. *A woman he'd once loved.* He wanted to tell her that he needed a moment, that he needed to be left alone to think, but what he needed to do was pick up the pieces of what he'd done, to make sure Sarah was as okay as she was claiming to be. *Even if all he wanted was to run.*

"Let's get your dog and then take you back inside," he suggested, trying hard to keep his voice even, to not let any of the anger surging through his body infiltrate his tone.

Sarah nodded, but she didn't move closer to him until he put his arm around her, forced himself to touch her even though he was terrified of holding her close. "I would never hurt you, Sarah. I am so, so sorry." Nate blew out a big breath.

She relaxed and let her head rest against him, like she was trying to prove that she wasn't frightened. "I only wanted to give you my keys," she said, producing them from her pocket. "I locked Moose in."

Nate took the keys from her and steered her toward the car, sucking back a breath and forcing himself to say something to ease the tension he'd caused. "I hope that dog didn't see what happened back there, otherwise he might eat me alive."

Sarah laughed, but from the nervous trill of noise she made, Nate knew she was feeling as on edge as he was. He could have seriously hurt her back then, and then what would he have done?

Because dealing with what had happened this year was enough pain and guilt to last him a lifetime.

CHAPTER FIVE

NATE was surprised that the dog had relaxed in his house, but he had no intention of letting his guard down, or making another mistake when it came to Sarah. The way he'd behaved earlier… He involuntarily shuddered. It made him sick that he was even capable of doing that.

"I think we need to move on to something stronger," he told her, holding up a bottle of whiskey he'd found in the pantry.

Sarah's eyebrows met as she gave him an uncertain look. "You want to drink?"

"The way I'm feeling right now isn't exactly lending itself to cups of tea or coffee." Nate had never been a drinker, but after everything that had happened it was exactly what he needed tonight. But the way Sarah was looking at him, like he was some sort of a wild man, was making him think he should skip the JD and just pour himself the cola.

"Just one," she said, still not looking convinced. "I have to drive so don't go making it too strong."

"On the rocks?"

She rolled her eyes and he added cola to the second glass, before putting a handful of ice in both. Clearly she wasn't any more used to drinking than she had been as a teenager.

"Nate, you're not, um, well..." Sarah took the glass he offered her and shuffled back into the sofa. It was the only place to sit aside from the small table in the corner, so he sat at the other end.

"What?" he asked.

"You're not drinking regularly, are you?" Her words came out in a jumble and her cheeks flushed red.

"I have plenty of problems right now, Sarah, but hand on my heart I've only had the odd glass of wine with dinner since I..." Now it was him faltering, his sentence trailing off instead of hers. "This is just soda." He held up his glass.

"Since when, Nate?" she asked. "You were about to say something."

He watched her hand as it cupped the glass tight, kept his gaze trained on her delicate fingers. "Since I left the recuperation facility."

If she was shocked she didn't show it. "So you weren't serving up until you arrived home."

Nate revisited his choice of drink, poured just a small nip of whiskey over some ice and slowly swallowed, grimacing as it burned a slow, steady trail down his throat. "If I tell you this, you need to promise to keep it to yourself." He wasn't even sure he wanted to tell Sarah, but it was killing him not having anyone to talk to, not being honest with anyone around him. "I haven't told my family any of this." Not that he had any intention of telling her *everything,* but even getting just part of his story off his chest would be a relief. "Except for my shrink, but given what happened earlier I think I need some more regular sessions."

Sarah's eyes were wide but he knew he could still trust her. "We spent years confiding in each other, Nate. I didn't share anything you told me then, and I have no intention of doing it now."

He refused to think about the past he'd had with Sarah. Because right now he needed a friend, and if he thought about the way things had ended, what had happened… He forcibly pushed it from his mind.

Nate crossed the room again to collect the bottle of liquor. He tipped a little more into her glass, deciding not to top up his own. But he couldn't sit down, not now, not with what he was about to tell her. Instead, he paced slowly back and forth.

"When I found out about Dad passing away I was still serving, but when the news came to me about the twin siblings we'd never known existed? I was already back in the U.S." Nate took another sip of his drink, trying to ignore the shake in his hand. He thrust the other in his pocket in case Sarah noticed it. "I'd asked my superior not to alert anyone to the fact I was back on home soil."

"Why did you want to keep that a secret? Your family would have loved having you home earlier than expected."

Nate laughed, but he could hear the cruel edge to it, was powerless to react in any other way. "Because I wasn't capable of dealing with anything then. What I've been through, Sarah…" He raked a hand through his hair, tugging at it in his frustration. "I needed time out and I didn't want anyone else to know that I was struggling or what I was struggling with. You've got to understand that I went from loving what I did to resenting it, and now I'm stuck somewhere in between."

They sat in silence, but he could tell that Sarah was thinking. She reached down to stroke her dog's head, like she was biding her time. Nate went back to sipping his soda for something to do.

"When you injured your leg, did something else happen?"

Nate tried not to react, to keep his face expressionless. *He wasn't going to tell her the truth about his injury, about what had happened that day, because talking about it would only mean reliving the experience all over again.*

"The past couple of years I've been part of Black Ops," he admitted. "I was recruited as a part of an elite squad and we had an operation go bad. After my injury, I spent a few months in a recuperation facility without my family being alerted, because I was considered *at risk.*"

He knew that Sarah would be desperate to know more, to understand more of what had happened and what he'd been through, but she nursed her drink without asking him another question.

"When you're ready to talk about it, Nate, you only have to say the word and I'll be here."

He nodded. "I appreciate that." Not that he had any desire to open up about anything else.

"So how about we make a toast to your dad?" she suggested.

"Good idea." Nate leaned forward and poured a small portion of whiskey into his glass. "To Clay Calhoun."

"To Clay," she agreed. "But, Nate?"

He raised an eyebrow in question.

"If we're going to keep drinking I might need some more cola. It's getting a little strong."

Sarah was in over her head. Way out of her depths. But she didn't know what to do.

Nate was in need of a friendly ear, some company while he was down, so she could hardly leave him. But a few more sips of alcohol and she wouldn't be able to drive home.

"What happened between us, Sarah?"

His words sounded blurry. She took another sip of her potent drink.

Did they have to be having this conversation now?

"Nate, I think we just need to let the past stay in the past. What happened to us…" She had no idea what to say to him. "It just happened, okay?" Stay down, she ordered in her mind. Now was not the time to get angry with him.

His face lost all expression as he sunk back farther into the sofa. "It didn't just happen, Sarah. I made a bad decision. *Bad decision after bad decision.*"

Sarah's pulse started to race, her heart beating faster than she was comfortable with. Since when did Nate admit to being wrong about something? But going back in time wasn't something she was convinced they needed to do, not with alcohol to fuel the situation.

"You left me when I thought we had something spe-

cial, something worth fighting for," she told him, knowing she had to at least be honest.

"And you ran straight into the arms of Todd when
we'd barely been broken up for a day," he fired back,
anger screaming from his rigid body. A vein had risen
on his forehead, one fist was clenched, and the other
hand looked in danger of crushing the glass he held.

"You know what? I'm sorry, Nate. I'm sorry for
marrying your best friend and I'm sorry for whatever
the hell happened to you these past few years." Sarah
reached for the bottle and poured herself another nip of
whiskey. "But don't forget that *you*—" she pointed at
him "—were the one who ended it. I was waiting here
and you told me it was over."

He sighed and reached forward, skimming her cheek
with his fingers before taking the bottle from her. "He
wasn't my best friend, Sarah."

She stared at him. "But—"

"You were," he interrupted. "Todd was a good friend
but you were my best friend. There was never any doubt
in my mind about that."

Tears stung Sarah's eyes; her throat was so tight she
found it hard to breathe.

"It's not your fault, Sarah, you're right. If anything,
when I left Black Ops it made me realize I'd prioritized
all the wrong things in my life. It's been one major
screw-up after another."

Sarah turned her head slightly so Nate couldn't see
her face, and brushed away the tears hugging her lashes.
"You're a highly decorated soldier, and you've just told

me you were in a special forces team. You've hardly been a screw-up, Nate."

He shook his head. "On paper, I've had it all. In reality?" He looked down into his glass. "I lost you, I lost my best friend from the army and now I've lost both my parents. Nothing has turned out like it should have."

"You lost a friend?" She'd known something had happened to him, that there was more than just an injury playing on his mind, something that ran deeper that he'd been unable to open up about before. She put down her drink, wishing she hadn't kept sipping away when it wasn't something she was used to doing.

"Yeah," he grunted. "We met the first year I served and we were recruited into Black Ops together. And now he's gone, too."

Sarah opened her mouth to ask more, but Nate's tearful shake of his head stopped her from pushing further.

"To your friend," she said, raising her glass instead.

"To fallen comrades," he agreed, holding up the bottle and taking a long sip.

Sarah did the same and then laid her head back on the sofa. The last time she'd drunk like this she'd probably been with Nate. And back then it had probably been Nate who'd convinced her it was a good idea. Just like now.

Nate opened his eyes slowly, one at a time. It seemed to help the thumping in his head.

What the hell had...oh.

There was a reason he'd woken up so comfortable,

before the sunlight had hit his vision and forced him to shut his eyes again.

Sarah lay half-curled up over him, her hair splayed out over his lower chest and part of his stomach, one arm slung across him. He tried not to smile at her faint snore.

Snore or not, though, Sarah was beautiful.

In the years he'd been away, even when he'd hated her so much for marrying Todd, when he'd known he'd never be able to forgive her, he'd always remembered her like this. And she'd hardly changed a bit in all these years. Not to look at and not to be around.

Her hair wasn't quite as long as it had been when she'd left for university, but it still had a slight curl and fell below her shoulders. Nate tried to resist touching it but he couldn't. He ran his fingers through the silky strand touching his chest, stopping himself from stroking her face. *She wasn't his anymore, and she never would be.*

Nate removed his hand and shut his eyes again, not wanting to ruin the moment but needing to keep at least an emotional distance from the woman still asleep on him.

And then he realized.

Last night had been the first night since Jimmy's death that he'd slept without waking. Without writhing, covered in sweat, reliving every moment of what had happened to him. Of what had happened to his friend, of firing over and over at the machine gun nests that had come so close to ending his life.

* * *

Jimmy looked at him. Made contact with his eyes—eyes that were so filled with pain Nate had found it hard to return the stare—before holding his gun up and starting to fire.

The silence that had engulfed them all, that had kept their presence hidden from the enemy, turned into a constant ricochet of gunfire. A noise that had filled Nate's head and made it hard for him to focus.

Until he'd realized that it was Jimmy. That it wasn't the enemy but his best friend firing like a crazy man, before turning the gun on himself.

Nate had run, had moved faster than he'd ever known he was capable of, but it was too late. Jimmy gave him one last look, before Nate could push the gun away, before he'd squeezed the trigger and taken his own life.

Nate had been hit, the bullet slamming into his leg like a blasting ball of fire, but he'd dragged his friend away. Managed to get him back to safety and fire at the enemy simultaneously, doing his best to ignore the spasms of pain.

Only it had been too late.

Was it Sarah or the booze that had given him a night's peace? Because it was always the same every time he shut his eyes, and he'd never imagined it would ever stop. Not that he'd even drunk much, except for a few good swigs from the bottle when Sarah had started to fall asleep on him.

"Nate?"

Sarah's sleepy voice pulled him from his thoughts and forced him to open his eyes again.

"Morning," he replied, watching as she fought to extract herself from him before one hand shot to her head.

"What did you do to me?" she moaned. "How did I end up…?" Sarah opened her eyes again, looking horrified. He watched as she glanced down, then at him. "Did we drink all of that?"

Nate followed her gaze. An empty bottle lay on the floor close to where her dog was still stationed. Asleep.

"I think it would be fair to say that you consumed more than me," he told her.

"This is all your fault." Sarah stretched, then slowly moved off him. "And my head is pounding."

"Ditto."

Nate laughed, then stopped himself. He'd gone one night without waking up in a sweat and now it was suddenly okay to joke around? *Not a chance.*

"Todd's coming back into town today," Sarah told him as she straightened her top and pushed at the creases in her jeans like she was nervous and didn't know what else to do, or maybe she was making sure she hadn't removed any of her clothing. "He wants to discuss some things and get me to sign the divorce papers. So he can marry his fiancée."

Nate swallowed an imaginary lump. What? "Did you just say fiancée?"

Sarah gave him a tight grin. "Yup, he's moved on pretty fast. I just wish I could shock the pants off him and make him realize that him leaving did me a favor."

His hands fisted at his sides, anger rising fast within

him. "Tell him you're marrying me, then," Nate said, wishing Todd was in front of him right now so he could show him just how pissed off he was with the way he'd treated Sarah.

Sarah let out a big hiccuping laugh. "I thought I was hungover, but I must still be drunk." She stared at him. "Oh, my God, you're serious, aren't you?"

Nate knew it was stupid, but right now in the mood he was in he'd do anything to protect Sarah. "You want to show Todd you're doing fine without him, and I want to get my family off my back. It's a win-win situation for both of us. We could just pretend for a while, watch out for each other."

Sarah had gone from confused to angry. Fast. "No, it's a stupid idea, Nate. I've already had one failed marriage, and I don't want to lie to anyone."

"Okay, stupid idea," he agreed. *What the hell had he been thinking, anyway?* The last thing he needed was to complicate things. "I'm not thinking straight, but what I do know is that I need a break from my family and I want to help you."

"Why?" Sarah asked, standing beside her dog now, even though her head must have been throbbing as hard as his was.

"Because I owe you one, Sarah. I owe you a favor for the way I hurt you, and because I need your help."

"Why can't you just be honest with your family? At least tell them what you told me?" she asked.

Nate folded his arms across his chest, as if he could squeeze the pain away by just hugging himself. "Because there's a whole lot more to my story than I'll ever be able to share with anyone, and I need some time on my own. Away from questions and too many people thinking they can save me."

"You're wrong about one thing, Nate." Sarah's voice was low.

He waited for her to tell him what she was talking about.

"You *can* be saved, and if I'm going to help you out with your family? Then I'll be making sure that *saving* you is my number one priority."

Sarah wished she knew the truth about Nate. About what had really happened that had messed him up so bad. She glanced back up at the main house again, her cheeks burning at the thought that someone might see her sneaking away from Nate's place.

"Mornin'."

Sarah squeezed her eyes shut and took a moment. Just a nanosecond to gather her thoughts. How had Johnny snuck up on her like that? And on a horse? She must have been way too deep in thought for her own good.

"It's not what it looks like," she blurted, wishing she didn't sound and feel so guilty.

"None of my business." Johnny tipped his hat, a big grin on his face. "I just thought I'd check in and see if we're still riding later?"

If it was possible to die of embarrassment, Sarah would have dropped on the spot. "Yep, sure. I'll see you later on," she mumbled, scurrying to her car.

She'd thought the whole town knowing about Todd

leaving her for another woman was embarrassing, but being spotted leaving Nate's place this early in the morning, in the same clothes she'd been wearing the night before? Hands-down worse than anything about her marriage breaking down.

Sarah opened the back door of her car, realizing how Johnny had known she was here. "Come on, Moose, up you get, bud."

The dog leaped in and she flopped down behind the steering wheel. Her head was still pounding, and her mind was a scrambled mess. On the one hand, it was nice not thinking about Todd anymore, but having her mind stuck like a broken record on Nate Calhoun wasn't exactly doing her any good, either.

CHAPTER SIX

NATE chugged back another glass of water in an attempt to leech any remaining alcohol out of his system. He wasn't convinced it was working, but he hoped a walk around the ranch would do him some good. Take his mind off the pounding ache of his mind working overtime, and give him some time to think about how the hell he'd gone from miserable and unable to talk to anyone around him, to opening up to Sarah and ending up asleep with her on his sofa.

He was still miserable. How could he not be? If it wasn't his leg giving him grief it was the memory of what he'd seen, the reality of the life he'd lived up until now.

His nostrils felt like they were burning, and his eyeballs, too. So much smoke, so many rounds fired...it was like dreaming of hell and not being able to wake. But he knew it was reality, because the screaming of his muscles from carrying the heavy frame of his friend was too real to be a nightmare.

Nate wished he could run, to see if he could somehow escape his mind when it raced off like that back into the past, but all he could do was limp. And wish to hell he'd have done something to save his friend's life before letting things go so far.

He glared down at his leg like it was to blame for what had happened. It was a constant daily reminder of what had happened, the bullet fragments that couldn't be removed stuck there forever.

What he needed was a horse to ride, and he knew exactly who to ask for one. If Johnny would lend him a mount for a couple of hours, maybe he'd stop feeling so helpless and sorry for himself. At least he could still ride—he'd figured that out when Sarah had insisted he haul himself up in the saddle the day before.

Nate walked as straight as he could down to the home field where he knew he'd find the man he was looking for, but no matter how hard he tried, he couldn't stop his fingers from finding a now-crumpled piece of paper buried deep in his pocket. A letter he'd been sent when he'd first arrived back in the States, passed to him by his superior and with him ever since.

Lucy. His friend's wife, and the woman he'd been meaning to contact ever since the full military funeral he'd attended in his best friend's honor. Then, he'd been on crutches and a complete mess, barely able to say a word let alone recount what had happened to the grieving widow. But now he knew he owed her at least a phone call, to answer her questions and tell her how sorry he was. To do his best to tell her how much she had meant to the man he'd trusted with his life on so many occasions over the past four years. How much Jimmy had meant to him, too.

Only picking up the phone wasn't going to be easy.

Because Nate knew that if he'd intervened, if he'd done what his gut had told him was right, then Jim might still be alive today. He might not be remembered as a hero, he might have serious issues to deal with and be pretty messed up, but he might be alive if Nate had spoken up and done something.

Instead, he'd lied for the man who'd been his best friend. And that lie had cost him his life.

Sarah had never been so pleased she'd worn makeup into town. She always made an effort to look nice, but today she'd worn a pink polo shirt that she'd never even taken the tags off before. Usually her riding attire consisted of a favorite T-shirt and worn jeans, but knowing there was a possibility of seeing Nate when she returned to the Calhoun ranch had made her spend longer getting ready than usual.

She stayed sitting in her car as she watched a familiar figure walk out of Nan's Bunk'n'Grill. The woman beside him wasn't so familiar, probably because she'd been shuddering with rage the one time she'd seen them together, but her husband sure was. *Soon to be ex-husband,* she corrected.

What was Todd doing back here with her? He was only supposed to be coming back to gather the remainder of his things and have a discussion with her over their settlement and divorce. There'd never been any mention of him bringing his fiancée, and he'd told her he wouldn't be arriving until late in the day and driving back the same night.

So long as he was still okay with her keeping the

house and him taking everything else, though, she wasn't going to be complaining. But both of them here? Her head was still killing her and her stomach was worse than delicate. She didn't need to be dealing with any of this right now, not when she was trying so hard to make a fresh start.

Seeing them together was only going to add to her nausea. And it wasn't because she still loved him, or that she was bitter about being lied to, because truth be told she'd known for a long time that her marriage wasn't working—that Todd wasn't right for her—but she'd been too darn loyal to make the decision to leave him when she'd thought he loved her.

She was upset because of the damn baby bump his new girlfriend was sporting. When all she'd ever wanted was a family, when she'd tried with Todd ever since their wedding night to conceive.

And now he was about to become a dad and she was never going to become a mom. Not with him, not with anyone else. Not ever.

A tap on her window sent her sky-high, fingers clasping the steering wheel as if it was going to save her from an intruder.

Sarah looked sideways and saw it was only Mrs. Sanders. An older woman she'd known since childhood, bending down and looking in at her like whatever she wanted to talk about couldn't wait a moment.

She plucked her bag from the seat, glanced at Todd walking down the road away from her and opened her door.

"Hi, Mrs. Sanders. How are you?" Sarah did her best

to sound bright and cheery. Knowing that Todd was back in town wasn't exactly helping her self-confidence— she hated the thought that people she'd known all her life could be talking about her marriage, or lack of. Or worse, pitying her.

"Well, dear, I wanted to ask you about the Fall Festival."

Sarah stifled a groan. She didn't mind a task to keep her busy, but right now she didn't want to be making small talk over the festival that she was *trying* to take a couple of days away from planning.

"I think there are a few things that didn't go as planned at the last festival, so I have a few suggestions to discuss with you," Mrs. Sanders told her, leaning in close like she was divulging a grand secret. "I'm sure you want it to be perfect, too, don't you, dear?"

Sarah did sigh this time. She couldn't help it. She definitely didn't need to be told what to do today, and she certainly didn't want to spend all morning discussing the festival or anything else for that matter. Today she just needed some time to gather her thoughts.

"Mrs. Sanders, I'm in a bit of a hurry this morning, but I'd love to hear your thoughts," Sarah answered politely. "There's a meeting at Gracie May's for everyone involved on Sunday night, so if you'd like to come along then, we can all listen to your suggestions. We're going to have supper while we run through everything."

She watched as the other woman struggled not to continue, clearly bursting at the seams to vent her thoughts. "Well, if you don't have a moment right now…"

Sarah raised her hand in a little wave. "I'll look forward to seeing you on Sunday," she said firmly as she walked away. She fought pangs of guilt gnawing in her gut. Usually she'd have stopped and given anyone her time freely, but she was starting to feel like too many people were taking her willingness to help time and again for granted.

Sarah fought not to let her shoulders slump as she searched the street with her eyes. She'd lost track of where Todd had disappeared to and she didn't want to bump into him. Not now when she wasn't prepared.

She might feel prettier than usual, but seeing Todd wasn't on her agenda.

Nate's words echoed through her mind as she walked into the store. *You can help me with my family and I can help you with Todd.*

She wasn't usually one for playing games or keeping secrets, but after seeing Todd before, it was starting to sound like an appealing option. Not Nate's ridiculous idea to say they were getting married when she wasn't even divorced yet, but maybe to something...

But could she cope with seeing more of Nate? She knew in her heart that she hadn't ever forgiven him, and maybe she never would, but with everything that was going on with her right now? Helping Nate transition back into civilian life would give her something meaningful to focus on over the summer break, and she wanted to help him so bad it was like a constant bruise to her heart. Anger aside, they'd once meant a lot to each other.

"Sarah?"

She looked up and realized she'd been in such a daydream she'd almost walked straight past her own mother.

"Mom! Just the person I need to talk to."

Her mom cringed and laughed at the friend she was talking to. "Oh, dear, that's my day gone."

Sarah took her mom's arm and propelled her to the checkout. She needed someone to talk to, and fast, and the last place she wanted to do it was standing in line at the grocery store.

"Who or what's got your knickers in a twist?"

Sarah grinned. She wondered if her mom would have used that phrase if she'd known what she was about to tell her after all she'd seen her go through in the past with the man in question.

"Nate's back in town," Sarah told her mom later over the table at dinner.

"Nate Calhoun?"

Sarah felt like a teenager talking about her first date. "No, another Nate."

Her mom raised an eyebrow at her like she didn't appreciate being made fun of. "It's nice he's back again. Is he just here for the festival? To do something for the commemoration on his father?"

She took a sip of her coffee. "It sounds like he's back for good." The thought struck terror through her body—just saying it aloud made it real. It was such a small town, and if Nate was back here to live, then she'd be seeing a lot of him, whether she wanted to or not.

"You're not thinking of—"

"No!" Her mom didn't need to finish her sentence for Sarah to know what she was about to say. She wasn't thinking about Nate like that; she would never think about rekindling what they had had...*or would she? That kiss...* She shut her mind off.

"Just remember that I was there when he left, when he promised that he was coming back for you and when he didn't. When he—"

"Forget I said anything," Sarah interrupted. "It's just that I saw him yesterday and with everything that's going on and what he's been through, it left me a little confused."

Her mom looked at her long and hard before clasping her hand and pressing a kiss to it. "You and Nate were wonderful together, sweetheart, and you know how much I loved him, but don't forget how hard you fell back then. You know I adored him, too, but you both went in such different directions and I don't want to see you hurt like that again, especially after everything you've been through lately."

Sarah moved around to the other side of the table to sit beside her mom and give her an impromptu hug. "Ah, who could forget my impending divorce." She made a face. "Maybe I should just forget men for good."

"Now Todd, he's a different story. At least Nate didn't *mean* to hurt you," her mom pointed out. "Whatever happened between you two, there was never any doubt in my mind that Nate loved you, and I know that calling things off must have hurt him more than he probably realized."

Sarah held up her hand and shook her head. "Let's

not even get started about the fact that they both left me or I might start to get a complex. And as for Nate hurting me back then? It was his decision and I still haven't forgiven him."

She hadn't missed the fact that she'd faced a whole lot of heartache in the relationship department in the past few years. So maybe even seeing Nate again as friends was taking things too far.

And that kiss... Argh. It kept popping back into her mind at the worst of times, her lips tingling as if it had just happened only a moment earlier. *Anger*. What had happened to her anger?

"Thanks for the pep talk, Mom, but I'd better go. Did I tell you that I rode Maddie for the first time yesterday?" Sarah took her chance to change the subject.

Her mom smiled. "That's exactly what you need. Out on horseback, just enjoying yourself."

Maybe she wouldn't tell her mom exactly where she'd been riding or with whom....

Nate grimaced as he swung his leg over the saddle. He was starting to get used to the ongoing pain, but sometimes when it twinged like that it still managed to take him by surprise.

"You all right?" Johnny called out.

Nate tipped his hat and nudged the horse forward with his inside leg. "Yep, thanks for the loan." He liked that his brother-in-law had left him to his own devices. Nate made a mental note to tell his sister how much he approved of her new husband.

He tried to force his heels down in the stirrups but it

hurt too bad, so he took both feet out instead and tried to relax. He was back on the land and he should, here of all places, feel at peace with his surroundings.

Nate needed to clear his head and work out what the hell he was going to do. How he was going to readjust again. Because while the rest of his family were busy thinking about the upcoming festival and moving on with the realization that they had siblings they'd grown up without knowing, that their dad had had a whole other life before he'd married their mom, Nate wasn't.

Because *his* mind was full of disturbing memories, his nostrils still filled with the acrid smell of too many guns firing at close range when he least expected it, and his leg ached every time he thought about his friend. Like it was somehow linked to his memory and what he'd lost.

Nate crossed his stirrups over the horse's wither so they wouldn't hit him in the ankles and nudged the horse into a trot and then a canter straightaway. He didn't fancy bouncing around at the trot, but he'd be darned if he couldn't still canter without stirrups and keep his balance.

He'd grown up riding horses as soon as he could walk and followed his dad around the ranch on horseback whenever he could as an older boy. So right now, the place for him to be was in the saddle. He needed to reconnect with the part of his past that didn't haunt him, remember how he used to feel at home, surrounded by his family.

Sarah had been right. Maybe not about him needing to talk, but about him riding and being out on the land again. Because he wasn't one of those guys who'd joined the army to be part of something. He'd loved it for that reason, but he'd grown up with a great family of his own, and he'd left here to make a difference, not to run away.

Sarah. Last night she'd momentarily reignited something within him that had been dead for months, but he couldn't act on it. She'd married his buddy and now she was most likely heartbroken and looking for a rebound kind of relationship.

And he wasn't about to be that guy. Because he'd loved Sarah with all his heart once before, and he had no intention of going there again. No matter how much he was craving her after kissing the hell out of those plump lips of hers the night before.

Sarah felt like her head was about to explode. Not from suffering the effects of too much wine anymore, but for how long it had taken her to get back in her car and to the Calhoun ranch. Organizing the festival was starting to become more work than she'd bargained for. Putting everything together wasn't the hard job, but dealing with so many old-timers with set views on what should and shouldn't happen was starting to wear her down. Especially when they seemed to seek her out wherever she went—another had accosted her on her way back to her car!

But now she was here she was starting to unwind again.

Every time she was in the saddle, it was as if the stress was sucked away and her mind was clear. Having her young horse started during her divorce was possibly the best thing she could have done.

Sarah gathered up her reins. "You ready to let off some steam, Maddie?" Sarah whistled out to her dog and urged her young mare forward. "Canter on!" she commanded.

She fought the urge to shut her eyes as the wind whipped at her vision. *And it wasn't just the wind.*

Seeing Todd before had brought everything back to her, made her wish so hard that it was she who was pregnant. It wasn't Todd she was grieving; it was the knowledge that she'd never be able to carry her own child, never be able to be the mom she'd dreamed of being all her life.

Her horse shied out beneath her and Sarah did her best to stay seated.

She swallowed a curse. *That was precisely why she needed to concentrate on riding and stop thinking about her problems.*

"Whoa, girl." She reached a hand down to rub Maddie's neck, letting the reins run through her fingers a little on one side. "You're okay," Sarah soothed. She coaxed Maddie on, only trotting now but trying to prove to her that there were no hidden bogey monsters in the trees they were approaching.

Only, her horse had been right. There was someone there.

Sarah sat back deeper in the saddle and pulled slightly on the reins to slow her mount to a walk. There was a horse tethered nearby, which must have been what had originally spooked Maddie, and a man asleep in the canopy of shade cast by a large tree. And from the length of the jeans-clad legs, and shape of the body attached to them, it was…damn it. It was Nate.

She could have kept riding and pretended like she'd never seen him, but she wanted to stop. They'd spent the evening before in each other's company, and she had no reason not to stop.

Other than the fact that she was hurting and had been on the brink of tears less than a minute ago, and seeing Nate again had brought back a whole heap of feelings that she wasn't keen on reexploring. Just when she thought she'd come to terms with her infertility, seeing Todd and then being around Nate had stirred it all to life again.

Sarah halted her horse and tethered her near to the other one. She seemed calm enough, no longer jumpy, so she left her and walked closer to Nate.

No matter how much she'd tried to hate Nate for leaving, for ending all the plans they'd made and dreams they'd once shared, she'd never been able to. She'd cried over him, cursed him and hated what he'd done and what had happened between them, but she'd never been able to *hate* him. Never been able to rip up the photos of them as a couple, either, or forget about what being with him had felt like. Angry, sure. But hate? *Never.*

Now he was back, nothing seemed to make sense. If Nate had never left they still wouldn't have been able to fulfill their dreams, because everything they'd planned to do one day involved a family. *Something that wasn't possible for her, no matter who she was married to.* Her doctor had made that blatantly clear.

And seeing Nate now… His legs were crossed at the ankles, sturdy boots protruding from his faded denim jeans. Nate had his cowboy hat over his face to block the sun, and her fingers itched to pull it away. So she could stare her fill, look at his full lips and strong cheekbones, drink in that chiseled jaw covered in what she imagined would be a sprinkling of stubble.

Sarah started when Nate moaned—made a series of noises that sounded more animal than human. His body started to shake, then he started to murmur, words coming from his mouth that sounded like apologies, like he was asking someone to stop, then whispering *no* over and over.

She couldn't just stand over him and watch him suffer, but she had to be careful. After his reaction yesterday when she'd walked up behind him in the dark… The memory of his hands around her throat and his heavy body pinning her to the ground made her shudder. He could have hurt her bad, but she still knew she had to do something.

Sarah slowly dropped to her knees and touched a hand to Nate's chest, over his heart. Bent to whisper to him, to coax him awake so he'd know she was there and she wouldn't give him a fright.

"No!" His scream echoed out at the same time as he sprang into action, grabbing her arms and flipping her onto her back before she had a chance to avoid him. Nate's eyes were wild, his grip tight. *Too tight.* Like he had no idea what was going on or who he was.

"Nate!" she begged. "Nate, it's me." Her voice came

out as a terrified whisper, her wrists burning as he held her down. *Please, not again.*

"Sarah?" The life came back into his eyes as he focused, his eyebrows creasing in the center, forming an arrow. "Sarah?" he asked again, like he knew who she was but couldn't figure out how they'd ended up like this or what he was doing to her, why he was holding her down.

"Nate, please," she begged, trying hard not to cry. "Let me go."

It took a moment, a slow moment as he seemed to realize what he was doing and what he had to do. When he did, his hands moved with lightning speed and he scrambled back, on his haunches, a few feet from her. The look on his face was pure terror—horrified of what he'd just done to her.

Sarah sat up, wincing as she rubbed gingerly at her wrists. Nate had hurt her this time more than she wanted to acknowledge, and from the disgusted look on his face, the last thing she needed to do was make him feel any worse than he already was. Not again. *He couldn't help what he'd done, but he'd sure scared the hell out of her.* What he needed was professional help, not her losing it over his actions.

"I'm sorry." His voice was low, almost pleading.

Sarah threw him what she hoped was a convincing smile, trying not to let him see how much it had affected her. "I shouldn't have snuck up on you like that. It was just that…"

"I was dreaming," he finished for her, looking up,

his eyes more haunted than she could ever have imagined them looking.

"Exactly," she confirmed. "So what happened just before wasn't your fault."

"It doesn't make me any less ashamed," he snapped, standing and staring off into the distance. "I could have hurt you, Sarah. Really hurt you this time." Nate shook his head. "For the second time in two days, I could have done something else I'd regret forever," he mumbled.

She shrugged even though she knew he wasn't looking. Did he mean something else when he said *forever?* "I don't believe that." Even with her wrists aching and her heart still racing, she hadn't truly feared him before. Not to the point where she didn't want to be near him because she knew he'd realize what was happening before it was too late. "You scared me, Nate, but you stopped yourself." She moved closer and reached out to touch his arm, gently trying to coax him into turning around. "That's all that matters."

"Don't try to downplay this, Sarah. I woke up and I thought you were part of my dream. I could have…" He turned back to her, shoulders slumping as anger crept back into his tone. "Damn it, Sarah, I could have snapped."

"But you didn't," she said straight back, not wanting to think what exactly he meant by *snapped.* "You didn't and I'm fine." She was the one being stubborn now.

He glared, eyes flashing. "Sarah, I don't know what you want me to tell you, or what the hell you think you're doing here, but I'm not the guy you used to know.

I'm *nothing* like him anymore, so I think you'd better go."

His anger, the hatred in his voice, made her recoil like she'd been slapped. Where had that come from? What was making him so angry, *at her?* She was the one who had a right to be angry with him, for *everything,* not the other way around.

"Nate, don't talk like that," she said, wishing she could do *something.* Anything to shoulder some of the pain he was suffering, to try to help him when he needed it most.

"You can't fix me, if that's what you think, Sarah. I'm not one of your school pupils having a bad day. A cup of hot chocolate and a cuddle isn't going to make me feel better, *so just go.*" His voice was low, rumbling with enough anger to startle her.

"No," she fired back, losing the fear that had temporarily taken over and fighting back instead. "You don't get to talk to me like that, and you don't get to act like you're a lost cause, either. You hear me, Nate? You don't have any right to be angry with *me.*"

He laughed. He actually had the nerve to laugh at her! A cruel, painful growl of a laugh as he stared her down.

Nate turned away, then whirled back around, closing the distance between them, his huge body blocking her path, looking down at her like he was about to explode. "I have nightmares every single night, Sarah. Every time I shut my eyes, I relive the horrors of what I've been through, and I thought for once that sleeping in the daytime, out in the open, I might actually be able to avoid waking up and thinking I was back in the depths of hell," he told her. "So when I tell you to leave me the hell alone, I mean it. Because no one can help me, not you and not anyone else around here. *Are we clear?*"

Sarah pressed her fingernails deep into her skin as she crossed her arms, refusing to blubber even if he did have her shaking in her boots. Literally. She'd never in her entire lifetime been spoken to like that—it was far more terrifying than what he'd done to her before. *This wasn't a man she knew, and she was starting to doubt it was a man she wanted to know, either.* Regardless of the past they'd once shared.

"The only thing we're clear on, Nate, is that you're nothing like the man I used to know." Sarah refused to break their stare, not willing to back down no matter how much she wanted to collapse into a trembling mess. "Because the Nate I knew would *never* have spoken to a woman like that, and he sure as heck wouldn't have spoken to *me* like that."

"Well, the Sarah I thought I knew would have waited more than a night after we broke up before jumping straight into bed with one of my best friends," he snarled. "So maybe we don't know each other as well as we thought."

Sarah burned with fury, her entire body alight with more emotion than she'd ever felt before. Her hand rose before she could stop it, slapping Nate with a flat palm across his cheek.

She snatched it back in a motion as fast as the act itself, horrified by what she'd done.

Nate just stared down at her, as motionless as a statue. His expression never changed, and he never said a word.

"Let's not forget that you ended our relationship, Nate. You told me it was over and I dealt with that the best I could. So don't you *ever* act like I was the one in the wrong."

Sarah turned and walked away from him. There were words she could have said, but she didn't. Because Nate wanted to be left alone, and the way she felt right now meant he'd sure made his point clear.

Tears pooled in her eyes, the second bout of tears she'd had to blink away within an hour, but Sarah never looked back. She reached her horse, mounted and rode away.

He could have called out to her, or come after her, but if he did she never heard him.

Sarah's palm still stung where she'd hit him, but she knew she deserved the pain. She hated violence, in any shape or form, and she couldn't believe she'd slapped Nate like that. Even if deep within her, she knew that he damn well deserved it.

Nate touched his cheek. He didn't care that it was on fire still from where Sarah had slugged him with her open palm, but he did care why she'd done it.

He'd behaved like a jerk. Said things that he never should have brought up, looked at her in a way that wasn't fair. Putting all his fear and anger into words that Sarah shouldn't have ever heard…but maybe she was right. The Nate Calhoun of old was gone, and right now he didn't even believe in himself enough to think that one day he might return.

Once, Sarah had been the most important person in his life. The person he'd imagined growing old with. Back then he would never have imagined speaking to any woman like that, let alone someone he cared about.

Nate roared. He roared like a wild bear with a thorn imbedded in his paw, before slamming his fist into the massive tree behind him. His hand exploded into a thick burst of pain, so intense that it sent him reeling. He collapsed onto the ground and cradled his hand, lying back with his eyes shut.

He didn't even know who he was anymore. Because the man he'd thought he was? It was as if he was gone and had lost all connection to the life he'd once led.

Nate cringed as he tried to move his fingers, forcing them to open and close.

Maybe it would be best for everyone if he just up and left. Because being back home was starting to hurt worse than being away had.

CHAPTER SEVEN

NATE glared at the computer screen but it didn't do him any good. The army physio wasn't going to go easy on him, which meant his only option to get rid of him was to shut the screen on his laptop. Given the circumstances, he doubted that would be the best option, and besides, there were other things he needed to discuss with him.

"Two more sets and we'll call it a day," the doctor told him.

Like he'd read his mind.

Nate grunted as he forced his leg up again, wishing it wasn't so hard. He was lucky to work remotely like this with anyone on his injury, he knew that, but it didn't stop him resenting the pain. Or how hard an exercise was that would have once been so simple for him to perform, and now left him sweating and cursing. The fact that his hand still hurt like hell from smashing it into a tree wasn't helping, either, although at least he could ice that for some instant relief.

A knock sounded out. Nate resisted the urge to get up and limp straight to the door.

"I'll let you off early to answer that."

"Thanks," Nate said, wiping the sweat from his face with an already damp towel. "But before I go, I wanted to ask you about talking to someone about some, er, some pretty dark night terrors I'm having. My counseling sessions have been pretty nonexistent lately."

The physio nodded. "Leave it to me, Nate. Someone will be in touch soon."

Nate felt the relief like a weight removed from his shoulders. "Thanks. Same time next week?"

"See you then. Keep up the good work."

Nate nodded and flipped the lid, ending the call. Another loud knock echoed out.

"Coming!" he called. Whoever it was they weren't the waiting type.

He didn't even consider that it could be Sarah. After the way he'd behaved yesterday? He doubted he'd be seeing her at all in the near future, if she had any control over it, and he wasn't exactly planning on seeking her out, either. Or at least not until he'd worked out an amazing apology to make up for what he'd said.

Nate pulled back the door, giving his face another wipe just in case it was…

"Holt," he said, seeing his brother standing on his doorstep.

"Hey, Nate."

There was a time when they'd never have had to knock on each other's doors, but now everything seemed strained. Completely unnatural when before everything they had done seemed like second nature, and Nate had no idea what to do about it.

"You, ah, want to come in?" Nate asked, not sure what else he was supposed to say.

"Nah, I've got a lot to do, but I promised Kathryn that I'd come over and ask you up for dinner tomorrow night." Holt stood with his hat in his hands, shifting his weight from foot to foot like he was as uncomfortable as hell. "I told her you'd probably say no, but..."

"I'll be there," Nate said, shaking off the desperate urge to tell Holt exactly what he'd expected to hear. Two family dinners within a few days would break some kind of record for him, based on the past couple of weeks.

"You will?" Holt looked up and made eye contact with him, holding his gaze steady.

Nate stared back at his brother, wishing things didn't feel like this between them. He loved Holt, wanted to spend time with him and hang out like they used to. But nothing was the same anymore—nothing felt the same no matter how hard he wished it did. What he needed was to know Holt wasn't going to ask him for details, want to hear what had happened or why he wasn't the same man who'd left Larkville.

"I need some time alone, Holt. But it doesn't mean I don't want to see you guys." A knot formed low in Nate's throat, thick like he'd never dislodge it. But he needed to *try.* "Anyone else be there?"

Holt smiled, the grin starting slow and spreading across his face. "My wife likes a crowd, but if you'd rather it just be the three of us, that's fine by me."

Nate pushed his shoulders up, then down, hoping it looked like a casual shrug even though he was shaking on the inside at the thought of another family dinner. *The last one hadn't exactly gone as planned, and he'd as good as walked out on his sister the other night, even if it had been for an entirely different reason.* He still hadn't made it over to her place to apologize, either.

"You don't want to come out and give me a hand with a rogue bull, do you?" Holt asked. "I can ask someone else but as far as I recall you were pretty good with the big fellas."

Nate laughed, taken by surprise. Holt grinned back at him, taking Nate way back in time, and it felt good.

"Let me get my boots on," he told his brother. "I was about to hit the shower but I might leave it till after."

"You might want to put some pants on, too. Those shorts make you look like a city boy."

Nate scowled back at Holt as he walked backward and flexed his muscles. "Watch it. I'll have you know I've been working out with the army doc."

Holt swallowed, hard enough for Nate to notice, and everything changed again—the easy banter ending like it had never existed. The unsaid things between them like a silent bubble that had risen to push them apart, Holt's eyes flickering back to Nate's leg, to his limp. Making it so obvious what he was thinking about.

I'm not the man I used to be. My leg will never be whole again, and neither will I.

"I'll be out in a sec," Nate said, biting his tongue against the words he was so close to snapping out, so close to telling his brother to screw the bull wrangling and spend the afternoon alone.

Holt looked uncomfortable again. "I'll wait outside."

Nate walked into his room and pulled a pair of jeans from the floor where he'd left them earlier. One minute he thought he'd made progress, that maybe there was a chance of things reverting back to almost normal again. And the next he came crashing back to reality, knowing that no matter what happened, he'd always be the outcast now.

He'd made choices that had changed his life forever, and he doubted anything would ever feel normal again, no matter what the future had in store for him. He'd loved his early years in the army, but now the one year that he'd hated seemed to tarnish everything in his life.

"You need to talk to someone, Jimmy. I can't cover for you any longer."

Jim inhaled the cigarette like his life depended on it, and Nate recoiled from the sharp aroma. "I'm fine. I just need you to get off my back and leave me the hell alone."

"If you're not focused out there, one of us could die. I need you to be all there, Jimmy, please. One last op and they might look at letting us retire early, okay? We can go home, get out of here and start over. Take a job training recruits or something. Get back to loving what we do every day."

He watched his friend shake his head, still drawing back hard on the cigarette. Nate hadn't known when Jimmy had started smoking, but now he seemed to go through packet after packet.

"You don't need to worry about me, all right? If I'm not okay I'll do something about it myself."

Nate tugged a fresh T-shirt over his head and made

for the door. It didn't matter where he was or who he was with, nothing could change what had happened to him. Because seeing Jimmy in his mind, reliving those conversations, the nightmares he had every night and the constant pain in his leg—they'd remind him of his past for the rest of his life.

He just knew it.

It was as if the bullet fragments left in his calf locked in memories that he would forever be powerless to forget.

Sarah's kitchen table was covered with papers and she had no idea where to start. Or she knew where to start, but her mind wasn't on the task.

She slumped down until her forehead met the cool of the wooden table and put her hands out palms down. *Her life was a disaster. A complete, utter disaster.* Everywhere she looked she seemed to see happy couples or pregnant women, like what she couldn't have was haunting her. Which was stupid, because she knew there were plenty of other options, even if she wanted to adopt or foster kids on her own one day.

And then there was Nate.

Argh. There had *always* been Nate, tucked away in the back of her mind if he wasn't right there at the front of it. Her marriage had ended because of plenty of things, but her not being able to fall pregnant had been a major reason. But if she was true to herself, she'd never felt for Todd what she'd felt for Nate. She'd always known it, but Todd was here and Nate had left her, and she'd tried to be a good wife to her husband, done everything within her power to make her marriage work.

But not being able to get pregnant hadn't been something she could control, and even though she'd slowly come to terms with it, her husband never had.

Her phone rang, its shrill noise making her jump and smack her knees on the table.

"Ouch!" She padded barefoot across the timber floor and reached for it. "Mom, I'm fine. Honestly," she said as she pressed the phone to her ear.

"Sarah?"

The deep, silky tone of the voice on the other end made her mouth go dry. *Walking-through-the-desert-all-day kind of dry.*

"Nate?" she asked, knowing full well that it was him on the other end. When he'd first left and she'd been under the illusion that he'd return, she'd held her breath waiting for the phone to ring. To hear that sexy-as-hell voice on the other end of the line. Now, his tone was an octave deeper, more a man now than the young guy who'd left back then. But it was undeniably *Nate*.

"Yeah, it's me," he said. She could hear the faint whisper of his breath as he paused and exhaled. She hadn't expected to hear from him at all.

"Are you okay?" she asked. Something must be wrong for him to be calling her.

"Can I come and see you, Sarah? Meet up with you somewhere?" he asked.

Sarah nodded before realizing that he couldn't see her. She didn't regret what she'd said to him yesterday, because it had been the truth, but they did need to clear the air between them properly. "Of course. Let's avoid town, though, shall we? I don't need the gossip mill firing into life over me again. Come to my place and we can have a coffee or something."

"I'll see you soon."

He hung up the phone and left Sarah with a shiver that patrolled its way up and down her spine, over and over again. She took a moment to collect her thoughts before walking calmly over to the desk and gathering up the papers she'd been shuffling.

She had plenty of time to organize the festival over the summer break, that wasn't the problem. But having Nate in her home? In the house she'd shared for so long with his friend? Now that was something she'd never be able to prepare for no matter how long she spent trying.

Maybe Nate was coming over to apologize, maybe it was something else entirely. Whatever the reason was behind his wanting to meet, though, she wanted her house to look presentable and she needed to have something to put out for him to eat.

Sarah glanced at her wristwatch. If he left the ranch soon it gave her less than fifteen or twenty minutes. Forget *the house*. If Nate was coming over, *she* wanted to look good. If her place was a little messy, then so be it.

She'd spent years wishing she could show Nate what he was missing, that she could make him remember what they'd had, to make him regret leaving her. Ending things the way they had. Because no matter how much he blamed her for becoming an item with his friend, he'd pushed her to it. If Nate hadn't left her, then she would have waited for him. *But a girl couldn't wait forever, and she hadn't.*

Nate had been the love of her life, but she'd wanted a family so badly, wanted to build a life here in the town she loved *with someone she loved.* The only problem was that she'd been missing one vital ingredient: Nate. Marrying Todd had been one of the biggest mistakes of her life.

CHAPTER EIGHT

NATE knocked at the door and stood back. He didn't really know what he was doing at Sarah's place or how he was going to apologize, but after the hour he'd spent in his brother's company he knew he had to do something.

Holt hadn't said or done anything wrong, but that was half the trouble. *It was what he wasn't saying, the questions in his gaze, the uncomfortableness between them, that was eating him up from the inside.* When all he wanted was to be around someone who treated him like there was nothing wrong.

He had no idea why, but Sarah was the only person he seemed able to tolerate right now, to be himself around, and yet he'd done a great job of trying to push her away already. When all she'd wanted to do was be there for him.

He stepped up to knock again just as the door was flung open.

"Hi!" A flushed-faced Sarah smiled at him from the doorway.

"Hey." Nate tried not to shake his head. He'd been brooding most of the afternoon and yet seeing Sarah had somehow made him want to smile again. Her hair was in a ponytail that was curling over her shoulder like she'd just been playing with it, her eyes bright even though he'd expected her to be angry. He would have forgiven her for still being wild with him.

"Come in," she told him, turning her back to lead the way. "Sorry about the mess but—"

Nate caught her wrist before she could take another step, forcing her to spin around. He kept the contact loose, his fingers curled around her soft skin, thumb stroking the base of her hand. "Sarah, I'm sorry," he said, not wanting to wait any longer when bringing up what had happened would be even more awkward. He needed to clear the air now while he still could.

Sarah didn't say anything. Her gaze was trained on his hand and Nate couldn't read her expression. Was she scared of his touch? Scared that he would physically hurt her again? *He hoped not.* And he certainly didn't want to hurt her with his words, either.

"I hope you know that I would never hurt you intentionally, Sarah." He took a deep breath, tried to find the right words, struggling to express how he was feeling. "What I said to you yesterday was rude and uncalled for, and I hate that I…"

She looked up when he stopped. "What?"

Nate squeezed her hand tight, then took a step back. "I hate that my dreams are so real, so vivid, that I don't even realize they *aren't* real. When I woke up and you were holding me, I freaked out. I thought I was back in Afghanistan, that you were the enemy, and instead all you were trying to do was help me. It's like I lose myself sometimes and it's hard coming back from that, but I am getting help for it. I promise."

Sarah's honesty was something he'd missed, something he'd craved since they'd been apart. She'd never been scared to say it like it was, to tell him when he was being an idiot or point him in the right direction. And he could tell that was exactly what she was about to do now.

"Nate, what you said before was the truth. I *did* take up with your friend, and it might have seemed fast to you because you were away, but I'd been on my own for almost two years. *Two years of not being with you.* So when we ended our relationship it was different for me than it was for you. It felt like it had been over for a long time when we finally called things off, and I was just so angry with you."

Nate swallowed. It was the truth, but it didn't make it any easier to hear. "Let's not go there," he suggested, hoping she'd agree. "Let our past stay in the past."

Sarah's smile was bittersweet. "I was hoping the same thing, but you brought it up, Nate." She raised her shoulders in a modest shrug. "Now we've started I think we have to clear the air."

She was right. "Bourbon again?" he asked.

Sarah laughed, the moment of humor making her entire face ignite into a burst of happiness. "After the headache I woke up with? I think we'd best stick to coffee. And while we're apologizing, I'm sorry, too, Nate. I never should have slapped you."

"Forgiven," he told her. "And I probably deserved it, anyway."

Nate followed her into the kitchen and sat in the chair closest to the counter. He watched as Sarah moved gracefully to the refrigerator and back again, before pulling down two cups for their coffee.

"What?"

Nate stopped thrumming his fingers on the counter. He hadn't even realized he'd been doing it until Sarah had spoken. "Huh?"

"What's wrong? You're staring at me and playing my counter like it's an instrument."

He grimaced. "Old habit. Sorry."

Sarah set his cup in front of him and moved around to the other side of the table. She sat down, fingers dancing around the handle of her own cup before letting out a big sigh. "Nate, what are we even doing here?"

"You mean right now?" he asked, not sure where she was going with her sudden line of questioning.

"I mean now, today, yesterday." Sarah shook her head and blew on her coffee to cool it before looking up at him again. "Why are we even putting ourselves through this?"

He wished he knew. "I don't know, Sarah, but what I do know is that it's been nice seeing you again. Not that you'd know it, from the way I've been acting, but you're the first person I've seen in a long while who's…"

She held her cup dead still, midair, and stared at him. "Who's what?"

Nate swallowed a hot swig of coffee, grimacing as it burned his mouth and throat. "You've made me feel something again, Sarah, and I haven't experienced that in a long while." There, he'd said it. "Even if we get angry at each other, at least I was feeling *something*."

Sarah slowly put down her coffee. "I don't understand."

He didn't know how else he could explain it. "I'm not into talking about my feelings, Sarah, you know that."

She looked down. Nate could see the disappointment all over her face.

He shook his head. *What the hell was he even trying to achieve talking to her about all this?*

"I've been angry, happy, sad—all those things since I saw you the other day, and nothing has even made me *feel* in such a long time. I just want you to know that somehow you've helped me. That's all."

She met his gaze, a shy smile back in residence on her face. "I saw Todd yesterday."

"He's here?"

"Yup. With his pregnant girlfriend, too. We were supposed to meet yesterday evening but he's put it off until tomorrow. Thankfully he left a voice mail for me, so I didn't actually have to speak to him."

Now Nate was angry. *Real angry.* It wasn't his place, but… "Do you want me to teach him a lesson?" Just thinking about him breaking Sarah's heart was enough to fill him with rage. His hands balled into fists beneath the table, just like they had the other night when they'd spoken about his former friend. But showing his face around here with his girlfriend?

"No," Sarah told him, her eyes never leaving his. "I hate that I'm about to become a divorcée, but the truth is that I wasn't in love with Todd—I hadn't been in a long time. I was ready for a fresh start, so him leaving wasn't the worst thing that could have happened. It was how it happened that stung."

Nate's pulse started to race. He shouldn't care, but hearing Sarah say that, telling him that she wasn't in love with her husband, was seriously affecting him. "So you're okay with seeing him back here?"

Sarah started playing with her ponytail, a sure sign that she either wasn't telling the truth or that she was struggling with…something that he couldn't figure out yet.

"It's not him, it's…" Her voice trailed off.

"What?" he asked.

Sarah sat back and started sipping at her coffee. "Nothing, forget I even said anything."

Nate was curious, but he wasn't going to pry. "You sure you don't want me to rough him up a little? Scare him perhaps?"

Sarah rolled her eyes. "Yeah, I want you to beat the guy up and end up in jail for assault. That would *really* help me out."

He held up his hands, pleased that they were at least having a civil conversation. After the way things had gone the day before, he'd have understood if she didn't speak to him at all, let alone sit in her kitchen joking around.

They sat in silence, both sipping their coffee. It didn't seem to matter that they weren't talking because it didn't feel strained, but he'd come here to ask for more than just her forgiveness.

"Sarah, when I told you that I'd help you out with

Todd, if you needed me to pretend that we were something more, I wasn't joking."

Her cheeks flushed, stained such a pretty pink that he had to look away. He hadn't meant to embarrass her.

"You don't need to do that," she told him, looking out the window like there was something she was interested in outside.

"Sarah?" Nate resisted the urge to reach for her hand, but he at least got her attention enough to make her turn back. "The reason I'm offering is because I need your help, too."

That made her turn her body back toward him. "With what?"

Nate took a big breath, hoping he'd know how to ask her in the right way. "I agreed on a full family dinner tonight, and the last one didn't exactly go well on my first night back," he admitted. "I was hoping that you'd come with me, just so, you know."

Sarah looked confused, but she collected their empty cups from the table and walked them into the kitchen instead of staying seated across from him. "Are you saying that you want us to pretend to be back together again, for real?"

Nate cringed. When she said it like that it didn't sound so great. "It would help me out if the heat was taken off me a bit, that's all. And I don't want to lie to anyone—I just want to take you with me. It'll be kind of like the other night, but with a few more Calhouns and me on better behavior."

She laughed as she put the cups into the dishwasher.

"It sounds to me like this would put a *heap* of heat on you."

Maybe, but… "It would take the heat off them asking about what happened to me before I came home, and about my leg and…" He paused. "I wouldn't be asking you if it didn't mean a lot to me. You don't owe me anything, Sarah, but I'd really appreciate if you would come."

Sarah stopped moving then and stared at him, long and hard. "If I say yes, you'll have to agree to my terms, too."

Right now he would agree to anything if it meant her coming with him to dinner. "Shoot."

"I want you to promise that you'll tell *me* about what happened before you came home, when you're ready."

Nate shut his eyes, pushing the inferno of memories away, the ball of fire that was so hard to shut out. "That's not something I can promise," he told her, forcing his eyes to remain open, to ignore the thoughts starting to circle his mind like vultures.

"Well, you're going to have to if you want my help," she insisted, all businesslike, as if they'd been bartering nothing more than goods.

Nate stared at her, long and hard. Why did she want to know so bad?

Sarah smiled. "On second thought, perhaps you were right about Todd. If I'm going to help you out, then maybe I should take you with me when we meet tomorrow."

Sarah watched Nate and hoped she hadn't pushed him too far insisting that he talk to her about his injury, but she knew that if she didn't no one else would. His family had clearly gone about it in the wrong way, and she had no intention of making the same mistake twice where Nate was concerned.

She'd tried being passive, but he wanted her to do something for him and she had to use that leverage if she had a hope of actually helping him.

"Yes to the second condition."

Sarah took a step closer, planting both hands on the counter and leaning toward him. "Yes to both," she insisted. "This isn't a negotiation here, Nate, it's all or nothing."

Nate scowled at her. "You must drive the kids in your classroom mad."

She shook her head. "I want to be there for you, Nate, and I'm not going to force you, so at least say that you'll try to tell me about what happened. What you can, when you can."

He stood, his large frame seeming massive in her kitchen. The table was like a child's version with him standing beside it, his height and breadth making her want to back down. *Fast.*

"Fine," he snapped. "But if I do deck your idiot husband when I see him, you'll only have yourself to blame for making me so angry."

Sarah touched her hand to his arm as she walked past him again. She knew it must be hard for him to think about Todd, doubted they'd ever spoken again since she'd started a relationship with him.

"Do you wonder how things would have turned out, if I hadn't left?"

Nate's husky-voiced question took her by surprise. She spun around, slowly, wishing she was in the middle of doing something so she didn't have to stand so close to him and look into his eyes when she answered.

"Often." She didn't know what else to tell him. Did he want to know how much she'd craved him? How many times she'd wished the man lying in her bed beside her had been him? How badly she'd hoped he would change his mind and come back for her?

"Do you think we'd have lasted? That we'd be married with a brood of kids?" Nate asked.

Sarah stared into his eyes. Into eyes that still seemed to have a pathway straight to her heart, that made her want to throw her arms around him and whisper in his ear that everything would be okay. That they could go back in time and change what had happened.

But it wouldn't have mattered if Nate had stayed or not, because they would never have had the family they'd often talked about, that he'd wanted.

"I don't know, Nate, maybe," she lied. "But let's not dwell on what could have been. It's not like you're never going to have the chance to marry a nice girl and have a family one day."

He chuckled. "You say it like it's a possibility for me and not for you."

Sarah did her best to keep the smile plastered on her face, to not let it waver. "I don't think that's what I want anymore, Nate," she lied.

She wasn't fooling him. "You were made to be a mom, we both know that."

Sarah bit her bottom lip to stop it from quivering,

dug her nails into her palm. *This was not a conversation she was ready to have with anyone, let alone Nate Calhoun, the man she'd always dreamed of starting a family with.*

"Things change, Nate," she told him, willing her voice not to crack. "Sometimes we don't get what we want."

He stared at her, his eyes narrowing. He didn't believe her any more than she believed herself.

"So dinner tonight, right?" she asked, doing her best impression of happy, as if his line of questioning hadn't bothered her at all.

Nate cleared his throat. "Yeah." He gave her another long, hard look before shaking his head slightly, like he was accepting that their conversation was at a close. "Want me to swing by and pick you up?"

She shook her head. "You don't need to come all the way out here to get me. How about we meet at your place?"

Nate brushed past her as he made for the door, and she had to stop herself from reaching out and pulling him back. Part of her was so desperate to go back in time, to rekindle something with Nate, but the realist part of her knew it would be a mistake.

He was a different man now, but he still deserved to be a dad. Even if they miraculously *could* rekindle what they'd had, it wouldn't work long term, and she couldn't bear her heart to be broken again. She'd already taken about all the heartache she could handle for a lifetime, and having to tell Nate that she was incapable of having a child, of their relationship slowly breaking down like her marriage had, wasn't something she could ever prepare herself for. Just because she was at peace with her infertility didn't mean he should have to be.

"I'll see you tonight, then," she said, leaning against the doorframe as he walked out onto her porch.

Nate turned, landing less than a foot or two away from her. She had to tilt her head back slightly to look up at him, to see his face, to watch the changing expressions there. He bent, so close, and Sarah shut her eyes. Lost herself in the faint scent of his cologne, of the feel of his body so near to hers.

Nate placed a featherlight kiss to her cheek, his lips hovering for longer than necessary, enough time for a shiver to trawl its way deliciously up and down her back, goose bumps tickling her skin.

"See you later," he said, voice low as he stepped away.

Sarah smiled, wrapping her arms around herself to stave away an imaginary coolness that was making her shiver. "Bye."

She watched as Nate walked through her front gate and around to the driver's side of his 4x4. His side profile was strong and masculine, his frame easily filling one side of the cab. He was so messed up from whatever had happened to him, far from the guy she'd known, but then he went and did something like that and made her realize that the Nate she'd once loved was still hiding in there. *Somewhere.*

Sarah smiled as he waved, hoping that he wouldn't notice the tears silently running down her face. She was powerless to stop them, unable to swallow away the emotion building with fury within her.

What had she done to deserve so much pain? Why had the man she loved so much left her, and then come home so damaged? Why was he finally home, finally within reach after so many years, and yet still so far away?

She shut the door, kicked off her shoes and made her way to the bathroom. Just because she was feeling sorry for herself didn't mean she wasn't going to look good. Being by Nate's side again, around his family, might be bittersweet but it wasn't exactly going to be difficult. She'd spent years around the table in the big ranch house, been part of their family on more occasions than she could ever count.

She'd loved Nate with all her heart once, and if she was honest with herself she doubted she'd ever stopped.

CHAPTER NINE

NATE was exhausted. Bone-achingly, mind-shatteringly exhausted. He let his head drop into his hands, fighting the fatigue that he battled on a daily basis. Why wouldn't his mind just shut off? He couldn't stop thinking about Sarah wanting him to talk, but if it was this bad inside of his own head, how would he ever cope with telling the truth? With speaking it out loud?

He ran his hands through his hair—hair that was still shorter than he'd once worn it. Back when he'd lived on the ranch, before he'd joined the army, his brother had always made fun of him, called him Goldilocks. *It seemed like a lifetime ago.*

A knock made him rise, shaking him back into action. *If only he could sleep, could actually fall into a deep slumber for an entire night and not be thrown back into the world he was trying so desperately to escape from, maybe he wouldn't feel like such a zombie.*

Right now, though, he had to pull himself together and deal with seeing all his family again for dinner, and figure out what the hell was eating Sarah up so bad. It was more than just Todd, he could sense it. Her idiot husband had sure caused her some definite heartache, but she was upset over something deeper than just her marriage failing.

Wow.

"You look amazing." Nate didn't even try to disguise it as he looked Sarah up, then down. She was more beautiful now than the day he'd first met her—there was a maturity to her face, to the way she held herself, that made her even more striking.

"You don't look so bad yourself," she said to him. Nate could see the blush creeping over her cheeks, though, knew that she was struggling with his compliment.

"I don't really think my jeans and shirt put me in the same league as you, but thanks."

She was wearing a dress, cut low enough on her chest to make his mind race in a different direction, but brushing the tops of her knees to make it more demure than he'd have preferred. Still, he more than liked it.

"Is it too much?" Sarah asked, her eyes flashing with what he guessed was concern.

Nate chuckled, forcing himself to look off into the distance for a split second, to stop thinking about how enticing the woman standing at his door was. *How jaw-droppingly beautiful Sarah was.* "Sarah, you look great. Maybe it's just because I've been around men for so long, but I'd forgotten how…" He paused, not wanting to embarrass her or say the wrong thing. "You're beautiful, Sarah, absolutely beautiful."

She stared at him before punching his shoulder softly. "Nate," she groaned.

He grabbed her hand before she could withdraw it,

his reflexes fast. His fingers curled tight around her wrist, holding it against him, her knuckles still brushing his right shoulder.

Nate knew he shouldn't have done it, that he should have just laughed and let her hit him, let her treat him like a brother or friend with her play punch, but damn it, he had no interest in being a friend to her.

Right now, he wanted more. A lot more.

"Nate?" Her voice was a low whisper, but she didn't move. Didn't struggle or try to pull her hand from his viselike grip.

He didn't know what to say to her, but he knew what he wanted to do.

Nate tugged her in closer, not letting go of her, forcing Sarah to pull up against his chest. She didn't resist, but he could tell she wasn't sure, either. Wasn't sure what he was about to do, and he had no intention of keeping her guessing.

Nate slowly moved her hand down, away from his shoulder, running his other arm up her body, caressing the small of her back with his fingers. She was a perfect fit against him, her shallow breathing only spurring him on.

He bent, inch by inch, until her chin tilted. Until her lips parted, inviting him, and he didn't hesitate.

Nate crushed her mouth to his, no longer gentle, needing to have Sarah against him, needing to feel her body tight to his. He fought against the urge to fist his hand in her hair, forcing himself to cup the back of her skull instead, to kiss her like he'd imagined kissing her all those lonely nights when he'd been on his own on the other side of the world. When he'd wished he'd been selfish enough to ask her to wait for him, so he could forge on with his career and know the woman he loved was still waiting for him back home. But asking her to keep waiting for years wouldn't have been fair, and he'd loved her enough to want to set her free.

Sarah's low moan brought him back to reality, made him pull his lips away from her, to take a breath and think about what he'd just done.

But Sarah had other ideas.

Nate found himself staggering backward as Sarah placed a hand flat to his chest, pushing him backward with a force he hadn't even imagined she possessed. Pain flashed through his leg as he took one more step, before finding his back pressed hard to a wall.

Sarah's hand was still holding him in place, but she never said anything. Instead, she reached up fast, her fingers twisting into his short hair, tugging him down, forcing his mouth to hers again.

And he had no reason to resist.

Sarah kissed him with a desperation that empowered him, that made him kiss her back with the same sense of recklessness, like they needed each other because their lives depended on it.

Until she removed her lips from his as suddenly as she'd kissed him, taking a step away and letting her hand trail away from him.

"Sarah?" His voice didn't even sound like his own, was deeper and confused.

She smiled and blushed beet-red. "I just need a minute to freshen up."

Then she walked away.

Nate laughed. He laughed like he hadn't laughed since he was a kid, tears falling down his cheeks as he stood alone, waiting for Sarah, wondering if he'd just imagined the fact that he'd been pressed against a wall in his own home and kissed in a way that had him desperate to call off dinner and take up where they'd finished off.

He had no idea where that kiss had come from, but he sure as hell wasn't complaining.

Sarah knew she was still blushing. Her embarrassment ran so deep that she was hot all over, and she could hardly bring herself to look at Nate. When she emerged from his bathroom, lipstick firmly back in place, they'd started walking up to the main house, but they hadn't said a word.

"Sarah, um…"

Until now.

"Please, Nate," she insisted, cringing inwardly as she kept her gaze trained ahead. "I don't know what happened before, so I think we should just forget about it." She was starting to wish a hole would open up and swallow her.

He chuckled. Nate was making fun of her! Right now she'd prefer quiet and brooding.

"It's kind of imprinted into my brain," he admitted.

When she didn't so much as look at him he caught her hand, swinging her around and forcing her to stop. "Sarah, it's not like we've never made out before."

She nodded, squirming on the stop as he watched her. *Not like that.*

"Sarah?"

Since when was he the chatty one? "I don't know what happened back there, Nate, but can we please not talk about it?"

He let go of her and raised both hands. "Fine by me. I'm just saying that we shouldn't be all weird about—" he paused "—kissing."

Sarah groaned and started walking again. This was going to be an uncomfortable night, and not because she regretted what had happened between them. Kissing Nate had opened her eyes, made her realize what she'd been missing out on all these years, shown her why she and Todd had never been right for each other. Because Nate's lips against hers had made her body tingle like a fire had been stirred to life in her belly, made her remember what it had been like when they were together.

But it had also shown her what she would never have.

Nate took Sarah's hand as they walked in the door. He'd hesitated, about to knock, then realized that it was about time he started acting like he was home rather than a stranger on the ranch.

"You did tell them I was coming, right?" Sarah asked him as she gripped his hand.

Nate quickened his pace to get inside, so she wouldn't be able to explode once he told her the truth. "Not exactly. I figured surprising everyone would provide a good diversion."

"By letting me take all the heat?" she murmured.

Nate tugged her into the kitchen, and almost instantly wished he hadn't.

Four faces turned their way, and they each held a different expression. Johnny smiled, like he didn't realize what the big deal was. Jess shook her head slightly and grinned, like she knew something that no one else in the room did. Kathryn was shocked enough to see him hand in hand with Sarah that she stopped whatever she'd been doing at the counter, and Holt… Nate could have laughed at the expression on his brother's face. When they'd been kids, he'd never been able to surprise his brother or do anything to shock him, anything that Holt hadn't already done. But tonight? Holt was still holding his beer in the air like his arm had frozen before he'd been able to bring it to his lips.

Maybe holding Sarah's hand had been too much. Arriving with a date might have been shock value enough.

"I hope we're not late," Nate said, unsure what else to say to announce their presence, to put an end to the empty silence in the room.

No one said anything for a moment and Nate felt Sarah's hand slide away from his. *Damn.* He'd definitely gone about this in the wrong way.

"Nate, I'm so happy you decided to join us," Kathryn said, breaking the silence and giving her husband a noticeable kick on her way toward him. The imaginary weight dragging Nate's shoulders down was lifted as his brother ignored her and took a swig of beer instead. Kathryn reached them and leaned forward to kiss his cheek before touching Sarah's shoulder. "You, too, Sarah. So long as no one wakes Izzy up, I'm sure we'll have a relaxing evening."

He watched Sarah nod, but she was flustered. "I was just telling Nate off for not warning you he was bringing someone."

Kathryn shrugged like they hadn't all received the shock of their lives when he'd arrived with a woman. "Don't be silly. We have plenty of food and a massive table. And besides, we're just pleased to have everyone together, right? The baby is down, the food's almost ready, and the company's great."

Kathryn turned to look at Holt, who seemed to realize he was expected to do or say something. "Yeah, it's, ah, good to see you both."

"Sarah, that horse of yours is looking good. I did some more work with her today," Johnny called out.

He watched as Sarah seemed to relax, leaving his side to head toward Johnny and Jess. Nate looked away from her to see his brother watching him, like he didn't know what to say.

"Beer?" Holt asked.

Exactly what they needed to settle things between them, shooting the breeze over a beer. "Sounds good."

He made his way over to where his brother had been seated and took the beer he offered when he returned. "Thanks for asking me over," Nate told him, knowing he was going to have to make an effort.

"Glad you could make it."

Nate didn't want to talk about Sarah after the conversation he'd had with Holt that first day he'd seen her again, but he knew he had to say something. "I should have called ahead and mentioned I was bringing someone."

Holt laughed. "I don't know if I'd call Sarah just *someone*."

Nate took another sip of beer, not sure what to say. It had been a long time since he'd just chatted like this and it was no longer something that came easy to him, especially with his brother. "It's been nice seeing her again." And he had to learn to open up, at least a little.

"You two were always good together. Made some of us wonder why you'd up and leave...."

"Don't go there." Nate hated the bite to his words but it was a knee-jerk reaction—he couldn't help it. "There are plenty of things I wish I hadn't done, Holt, and leaving here like that is one of them. I didn't exactly manage to achieve the right balance."

They sat in silence, staring at each other. Nate stood. "Maybe this wasn't such a good idea."

Holt stood, too, but he didn't look angry. He held out a hand instead, and when Nate didn't clasp it he grabbed hold of his upper arm, looked him straight in the eye. "Nate, I know I seem to keep saying the wrong thing, but don't walk away from us."

Nate stayed still, eye to eye with his brother. He knew the rest of the room had gone silent and he wished they were having this conversation in private. "There are things I can't talk about, Holt, and I need you to respect that." He was trying to stay calm but it didn't come naturally to him anymore.

Holt nodded and let go of his arm. "I don't want to be the enemy here, Nate. The truth is we're all pleased to have you back, even if things are a bit rough at the moment."

Nate shut his eyes, forced his anger away and held out his hand to Holt. His brother clasped it straight-away, holding on tight as they kept the grip for longer than they should have.

"You need to understand that I need time, Holt. I'm not, things aren't…nothing's the same for me right now."

Holt let go of him and sat back down. Nate did the same.

"Whatever you need, Nate, I'm here for you. Don't you forget it."

A hand on his shoulder made Nate jump, but he willed himself not to overreact. He was in his broth-er's home, not on some foreign battlefield. The conver-sation he'd had with the army counselor played back through his mind, the sense of calm he'd felt after talk-ing to him on the phone earlier in the day.

"Hey." Sarah's warm, soft voice made him relax.

Nate touched her hand, let his fingers settle over her skin. *He was glad she was here, that he had her with him tonight.*

"You want to sit down?" Nate wished he could go back in time, was still close enough to Sarah that he could pull her around and down onto his knee. That she would happily sit on his lap and lean back into him.

More thoughts, more feelings, that he needed to sup-press.

Sarah touched the back of his neck before walking off toward Kathryn. "I'm good," she said, but the look she gave him told him something else entirely. *She was nervous and he'd done little to help her fit back into his family's fold.* Everyone had always loved Sarah, but she was here for him and that meant he needed to make an effort where she was concerned, too. *It wasn't all about him and he needed to remember it.*

Nate watched as Jess followed close behind Sarah. Johnny was hanging out with Brady in the adjoining room.

"I think I'll join the girls for a drink," Nate said, suddenly not able to take his eyes off Sarah, the one person in the world he'd come close to opening up to, and who he'd treated like crap these past few days. And yet she was still there for him, pretending their relationship was something more just to help him out.

Well, maybe they shouldn't be pretending.

"After you." Holt gave Nate a wink, like he'd known what he was thinking, or at least that he knew he'd been thinking about Sarah.

Sarah looked up, too, like *she* knew he was thinking about her, as well, but instead of the knowing look his brother had given him, Sarah's was shy. *Did she want this to be real, too, or was she just really good at make-believe?*

There was only one way to find out, and Nate wasn't going to waste time figuring that out. He spent enough time already inside his own head, thinking about things that he couldn't control, that he couldn't go back in time and fix, but this was different. *This he could do something about.*

* * *

Sarah tried to focus on what Kathryn was saying to her, but she was having a hard time remembering what their conversation was even about. When she'd looked at Nate before, she'd been worried he was about to walk out and that things were about to become difficult, but now it was him watching her and she couldn't ignore it.

She looked across at him. Now he wasn't just looking at her, he was headed in her direction.

"Hey," he said, snaking his arm around her waist. "You okay?"

Sarah tried not to tense up but it didn't come naturally. Having Nate so close, his body so warm and… She took a slow, deep breath. "I'm good. Thanks." *Was he playing pretend still or was something else going on?* Regardless of what was going on between *them,* he looked happier than she'd seen him since he'd been back. More relaxed, and clearly getting on better with his family.

She glanced sideways at him, tried to ignore his arm still around her waist, loosely tucked behind her back like it belonged there. Part of her wanted to snuggle closer, but the other part of her, the sensible side that remembered how much it had hurt when he'd left her, told her to steer clear. Friendship, sure, but nothing more.

No matter how good his kisses were.

"Do you need a hand there, Kathryn?" she asked.

"Sure. How about you carry this to the table for me?" the other woman suggested. Sarah nodded and sidestepped away from Nate. She took the large serving dish and crossed the room, placing it on the middle of the table.

"Oh."

"I didn't mean to scare you."

Nate was standing behind her when she spun around.

"Is something wrong?" she asked, struggling to meet his gaze. Something had changed, something that she couldn't quite figure out.

"I just wanted to say thank-you for coming with me tonight. If you hadn't agreed to join me, I don't know if I'd have come at all, and you were right."

She tilted her head slightly, looking up at him. She forgot sometimes how tall Nate was. "About what?" she asked.

He held out a hand and she looked at it, paused before tucking her palm against his. There was something unnatural about touching him, about pretending, but there was also something comforting, too.

"You said I needed to give my family a chance, and you were right. It was never going to be easy, on them or me, but I need to try. Otherwise where am I ever going to belong?" Nate clasped her hand more tightly and used their interlocked fingers to draw her closer. His other hand rose to her face, cupping her cheek.

Sarah resisted the urge to close her eyes and lean into his touch. She couldn't go there. Anything that happened with Nate couldn't be permanent, couldn't be what they'd both once wanted, but would it be so bad to give in to her feelings *just for now?* "Nate, this doesn't feel like pretending anymore," she whispered.

His grin was lopsided when he smiled at her, his head moving slowly from side to side. "Maybe we're not."

Sarah took a quick step back when a throat was cleared, loudly, behind Nate.

"Sorry to interrupt but…" The sound of Holt's voice made her groan, but Nate didn't let go of her hand, not until she looked up at him, until their eyes met one last time.

"Of course," she said, in the bravest voice she could manage. "Dinner smells delicious."

Sarah kept her head down as she walked around to the other side of the table, hoping that Nate wouldn't follow her. Everyone sat down and Brady took the heat off her and Nate with his chatter as he play-fought with Holt for the head-of-the-table seat.

But the heat never left Nate's gaze—she could sense him even without looking at him. Something had changed, *the game had a whole new set of rules that she didn't know about,* and the thought terrified her.

"Sarah, how's the festival coming along?" Kathryn asked as she took her seat.

"Are you offering to help?" Sarah quipped, pleased to have something to focus on other than Nate, even if it was just for a moment.

Everyone laughed, leaving Kathryn looking slightly bewildered.

"It's okay," Sarah told her. "They're just thinking about how much they *all* want to help me, right?" She made the mistake of looking at Nate then, while everyone else erupted into chatter about the festival. His smile spread slowly across his face as she watched him, his eyes finally sparkling like she'd remembered, the way they'd looked at her for so many years when they'd been in love.

"Thank you," he mouthed, gesturing with his head toward his brother and sister.

It *was* nice, being around the Calhoun family, being seated at a table and surrounded by happy people who loved one another. She'd be a liar if she didn't admit to still loving this family, and Nate, too, but it only made her fate more bittersweet. Her own table would never be surrounded by a brood of their children and their partners, if they did let something happen between them again. Because she might have come to terms with not being a biological parent one day, but it didn't mean Nate should have to make that compromise.

And there was nothing she could do about it. Not a thing.

Nate slapped his brother on the back, dropping a kiss to his sister's head as he passed, and to Kathryn's cheek, too.

"Thanks for having us," he said, taking Sarah's hand and leading her out onto the porch.

"It was lovely, thanks," Sarah called out, holding up her hand in a wave as they walked away.

"Nice to see you two lovebirds." Holt's laughter rang out behind them as they walked.

Nate shook his head and slung his arm around Sarah's shoulders, giving her a squeeze. "Kind of weird stepping back in time like that."

She sighed. "You can say that again."

They kept walking in the dark, side by side but not saying anything.

"Sarah, what I said before about not pretending…"

She stopped and looked up at him. "What are we doing, Nate?"

It was him sighing now, putting both his arms around Sarah's waist. "I don't know if I can answer that, but you know what?" He looked up at the sky, then back down at her. "All I know is that being back home was hard, *really hard,* until I saw you again. And somehow you've helped me to pull everything together."

She stepped toward him and placed her cheek against his chest, arms looped around his waist. "We can't just go back in time, Nate. Things have changed, *I've changed,* and you have a heap of stuff to work through."

Nate turned her in his arms so her back was pressed to his chest instead, tilted her back slightly to point up at the sky. "You see those stars up there?"

She nodded against him.

"I don't know anything about the constellations, but what I do know is that for years I stared up at the stars in whatever hellhole I was posted to, and I thought of you. You were always with me, even when I was so pissed with you for taking up with Todd, even though I knew deep down that I didn't have a right to be."

She stayed silent, warm against him, and he wrapped his arms around her tight.

"There's so much we need to say, so many things that we need to talk about, Nate."

He let her go when she pulled away, but she didn't go far.

"Like what?" Was there something going on with her that she needed to tell him? "What's wrong, Sarah?"

She reached out for him and placed her palm against his. "Being with your family tonight was a great first step, but you need to talk to someone about what you've been through. About—"

"Is this about what happened when I grabbed you? Sarah, you have to know that I would never hurt you. I know I scared you but, hell." He ran a hand through his hair, losing contact with her to do so. "I wish I could take it back. Both times. And I've already had my first counseling session."

"That's great, Nate. Because you need to deal with what's going on with *you,* get yourself in the right head-space, before we can even think about something happening with us."

Nate started to walk again, needing to move, and Sarah followed. She was right, Sarah always seemed to be right, but that didn't make her words any easier to digest.

"Do you know that Holt could hardly look me in the eye after I saw him looking at my leg earlier today?" he asked Sarah. "It was like a great white elephant was suddenly in the room with us, and I didn't know how to talk to him. Whether to make a joke or tell him to buzz off."

Sarah would have noticed he was limping, that there was no way he could walk this far or at this pace without it being obvious, but it was like she didn't even see it. Or maybe she just honestly didn't see it as a big deal.

"That's what I'm talking about, Nate," she said.

They reached his house and he unlocked the door, opening it for her to walk through. "Some things are better left unsaid," he told her.

"You can talk to me, Nate," Sarah told him, standing behind him when he whirled around. "I didn't mean to ruin our evening, but you need to talk, Nate, and I'm here to listen. About anything and everything, or just what you're prepared to tell."

CHAPTER TEN

NATE didn't know what was worse, the fact that Sarah seemed not to see his injury when everyone else seemed to notice it constantly, or that she had no problem asking him outright about what he'd been through.

His family had only seemed to feel sorry for him, wanted to know why he wasn't the same person who'd left when they'd asked him questions. Sarah? She wanted to know what he'd experienced, what had happened…the truth behind his experiences rather than just the end result.

"I don't think you understand what you're asking," he said, trying not to be angry with her, to acknowledge how strong and brave she was being.

Sarah's eyes looked like they were glowing, but on second look he wondered if they were tears making her usual amber gaze appear so different.

"Nate, you have to talk to someone about more than just your night terrors. It doesn't have to be me, but if you want to fit in here again? If you want to be part of your family again and live the kind of life that I know you want, then you can't keep it all bottled up inside."

He wanted so badly to walk away, to tell himself that

Sarah didn't know what she was talking about, but it was impossible. Because she meant something to him, and no matter how angry he became or how much she got under his skin, that wasn't going to change. And tonight he felt different. Something *had* changed between them, or maybe it was just something within him that had changed, but one thing he did know was that he didn't want to hurt her. Not again.

"Unless you've been where I've been, seen what I've seen, there's no way you can understand." Nate kept his voice as low as he could, controlling the pain and anger that surged within him whenever he spoke about his past. About his last year in Black Ops, what he'd been witness to, what he'd lost.

Sarah shook her head and leaned toward him. "I don't need to understand, Nate, but you do need someone to talk to." Sarah pressed her palm to his cheek, her eyes now obviously glistening with unshed tears—tears that he could only guess were for him. "What's it going to cost you to try me?"

Nate stood and walked away, paced to the door before whirling back and glaring at the woman looking up at him so expectantly. Giving him a chance to open up, even though he was so angry with her right now for asking him to do something he found so hard. But he didn't want to be that guy, the one freaking out whenever someone tried to talk to him about what he'd seen.

"Everything, Sarah," he choked out. "It already feels like it's cost me everything, what I went through."

Nate watched as she swallowed.

He ran as fast as he could, taking down the machine

*gun nest as he covered the ground. Jimmy was crum-
pled, collapsed, lying unprotected as round after round
echoed out around them.*

"I lied for someone I cared about, okay? Are you happy now that you've heard the truth?" The words snapped out of him, even though he didn't want them to. But talking about Jimmy, about what he'd witnessed, wasn't something he'd ever planned on sharing.

Sarah shook her head, her mouth hovering into a frown. "I'm happy that you're finally talking again, and that you're telling *me* the truth."

"I've never lied to you, Sarah. Never," he told her, wishing he could keep his anger in check but failing miserably now. "But reliving the past isn't going to help me!"

This time it was Sarah glaring at him. "Never lied to me? How about when you promised that you'd come home, that I was as important to you as the army was? How about when I waited for you, put my life on hold for you, and *you never came back?* I was so proud of you, Nate, of what you were doing, but I hadn't expected it to cost us our relationship."

He wanted to turn away from the tears he could see only barely restrained by her lashes, but he couldn't pull his eyes away from her face. "I said I'd never lied to you, not that I'd never broken a promise to you." Damn it, he knew he'd hurt her and what he'd done was wrong. He should never have left, never have ended things with her.

She laughed. "Oh, *I'm sorry.* I didn't realize there was any difference between the two."

It was something he'd never forgive himself for, and never stop regretting.

Nate cleared his throat, wishing he could walk away from a fight they were long overdue to have, but one that he'd hoped he'd manage to avoid. "When I told you what you meant to me, I wasn't lying, Sarah. Deep down, I know you believe that." He paused, not sure how to tell her what had happened, why things hadn't worked out the way they should have. "I never wanted to work on the land and I didn't want to give up doing what I loved, but when I joined up I hadn't realized how hard it would be fulfilling my dreams and feeling guilty about leaving you behind."

"If I'd known I was holding you back I would have finished our relationship myself." Her words were almost cruel, angry. "And don't give me that crap about not wanting to work the land, because you had a dream once, Nate. A dream you shared with me, and that was you serving our country and then coming back. Don't you remember? You wanted to spend time away, then come back and find a way to make a living here on the ranch, and then start a family here with *me*."

"I remember, Sarah. I will always remember," he said, reaching for her hands. "But you were brave enough to let me go, and I'll always admire you for that. It was just that, I don't even know how to explain this, but…" How had they ended up going back this far into the past, into what had happened between them, when only moments before he'd been starting to tell her about Jimmy? His plan had changed, what he wanted had changed, but the way he felt about her never had.

Sarah waited instead of pushing him away and Nate knew he had to continue. That if he didn't speak now she *would* walk away and he might never have the chance again.

"When I was offered the chance to become part of a special forces team, I would have been a fool not to accept. Or at least that's what I thought at the time. I was so young and it was something I'd dreamed of since I was a schoolboy."

"So why are you back here, then?" she asked. "Tell me what brought you home, Nate. *Tell me.*"

Nate gripped her hands tighter, needing all of her strength as well as his to be honest with her about what had happened. He wasn't angry anymore, but talking was never going to come easy to him, not with his friend and the army as the subject matter.

"When I heard about you and Todd, I thought it was a sign that being Black Ops was what I was meant to be doing. Part of me had hoped you'd still wait, but it was stupid to even think that, when I told you it was over. But within a couple of years, I wanted out. Jimmy did, too, and we both tried. He was struggling and I didn't want to end up the same way. I knew something wasn't right with him, and not saying something, not interfering when I could have, cost him his life." Nate shook his head. "I went from loving my job more than anything to hating it."

Sarah was nodding and squeezing his hands in return. "Why did you want out?" Her anger had turned into concern.

Nate sighed. Talking wasn't getting any easier, but

Sarah was there for him and he had to try. There were things he could tell her, because of what they'd shared in the past, that he knew he'd never be able to divulge to anyone else. Not even his family.

"Because it didn't feel right. And because..." Nate gulped and watched as Sarah did the same. "Because after losing you, and then Mom passing away, I realized that I'd left the place I actually belonged. I'd been searching all this time, wanting to serve my country and prove myself on my own, and at the same time I'd managed to lose everything that was important to me. I might not have realized it straightaway, but hand on my heart it's the truth. All I wanted was to come back here, but now that I'm here it's like I no longer fit in anywhere."

Sarah looked numb, like she was in shock and didn't know how to respond. "Then when Dad passed away and my friend, too, it was like everything had been taken away from me. Like I had nothing left." He looked up and into Sarah's beautiful, amber-gold eyes. "Until I saw you again."

Sarah's cheeks turned the softest shade of pink as she smiled. "You don't need to say that, Nate. Flattery won't get you anywhere with me."

He stroked her face from the edge of her eye to the curve of her mouth, then cupped her chin. *"But it's the truth.* I came home a broken man, and when I thought I was beyond repair, somehow you managed to save me."

"What happened out there, Nate? What happened to your friend?"

Nate's body shuddered like a bolt of lightning had hit

it. No one else in the world knew what had happened out there that day, no one but him. *And the friend he'd watched kill himself.*

"You have to realize that when I joined the special forces, when I became part of one of the most elite military operations in the world, I pledged to keep what I saw, where I was and what I did a secret." Nate sucked in a big breath. "What happened on tour had to stay on tour, no question about it."

Sarah tucked her arms around his torso and hugged him tight. "But something happened over there, Nate. Something that you need to talk about before the secrecy of it eats you alive." She paused. "This isn't me asking because I'm nosy, this is me asking because I want to help. And if it's not me you talk to, then it has to be someone else, and soon."

Nate had no idea how she could be so compassionate toward him when he'd already hurt her so bad, when only moments before they'd been arguing.

Jimmy's lifeless, heavy body weighed him down so much he could hardly walk. The pain in his own leg was so intense that Nate thought it might have been on fire. That it had somehow been set alight.

He was yelling, over and over, screaming for someone to help Jimmy.

And knowing that no matter what happened, he was never going to be able to tell the truth. Not to anyone.

Except Sarah. Right now.

"Once I tell you, I need you to not ask me about it ever again. But I need to know that you're sure?"

"Sure that I can keep it a secret or sure that I want to know?"

Nate held her hand, pleased that for once he wasn't trying to fight having her near. "I already know I can trust you with a secret, Sarah. What I need to know is whether you want the burden of knowing what happened to me that day."

Sarah smiled at him, honesty shining from her eyes with an unmistakable glow. "Tell me, Nate. When I said I was here for you it wasn't an empty promise. I don't say anything I don't mean."

Nate pulled her hard against him in a fierce embrace before letting go so he could face her. They sat on the sofa, Nate staring into Sarah's eyes.

"When I said before that Jimmy was struggling, *he was really struggling.* He had been my best friend for years, and I knew him as well as anyone in my life. There were days near the end that I had to cover for him constantly, because I knew he wasn't capable of doing what was required of him, what was expected of us. And I knew he was getting worse. We'd served together before Black Ops, so I knew something was wrong because we were so close we may as well have been brothers."

Sarah nodded, encouraging him to continue.

It was a fight to expel the words. They were in his mind but stuck in his throat before he could tell her what he suddenly wanted to share so bad it hurt. Like a knife being twisted in his chest.

"I knew things were bad, but I couldn't bring myself to do anything about it. He kept insisting he was fine, or he wouldn't talk about it at all, and if I'd said something to our superior then, I knew he'd be out. And what would that have meant for the rest of his life? For his wife waiting at home? What would a dishonorable discharge have meant for him?"

"And now you think you did the wrong thing in not saying something?" Sarah asked, her voice soft and full of concern.

"I don't think, Sarah, *I know.*" Nate tried hard not to let himself be sucked back into the world he was trying so hard to pull away from—the world of memories that never seemed to stop hunting him out. "The official records tell of enemy fire taking out my best friend. About me being injured when our operation went bad. I've never told anyone that I watched as Jim turned his gun on himself and took his own life, or that I was shot because I ran as fast as I could to save him, firing at two separate machine gun nests, and got shot in the process. But that's the truth of it, Sarah. Because I didn't speak up and do the right thing, I cost my friend his life."

Nate was suddenly gulping for air, fighting to breathe. His body began to convulse, before a massive sob erupted from his chest.

"Nate, oh, Nate. Come here." Sarah grabbed him tight and tucked his head to her chest, cradling him like she would one of her young pupils.

"I'm sorry, I…" Nate couldn't even talk, he was crying so damn hard and he couldn't stop it. *He was crying like a baby in front of the one woman in the world that he wanted to be strong for.*

"There's no shame in crying, Nate. I'm here for you, I'm here," she whispered, her lips close to his ear.

She was right. *Sarah wasn't the girl he needed to impress; she was the one he could be himself with.*

Somehow her words pulled his emotions back in check. He took a deep, shuddering breath and reached for her face, cupping her cheeks gently in between both his hands. "I love you, Sarah."

Tears sprang into her eyes then. "Nate, you don't need to say that," she mumbled.

He didn't let go of her face even when she tried to look away, to force his gaze from her.

"So all of a sudden you don't want me to be honest with you?"

Her bottom lip had started to quiver. "You mean it, don't you?" she whispered.

"I only say what I mean, Sarah," he told her, bringing his face closer to hers. "I'd rather stay silent than lie, and you're still the only woman I've ever said *I love you* to."

That got her attention. He could see the question in her eyes, the disbelief, but it was true.

"Are you sure?" she asked, a shy smile kicking up the edge of her lips.

"It's not the sort of thing I'd forget," he told her, trying not to laugh. "*I love you, Sarah.* Always have, probably always will. Hand on my heart, you're the only woman I've ever told, aside from my mom and my sister."

She shook her head, her bottom lip caught between her top teeth as she watched him. Nate took his chance.

Talking to her had helped, had felt right, but he knew what would make him feel a whole heap better.

Kissing Sarah again.

Nate knelt and tugged Sarah from the sofa, pulling her down to his level. She obeyed, her eyes trained on his, not resisting when he pressed his lips to her throat, pushing away her hair with one hand and holding her close with the other.

"Nate?"

He trailed more kisses down her collarbone. "Mmm?"

"Are you sure this is a good idea?"

He chose not to answer with words. Nate cupped Sarah's face with both hands, eyes focused on her full lips. They parted when he kissed her, her body softening against his, hands snaking around his hips.

But it didn't last for long.

Sarah's confidence seemed to have grown. She was no longer blushing but smiling at him when she pushed him away like she was a woman in charge of her own destiny. *And right now he hoped that immediate destiny included him.*

Nate groaned as Sarah placed her palm to his chest. *Last time she'd taken charge he hadn't exactly minded, and her plans this time didn't disappoint him.*

She slowly pushed him, more gentle than she'd been earlier, but her message was clear. Nate grimaced as his leg bent in an uncomfortable position.

"Are you okay?" She stopped moving, her hand fluttering away from him.

"Fine," he growled, grabbing her hand and placing it back flat to his chest. Nate lay back, trying hard not to take over and lay claim on Sarah with his hands, pulling her down on top of him instead.

But Sarah was setting the pace, and he wanted to let her, wanted her to decide what she was comfortable with.

She sat astride him and Nate didn't fight it, even though he wasn't used to anyone else taking charge of anything in his life. He'd resisted contact with anyone for so long, jumped when he was touched, needed to be in charge. *Until now.* Because Sarah wasn't going to hurt him, wasn't doing anything other than be there for him, and he was ready to at least try to trust again. "You're gonna have to go slow with me," he joked, pulling her farther down onto him. Her hair fell over the sides of his face, tickling his throat.

"This slow?" she joked, giggling as she pressed tiny kisses across his jaw.

"Just hurry up and kiss me, woman," he growled, flipping her over so she was trapped beneath him, his patience long expired.

Sarah loved the indent of Nate's body above her, the weight of his large frame. She could do this. How long had she thought about Nate? Remembered the way things had been between them?

It didn't matter what couldn't be, it was about *right now.* Being loved, even just for one night, by Nate. Even if she had made him tell her everything without sharing her own fears, her own secrets, that she was terrified of confessing to him. Even if he had said *I love you.*

"Do you want me to stop?" Nate's question, his voice

low as he whispered in her ear, made her wriggle beneath him, searching out his eyes.

"No," she whispered back, shaking her head. Sarah hated that he'd taken some of his weight off her, had liked feeling crushed beneath him, his hot breath on her neck, hands skimming her body. "No," she whispered again.

Nate stroked her forehead, his fingers trailing slowly down her face with a delicateness that made her squirm, body shuddering as his thumb dipped into her mouth on its way to her chin.

"Nate." She had no idea why she wanted to keep saying his name, maybe to believe it was real, that this was actually happening.

"You're sure?" he asked.

Damn it, did he have to keep being such a gentleman? Did she have to spell out exactly what she wanted him to do to her? *The thought filled her body with heat.* No way could she talk to him about what she wanted.

Instead, she nodded when his fingers brushed her face, before grazing his lips against hers, his weight against her body again, nestled snug into her. "You're even more beautiful than I remembered," Nate told her, his lips so close to hers as he spoke that she could feel his warm breath against her skin.

Sarah murmured; she wasn't capable of anything else.

"I mean it, Sarah." The look on Nate's face, the tenderness in the way he touched her, like she was the most cherished of possessions that he couldn't bear the thought of hurting, made her heart beat too fast. Made her light-headed, made her crave his touch like she'd die without the attention of his hands on her body. Without his lips cradling hers.

"Nate?" she whispered, pressing him back ever so slightly with one hand.

"Mmm-hmm," he mumbled, pushing her cheek slightly so that her lips were aligned perfectly beneath his again.

Nate slipped one finger under the strap of her dress, pushing it gently down to expose more skin.

Sarah heard the moan rise from her own throat, arched her back as Nate's lips left hers and started to burn a heat-filled path down her neck, past her collarbone, to her...

"Nate," she managed, choking out his name.

His grin was wicked, a lazy, conceited smile spreading across his face as he stopped, looked up and met her eyes.

"You *do* want me to stop?" he asked.

She giggled, unable to stop herself. "No," she said, her palm cupping his jaw as she stroked his cheek. He was so handsome, so chiseled yet masculine, tough in the most desirable of ways. "I want you to turn the lights out."

He looked like he was about to disagree, to decline her wish, but the devilish grin was back as quick as it had disappeared.

"Follow me," he ordered, pushing against the carpet as he rose to his feet, offering her a hand to do the same.

Sarah hesitated, wasn't sure whether she'd completely ruined the moment or somehow made it better. She took his hand for him to help her up, but Nate swept her off her feet and up into his arms before she could even steady herself.

"What are you doing?" she demanded, wriggling to break free from his grip. But he held her tight, so snug against his chest that she couldn't move an inch.

"I'm taking you to the bedroom," he informed her, the determined look in his eyes making her stomach flip.

She tried wriggling again. "I'm too heavy, your leg…"

His gaze flashed with anger then, his arms tightening even harder around her. "Don't go there," he warned.

Sarah didn't need to be told twice. She scooped her arms around his neck, hands locking in the air behind him, and offered her mouth to Nate. *And he took it without hesitation.* If he said he could carry her, he could carry her.

"Bedroom?" he asked, voice husky again.

"Yeah." Sarah breathed out the word, her heart racing again, pounding hard.

This time Nate didn't pause to ask if she was sure. He stormed toward his room with a determination that terrified her.

CHAPTER ELEVEN

SARAH lay wrapped in one of Nate's arms, her leg curled over his, head flat to his chest. She'd fallen asleep, too, but something had woken her.

Ow. Nate's comfortable hold on her tightened, his arm squeezing her hard, then releasing again. *At least now she knew why she was awake if he'd done that before.*

Sarah didn't move, not sure what to do. She knew Nate wouldn't hurt her intentionally, but the last time she'd tried to comfort him when he'd been obviously having a dream hadn't exactly worked out that well for her.

His arm tightened again but she stayed still. *She had no idea what to do, whether she should slip away from him and wriggle to the other side of the bed, or stay put and try to comfort him.*

Nate started to shake then and Sarah did move. She wasn't scared of him but…she swallowed and held up a pillow to cuddle, clutched to her naked body. She suddenly felt supervulnerable. His body shuddered violently, one arm thrashed out, but Sarah was still frozen, unsure what to do. When he started to mumble words she couldn't understand, she fumbled and flipped the bedside lamp on, hoping the light would wake him.

But it didn't. All it did was make his distress more obvious. His forehead was glistening with sweat, his body was twisting in the sheets, face pained.

She had to do something.

Sarah edged closer, wished she wasn't naked so she'd feel more confident, but she couldn't take her eyes off Nate. Was powerless to leave him for even a moment, despite the fact she had no idea what to do, how she could help him.

He didn't need to be jolted from sleep, and he needed to know where he was, who was with him, as soon as he woke.

"It's Sarah," she said, her voice a low whisper, wrapping her arms tight around herself and resisting touching him. Not letting herself wriggle any closer even though her instinct was to hold him, to cocoon him in her arms. "It's Sarah. I'm here, Nate, it's Sarah," she said, braver now, her voice stronger. Nate wasn't thrashing now but his eyes were still shut. The sheets were a tangled mess on his side of the bed.

"It's Sarah, Nate. Sarah," she repeated, still desperate to reach out to him.

Nate woke then, leaped up into a sitting position, his eyes wild, like a stranger sitting before her.

But it was Nate. He wouldn't hurt her, do anything out of character, so long as he knew it was her.

"Nate, it's Sarah, look at me."

The wildness disappeared from Nate's gaze almost immediately. He ran a shaky hand through his hair, looked around, then brought his knees up to his chest, dropping his forehead to rest on them.

Sarah took her cue. He wasn't a danger to her anymore, knew it was her.

"Nate," she whispered, scooting over to him, no longer caring that she was naked. *This was Nate she was with, not some stranger.* Sarah put her arm carefully around his back, her other hand touching his hair.

When he drew back, made eye contact with her, she knew he'd be okay, that she could at least be there for him and that he'd let her.

"You're going to be okay," she told him, her lips to his ear as she held him tight.

Nate's body went stiff, then relaxed, his arms going around her to hug her back.

"Every night," he said, his voice muffled against her hair. "There's not a single night that I go to bed and that doesn't happen."

Sarah swallowed furiously, willing herself not to cry. Nate didn't deserve this sort of pain, not after what he'd been through, what he'd seen…*what he'd done for a friend.* "Are you reliving what happened?" she asked, hoping she wasn't pushing it by asking more.

Nate let go of her and leaned back, his head resting against the wall behind the bed. "I see everything," he told her. "I see Jimmy, I see blood, explosions—you name it, it's in my nightmares."

Sarah lay down, her head nestling into the soft pillow, and held out her hand for Nate to join her. He didn't move to turn off the lamp and neither did she.

Nate lay down beside her, on his side, so they were

nose to nose, mouth to mouth. He skimmed the side of her body, running his hand down her arm, over her backside and to the top of her thigh. "I thought that being with you, having you beside me, might help."

She wished it had, too. Now that she'd witnessed what he went through, had seen him transform from peaceful sleeper to a man plagued by night terrors, she could understand why he'd almost strangled her in the state he'd been in. Why he'd mistaken her to be someone from his dreams, and how much it must have hurt him when he'd realized what he'd done.

"I'm not scared of you, Nate, if that's what you're worried about," she said, touching a slow kiss to his lips.

Nate pressed into her, the length of his body fitted to hers. "The other night, when we were drunk and asleep on the sofa, was the first time I've slept through without waking like this."

Wow. "But you haven't woken from a nightmare to this before, have you?" Sarah asked, smiling as she wiggled against him.

Nate chuckled, a deep noise followed by his hand grasping her bottom. "No, Sarah. I haven't."

She pretended to protest, to fight him when he held both her hands down and lay above her, settling enough of his weight over her that she knew she'd never get away even if she wanted to.

"I've never told anyone about this, either," he whispered, placing a teasing kiss to her neck, then the other side, before finding her mouth. *"Ever."*

She looked into his eyes, could sense the level of trust he was instilling in her. Nate wasn't the kind of man who'd like anyone to know his weaknesses, would never like to burden anyone else with his problems. And she had no intention of divulging anything he told her to anyone, no matter what.

"Your secrets are always safe with me, Nate."

If only she could share her secrets with him.

Nate woke with a sense of calm that surprised him. Usually, after he'd woken from a night terror, he'd never fall back into a comfortable sleep. It was why his eyes felt like they were hanging from their sockets most days, and probably why his temper was too quick to leap to the surface. Especially where his family were concerned.

He briefly shut his eyes and focused on the softness of the woman lying beside him. *Sarah.* He'd never imagined he'd be sharing a bed with her again, that he would have her in his arms, that he'd have *loved her* like he had last night.

She sighed in her sleep and moved, snuggling in closer to him. Nate turned so that his arms were around her, studying her face as she stirred. He traced the smoothness of her skin with his eyes, drank in her soft lips, smiled as he slowly reached a hand toward her face and plucked a soft curl that was draped over her cheek.

"Hey," she mumbled, lips parting but her eyes still shut. "I can tell you're looking at me."

Nate put his arm back around Sarah and pulled her closer. Never in a million years, after what he'd been through and the way he'd felt these past few months, had he ever imagined being with Sarah again. Opening up to anyone about his experiences or the secret he held. But she was starting to change the way he thought, the way he behaved. Even if it had been slow progress up until now.

"Sleep well?" he asked.

She grinned and opened her eyes. "Yes. Better than I have in a long while."

Nate touched her cheek with the backs of his fingers. "Divorce keeping you awake at night?"

A look passed across Sarah's face that he couldn't read. But it was one he recognized from that first time he'd seen her, under his tree. Like she was upset, couldn't help from showing it, but wiped the emotion as quick as she could. *But not fast enough for him not to notice.*

"Sarah?"

She shook her head against the pillow, pulling back from him slightly. "It's nothing, Nate."

He wasn't buying it. "If you do need to talk, about Todd, or anything—" he tried hard not to grimace when he said his former friend's name "—I'm here for you just like you were for me."

Sarah wriggled and kissed him, her arm circling his neck. "Thank you," she said.

Nate was curious to know what was wrong, but whatever was keeping her up at night wasn't something she wanted to talk about and he understood exactly what that felt like.

"How about some breakfast?" he suggested, changing the subject so she didn't have to.

Sarah cringed, not exactly the response he'd expected.

"Did I say something wrong?" he asked, rising and pulling on the jeans that he'd shed way too fast the night before. They were crumpled in a heap on the floor.

"Oh, my God." Sarah's hand flew to her mouth, sitting up and drawing the sheets to cover herself.

Nate's eyebrow shot up in question. "What?"

"You never struck me as the commando type." She giggled.

He planted his hands on the bed and leaned toward her, kissing her before grabbing the sheet between his teeth and pulling it away from her.

"Nate!"

He laughed and jumped back. "I'll have you know it's only a morning kind of thing. I didn't know how fast you'd want to be ripping off my pants again, so I thought I'd make it easy for you."

Sarah rolled her eyes, but he didn't miss the pink blush as it frosted her cheeks. He didn't remember her blushing so much when they'd been together even though she'd been a whole lot younger then, but she seemed to do it all the time now.

"I'll have you know that it was you who initiated—" she paused and held the sheet up again to cover her breasts "—*this*."

Nate stood and walked to the door, before turning back. "What was it you were going to tell me before?"

She sighed and Nate wished he'd just forgotten about it and not asked.

"I had a phone call from Todd before I arrived here last night. He confirmed our meeting today."

Nate nodded, probably for longer than he needed to. "You still want me to be there?"

Sarah smiled, meekly this time. "Yeah, but only if it's not a problem. I mean, if you have something else on, or you need to be somewhere…"

Nate gave her a quick salute, followed by what he hoped was a convincing smile. "I'll be there."

They stared at each other for a moment before Nate remembered where he'd been heading. "I hope you like omelets," he called out as he walked away from her. "'Cause it's all I know how to make!"

Nate reached the kitchen and leaned against the wall, needing a minute to think about what he'd just agreed to. He did want to help Sarah, but the reality of seeing Todd again wasn't exactly appealing, even though he'd told her yesterday that he'd do it for her.

He still had so many issues to deal with, was struggling with his own problems, but Sarah had been there for him and he'd promised the same of her.

Nate opened a drawer to find the utensils he needed, but his fingers first connected with a folded piece of paper. *Jimmy's wife. What he needed to do today was muster the courage to phone her.*

He pushed it to the side, like he'd been doing for months, and set about making breakfast. Maybe he should tell Sarah, or maybe he should just quit stalling and do something about it.

CHAPTER TWELVE

SARAH was beside-herself nervous. Nate was sitting on her sofa and surfing the channels on her television, and she was starting to pace. Was he seriously okay with this kind of normality? And what had the verdict been on whether they were still pretending or not? Because what had happened between them had her seriously confused, and if they were starting something here, then she needed to get something off her chest.

Argh. Being with Nate, dealing with Todd, it was all too much.

"Nate," she said, straightening her shoulders and moving to stand in front of him. He laughed and leaned around her to use the remote, switching the television off.

"Come here," he said, trying to loop his fingers into her jeans and tug her down.

"Nate!" she scolded, standing her ground. "I'm trying to be serious here."

"So am I."

She swatted at his hand, almost wishing things didn't feel so good between them. She should have just told him to start with, admitted why Todd's having a baby had upset her so much when she'd first found out.

Moose couldn't resist any longer and leaped up, nosing at her like he was making sure she was okay. He'd been watching Nate with a wary expression ever since he'd arrived, but after spending the night before being babysat by her mom, he seemed pretty pleased to be home.

"Shoot," he said, pulling her down slowly so she could sit on the arm of the chair. "And tell that dog that he's going to have to get used to me."

She wished that was all she had on her mind, worrying about her overprotective dog not liking Nate when animals usually loved him, but she needed to get this off her chest. It was time she was honest with Nate, opened up to him about what had happened to *her* these past few years, the pain she'd been through. Telling him now before things went any further between them, before she risked being hurt again, was the only way forward. Especially after he'd been so brave talking to her.

"Sarah?" he asked, his playful expression turning into a frown as he watched her.

"Nate, there's something I—"

"Well, isn't this cozy."

Sarah leaped up and nearly tripped over her rug at the sound of Todd's voice. "Have you heard of knocking?" she demanded, furious that he'd just walked in like that when it wasn't his home to do so anymore.

Todd looked at her, then back at Nate, eyes wide with what she could only guess was disbelief. Sarah dropped her hand to her dog's head when she heard his low growl, which turned into a muttered whine at her touch.

"From memory I'm pretty sure the house is still half-mine, so I didn't know I had to knock," Todd said, watching Nate closely. "But then I wasn't exactly expecting to find you shacked up with someone so soon."

Sarah tried to stay calm, didn't want to engage in a fight with Todd and especially not in front of Nate, but she was so angry her hands had started to shake. "Todd, let's not argue, and please don't accuse me of anything when you've hardly been the world's best role model, okay? I saw you with your fiancée in town and I guessed she'd be with you today."

If she was angry, Todd looked wild. "All these years I knew you were pining over *him,* but I tried to tell myself it was stupid. That you weren't still in love with a guy who'd decided he had better things to do than come back to you."

"I think that's enough, Todd." Nate's deep, commanding voice sent a shiver through her.

"Don't you tell me what to do in my house to *my wife.*" Todd was red-faced and beyond angry now, the testosterone and tension in the room overwhelming.

Tears fell down Sarah's cheeks and she couldn't stop them, but Nate's body beside hers when he rose, his hand on her hip, made her stand strong. Todd was the one at fault here, not her, and she wasn't going to be made out to be the bad guy. She had been faithful to him and done everything she could during their marriage, to make it work, and while she'd thought of Nate often she'd never treated Todd like she didn't love him.

"Todd, I signed the divorce papers and sent them back yesterday. I think you'll find that I'm no longer your wife." Her voice was cooler, calmer, than she'd expected. "You've moved on, and now so have I."

Todd stood there, glaring at her and Nate like he wanted to set them on fire with his gaze alone. Why was he even angry when he'd so clearly moved on?

"Was this going on during our marriage?" Todd demanded, directing the question at her and pointing at Nate.

Sarah shook her head. "No." From the corner of her eye she could see the determined look in Nate's eyes, the hard line of his jaw as he kept his mouth clamped shut, like he was desperate to interfere and put Todd in his place, but trying so hard to let her deal with the situation on her own. "You were the unfaithful one, Todd, not me. I never did anything other than try to make things work between us."

Todd started to walk backward to the door, like he'd had enough, his expression pure hatred, but not yet ready to turn away. "Have you told him the truth yet, Sarah?"

Her lip quivered but she took a step toward him, praying that he'd stop, that he wouldn't tell Nate. But he only sensed her discomfort and laughed, like he couldn't wait to make a fool of her, to make sure she didn't find happiness with anyone else. He'd been so cruel toward her at the end when she'd been trying so hard to make things work, to deal with what she was going through, coming to terms with how the news from her doctor would change her life forever.

"Todd, please," she begged, shaking her head and pleading with him as she looked him in the eye.

"Ah, I see. Lover boy doesn't know that the happy little family you were always talking about before he left can't happen. That you'll never be able to have his kids. I wonder if he'll still want you now, sweetheart?"

His cruelty made her feel like she'd just been cut in half. She'd come to dislike him at the end of the marriage, been furious for what he'd done, but she'd never known he could be so full of hatred, that he could want to hurt her that bad for something she'd had no control over.

"Just go, Todd. Get out of my house," she said, her voice so quiet that she wondered if he'd even heard her. "The next time you want to discuss our settlement you can do it through my lawyer. I'm done playing nice."

He walked out and left her standing there, wishing she'd never asked Nate to be witness to their meeting. She should have known how badly Todd would react to him, even if he did have a new partner and baby on the way. Nate's had always been a name that wasn't mentioned in their house, for the very reason that they had a history together that everyone in the district knew about, especially Todd. She'd been stupid asking Nate to come, even if it had seemed like the right thing to do at the time.

"Sarah?"

Nate's hand on her back told her it wasn't all just a bad nightmare, either. *It was real.*

"Just go, Nate. Please." She couldn't face him, not after being humiliated like that.

Nate walked around her when she refused to turn so she couldn't ignore him. "Sarah?" He tried to tilt her chin but she looked away.

"I'm sorry you had to witness that, but Todd's right," she told him, in a voice far braver than she felt inside. "I can't have children, Nate, so whatever happened between us last night doesn't mean we can just pick up and go back to what we used to have. I'll never carry a child, not with you, not with *anyone*."

She couldn't read Nate's expression and she didn't want to. Maybe he'd just wanted to have some fun, maybe he wasn't thinking the same things that she'd been hoping, wishing they could step back in time. But if she knew Nate like she thought she did, he wouldn't have just slept with her if it didn't mean something, not with the history they shared. And he'd be furious that she hadn't opened up to him, especially when she'd been so demanding of him facing up to his issues.

"You should have told me," he said.

Sarah met his gaze, defiant. "Why? You had enough of your own problems to deal with without me offloading mine. I can't ever get pregnant, Nate. Not now, not ever." She shouldn't have been angry with him, but she was. Or maybe she was just angry with herself. "But I'm at peace with that now."

He shook his head, his expression sad. "I'm sure there are plenty of specialists, or doctors you could talk to. There must be—"

"Stop, Nate, just stop," she ordered, battling tears again. "Don't you think I've done everything I can? That I've investigated every possible way for me to have a baby? I can't and there's nothing anyone can do for me, okay?"

He nodded. "I'm sorry."

"Well, I don't want your pity and I don't want you to pretend like it doesn't matter, so I think you should just go."

He shuffled toward her, arms open. "Sarah, I know you're hurt but—"

"But what, Nate? You want a family, and so do I, but we can't ever have one together. Not like we always talked about, anyway. I've been with a man who said it was okay, and now look at him? Shacked up with another woman already and about to become a dad." She took a big breath and let it out on a slow exhale. "You have no idea how he treated me when he found out, after we'd exhausted every option and I *still* couldn't get pregnant. So I'd rather never put myself through that again."

Now it was Nate who looked angry. "I'd never treat you the way Todd just did, *never.* You know that, Sarah, and if you don't, then you don't know me at all."

"But?" she asked.

"What do you mean, *but?*"

Sarah touched his cheek before she walked away from him. "But you still want to be a dad, Nate. You might say *no* now, but I've seen the way you are with Brady. *I know you,* and you're going to make someone a great husband and be a great father one day. Of your own biological children."

He stared at her, his expression like carved stone.

"Maybe I was right, then. Maybe you don't know me

at all." Nate gave her a look she'd never seen before—a sad, haunted expression that sent an icy blast through her body. Chilled her to the bone and made her wish she'd just kept her mouth shut.

And then he did exactly as she'd asked and walked out her door.

Sarah dropped to her knees and curled up beside her dog, the tears falling freely now. She could deal with her marriage being over, but she didn't know if she'd ever cope with losing Nate. *Not again.*

CHAPTER THIRTEEN

NATE was in a foul mood, but he didn't want to take his anger out on anyone or anything. Which was why he was sitting on the sofa on an otherwise perfect afternoon, instead of riding or helping out on the ranch. He should have gone out and found Holt, but given his recent track record, he didn't want to say something to his brother that he could regret later.

He was fuming about Sarah and trying not to think about her simultaneously, and it wasn't working. He couldn't give a crap about her not being able to have children, except for the fact that he hated how deeply she must have hurt when she'd found out. What he was furious about was her not telling him, not opening up to him. That he'd had to find out from Todd.

Nate looked up, stared at the kitchen, before rising. If he was going to sit around inside, he needed to do something productive, and he knew exactly what that something was. If Sarah had taught him one thing, it was that he needed to be honest, to deal with his emotions and not push people away. Well, there was one person he should be offering a helping hand to, and she deserved at least a phone call from him.

Nate strode across the room and pulled out the piece of paper. He reached for the phone and dialed the number, wishing he could stop his hand from shaking.

She answered almost immediately.

Nate swallowed and tried to push the memories away, tried to stop thinking about Jimmy and how he'd looked when he'd died. What it was like seeing his best friend lying with blood seeping from him.

No. He was stronger than that. He had to be.

"Lucy, it's Nate. I've been meaning to call you for months now."

The kind, gentle voice at the other end settled his nerves.

He wasn't going to tell her the truth about how Jimmy's life had ended, but he was going to tell her about how brave her husband had been leading up to that day, and why he'd been such a good friend when Nate had needed him most.

That he'd done his best to save Jimmy, to be there for him, and that Jimmy had had his back on every mission they'd been on. Not the last one, but in Nate's books that didn't count. Jimmy had been his best friend, and his best friend's widow deserved to know just how damn special her husband had been.

Sarah walked slowly with her dog, as far away from the dwelling as possible. She didn't even want to make eye contact with the guesthouse Nate was living in, and she sure as heck wasn't going to look over at his tree. The one they'd sat under together so many times, and the place where she'd found him such a short time ago.

She missed him like hell already and she didn't want to think about him.

"Come on, Moose," she called.

Sarah came to the gate closest to where her horse was grazing and she let her dog through before doing the same. Then froze on the spot. From where she was standing she could see Johnny and Brady, and *there was Nate.* Playing with his nephew, touching his hand to his head, before mounting one of Johnny's horses.

Where was he going?

Sarah stayed still, hoping Nate wouldn't turn around and see her standing there, and he didn't. As soon as he was out of eyesight she made her way over to Maddie and took hold of her halter, before leading her toward the far gate so she could get her gear and saddle up.

She bit her lip and kept walking, waving out to Johnny as he turned around. Just because things were through before they'd started with Nate didn't mean she was going to stop riding. She loved the Calhoun family and Holt hadn't seemed to mind her horse spending some time here over the summer, so that wasn't going to change.

She had to forget Nate all over again, no matter how much it hurt. Her future wasn't going to be what she'd hoped it would be, but she was going to do her best to move on. She owed it to herself, and she owed it to Nate to let him go.

Nate was starting to regret not bringing more clothing. Johnny had told him to watch the weather, and now after an hour of riding he wished he'd heeded his warnings. There was a storm brewing—he could feel it in his bones—and that meant he needed to get back fast. He might have been away from Texas for a few years, but he'd never forgotten the thunderstorms that could blast a tree in two, even in the middle of summer.

He'd taken the stirrups off completely today instead of crossing them over the pommel of his saddle or letting them swing free, and it had been the right decision. He was able to nudge the horse into a canter without worrying about them, and it made it easier on his leg. He could grip with his knees and not put any pressure on his lower leg, and so long as he could keep his balance he'd make it home, fast, before the worst of the storm hit.

As they settled into a steady rhythm the first raindrops fell, heavy plops that soaked straight through his shirt. Nate urged his horse on, forgetting everything other than the stretch and pull of the animal beneath him.

"Easy," he called, one hand touching the horse's neck as a low rumble of thunder sounded out.

She calmed for a moment and then pulled on his hands, fighting for her head. Then Nate saw what she was becoming so excited about. There was another horse in the distance, *a rider in trouble*. Nate didn't ask his horse to go any faster, with no stirrups they were already cantering too fast, so he did his best to keep her steady and calm.

And then he recognized the horse and rider. *It was Sarah, and she was only just managing to stay in the saddle*. Shit. This was not good weather to take a freshly broken horse out in. What the hell did she think she was doing?

"Steady, girl," he told his mount, "nice and steady." He asked his horse to slow as they approached, sitting deeper in the saddle and being firmer with his hands. "Whoa."

"Nate!" Sarah's usually calm voice was ear-piercingly high.

"Stay calm," he ordered, asking his horse to walk slowly toward Sarah and her nervous mount. "Get those shoulders back and tell her who's boss." He might be a fan of natural horsemanship, but the horse still had to know who was in charge, and right now Sarah wasn't doing a very good job of making that clear. They were flight animals; if she wasn't assertive, the situation was going to get dangerous.

He neared the skittish horse and made a grab for the reins, trying to keep his balance. Damn it! If his leg wasn't buggered he would have jumped off and taken hold of the young mare and settled her, instead of struggling to even keep control of his own horse. *But then if he wasn't injured, maybe he would never have come home.*

"Hey, girl," he said, pulling back hard to keep Sarah's horse steady. "We're okay."

Another rumble of thunder followed by a crack of lightning made the horse's eyes roll and Nate was finding it harder to stay in the saddle, especially with his own horse becoming jumpy.

"Sarah, you okay?"

He glanced at her quickly, saw the terror in her face, how white her cheeks were.

"Don't let go, Nate."

"Come on," he said firmly. "We need to either get back right now or unsaddle the horses and let them go. It's your call." He hoped she agreed on the first option, but he'd do whatever she was most comfortable with. If she was that frozen with fear, riding back might not even be an option. "Sarah?"

"Let's go," she agreed.

Nate took control, not wanting to take any risks, not where Sarah was concerned. "Let's start at the walk. If we can keep them calm enough, we'll trot back."

Sarah nodded and he saw the determined look in her eyes that had been missing before. The glint that he usually associated with her attitude to everything she did, her confidence returning.

Sarah's horse jig-jogged, nervous as hell, but she stuck to his mount like glue, not wanting to break away on her own. "We're going to be fine," he called to her, raising his voice over the now-insistent drops of rain and rumblings of the fast-approaching storm. "She's not going to break away from my horse and I think we need to speed things up." At this rate, Nate knew they didn't have a chance at making it back to the house or stables. But there was a barn they could get to, where they'd all be safe, *so long as lightning didn't strike too close.*

"You okay trotting?" she asked.

Nate gritted his teeth together as they broke into a fast trot. Given the fact he had no stirrups, bouncing along wasn't exactly his favorite gait. "How about we canter?"

He could see her confidence had returned, at least temporarily. "I'll give it a go."

The horses were jumpy but they rode side by side, the rain starting to pelt down and soak through his shirt. Nate saw the barn he'd had in mind, somewhere they usually stored hay at the end of each season if they had need to, and one he hoped was empty. He pointed to Sarah, his eyes blurry from rain as he gestured where they were heading. They both slowed to a trot, then a walk, pulling up outside it. They never would have made it back to the stables or close to the house.

"Let's dismount and lead them in. There's a few old wooden gates in there and a center divide, so if you're okay holding them I'll erect a makeshift stall for the pair of them," he called out to Sarah, stretching his legs and rotating his ankle before swinging his leg over his horse and landing with a thud on the wet earth below.

Son of a... Nate swallowed the curses ready to burst from his mouth. Damn it if his leg didn't hurt like hell, but he had a task to do and no time to fool around. Sarah was already on the ground, watching him, her eyes asking questions even though she didn't actually say a thing.

"Here," he said, passing her the reins. "I'll make it quick." Nate wanted to get out of the rain but he also wanted to get Sarah out of harm's way, and he wasn't convinced she'd be able to keep hold of both horses, who were leaping around like a pair of idiots, if the storm came so much as an inch closer.

Nate limped into the open barn, grabbing an old ball of string and dragging two of the old gates leaning against one of the walls. He tied them together and hauled a few of last season's bales of hay over, too. "Bring them in," he called out.

Sarah started toward him but lightning cracked close by, making her horse rear up in fright. Nate made it to her just in time, grabbing her horse. "Whoa, girl, let's get inside." His voice was firm and so was his hold as he led her in. Sarah brought his horse in and he passed her the reins again, before hauling the hay bales into the gap and building them up.

"Shall we take their bridles off?" Sarah asked, her voice shaky.

Nate gave her what he hoped was a confident smile. "Nope. Let's put the reins back over their heads and knot them. That way if they get away they won't break their necks tripping over them, and we can still get hold of them quick if we need to."

Sarah climbed over the gates with a hand from Nate once they'd settled the horses as much as they could. He'd passed some decent-looking hay over, which was keeping them happy for now, even if they were still understandably frightened.

She went to let go of Nate's hand, then grabbed it again, her legs wobbly. She could have been badly injured out there, could have had a bad fall and been left out in the storm for hours or even longer before anyone found her. *She'd been trying to avoid Nate and somehow he'd ended up saving her.*

"I should never have ridden out in that weather. Johnny warned me, but all I could think about was needing to get up in the saddle and clear my head," she admitted to Nate. "I'm not usually one to take risks, but…" She didn't even know what to say. Thank goodness she'd left Moose behind to play with Brady; the last thing she'd have needed was him to worry about, as well.

He put an arm around her, but she could tell from the awkward angle he was on that something was wrong. "You're okay now, so don't even think about it. Maybe we should both listen to Johnny more often, though—sounds like he has better brains than the pair of us combined."

"Nate?"

He looked at her. They'd both stopped walking.

"Your leg's bugging you, isn't it?" she asked.

Nate steered her toward some hay bales and sat down, his leg stretched out in front of him. "Bugging me would be an understatement," he admitted. "Hurting me like someone's stabbing me over and over in the calf might be a better description."

Her shocked expression as she sat down beside him made him laugh.

"Okay, maybe I shouldn't have been quite so honest. I'm fine, Sarah, please don't worry about me."

She shook her head, slowly, before tucking her knees up and wrapping her arms around her legs. Now that they were sitting, the adrenaline rush of riding and securing the horses over, she'd realized how cold she was.

Her shirt and jeans were sodden, completely soaked through, and it was taking an effort to stop her teeth from chattering. The last thing she needed was to be miserable and get sick, too.

"Great summer weather, huh?" Nate asked.

She nodded. "Yeah."

They sat there, not saying anything, the only noise the pounding tap on the roof as the rain fell furiously, the storm surrounding them. Sarah stared into the torrential rain, watched the jagged lightning in the sky as it lit everything around it.

"Come here." The softness of Nate's voice made her look up. "I'd come to you but…" He pointed at his leg. "It might be easier for you to come to me."

Sarah wanted to resist, didn't want to be close to Nate, to remind herself of what she was missing out on. *But she couldn't.*

Sarah stood and crossed the distance between them, sitting down beside him. Nate's arm automatically went around her, pulling her tight against his body. Letting her steal some of his warmth, even though he was as wet as she was.

"You're freezing," he said, sitting up more and putting his other arm around her to try to warm her up.

Sarah wasn't going to deny how cold she was, especially with the heat coming off Nate. She had no idea how he could still be so warm given the storm they'd both been stuck out in.

"Why aren't you freezing, too?"

He chuckled. "I am, but I'm kind of used to extreme

temperatures. I've been trained for years to cope with this sort of situation, and I've seen a lot worse. Sometimes heat is worse than the cold."

"Nate?" she asked, burying her face against his shoulder, not strong enough to pull herself away from him. *She should have stayed on the other side of the barn, but there wasn't a chance she was going back there now.*

"Yeah?" His mouth was touching the top of her head, her hair.

"I'm sorry about your friend, and about your leg, too. I wish things were different for you." She didn't know why, but telling him how she felt, what she'd been wanting to say to him and not known how to, seemed to take a weight off her shoulders.

Nate grunted, half chuckle, half throat-clear. "Me, too." He hugged her closer and she held on tight. "And I'm sorry about the whole baby thing, as well." Nate's voice was low and husky, like he hadn't known what to say or whether to mention it.

"Me, too," she said, listening to the steady beat of his heart through his wet shirt, enjoying the constant rhythm against her ear. "Me, too." She'd had a while to come to terms with it now, but the reality that she'd never be able to have a baby with a man she loved one day still hurt sometimes.

Nate let go of her with one arm and started to stroke her hair. She shut her eyes and leaned into him, craving him more than she'd ever like to admit, even to herself.

"Sarah, just because you can't have children doesn't mean you can't be a mom," he said. She squeezed her eyes shut even tighter. "You could easily adopt one day. Don't give up on your dreams just because the journey's too hard—there are plenty of kids out there in the world in need of a great mom. If it's what you want, I know you can make it happen."

What did she say to that? Of course she knew her options, but hearing it from someone else, *from Nate,* was kind of reassuring. That it wasn't just some line she'd been feeding herself to make herself feel better. "Thanks, Nate."

He pushed back from her. "Let me finish."

A loud bang of thunder made her jump back into his arms, pressed tight to his side. The horses were starting to skitter, too, kicking against the side of the barn.

"Settle down, girls. We're all okay," Nate called out to them, rising slightly to look in at them. "No need to be scared."

Sarah fiddled with the hem of her wet shirt, hating that they were stuck here, soaking, and having a conversation she'd rather not be engaging in. She could feel him watching her, then his hands covered hers to stop her nervous fiddling.

"Just because one man couldn't deal with your infertility doesn't mean you're not going to meet someone else. Someone different," he told her. "You have options, and *you* deserve someone who can understand that."

She looked up, met his gaze and stared into his bright blue eyes. "Maybe you're right, but right now I think I might be better on my own. Given my current track record."

The left side of his mouth kicked up into a curve. "Or maybe you're just not giving the right guy a chance."

Sarah's heart started to beat too fast. Her mouth became way too dry for her liking. She needed to deal with this right now, tell him how wrong he was before the conversation went any further. Before he said something, or did something, that would stop her from telling him how she felt.

"Nate, I've seen you with Brady. I know how great you'd be as a dad, and I don't want us to…" She shrugged, pulling her hands back from his and forming a knot with them instead. "I can't deal with losing you again and I know we can't work."

He glowered at her. "And you think that's a decision you can make on your own? Without asking me how I feel?"

Sarah bit down hard on her lip, wishing she could walk away. A quick glance out at the storm told her otherwise. The rain was so thick and hitting the ground hard, so there was no chance of escape. Especially if she didn't want to risk becoming lost or zapped by a lightning bolt, not to mention hypothermic if her body temperature dropped any lower.

"Let's not make this harder than it has to be. What we used to have was great, seeing you again has been amazing, but we don't have a real future together."

He touched her cheek, shuffling closer, forcing her to stare back at him. "Don't tell me that," he said. "I don't care if you can't have kids, I don't care what's happened in the past. What I care about right now is *you*."

He smiled. *"You and only you,* Sarah. When I told you that I loved you, I meant it."

"Nate, if you left me again…" Sarah's voice quavered. *She wasn't ready for this, wasn't prepared to have this sort of discussion.*

"I'm not going to. At least not like that."

She had no idea what he meant, but…

Nate's mouth met hers so fast she didn't have time to think, to push him away. His lips were soft against hers, warm, taking all the cold from her body and replacing it with heat. He kissed her hard, like he didn't ever want to stop, and she didn't ever want to let him.

When Nate pulled away, his lips hovering over hers, she didn't move a muscle.

"When you reminded me the other day about my dreams, what I used to want, you were right," he said, touching his nose to hers before sitting back. "I want to do something on the land, think about the tourist stuff we used to brainstorm about. I don't know, horse trails or luxury camping or *something* that makes money and lets me stay around here and be useful."

Sarah placed her hands on her lap now, trying to stay calm. Her stomach was still full of flip-flops, but she wasn't as nervous as she had been. She wanted to hear what he had to say, even if it scared her. She owed it to herself to listen.

"What I need is some time to figure out what I want, Sarah. What I want to do with my life."

She wasn't sure what he was trying to tell her, if he was asking her something. "You need to do whatever feels right, Nate."

He grinned at her. "What feels right is us, *you*," he told her. "But as much as I want this to work, I need to sort myself out first. Otherwise I have nothing to offer you. I need a month, Sarah. A month of figuring things out and spending time on my own, so we both know where we stand and what our future could be."

Her hands had started to shake. *Had she heard him right?* "I don't understand. Do you still want to be with me?"

Nate opened his arms and pulled her into his chest. "More than ever. If you can forgive me for leaving you all those years ago, I promise I'll spend the rest of my life making it up to you."

Sarah looked up at him, her arms wrapped around herself and her back twisted so she could stare up at his face. "I forgive you, Nate. Of course I forgive you." *How could she not?* Truth be told, she'd forgiven him a long time ago, because the years she'd spent with him had been the best of her life.

He laughed and dropped a kiss to her head. "And no more baby talk, okay? I need you to know that I don't give a damn about you not being able to have kids. Right?"

She shut her eyes, hoping he wouldn't regret what he was saying. She knew how much he loved children; watching him with Brady was reason enough to see that he would be a great dad. "But if you do…"

He tilted her chin back up with his thumb. "I won't. What I want is you. And if it becomes something we both want, then we'll do something about it. Okay? We can find a kid who really needs us, who's already out there in the world." He sighed. "I saw plenty of children when I was away, kids in desperate need of someone to love them, so I'd love to help even one child, one day. To do something out of love."

She shook her head. He'd managed to amaze her again. "I can't even imagine what you've seen, Nate, what you've been through."

He dropped another kiss to her head, and she didn't pry. He'd keep opening up to her, when he was ready; she just had to be patient.

Sarah looked outside, suddenly realizing that there was no longer a constant drumbeat of rain in the background. The storm had passed as fast as it had arrived. Where else but Texas would a summer storm like *that* hit?

"Nate, it's over," she told him, gesturing with her head.

He grunted like he wasn't that happy about it, so she kept hold of him, tucked against him. She might have wanted to run before, but now that all the hard stuff was behind them, the discussion she'd been so scared of having now out in the open, staying with Nate in the barn wasn't sounding like such a bad idea.

"When you said you wanted a month…"

"I want to leave here and travel around a bit, see what my competition is in the tourism industry and take some time to get my head in the right place," he told her.

So where did that leave them? What did he actually want?

"But," he continued, as if he could sense her question, "it doesn't change the way I feel about you. I need you to know that. Sorting my head out is about dealing with what happened to me back in Black Ops. I want to visit Jimmy's widow and go to his grave, spend time on some other ranches and see what they do. Me going away is not for thinking about whether or not I want to come home to you, Sarah. Because right now that's the only thing I *do* have clear in my mind." Sarah smiled at him when he looked at her. "When I said I wasn't going to leave you again, I meant it."

Sarah shivered in her still-wet shirt. "But if you do…"

"I won't," he insisted. "What I want is for you to deal with your divorce, make sure this is what *you* want. So that we can both start over."

The horses were starting to stomp again, their cue that it was time to get a move on.

"And you're sure about this?" Sarah asked, her cheeks flushing as Nate rose and then pulled her to her feet, so she landed smack-bang against him. *It sounded too good to be true, like she was imagining the words he was saying to her so openly.*

"What I'm sure about is that I love you, Sarah. I love you now and I always have."

Sarah giggled like the first time he'd told her, under the tree that they'd spent so many hours making out beneath. "I love you, too, Nate."

"Then promise me that we're going to make a real go of this. Of us," he asked, arms slung around her waist to keep them locked together.

"I promise," she told him, tilting her head back for another kiss. "I promise."

And she did. This was Nate, *the love-of-her-life Nate. And he'd finally come home for good.*

CHAPTER FOURTEEN

SARAH stood on the steps of her porch, watching as Nate loaded his two bags into the trunk of his car. Her hands were starting to shake so she linked them behind her back. This was tough. The last time she'd said goodbye to Nate, he'd never come home to her. And now she had to take a huge leap of faith and believe that this time was going to be different.

"I think that's all," he said, joining her on the porch.

Sarah nodded, starting to panic. "And you definitely have to go, right?"

Nate chuckled and pulled her hands away from her back, slinging them behind him instead. They stood pelvis to pelvis, Nate's head dipping down slightly so he could gaze straight into her eyes.

"I love you, Sarah. You do know that, right?" Nate's voice was low, like he was struggling with leaving her as much as she was struggling with being left.

"I know," she mumbled. *And she did know; he'd made it more than clear. But it didn't help how she was feeling right now.*

"I promise I'll be back by the end of the month. You don't have to worry about me coming home, because there's no part of me that doesn't want to come back to you." He paused, dropping a soft, slow kiss to her lips. "And that's a promise."

She could have held on to him all day, kept her body pressed to his and snuggled close for hours, but she knew she had to let him go. "I'll be fine, it's just…"

"You're worrying it'll be like last time?" he finished for her.

Sarah nodded. "I know it won't be, but part of me keeps thinking that maybe this is the last time I'll see you."

Nate sighed, kissed her again, before stepping back. Just enough so that his arms were free. He took her hands into his and raised them up, slowly kissing each of her knuckles before meeting her stare again.

"You're the best thing that's ever happened to me, Sarah. I need you to know that," he said. "And when I come back, there's something I'd like very much to place on this finger." Nate plucked at one of the fingers on her left hand with his teeth, before grinning up at her.

"Don't forget about the festival, either?" she joked, blushing furiously after his ring comment and ignoring it simultaneously. "You have to come back to meet your new siblings and help me organize all the finishing touches. Not to mention the dedication to your dad."

Nate groaned. "Are you sure we can't skip the festival and go away somewhere instead? I'm not that sure about meeting all these new people."

Sarah swatted at him, aiming to punch him in the arm, but he grabbed her hand before she'd managed to connect. "I'll have you know that your new sister,

Ellie, is a good friend of mine now. What's she going to think when I tell her you've skipped town already without meeting her?"

He didn't seem to care what she said. "Come here," he ordered, keeping hold of her hand.

"I do care, you know that. But what I care about most is you." Nate put his arms around her and held her tight, his face buried in her hair. "I'll be home before you know it, and I'll phone you as soon as I get to Jimmy's house."

Sarah gave him one last squeeze, shut her eyes and tried to lock the way he felt in her arms into her memory. "I love you, Nate."

"Baby, I love you, too."

He walked down the porch steps and stopped at the bottom, turning around to blow her one final kiss. "I'll see you soon."

Sarah nodded and held on to the railing. A wet nose nudged her hand and she looked down to see Moose now sitting beside her. She couldn't help but laugh at him, staring down at Nate like he was pleased to be rid of him, like he was the man of the house and he didn't like being challenged.

"You better train that dog to like me before I get back!" Nate called out to her, waving through the open window.

Sarah was laughing so hard she couldn't even manage to answer him.

Who would have thought she'd ever be sharing a laugh with Nate Calhoun again, let alone waving him goodbye and waiting for him to return?

EPILOGUE

SARAH walked out to check the mailbox. The sun was bright so she held up her hand as she peered inside, not expecting to find anything other than a bill inside. She was wrong. She pulled out the card, smiling to herself at the rodeo scene depicted on the front.

Nate. She flipped the card and looked at the familiar writing on the back. Messier than it had been when they'd written to each other while he was away serving, but she'd still recognize it anywhere.

Her heart started to race, then fell back to a more steady rhythm. *So much for being home by the end of the month.* She'd hoped to only have a few more nights without him, but from what he was telling her on the card, she doubted she'd see him for a while yet.

"Come on, Moose," she called to her dog, turning to walk back inside.

"And here I was thinking you'd be pleased to see me."

Sarah stopped. Stood dead still, knowing it couldn't be him. That the deep, teasing voice she'd just heard had to be her imagination, because Nate must still be hours away from Larkville. If not farther.

She spun slowly on the spot.

Oh, my God. "Nate!" She laughed and walked toward him, not letting herself run at him and throw herself into his arms like she wanted to. "But I just got your…" She held up the postcard in one hand as she stepped into his open arms to explain her confusion.

"I just put it in your mailbox. I wanted to see how disappointed you'd look if I told you I wasn't coming home yet. You know, just to make sure you were still into me."

Sarah didn't hold back when he bent to kiss her, looped her arms around his neck and let her lips dance across his, even though she should have told him off for his prank. "You are *so* mean," she murmured, pulling back so she could look up at him. See that it was really him.

"Distance can make a guy worry," he confessed, slipping his fingers into the loops of her jeans.

"Well, you didn't have to worry about me," she said with a sigh, standing on tiptoe and kissing him again. "Not at all."

Now it was Nate clearing his throat and moving away from her. He looked…*nervous.* Sarah watched him closely, wondering what was wrong. Oh, no, had he had a change of heart? Was that what this was about?

"Sarah, I'd hoped to speak to your mom first but now that I've seen you I don't think I can wait." Nate was smiling but his eyes were darting around, like he was nervous, and Nate was *never* nervous.

"Is everything okay? Do I need to sit down?" What was he going to tell her?

Nate's shoulders rose up, then came down. "No."

Sarah closed the distance between them. "Whatever it is, Nate, you can tell me."

He laughed and pulled something from his pocket. He held his little finger out to her, a big smile on his face.

There, perched on the smaller half of his finger, was a ring. A diamond surrounded by a cluster of smaller diamonds that threaded all the way around the band.

"Wow." Sarah couldn't take her eyes from it, not even to look at Nate. It was amazing.

"I don't want to push you if you're not ready, but I love you, Sarah. Always have and always will." Nate's voice was tender, his words making tears flood her vision almost immediately. "This is me telling you," he said, taking her hand and placing the ring in her open palm, before closing her fingers around it, "that I will never leave you ever again. That I love you for *you*."

Sarah stared up into Nate's eyes, shaking her head slowly from side to side as his words sunk in. She opened her palm and looked at the ring sitting there, before slipping it onto her finger.

Nate's hand nudged her chin up, forcing her to confront his gaze. "Marry me, Sarah? You don't have to say yes now, you don't even have to wear the ring yet if you don't want to, but I want to make my intentions clear." His mouth met hers, lips so tender and soft that she found herself clutching on to his shirt, trying to pull him closer. "I want you to be my wife. *For now and forever.*"

Tears did fall then. She couldn't help it. They trickled freely down her cheeks and Sarah was powerless to do anything about them.

"Yes, Nate. Of course my answer is yes."

His eyes widened. "It is?"

"Yes, I want to marry you, Nate," she said with a laugh, finding it hard to believe that he was even standing in front of her, let alone proposing. "Yes, yes, yes!"

Nate grabbed her around the waist and swung her around, his smile as wide as hers felt.

There was something different about him, something more open and happy about Nate than before he'd left, and she liked it. As if the more grown-up Nate that she'd fallen in love with since he'd returned had merged with the old Nate, the happy young man she'd loved since she was a teenager.

"I think we should take this inside," he whispered in her ear. "I'd hate to upset your neighbors."

Sarah tilted her head back and giggled as he kissed her neck. "There's one problem," she told him.

A low growl echoed out behind them, as if Moose had read her mind.

"If you'd warned me you were coming home, I'd have spent more time training someone to like you."

Nate held her up in his arms, spinning her around so she faced her dog. "Are you sure we can't find him a new home?"

Sarah gave him a pretend slap across the face, suppressing a squeal when he grabbed her hand and stole a kiss from her.

"Nate, he's my baby," she complained, smiling down at her dog. "Aren't you, darling?"

Nate glared at the dog, but Sarah could tell he was trying hard not to laugh. "Well, only one of us gets to sleep in bed with her, buddy, and that someone just happens to be me."

Sarah cringed. "Um, Nate, about that…"

He looked down at her and shook his head. "You're kidding me, right? We have to share your bed with the dog?"

Sarah laughed so hard she had tears streaming down her cheeks again. "'Fraid so."

Nate put her on her feet and took her hand. "When I proposed I had no idea what I signed up for, did I?"

She slipped her hand from his and pressed her palms against his cheeks instead. "I do love you, Nate."

"Yeah," he said, glancing at the dog. "Me *and him*."

Sarah dragged him by the hand up the porch steps and through her front door. "I have two men in my life. You're just gonna have to get used to sharing me."

But only Nate would ever make her feel the way she did right now. Loved for who she was.

Nate pulled the door shut behind them before backing her up against the wall, pinning her hands above her head and pushing his body against hers. "I don't share," he whispered, "especially when it comes to you."

Sarah couldn't stop laughing as he nibbled at her ear, then kissed her collarbone, before tracing a path back to her mouth.

"Are we clear about that?" he asked, his eyes shining.

"Oh, we're clear all right," she affirmed, wriggling her body closer to his. "It's just you and me, soldier."

"Damn right," he murmured in her ear. "I'm not ever letting you out of my sight again."

Sarah tilted her head back and shut her eyes. This was…bliss. And she didn't *ever* want Nate to stop.

* * * * *

A sneaky peek at next month...

Cherish™

ROMANCE TO MELT THE HEART EVERY TIME

My wish list for next month's titles...

In stores from 15th March 2013:

❑ Baby out of the Blue – Rebecca Winters

& The Billionaire's Baby SOS – Susan Meier

❑ Guardian to the Heiress – Margaret Way

& Winning Back His Wife – Melissa McClone

In stores from 5th April 2013:

❑ His Country Cinderella – Karen Rose Smith

& The Hard-to-Get Cowboy – Crystal Green

❑ Little Cowgirl on His Doorstep – Donna Alward

& Mission: Soldier to Daddy – Soraya Lane

Available at WHSmith, Tesco, Asda, Eason, Amazon and Apple

Just can't wait?

Visit us Online

You can buy our books online a month before they hit the shops! **www.millsandboon.co.uk**

0313/23

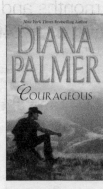